CALLED OUT

To Fred, From one Chicagoan to another!

CALLED OUT

A novel of base ball and America in 1908

— —

FLOYD SULLIVAN

Floyd Sullivan

BOOKS BY FLOYD SULLIVAN

Called Out

AMIKA PRESS

Old Comiskey Park
(editor)

Waiting for the Cubs

MCFARLAND

First Edition   ISBN 13: 978-1-937484-51-4
AMIKA PRESS   466 Central AVE #23 Northfield IL 60093   847 920 8084
info@amikapress.com   Available for purchase on amikapress.com
Edited by Jay Amberg and Ann Wambach. Cover art & design by Jeanne Sullivan Meissner and William Brese. Cover photography courtesy Library of Congress. Author photography by Lucy Sullivan. Designed & typeset by Sarah Koz. Set in Farnham, designed by Christian Schwartz in 2004. Title set in Gloucester Extra Condensed, designed by Monotype in 2001. Thanks to Nathan Matteson.

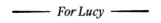 *For Lucy*

Part I

Pulliam folded back the sheet and set his bare feet on the hardwood floor. Something thin and dry crunched under his left foot. He pulled his leg over his right knee and brushed the remains of a gray paint chip off his sole. He looked up and saw where small leaf-shaped flakes peeled away from the ceiling.

He sighed and glanced at his lover. "I'm sending you back to Louisville," he said softly.

"Pardon?"

"You heard me."

"Sending me? You talk to me as if I were your wife. Or your nigger."

"It's not safe." He stood and crossed the room to the closet.

"You're angry with me because the paint's chipping, Harry? I watched your eyes." Pulliam didn't reply. "Do you have someone else?"

"Of course not." He began to dress.

"Then why do you want me to leave?"

"I don't want you to leave. Quite the contrary." He reached for the hanger holding his suit. "It's dangerous for us here."

"How do you mean us? It's not dangerous for me."

"Yes, it is." As he was about to put on his suit jacket, he looked for his gold silk handkerchief in the upper pocket, but it wasn't there or in any pocket. He made a point of being very careful about every detail of his clothing. They had men watching him. If he left looking any different than when he arrived, they would nod and jot down in their notebooks that he had lost his handkerchief while visiting the flat on Bleecker Street.

He turned back to confront the beautiful face that questioned him

1

from the pillow. "Do you want your name to be associated with a love nest in Greenwich Village? Do you want your family to read about it? Or hear about it from friends? Or enemies? A Russell of Louisville caught in a love nest? A fairy love nest?"

"But this is New York. Nobody cares."

"They will care in the National League, and so they will see to it that they know in Louisville." He found the handkerchief on the closet floor.

"Is it a woman? There are always pretty women around base ball players and base ball men."

"Don't be silly."

"Women like you. I see how they look at you."

Pulliam shook his head. "I will not discuss this with you now."

"At least you admit it's a discussion."

"That was a mistake." Pulliam sat on the edge of the bed and leaned over to tie his shoes.

"I will not go back. I detest Louisville."

"I mean to give up this flat." Pulliam saw that his black shoes needed polish. "I plan to call the agent tomorrow."

"Tomorrow is New Year's Day."

"The day after then."

"Will you see me tomorrow? Since you are about to leave me? I don't want to be alone on New Year's Eve..."

"You won't be alone."

"...while you attend some perfectly horrible base ball banquet where I'm not welcome."

"I won't be entirely welcome, either." He paused. "I told you. I am doing a favor for a friend, and I am already late."

"Your friend is dead."

"A favor for his family. I am obligated."

"Aren't you worried that I'll misbehave?"

"No more than usual." He returned to the closet for his coat and hat.

"Set me up in the club."

Pulliam laughed. "That would be just perfect."

"Why not? I'm a man. I'll fit in."

"You don't fit in. It's a different world."

"Then you don't want me."

"Of course I want you, Ted. Didn't I just show you that I want you?" He stood and went to the door. "But they are watching me, and they will crucify us both."

"It's a stupid game. A vile game. Why do you work for them?"

Pulliam lowered his voice to a whisper, pronouncing each word with a clipped firmness. "Never, ever speak of the game in those terms. It is not the game. It is the men who own the game that drag it down."

"And you are on a noble mission to save the holy game. Jesus driving the money changers from the temple."

He stared at his lover, now sitting up, his head against the wall, his torso exposed to the waist. *Why didn't Ted appreciate the game? How could he not appreciate the game?*

Pulliam had once risked bringing Ted to Washington Park in Brooklyn to watch the Superbas play the Philadelphia team. He tried to teach him the basics of the game and show him how at its best it could be as uplifting as fine art or music. But it was hopeless and always would be.

"Be ready to leave here by the end of next week."

"End of the week? I can't and you know I can't." Ted slid back down onto the pillow. "The gallery needs me at least until the exhibit opens in February."

"But you told me you hate the gallery."

"I have obligations, just as you do."

"Is it an exhibit of the painter I met at Mouquin's?" He checked the inner left pocket of his suit jacket for the sheet of paper on which he had scribbled the toast he was scheduled to give at the banquet.

"Yes, and seven others. The exhibit opens February third. Macbeth will need me until then."

"His name fits," said Pulliam as he walked to the window and looked down onto a dark Bleecker Street, illuminated only by the light spilling out of several windows along the lane and a lone gas streetlamp three doors away. "A group show then? Do they all celebrate what is ugly in the world, like your friend?"

The black carriage remained parked directly across from the flat.

The driver sat atop his perch, bundled in a long brown coat, a dark scarf wrapped around his head under his top hat.

"It's not the art that's ugly," said Ted. "It's the men that own the art who bring it down."

Pulliam spun around. "I mean to give up this flat as soon as possible," he said. "I will continue to subsidize your rooms at the Prince George until the end of January. You will need to find other lodgings through February third." He went to the door.

"Will you visit me in my rooms?" asked Ted.

"You know I cannot be seen with you at your hotel. Why do you insist on...insist on..." He opened the door and walked out of the flat without looking back.

Thomas stood with his cab at the corner of Bleecker and MacDougal. Pulliam climbed into the hansom saying, "Delmonico's, Thomas." He rubbed his eyes and his temples. He felt the beginnings of what he knew would be an intense headache. Fighting with Ted inevitably made him angry with himself, and the strain could make him physically ill.

He would call Ted in the morning and invite him to dinner at Mouquin's where they would chat about his artists and the upcoming show at the Macbeth Galleries. They would have fun together. It would ease the tension between them, and perhaps he would convince Ted that some time away from New York would be best for them both.

He would then phone his sister Grace and wish her and her family a happy 1908. Her son, his namesake, would be two years old in ten days and talking more clearly than ever. The thought of speaking with him eased the pressure behind his eyes.

A dram of whiskey might kill the pain in his temples, and he knew John Brush would have a selection of the best bourbons at the National League banquet. Perhaps he would have two drams.

The hansom turned up MacDougal Street and approached Washington Square. Pulliam tapped on the rear wall behind him and shouted, "Thomas, is a carriage following us?"

A few moments passed. Pulliam imagined Thomas turning in his seat to check the street behind them.

"There is a carriage behind us, Mr. Pulliam."

"Does the driver wear a brown coat and a scarf?"

"It's difficult to see, sir. He wears a dark coat and scarf, much like my own. Shall I pull over and let them pass?"

"No. That won't be necessary. Just try to keep your eye on them."

They turned at Waverly Place and drove along the park.

"Sir?" shouted Thomas.

"Yes, Thomas?"

"The carriage continued toward Eighth Street."

"Thank you, Thomas."

Of course it did, Pulliam thought. *They know I'm going to Delmonico's. Brush would have given them instructions to take a different route to Forty-Fourth Street and wait for me there.*

He put his head in his hands. The pain behind his eyes began to throb.

Squeezing herself into the corner of the last seat of the car, Lenore tried to ignore her fellow subway passengers, most of whom were quite drunk. At each stop more stumbled on board, bottles in hand, hugging and laughing and swaying freely with the movement of the train. The passenger next to her, a girl who could not yet be twenty, had turned away from her, legs in the aisle, in order to respond to the open leering of a young man standing above her. When the train turned in the tunnel, the force pushed the girl into Lenore's side, but the couple continued flirting as if Lenore existed only to stabilize the girl's balance.

When the train stopped at Seventh Avenue she waited until the revelers had left the car before she followed them onto the station platform. The joyful din of the New Year's Eve crowd in Times Square floated down the exit and echoed in the hollow of the subway tunnel. Passengers from the cars behind her rushed past to join the party on the street. The volume of the noise grew as she climbed the stairs.

On the sidewalk, the crowd was so thick that she could barely move.

She worried that she would be late, and she did not want to be late or it would be her last performance.

She could do nothing to avoid the pressing throng of young men in their bowlers and women in their huge, flopping Merry Widow hats. They were bundled up against the cold, but most had long since loosened coat buttons and untied scarves. Some blew horns, some waved rattlers, and others rang bells. Many just hooted and hollered for the sheer drunken joy of it all. Couples embraced openly.

She had difficulty distinguishing the prostitutes from the casual merrymakers, and she knew a working girl when she saw one. So many of her theater friends had in desperation turned to brothels, or walked the streets, to make ends meet. The banquet at Delmonico's would be a temptation for others to slip into their ranks. They would be encouraged to do so. When her friend May recruited her to join the small chorus line that would perform for a private New Year's banquet, she knew she could be among them.

If it were a dinner for Morgan or Hearst or Standard Oil, she would have been flattered as only the best dancers in the line were invited to perform for the most important businessmen and politicians. But May told her the banquet was for base ball men. She liked base ball and had met many base ball players and several team magnates when her father was alive. But she had also heard too many stories about John McGraw's pool halls in Herald Square and the parties in the uptown hotels near the ball parks. Her performance, she assumed, was expected to include a one-on-one after their dance, especially since they were to present a version of "Take Me 'Round in a Taxicab" being developed for Grace Leigh, one of the stars of Mr. Ziegfeld's new review. Her costume was little more than an "On Duty" sandwich sign over a tight, strapless bodice that covered less that a bathing suit. They would flail around the banquet room and wait to be hailed by one of the guests.

She wondered for a moment if any of the base ball magnates would recognize her, but quickly dismissed the thought. She had been very young, barely in her teens, when she had last met base ball men at her father's memorial service.

She fought the crowd up Seventh Avenue to Forty-Fourth. She had never seen Times Square so bright. The Hotel Astor stood ablaze with brilliant electric illumination, every one of its dozen floors projecting a steady flow of warm Edison light out from the elegant, red-brick façade. The last of the brownstone row houses stood as narrow shadows overwhelmed by the mass of the new hotels and theaters. Times Square, or Longacre Square as she still thought of it, was no longer a residential neighborhood.

She paused and looked up at the Jardin de Paris, atop the New York Theatre, where Ziegfeld's first review had made its unexpected success the previous summer. May told her that if she did as she was told tonight she would get a second audition, this time in front of Mr. Ziegfeld himself.

"I put in a good word for you with Abby," May had said. "Don't let me down." Lenore didn't believe her, but she didn't know what else to do.

A blizzard of confetti and ticker tape swirled through the air. The noise grew to an earsplitting pitch. Lenore turned and looked back toward the tall new Times Building at the bottom of the square. It reminded her of the Flatiron Building in Madison Square, but with a wedge cut out of the top ten floors. A huge illuminated globe sat at the top of the building's flagpole. She had read that they would experiment with dropping it at midnight instead of setting off the traditional fireworks.

Perfect, she thought. *A huge electric base ball signaling that 1907 was now 1908.*

Henry T. "Monkey" McBride sat at Forty-Seventh and Broadway on the smaller of the Engine Fifty-four fire wagons, looking down into the flowing crowd. This New Year's Eve would be easy duty because it was just an electric ball instead of fireworks. Nonetheless, someone had to keep watch, and so there he sat reining in the damn horses that would never get used to the whistles, horns, and rattles. But he was content to watch the party. It could have been worse. Normally he would have been on call, ready to climb into some fourth- or fifth-story tenement inferno.

To his left, at the end of the square in the middle of Broadway, he noticed a wide circle of women tormenting a stumbling, obviously drunk young man in their center. He wore a black bowler, slightly crushed and tilted on the side of his head. He wobbled and made a run at their locked arms, attempting to break through. They held firm and flung him back to the middle of their circle, howling with laughter as he fell to his hands and knees. His hat stayed on his head.

Whores, thought McBride. *Having a laugh at the expense of a drunk, one of my own neighbors from the Tenderloin, no doubt. Good for them. Let him have it, the silly bastard.*

The young man struggled to his feet and tried again, with the same result. Again the women laughed, slapping their thighs and clapping their hands. This continued for ten minutes until several police arrived. They playfully swatted the girls' linked arms with billy clubs, hauled a couple away, and freed the young man to make his way into the crowd below Forty-Seventh.

I was right, thought McBride. *Whores. The police wouldn't treat a decent lady like that.*

He watched the drunk for several minutes, following his bobbing derby hat as it weaved down Broadway into the square. The shouting and noise grew louder. He looked up and saw the glowing white ball begin its descent.

Looks like a big electric base ball, he thought.

One of the women who had tormented the drunk followed him into the crowd, but he didn't notice her. He looked up to see the big bright ball slide down the flagpole. The crowd cheered. Arms waved high. Whistles and horns blew in a piercing cacophony. Hats flew through the air. The whore reached up, swiped his bowler, and flung it over the crowd. The man was too drunk to notice who stole his hat, but knew immediately that he would never find it among the hundreds being crushed on the street.

A damn pity, he thought, *that such a good hat should be gone, just like that, trampled and smashed and made useless on a cold night like New Year's Eve.* He decided right then and there that as soon as he had the money he would buy a new bowler, better than the one he had just lost. And the new one would be brown so next year he could easily find it among all the black hats on the street. He almost picked up one of those black bowlers to replace the one he lost, but decided against it. *Who knows what kind of vermin lives in the hair and hats of the type of blokes who would be in Longacre Square on New Year's Eve?* He shrugged and turned west toward the Ninth Avenue El.

Certain she would be late, Lenore pushed her way onto Forty-Fourth and proceeded east. Amazed at how dark and empty the crosstown street became as soon as she left the square, she gathered up her heavy, full-length, black wool skirt and ran as best she could. It took several minutes to cover the long block to Sixth Avenue, cross under the El tracks, pass the huge red Hippodrome Theater, and then arrive at Fifth Avenue, across the street from Delmonico's.

It resembled an Italian villa rather than a restaurant. Ornate, terra-cotta-trimmed windows glowed golden yellow, an occasional shadow passing through the soft light. There was no flickering from candles, gaslight, or the simple lamps fueled by Rockefeller's Standard Illuminating Oil or kerosene, as in the windows of the city's tenements. Delmonico's was as fully wired for electric lights as the Hotel Astor in Times Square. The brightness of the third floor's tall double windows, each with a round porthole window above it, spilled onto Fifth Avenue and the three canopies that sheltered the busy Forty-Fourth Street entrance.

Lenore crossed the avenue and found the side door that led into the basement kitchen. The sudden change from the chill of January in New York to the tropical heat of the kitchen all but knocked her over. A large man in a long-sleeve, institutional white shirt; filthy apron; and squat toq held out an arm and stopped her.

"Which party?" He sized her up as if she were a hog belly ready for his butcher's knife.

"The base ball dinner," she answered.

"Ah. Okay. You are a taxicab, no?"

She nodded.

"Okay. You late." He gestured toward the far side of the kitchen.

She hurried past a long row of polished copper prep counters where a gauntlet of cooks worked under hanging racks of huge metal pots with lids the size of hand cymbals. They looked her over and leered as they sliced meats and prepared sauces, insulting her in a rich mix of languages. She silently wished each of them fewer digits in the New Year.

As she turned the corner at the last counter she heard a man call, "Hey, taxi!" She glanced at him. An overweight, middle-aged cook with a thick drooping mustache grinned at her. Sweat beaded on his forehead and ran down his nose. He pulled the bottom of his apron away to reveal his open pants and a huge, gray-red salami hanging out of his unbuttoned fly. "You want some of my meat?"

"Lenore," called May. "Come on already. You've got one minute to change. Here," she said as she tossed a cardboard placard and bundled fabric at her. "A good thing there ain't much to change into."

"Where do I dress?" Lenore started to ask.

"Undress is more like it. Right here," answered May. "You got no time to find the ladies'."

Lenore glanced at the other eleven dancers in their "costumes," sandwich signs that covered bodices cut low in harlequin colors of black and ruby red. She looked at the cooks who were now clapping and cheering, and then she stepped behind the line of girls, hiding herself as she stripped. The entire kitchen booed loudly. She balled up her clothes and held them under her arm as they made their way up the service stairs to the third floor.

The idea of the New Year's Eve banquet distressed Pulliam. He had to cancel plans and hurt Ted in order to attend. But Brush had invited him and made it known that George Dovey was coming down from Boston, Gary Herrmann from Cincinnati, and Charlie Murphy of the Cubs all the way from Chicago. His old friend and former employer Barney Dreyfuss would be in from Pittsburgh. The locals, Charlie Ebbets from the Brooklyn Superbas and Frank Farrell of the American

League Highlanders, would be there as well. And he would have to deal with John McGraw. The Giants' beady-eyed, squat little manager made Pulliam sick. He represented everything that was wrong with base ball. His foul mouth and childish, mean-spirited histrionics on the field dragged the game back into the nineteenth century.

Christy Matthewson would attend with McGraw. The wide-eyed and naïve lad from Pennsylvania was the Giants', and perhaps the game's, best pitcher. Why he socialized with McGraw away from the ball park Pulliam could never understand.

But O. P. Caylor's daughter Lenore would be there, and so perhaps Jane Matthewson, Elsie Brush, and other wives. Their presence would temper the behavior of the men.

Pulliam jumped out as the hansom pulled up to Delmonico's Forty-Fourth Street entrance, busy with revelers either just arriving to celebrate the beginning of 1908 or leaving for parties elsewhere in the city.

"Thank you, Thomas," he said. "I will find a cab after the banquet."

"I don't mind waiting, sir. There might be too few cabs this night."

"But I will be taking a young lady home. She lives all the way uptown near 110th Street. And then it will be back to the club. You should go home."

"I will be perfectly fine right here, sir. Enjoy yourself."

Pulliam hesitated. "Very well, Thomas. Thank you. I am very late for the banquet so I anticipate it will end soon. It's already," he took his watch out of his vest pocket and flipped it open, "it's already ten after twelve. Hmm. I guess I missed celebrating the stroke of midnight."

"Happy New Year, sir."

"Happy New Year, Thomas."

He turned and walked up the steps under the middle of three canopies that extended to the curb. A uniformed doorman held the entrance open. Pulliam paused and handed him a coin.

"Do you see the hansom just now turning to wait across the street?"

"Yes, sir."

"Please see that he gets a pot of fresh coffee and a flask of Courvoisier. I'll settle the bill on my way out."

He rode the elevator to the third floor with a young lady in a mink coat that reached the floor and an older gentleman in tails and top hat. The woman smiled at him. "Happy New Year, sir," she said cheerfully.

"And to you, madam. Sir." He nodded to the couple.

"Happy New Year," said the man.

The elevator operator stopped at their floor and opened the gilded wrought-iron, inner gate followed by the outer doors.

"The base ball banquet?" asked Pulliam.

"Double doors to your right, sir."

"Base ball?" said the woman. "What fun!"

"Where do you see the Giants in '08?" asked the gentleman.

"I think it will be an exciting season. The pennant chase will be close."

"Well," said the man, "just so the Cubs don't win again. They are beginning to annoy me."

"Enjoy the evening," said Pulliam.

The woman smiled again as the man took her elbow and ushered her to the left.

As he approached the double doors, one opened. John McGraw exited, the sounds of men loudly celebrating escaping from behind him. McGraw looked up at him.

"Well, well," said McGraw. "The boy president decides to honor us with his presence after all."

"Happy New Year, Mugsy."

"You missed dinner, Harry."

"I ate. Thank you for your concern."

"I'm sure you did," said McGraw and laughed. He continued past Pulliam and down the hall.

Pulliam caught the door before it closed and entered the room. Through the thick gray haze of tobacco smoke he could see that there were no women present.

He entered and slowly walked through the small banquet hall, greeting the other guests with best wishes for the New Year. Busboys moved chairs and carts, making room for some kind of presentation at the front. He took a seat between Farrell and Dreyfuss at the huge oval table cluttered with used silver flatware, burning tapers in baroque sterling holders, floral centerpieces, and casually discarded table linens. Heavy, red velvet drapery framed white lace curtains covering the tall windows. At one end of the room the American flag, the National League flag, and the Giants' 1905 championship pennant had been carefully hung in an elegant rounded sweep, partially obscuring a floor-to-ceiling mirror.

"Where you been, Harry?" asked Dreyfuss.

"A dinner engagement I couldn't miss. Family. Sorry I'm late."

"Don't apologize to me. But I think John was a little upset. You're scheduled for a toast, aren't you?

"Yes. I'm ready. Mr. Brush's festivities will proceed as scheduled." He gestured at the room. "I was led to believe that the wives would be here."

"By who?" laughed Dreyfuss. "It's just us boys tonight. And I think John has something special planned for us."

Pulliam suddenly realized that Lenore Caylor might be part of the something special and the thought sickened him. No wonder her mother sounded so worried on the telephone.

Dreyfuss quickly changed the subject. "We have a good chance to beat Chicago this year," he said, "as long as I can sign Hans."

"I don't understand him," said Pulliam.

"What's not to understand about money?" Dreyfuss shook his head. "Can't you talk to him, Harry? You recruited him in the first place. The league needs names like Honus Wagner to maintain the integrity of the game."

"I'd like to, Barney, but I recruited him when I worked for you. I am obligated to remain neutral in any financial negotiations between individual players and their clubs."

"But it's good for the league to have Hans on the Pirates. You can't let the Cubs win year after year. People won't turn out for the games anywhere but in Chicago."

"Integrity of the game, you say?" said Farrell, leaning over to look at Dreyfuss on the other side of Pulliam. "I'll give you Hal Chase and my ball park for Hans Wagner and pay him what he wants."

Dreyfuss laughed. "At least Hilltop Park is on high ground. Every time it rains, which is just about daily in Pittsburgh, I lose a year of my life worrying that the Allegheny is going to wash over my field. I'm moving, I tell you. It's higher ground for me."

"We've heard the rumors about Chase," said Pulliam.

"Rumors?" said Farrell. "All you have to do is watch him for a game or two and you can see what's going on."

"I have to admit," said Pulliam, "that I'm a little relieved that both Chase and Cobb are in the American League and not ours, as good as they are."

"Cobb's a psychopath, sure," replied Farrell. "But Chase? A talent like that lying down for gamblers? It's disgusting. And a waste."

The lights flickered and John T. Brush pushed himself up at his place. Pulliam noted that he looked thinner and more stooped, and moved with more difficulty. His suit hung loosely on his skeletal shoulders and limbs. The president of the New York Giants knew his way around showgirls all right, he thought, but his indiscretions were slowly killing him.

"May I have your attention, please?" said Brush, clinking his wine glass with his knife to quiet the room. "Now, boys. Now, boys. Quiet, please." He paused as the conversations around the room faded.

The door opened and McGraw entered and took his seat to the right of Brush.

"Thank you." He cleared his throat with a loud wrenching gurgle that seemed to originate in the bottom of his lungs.

"Now," he turned and looked at Pulliam, "now that we're all here, I think we can proceed with the evening's fun. The 1907 season was great for base ball. It could have been better," Brush paused to allow the attendees to laugh, "but it was Chicago's year after all, and so I'd like to read a few telegrams of congratulations to the Cubs from a few of our colleagues in the new league. It's only right seeing as Charlie took the train all the way from Chicago to be with us this New Year's Eve."

Brush looked down at his place and picked up several yellow Western Union forms. "First, from our friend, the president of the American League." He glanced at Charles Murphy. "By the way, Charlie. I'm surprised you couldn't convince old Ban to ride the Twentieth Century to New York with you." Several of the base ball men chuckled.

Brush cleared his throat and brought the telegram closer to his eyes. "From Ban Johnson, 'I extend congratulations to the National League, President Pulliam personally, and President Murphy on your splendid victory in the World's Series last October. May you have a most convivial time in celebrating the event.'"

The diners clapped and raised glasses.

Farrell turned to Pulliam. "Times have changed, Harry," he said. "A few years ago Brush would have sooner shot Johnson through the heart than look at him. Congratulations."

"Thank you, Frank," replied Pulliam.

Brush raised his hands to silence the diners. "Here's another. This one is from the esteemed manager of the Detroit club. 'Feeling it honorable defeat to go down before so valiant a foe, the vanquished tenders its congratulations to the victorious, but if we meet next year no mercy. Hugh Jennings.'"

Farrell stood and raised his glass high above his head as laughter filled the room. When he sat down he again turned to Pulliam. "I have to root for someone in our league. Heaven knows my Yankee Highlanders don't have a sporting chance."

"That's not what your man Joe Vila says," said Pulliam.

"My man? A base ball writer? No offense, Harry."

Brush looked down at the last sheet of paper and began to read. "Finally, this. 'As an American League club owner and Chicagoan, I fully appreciate the strength of the Cubs and regard them as a worthy successor to the White Sox as World's Champions. Charles Comiskey.'"

"And now," continued Brush, cutting off any further applause, "I believe our own league president will close the toasts with a statement. Harry?"

Brush sat. Pulliam stood at his place. "Thank you, John." He pulled the sheet of paper from his inside jacket pocket. "Point of fact, George Dovey's friend, and tireless Boston rooter, Mike Regan, penned a little verse that I believe speaks for all of us.

It's a grand old flag
And helps Charlie to brag

About his club, the best in the world
And certainly last fall
The turn he did call
When he set all brains in a whirl
He is Charlie Murphy by name
And the president by fame,
Of a club that makes all others look like dubs.
Hats off, say we, to Charlie Murphy,
And hurrah for the dear old Cubs!

The entire gathering, except Murphy, rose to their feet and cheered. The heavyset president of the Cubs smiled, his ruddy, fleshy face flush with drink, and extended his glass to each of the guests in turn as they broke into a very loud, off-key rendering of "For He's a Jolly Good Fellow."

Pulliam shook hands with Farrell and Dreyfuss and then made his way around the table, slapping backs and returning best wishes for a successful 1908 season. When he came to Garry Herrmann he said, "And thanks, Garry. I appreciate your support for me last year."

Herrmann sat with a sigh as if keeping his bulk on his feet for too long had exhausted him. His neck disappeared into his stiff white collar. "Time to put things behind us, Harry," he said. "Base ball is growing everywhere, and we can't let ourselves lose sight of that. There's a lot of money to be made for everyone if we can avoid hurting each other. We're not competitors."

Pulliam smiled and moved on, hoping he could finish his social obligations and make a quick exit. Perhaps there was no final entry on Brush's agenda and Miss Caylor wasn't there at all. He would slip out and have Thomas take him home.

He passed Brush on his way to the door. The gaunt president of the Giants looked exhausted, but determined to stay on his feet. He propped his emaciated body up by holding on to the edge of the table.

"Say, Harry," said Brush. "That was one of the worst pieces of doggerel I have ever heard. You should have read one of your own poems."

"I couldn't exactly pen a verse about the Cubs, could I, John? It would look as if I favor one team over another, wouldn't it? We couldn't have that."

"You still write poetry, Harry?" Pulliam didn't answer. "No? Maybe you should go back to writing poetry. You're better suited for it."

Pulliam smiled. "And miss next year's banquet celebrating the Giants' 1908 World's Series championship? I wouldn't dream of it. I'm enjoying myself so much tonight. Thank you again for your hospitality."

Brush looked like he needed to spit again. "My pleasure," he whispered through the phlegm. "And you don't want to leave just yet. The best is yet to come, although it may not be to your personal taste, come to think of it."

The young women squeezed through a narrow hallway lined with low rolling carts that carried the skeletal remains of several large fish, oyster shells on beds of melting ice, wooden serving bowls with slivers of carrots and lettuce, scraps of beef roasts on sterling silver platters, and the rinds of cheeses, as well as empty wine and spirits bottles of all kinds.

"Jesus," said May. "Do you suppose they've had enough to eat?"

One of the girls near the front of their line turned and said, "Not likely. We're next on the menu."

Lenore cringed. Other girls giggled.

The door opened and a stout woman of about fifty entered from the banquet room. Lenore didn't recognize her but assumed her to be the much-feared Abby, producer of special showgirl events and madam extraordinaire. "All right, ladies. You're on. Make me look good or you'll be off the stage and on the street by tomorrow midday."

May turned to Lenore and whispered, "On our backs she means to say."

Lenore reached out and dropped her bundle of clothes on the far side of the row of carts, just missing a bloody beef platter as someone poked her from behind. She turned to see Lillian Lorraine. "Oh it's you, Lillian," she said. "And I thought I was the last one in the line."

"I'm supposed to be in the middle," slurred Lillian, obviously drunk.

"Can you cover for me, Lenore? I'm sorry. It's my birthday. I was at a party."

"I think so. Happy birthday."

"Thank you." She looked around Lenore toward the front of the line. "This is a big chance for us, you know."

"No doubt. How old are you?"

"Sixteen." She fussed with her hair and then looked down at her costume. She shrugged. There wasn't much to be done with two pieces of cardboard held together by thick, scratchy twine. She glanced up at Lenore. "You know what can happen. Think of Millicent Willson. Mr. Hearst saw her in *The Girl from Paris* just about ten years ago, and now Millie and her sister are sitting pretty, aren't they?"

"These are base ball men, Lillian," replied Lenore. "Hardly the same as William Randolph Hearst."

"So what?" said Lillian, as the line of showgirls inched closer to the door of the banquet hall. "Let me tell you something, Lenore. Do you know who set this up?"

"No. What difference does it make?"

"Old Elsie Lombard, that's who."

"Who?"

"Elsie Lombard Brush, that is." Lillian tried to fold her arms over her chest in triumph, but the cardboard sandwich board wouldn't let her.

Lenore remembered the name. "Mr. Brush's wife? Mr. Brush of the Giants?"

"She was a dancer like us and married this base ball man John Brush who owns the Giants and a big department store in Indiana, and now she's sitting just as pretty as Millie as far as I can see. Maybe it's base ball instead of newspapers, but can you count higher than fifty thousand dollars or a hundred?"

Lenore smiled. "So you're not holding out for John D. Rockefeller?"

"Him?" said Lillian. "Never see him at one of these, and if you did you couldn't get near him. As straightlaced as they come, they say he is."

Brush tapped on his glass with his table knife.

"Boys? Now, boys," he looked at McGraw, who nodded and shouted over the din of the celebrating magnates.

"Hey! Shut up!" The attendees turned to face McGraw. "Mr. Brush has one more item on his agenda and I'm sure you'll all enjoy it."

"Thank you, John." Brush waited for his guests to retake their seats. "Thank you." He took a sip of water. "I talked to Flo Ziegfeld a couple of weeks ago, and he told me that he was working up a new number that he'd like to try on you boys. If we like it, he'll put it in his new show. They're all set to play this summer back at the Jardin de Paris." He pronounced the theater's name as spelled, with no attempt at a French accent. He struggled and paused, his face turning deep red. He coughed and looked from side to side. A waiter ran up to him with a cuspidor. He spat.

"Excuse me, boys. I got a little excited about the show, which you all will, too, once you set your eyes on the line of pretty girls waiting out there in the hall." The magnates of base ball cheered. Pulliam grimaced. "So without wasting another minute, here's the New York Giants' New Year's gift to base ball. A free taxicab ride to the ball park!"

A stout woman pounded out a few chords on an upright piano that stood in the corner of the room. A small door in a wall to Pulliam's left opened and the first of the girls danced into the room, cardboard sandwich "On Duty" sign vibrating as her breasts bounced behind it. The rest of the line followed, signs jiggling in random rhythms determined by the sizes of their chests.

Lenore looked up and through an open door saw the bright bulbs of a large crystal chandelier, clouded by smoke. A lustful male uproar almost drowned out the piano that tinkled their cue. The front girls began to sing in high, nasal voices.

There's a new fangled cab,
That's designed to keep tab,
To show you how far you may go;
But if you're discreet,

It is easy to beat,
As any wise person must know.

May took a deep breath and leapt into the room. Lenore counted two measures for her turn, raised her arms to the correct position, and stepped through the doorway. Behind her, Lillian belched, stumbled on the threshold, and bumped into her back. Lenore lost her balance and dropped to her knees.

Pulliam's first thought was that they'd have to work on wardrobe. Those signs would never do on an actual stage, especially Ziegfeld's. But the base ball men didn't care. Most leaned this way or that, maneuvering for a glimpse behind the cardboard.

As the showgirls danced before him he saw the eyes of his colleagues widen in anticipation. He didn't want to know who would leave with a girl and who would simply watch and then return home or to a hotel, faithful to wife and family. He especially didn't want to know what Christy Mathewson would do. The all-American boy. The symbol of what was best in base ball. Tall and blond and wholesome. The college graduate raised on Christian purity in the Pennsylvania countryside. He hated to see Mathewson at the banquet, gawking at the female flesh like the rest of them.

Pulliam himself would have to perform for the magnates because he was thirty-eight years old, handsome, and, unlike the others in the room, unmarried and unattached. He wasn't sure how he would do it, but he was determined to step out ahead of his colleagues, perhaps find Miss Caylor and get her out of Delmonico's as fast as he could, all under the guise of "selecting" her as his personal entertainment. And he must accomplish this before any of the other base ball men recognized O. P. Caylor's daughter.

He stood behind his chair, wishing for it all to end quickly until he saw the dancer who almost fell on her face. Lenore Caylor. He hadn't seen her since he last visited her father more than ten years before, but it was Lenore.

He glanced around the room. The other men laughed and pointed. The woman at the piano, a dance supervisor of some kind he surmised, turned red with rage. He waited no longer and stepped toward the dancers. Turning to McGraw he shouted, "Hey, Mugsy! Keep your hands off her because she's mine, two left feet and all." McGraw fumed. The others cheered. Mimicking the girls' steps he danced to the one who had faltered. Seeing Pulliam approach, she began exaggerating her steps in a vain attempt, he was sure, to convince him that her stumbling was part of the act.

He reached out, gently pulled her to him, and swung her around. The last girl through the door stopped and covered her mouth for a second, but kept right on dancing. He guided Lenore's hand to the girl's shoulder and pulled the knot in the twine that held her sign in place. The cardboard tumbled to the floor. And with that, the magnates and players stumbled over each other to get around the table to the rest of the girls. The music's tempo accelerated. The room became a chaotic swirl of pink flesh and dark suits.

Henry McBride took a last look at the square and reasoned that it had cleared enough for him to return to the engine house. He turned the team of three horses, smiled at the large pile of steaming droppings that would greet some hungover "White Wings" street cleaner, and headed back to the engine house just the other side of Eighth Avenue. Along the way he passed the occasional drunk who hadn't quite made it home, sleeping in the cold of a doorway or stoop. A laughing woman ran past, back toward the square, a stumbling young man in tow. In spite of the Times Building, the Hotel Astor, and the new theaters, the square was still the working girl's promenade it had always been, and always would be, near as he could tell. A few years before, he sometimes strolled over to Forty-Second Street or Forty-Third Street from the engine house with an extra dollar in his pocket and no chance of love in the near future. But now? Now he had his Maureen and glad he was that he had never caught anything nasty in Longacre Square.

It was a crapshoot and he had rolled sevens until he respectfully left the game.

Lenore let the man lead her out of the banquet room. The noise they left behind continued to rise in volume.

"Where are your clothes?" he asked.

"Behind there," she answered, pointing at a cart. She watched as he pushed two of the carts aside, located her rumpled bundle, and carefully handed it to her.

"Now, I think you'll need the ladies' restroom," he said with a thin smile and a hint of a bow.

"I don't know where it is," she replied. "I changed in the kitchen. In the basement." She stood still, watching him.

"I see," he said. "Well, it appears I will have to do some scouting for you." He smiled again, turned, and looked down the hall. He walked to a door and opened it. Frowning, he closed it right away. "Electrical closet," he said. He went a bit farther and opened another door. "Ah. This will do." He nodded for her to join him. She waddled toward him, more aware than ever of the ridiculous, awkward boards covering her body. He gestured and she looked into a large utility room full of chairs stacked high, collapsed tables, and assorted buckets and mops. He found a light switch and turned it, illuminating the dingy space. He nodded again. She entered, fully expecting him to follow, but he closed the door behind her and remained in the hall.

As she dressed she worried about what she would say. There was no other way out of the utility room. She would have to confront him and tell him good night in no uncertain terms. She ran her hands through her hair, brushed the front of her skirt, and opened the door.

He stood leaning against the far wall. He smiled and pushed off. "This way," he said and gestured to her right. She exited the storage room and started down the hall. She felt the light touch of his hand on her left elbow. "There are double doors just ahead that lead into the main hall. We can take the elevator from there."

Through the doors the building was transformed from the dim

blandness of the service hall into its more public palatial splendor. But she had little time to appreciate its beauty. The man ushered her onto a waiting elevator.

"Ground floor," he said to the operator.

"Yes, sir."

She wanted to tell the gentleman that, in spite of appearances, she was not what he assumed. And she would never be. No she would not. Not with this gentleman or anyone else and not for any promised audition or stage role or any amount of money. Once they had left the restaurant she would thank the man and be on her way. She would return to the West Side and go to Barclay's Coffee Shop and wait the two hours until she was to meet May and rehash the evening over an early breakfast.

The elevator operator opened the doors onto a crowded throng of well-dressed diners in various states of inebriation. The man led her through the lobby to the checkroom to retrieve his hat and coat, and out onto Forty-Fourth Street. The doorman offered to hail a carriage, but the man said, "No need," and glanced down the street.

"Thank you very much for everything," said Lenore, "but I'll be on my way now."

"Nonsense. I will be happy to drop you off at your home."

"No, thank you," she said. "I'm used to these hours. Being in show business."

"I insist," he said and, taking her arm, led her to a hansom waiting across the street. "Here's Thomas."

The stout uniformed driver jumped down from his bench and opened the door.

"Thomas, this is...," he paused and looked at Lenore with a conspiratorial smile, "this is Miss Lenore Caylor."

Her eyes widened. "You know me? How do you know me? Who are you?"

"Pulliam," he answered. "Harry Clay Pulliam. And this is Thomas."

"Uh, nice to meet you, Thomas," she said and stared at Pulliam. "I've heard your name before. You knew my father, didn't you?"

"I was very honored to count your father among my dearest friends.

Please," he said, nodding at the hansom. She hesitated but climbed in. "Thomas, 503 West 111th Street."

"Shall I take Sixth Avenue, sir? To the park?"

"Yes. We should avoid Times Square."

"Amsterdam Avenue crosses 111th in the Heights on the other side of Morningside Park."

"Amsterdam Avenue will be fine."

"And, sir?"

"Yes, Thomas?"

"Thank you for the coffee and spirits."

"It was the least I could do. Which reminds me...I'll be right back."

Pulliam climbed the steps and found the doorman. "Please charge the coffee and Cognac to Mr. Brush's party."

"Yes, sir," said the doorman, bowing.

Pulliam handed him several coins. "For your trouble."

"Thank you, sir." The doorman tipped his hat.

Returning to the hansom, Pulliam climbed in next to Lenore. Thomas slapped the reins. They pulled forward and crossed Fifth Avenue.

Lenore stared at him. "How do you know my address?"

"I spoke with your mother."

"You spoke to my mother?" She turned and looked out at the street. "How did you know my father?"

"Your family lived here in New York when I first began writing for the Louisville *Commercial*. Your father covered base ball for the *Herald*. We met at a game between the Giants and my Colonels, oh, about fifteen years ago."

"Here in New York?"

"No. In Louisville. We had much in common. We both studied law and worked as newspaper writers." Pulliam looked down at his hands. "I last saw him when I accompanied Mr. Dreyfuss and Mr. Clarke to watch Hans Wagner play in Paterson, New Jersey. That would have been in 1897."

"Father was already very ill."

"Yes. But he was nonetheless very gracious, advising us on how to find our way across the Hudson to Paterson. We were in town playing the Brooklyn team." He turned to Lenore. "You were already quite a lady."

She laughed. "Quite a lady. All of fourteen."

"But I recall very well your devotion to your parents. You stayed at your father's side, both to give him comfort and to relieve the burden his illness placed on your mother."

She hesitated for a moment and then turned to face Pulliam. "I should have anticipated that I would see some of Father's former associates at a base ball banquet. Do you still work for one of the teams?"

"No. It's worse than that. I'm afraid I'm the president of the National League."

Lenore raised her eyebrows. "So all of those important base ball men upstairs work for you?"

"The other way around, actually. They vote for and hire the president."

"You say that many of them knew Father."

"Some of them. But don't worry. No one recognized you. Except myself. You see, I was looking for you."

"Of course you were. What did Mother say?"

"She said you told her that you were to attend a base ball event on New Year's Eve and that you would be safe with many of your father's old friends. She asked me to watch for you because she didn't like the idea of you going unescorted."

"My mother called you and so you came to rescue me? This is a little difficult for me to understand."

"I won't deceive you. Your mother asked, in your late father's name, that I convince you to leave show business."

"I didn't know she followed my career so closely. Well, after my grand entrance just now, I can assure you my future on the stage has completely evaporated. You have accomplished your mission without trying."

Pulliam smiled. "Not completely."

She turned from the window and stared at him. "How do you mean? What comes next? Will you propose marriage, perhaps? Make an honest woman of me?"

"Very amusing. No. I was thinking more in terms of employment.

You see, the National League office needs a stenographer, and I happen to know that your education qualifies you for the position."

"So you plan to interview me for the post tonight?"

"I assure you not. I hope you will come to the office next week, at your convenience, and meet with myself and Mr. Heydler, the league secretary."

She looked away. "I can't go home now."

"Why is that?"

"I promised my friend May that I would meet her at Barclay's at about three. I told my aunt and my mother I would be staying with May in Brooklyn." Pulliam stared at her for a moment.

"But your mother is expecting you. I gave her my word. She is very worried about you."

"I find it quite surprising that she called you. She...she has trouble with telephones."

"I assure you I wouldn't have ushered you out of that room if I hadn't talked to your mother."

She remained silent for a moment, looked out at the passing buildings, and sighed.

"So," he began as the carriage sped up Sixth Avenue, under the elevated tracks, "do you follow the game?"

"Of course. It's in our blood, as you know."

"The Giants?"

"I follow the Giants because we live in New York. Also the Superbas. But at home we are partial to Cincinnati because of my father. After all, he founded the team."

"And what about the Highlanders in the new league?"

"The American League?" she laughed. "Well, we really didn't like them at first. They were intruders, as far as we were concerned, trying to take something away from us."

"That's how Brush and McGraw of the Giants felt, too."

"I'm certain there were many in the National League who held similar opinions."

"Mr. Brush thought he was losing money to them. Their ball park is very close to the Polo Grounds. So when the Giants won the pennant a few years ago he refused to play in the World's Series. I guess he thought that would make the American League go away."

"I remember when Mr. Brush owned our Reds, when I was a young girl. I recall hearing that he bought the Giants several years ago."

"Yes. He owns the Giants."

The hansom turned west at Central Park and continued toward Columbus Circle.

Lenore gestured toward the back of the hansom and Thomas's perch. "He agreed to work for you on New Year's Eve?"

Pulliam nodded. "Thomas has no family. He'd rather work holidays."

"No family?"

"I don't know why, and I would never ask."

Pulliam glanced out at Central Park, lampposts dotting the otherwise pitch-black expanse with flickering, warm yellow gaslight.

"How did you come to be a dancer?" he asked.

"The usual story. When we lived in New York, Father would take Mother, Aunt Trudie, and me to the theater."

"Aunt Trudie?"

"My mother's sister, but she's more like a sister to me. She's only thirty-two. She lives with us."

Pulliam sat up. "Wait a moment. Gertrude, uh Pitt..."

"Gertrude Pittenger. Yes. You remember her?"

"Of course. Your father asked that I escort her to the theater one evening many years ago. She must have been under twenty at the time. We had a very pleasant evening."

"Then you have quite a history of escorting the unattached women of my family."

The hansom turned uptown at Amsterdam Avenue.

"I was very happy to hear from your mother. I apologize for not keeping in touch with your family since your father's passing." He paused. "But you were telling me about your career in the theater."

"Not much of a career, really. I fell in love with the stage and wanted very much to become a part of it. I took dance as a child. I was told that I was somewhat skilled and should join an amateur ballet company. Father approved. He wanted me to continue my education in the classical arts. You know, something to keep the women occupied while the men did as they pleased."

"My goodness. I suppose you're a suffragette, too?"

"I believe that I should have the right to vote."

"I've marched for that right myself."

"I have not," she said, "but speaking for American women everywhere, I thank you for your support."

"Now, how did we get off the subject of your background?"

Lenore sat back in her seat and placed one hand over the other on her lap. "Just after the turn of the century we moved to our current address. It was a nice, new building. My aunt moved in with us. My mother," she hesitated, "my mother was not up to the task of raising me alone."

"When did you begin your professional career?"

"Soon after we moved. It went well for a couple of years."

"And now?"

"To be perfectly honest, Mr. Pulliam, I believe at twenty-four I am too old to dance on the stage."

"Nonsense."

"Did you see the girl who was behind me?"

"The one who knocked you down?"

Lenore laughed. "Yes. Poor Lillian. She's just sixteen, but she's the future of the New York stage. If alcohol doesn't destroy her first."

"I assumed she had been drinking."

"But enough about dancing," said Lenore. "Tell me about your offer of employment."

"Well, in short, we need a new stenographer. The woman who previously held the post resigned before Christmas."

Lenore smiled. "Why? It must be very amusing. The business of base ball instead of, I don't know, insurance for example."

"She hated it."

"Hated it?"

"I'm afraid so. She wanted to work downtown where all the money is. But in all honesty I am very happy she's gone. It's worse having someone who's miserable than no one at all."

The hansom paused at 110th Street. Pulliam leaned out the window. "Thomas, is the carriage from MacDougal Street still behind us?"

Lenore could not hear the coachman's reply. "Is someone behind us?" she asked

"I apologize, Miss Caylor. Everything is fine. We are almost there."

The hansom turned left at 111th and pulled up in front of a six-story, brick apartment house with a small limestone front porch and second floor balcony supported by three round columns. Pulliam jumped onto the curb and held out his hand. Lenore took it, stepped down, and stood close to him. He quickly released her hand.

"Will your mother be waiting for you?"

"I expect so, if you promised to deliver me safely home. Aunt Trudie will still be awake as well."

A carriage passed them heading west. Pulliam followed it with his eyes. "Well, I will walk you to your door. If your mother and aunt are awake and, how shall I put it?"

"Dressed?"

"Yes. Of course. If such is the case then I must pay my respects, even at this late hour." He turned to the hansom. "Thomas, I may be a few moments. Feel free to continue home. I can find a cab on Amsterdam Avenue."

"I'll be waiting here, Mr. Pulliam."

"Very well. Thank you." He took Lenore's arm and they walked to the door. "No matter how I try I can't be rid of him," he joked. She smiled and opened the door with a key. She led Pulliam through a small lobby and a second door. They took a narrow stairway to the second floor.

They continued down a nicely finished, carpeted hallway to the last of five doors. "Let me make sure Mother and Aunt Trudie are up and respectable enough to receive a gentleman." She unlocked the door and entered. Pulliam noticed that the interior of the apartment was brightly illuminated and so assumed O. P. Caylor's widow was awake.

Lenore returned, opening the door wide. "Please come in, Mr. Pulliam. My mother and aunt have been expecting you."

They walked through a short hallway and turned left into a small parlor. Squat electric lamps with tasseled, ivory shades sat on three small tables, two on either side of a green-on-green striped Queen Anne love seat, and the third on a small table next to a large matching chair with ottoman. An armed wingback chair with deep blue and gold tapestry upholstery faced them from the opposite corner.

Mrs. Caylor and her sister stood in the center of the room almost formally dressed in floor-length, lace-trimmed gowns. They were slender and of equal height, several inches taller than Lenore. Pulliam thought Luella Caylor, whose hair had turned completely white, looked much older than her perhaps fifty years, while Lenore's Aunt Trudie looked younger than thirty.

"Oh, Mr. Pulliam," said Lenore's mother. "It's so good of you to call on us." Pulliam looked at Lenore, who stood expressionless, and then back at her mother. But before he could reply, Mrs. Caylor spoke again. "Do you think the Chicagos will win it again, Mr. Pulliam? You know Mr. Caylor, Lenore's father, always said that you couldn't count the Chicagos out. They always seem to come back with good teams. Do you remember Cap Anson? His teams always won. Do you remember Cap Anson? I'm sure you do. Is he still with the Chicago club? Do you remember that Anson fellow? He was the best in the league and you just couldn't beat him. Mr. Caylor always talked about Cap Anson. Do you know Mr. Anson?"

Lenore's aunt spoke. "Luella, why don't you sit down while I make a pot of tea." She guided her sister to the wingback chair.

"Oh, yes, of course. Thank you." Mrs. Caylor sat and smiled at Pulliam.

"Aunt Trudie," said Lenore, "I'll make the tea. You sit with Mother and Mr. Pulliam."

"Thank you, Lenore," said Aunt Trudie. "Mr. Pulliam, it's very nice to see you again. I don't suppose you remember me."

"Of course I remember you, Miss Pittenger," replied Pulliam. "We spent a very pleasant evening together in the company of your sister and Mr. Caylor."

"Yes. I enjoyed it very much as well."

"We saw Lillian Russell at Abbey's Theater," he continued, "if I recall correctly."

"Indeed we did, Mr. Pulliam. They call it the Knickerbocker Theater now, I believe. I haven't been there in years."

"We shall go, Trudie," said Mrs. Caylor. "Perhaps Mr. Pulliam would like to join us? And Lenore could come as well. Perhaps a matinee. Lenore is old enough to attend a matinee now. She likes to dance, you know."

"Yes," said Pulliam. "She mentioned that to me this evening."

"How does 1908 look, Mr. Pulliam?" asked Trudie. "For base ball."

"It should be an excellent season, Miss Pittenger. Chicago will contend again, but I expect the Giants and the Pirates will be right there with them. The American League looks close, too. I'm sure Mr. Comiskey will work hard to bring a city series back to Chicago."

"Yes. The 'Hitless Wonders,'" said Trudie. "Two years ago."

Pulliam nodded. "The White Sox were quite the surprise of that Series."

"Especially to the Cubs."

"Mr. Pulliam," said Mrs. Caylor. "Do you remember Cap Anson? Is he still with the Chicago team?"

"No, Mrs. Caylor. He retired from the game a few years ago."

"Thank heaven for that," she replied. "Now maybe our Cincinnati team will win some games."

"I'm sure they'll have a good year, Mrs. Caylor."

Lenore entered the room carrying a tray holding a floral-patterned porcelain teapot with matching cups and saucers. A small platter held biscuits and small cakes. "Here we are. Nothing like a pot of tea at two in the morning. Perhaps you would prefer a glass of sherry, Mr. Pulliam."

"No, thank you. This is perfect."

Trudie stood and helped her niece serve the tea. Pulliam's eyes wandered until he noticed a framed photograph of O. P. Caylor on one of the tables next to the love seat.

"That's a wonderful likeness of your husband, Mrs. Caylor."

"Thank you, Mr. Pulliam," she replied.

"By any chance, would you have another copy?"

"Why, whatever for?"

"I would like one for my hall of fame."

Lenore brought him a cup on a saucer. Trudie followed with an empty bread and butter plate and the platter of biscuits and cakes. He selected one oval biscuit.

"Thank you."

"Your hall of fame, Mr. Pulliam?" asked Lenore.

"Hall of fame, yes. You see, I think we should honor the best players and teams."

"Are all of the men famous in your hall of fame?" asked Lenore.

"Some. To base ball fans at least. But they've all demonstrated skill and dedication to the game. They've accomplished great things on the field."

"Then why don't you call it the hall of greats?" asked Mrs. Caylor. "A hall of fame could include anyone who's famous. I'm sure that my Mr. Caylor was never very famous. He was a terrible manager. Always getting fired. He was much better as a newspaper man. I don't believe a newspaper man belongs in your hall of greats. Is Cap Anson in your hall of greats?"

"I suppose," said Pulliam, "that 'hall of greats' sounds more accurate. But I like the sound of 'hall of fame.' It rolls off the tongue nicely. And I believe that your late husband belongs there. He did many great things for the game, besides his years as a manager."

"But he was a terrible manager, Mr. Pulliam." Mrs. Caylor smiled and sipped her tea.

Lenore set the platter down and said, "I'm sure we have another photograph. Let me look for one. Excuse me a moment."

She returned a few minutes later with an envelope large enough to hold a small photographic print. Pulliam stood. "Thank you, Miss Caylor. Your father will join our hall of fame as soon as I return to the office on Thursday."

Mrs. Caylor replied, "It is we who should thank you, Mr. Pulliam. Father would be very pleased."

"It makes me very happy to hear that, Mrs. Caylor." He took the envelope from Lenore. "Now, I must be on my way. Thank you for the tea and biscuits."

Lenore walked Pulliam down the hall as far as the staircase. "Thank you, Mr. Pulliam. You've been very kind."

"My pleasure, Miss Caylor. I will call you on the telephone in a few days to schedule that interview. Unless Mr. Ziegfeld has hired you in the meantime."

"I'll be happy to visit you in your offices."

He turned to leave but stopped on the top stair. "By the way, Miss Caylor. It was your aunt who called me on the telephone. There's no doubt in my mind."

"I realized it must have been Aunt Trudie. I saw the expression on your face as she first spoke to you this evening," said Lenore. "I suspected you recognized her voice. Anyway, as I mentioned, my mother has trouble with telephones."

"Good night, Miss Caylor. I hope I haven't caused any trouble between you and your aunt."

"Not at all, Mr. Pulliam. Good night."

He arrived at the New York Athletic Club at, according to his watch, 3:09 AM. He slowly walked through the lobby and paused at the front desk.

"Happy New Year, Mr. Pulliam," said the clerk, a tall, blond man of about thirty, dressed neatly in the club uniform of bow tie, stiff high collar, black waistcoat, and charcoal gray coat with tails, circular club seal with winged foot stitched over the left breast.

"Thank you, Robert. I trust you've a had an enjoyable evening here at the club?"

"Very festive, sir. But the party ended an hour ago."

"To your relief, no doubt."

"Yes, sir."

"Robert, will you ask Gordon to telephone the Prince George Hotel? Ask the front desk for Mr. Russell. I don't expect him to be there just now, it is New Year's Eve after all, but if he would try every thirty minutes and then put the call through to my rooms when the party answers, I would appreciate it."

"Certainly, Mr. Pulliam. Shall we make the first call at 3:30?"

"That will be fine. And don't worry about whether I'm asleep or not. I need to speak to the gentleman at that number."

"Very good, Mr. Pulliam." The clerk smiled.

Pulliam stared at him, struggling to interpret the look on his face. Was it a knowing sneer? Was he simply doing his job by trying to be pleasant?

"The business of base ball," said Pulliam, "knows no holiday."

"Of course, sir. Good night, sir."

Pulliam turned toward the wide, winding, carpeted staircase, as was his habit, but decided he was too tired to trudge up to the third floor. He walked slowly to the bank of elevators.

He went straight to his bedroom and changed into a white cotton night shirt. Turning on the lamp on his bedside table, he picked up a slim volume of poems by William Stanley Braithewaite, *Lyrics of Life and Love.*

> 'Tis strange that we should fall apart
> And live divided nights and days!
> What loneliness crowds on the heart,
> What vacancy in eyes that gaze.

His eyes closed as he read the first words of the second stanza. The switchboard did not interrupt his troubled sleep.

He awoke to sunlight streaming in around the perimeter of his windows' shades. Sitting up quickly, he was confused until he remembered that it was New Year's Day. He reached for his watch on his bedside table, but it wasn't there. This upset him. He always placed his watch on the bedside table to confirm that his daily wakeup call from the lobby was on time.

He reached for his telephone and lifted the earpiece off of its hook.

"Good morning, Mr. Pulliam," said a very young male voice.

"You're not Gordon," said Pulliam.

"No, sir. Gordon is off duty now. My name is Carl. How may I help you?"

Pulliam paused and then said, "Good morning, Carl. Did I not leave instructions to call me at a certain hour?"

"You did leave instructions, Mr. Pulliam. Let me review the note." Pulliam heard a faint rustling of paper. "I was to call the Prince George Hotel every half hour, ask for Mr. Russell, and ring you when the party was reached."

"And at what time did you last attempt to reach Mr. Russell?"

"Eight o'clock, sir. Twenty-one minutes ago."

"Thank you, Carl."

"Yes, sir. Shall I continue to make the calls?"

"No. Thank you. That won't be necessary."

"Will you take breakfast in your rooms today, Mr. Pulliam? Or perhaps in the dining room?"

"Oh. Yes. Of course."

"Sir?"

"Please send up," he paused, "one boiled egg, not too runny, one slice of toasted bread with butter, orange juice, and coffee."

"My pleasure, Mr. Pulliam."

"Thank you." He began to hang up the earpiece but stopped. "Nice to meet you, Carl."

"Thank you, sir. Happy New Year."

"Happy New Year to you, Carl."

Pulliam debated whether or not to take a cab downtown to the Prince George. He decided that he would upset himself too much no matter what or whom he found there.

He would turn to the game. The game would help keep his thoughts away from Ted and the flat on Bleecker. The good work of the game would keep him sane. He determined to take the Sixth Avenue El to Twenty-Eighth Street and walk from there to the office. There were less than two months to prepare for the National Commission, National League, and Joint Rules Committee meetings that came one after another at the end of February. Luckily, this year they would be in New York at the Waldorf-Astoria, just up Fifth Avenue. He needed to name the National League representatives and to study the topics to be discussed, especially the proposed rules changes.

Along Twenty-Eighth Street he considered continuing across Broadway and Fifth Avenue to Ted's hotel, but turned downtown toward the league offices at Twenty-Sixth Street.

A knock on her door woke Lenore at 9:40.

"Lenore?" It was her mother. "Telephone call, Lenore." Three more knocks. The message was repeated.

"Yes, Mother. I'll be right there."

She threw back her top sheet and quilt and stepped into her plaid cotton slippers at the side of her bed. When she opened her door, her mother stood smiling, wearing a slightly soiled, blue gingham apron.

"I'm sorry, Mother," she said quickly. "I guess I overslept."

"I'm sure you needed your sleep, darling. We'll have breakfast ready for you as soon as you're done with your telephone call. It sounds like a lady."

She moved away from the door. Lenore walked down the hall to the wall phone and picked up the earpiece dangling under the oak box.

"Hello?"

"I am so sorry, Lenore." It was May. "Did you go to Barclay's?"

"Hello, May. No. I'm sorry."

"Don't fret. I didn't make it either. But you did all right for yourself, didn't you? President of the base ball league and all."

"It was an interesting evening."

"Interesting? I would think so," May laughed. "He was a handsome young man, not like the fat old beast that went for me."

"He's a friend of the family."

"Pardon? A who? Oh no, Lenore."

"He offered me a job, May. That's all."

"A what?"

"Employment."

"What kind of employment? You're not going to work for the president of the base ball league, are you?"

"I'm considering it."

"He must be a good man, as well as young."

"Why don't we meet somewhere downtown for lunch. By City Hall."

"How about Shanley's, near the theater." May paused. "It's just ten. Can you meet me there at two?"

"But that's all the way up in Times Square. Can you make it there from Irishtown on a holiday?"

"I'm not home right now, Lenore. I'm near the Flatiron Building."

"Oh. I guess you can just walk up Broadway," said Lenore.

"I don't think so. Too chilly. I can afford a cab today. And I can afford Shanley's. Meet me in the ladies' restaurant on the second floor."

Pulliam reached Ted at one fifteen that afternoon.

"How are you feeling?" he asked.

"Terrible, but not sick." Ted voice sounded deep and rough. "How was your base ball banquet?"

"Terrible."

"Did you find your family friend?"

"Yes. It was very nice to see her."

"Aren't you going to ask me where I spent New Year's Eve?"

"No. I called to invite you to dinner tonight at Mouquin's uptown."

"You'll come down here to meet me?"

"I'm at the office."

"The office? You are ridiculous." He sighed loudly. "Very well. Eight o'clock?"

"That will be fine," said Pulliam, knowing that Ted would need those hours to recover from whatever trouble he found the night before.

"What will you do?" asked Ted. "I hope you don't mean to work until then."

"I'll take a walk through the park. I'll read the newspapers. Don't worry about me."

"Harry, I do worry about you. I fear that as much as you love your game, it doesn't love you in return."

"I'll see you at eight, Ted."

"All right. Yes."

Pulliam waited for the click to tell him that Ted had broken the connection at his end.

At exactly eight o'clock he left the St. James Building at Twenty-Sixth and walked up Broadway to Twenty-Eighth Street. He turned and passed the row of music publishing houses, silent and dark, and continued to Sixth Avenue. The night was cold, but there was no wind so he found his walk to be pleasant. He let his white scarf hang loosely over his shoulders, left his topcoat open at the neck, and tilted his bowler slightly back from his forehead.

He was surprised by the life on Sixth Avenue. He thought of the first of January as a day to stay home with family. But hansoms and carriages stood two deep and a dozen long in front of Mouquin—a four-story, yellow wooden building, set back between two more recent brick wings that opened onto the sidewalk. Pulliam climbed the canopied stairs to the second floor entrance.

The dining room was crowded and lively. The tall mirrors that lined the walls magnified its spacious size.

Ted stood at the bar talking to a young, very handsome gentleman in a nicely tailored, black pinstriped suit. Pulliam stopped and examined him from head to foot. His left hand held his coat open to reveal a bright blue vest with deep red piping and matching bow tie. His straight dark hair was parted in the middle, free sweeping strands flowing down over the corners of his forehead. His button shoes were new and spotless.

He was exactly the kind of man that would attract Ted. Pulliam waited a moment, gathering his composure, tamping down his jealousy.

Not logical, he thought. *Not smart. Why would Ted openly flirt with this man knowing that I would arrive any moment? To annoy me? To show me that if I want to keep him I had better keep him in New York?*

Pulliam slowly proceeded to the bar. Ted saw him and smiled. "Harry," he said. "Good of you to come." He gestured at his companion. "Please allow me to introduce you to Mr. Everett Shinn. Everett, this is an acquaintance from Kentucky, Mr. Harry Clay Pulliam."

The two shook hands.

"Mr. Pulliam," said Shinn. "I'm honored. Please, can I buy you a drink?"

"Very nice to meet you, Mr. Shinn. Thank you, but I believe our table must be ready."

Ted frowned. "I've spoken with the maître d'. He said we have a ten-minute wait." He gestured to the bartender. "Your best bourbon, please. Two drams. A drop of water."

"From Kentucky," said Shinn. "And what brings you to New York, if you don't mind my asking?"

"Base ball."

"But it's winter," laughed Shinn.

"And you, Mr. Shinn? Are you from New York?"

"Philadelphia, actually. Originally New Jersey, across the river from Wilmington."

Ted smiled and said, "Everett is one of the artists in the exhibit planned for Macbeth next month."

"Oh, yes," said Pulliam. "I believe it is to be a group show? I met a Mr. Sloan here several weeks ago."

"Yes," replied Shinn. "There are eight of us."

"I look forward to it. And how are you finding the art market just now?"

Ted broke in, "Everett does very well in several professions, all related to the arts. Sales of his paintings are not his only source of income."

"Is that so?" asked Pulliam.

"Harry, you've been to the new Stuyvesant Theater, haven't you?" Ted turned to Shinn. "Mr. Pulliam enjoys the theater, poetry, music, painting...everything. Although his passion is base ball."

Pulliam tried to smile. "I've been to the Stuyvesant. I saw *A Grand Army Man* there just after it opened last autumn. A beautiful theater."

"Everett painted the murals."

"My goodness!" said Pulliam. "You're quite accomplished, Mr. Shinn."

"It is my goal to become reasonably conversant in a variety of disciplines," said Shinn. "Some of my colleagues limit their horizons to the arts of drawing and painting. I, apparently like yourself, Mr. Pulliam, refuse to discount the possibility of success in anything I pursue."

"Everett was just telling me about his plans for a theater attached to his home," said Ted.

"Your home?" asked Pulliam.

"I live in Waverly Place. Are you familiar with Greenwich Village?"

Pulliam nodded and immediately wondered if this attractive, well-dressed Mr. Shinn had visited Ted on Bleecker Street.

"There is a coach house on my property that I mean to rehabilitate as a small theater."

Shinn was suddenly distracted, looking beyond Pulliam to the entrance. "But here's Flossie. I must go. A pleasure to meet you, Mr. Pulliam. I will see you at Macbeth, I trust."

He extended his hand to Pulliam. As they shook, Shinn turned to Ted. "See you at the gallery, old boy." He dipped his chin and whispered, "It's a good thing she sees me with you two gentlemen." He slapped Ted lightly on the back and approached a thin woman dressed in a royal blue broadcloth suit with pleated skirt and a cream-colored Merry Widow hat trimmed with a small bouquet of blue feathers.

"His wife," said Ted.

"Wife?"

"Yes. Florence Scovel of the Philadelphia Main Line Scovels. Her family disapproved. Now I fear she disapproves as well."

"How's that?"

"He's an unrepentant womanizer. There isn't a skirt in Manhattan he hasn't pursued." Pulliam sighed audibly. "I suppose you thought I was flirting with him."

"He's your type."

Ted laughed loudly and slapped his thigh. "Of course he is. He looks and dresses just like you." He turned to the bar. "But let's not fight tonight. Look. Your drink has arrived."

The subway crawled along its route from the Upper West Side, across town under Forty-Second Street, and down Fourth Avenue. Lenore had boarded at 110th and Broadway and had her choice of seats. Mr. Pulliam had generously scheduled their meeting for late morning so Lenore might, as he said on the telephone, "avoid the crowded early trains and enjoy a relaxing ride downtown." Her timetable detailed that it should take eighteen minutes to Twenty-Third Street on the local, but according to Aunt Trudie's watch she had been in her seat for twenty-one minutes and they were just at the Grand Central Station stop.

Trudie had prepared her a full breakfast of eggs, pork, potatoes, toasted bread, and tea. "You can't meet Mr. Pulliam hungry," she told Lenore the evening before. "What if your stomach growls during your meeting?" And she had starched and pressed Lenore's best pleated white cotton shirtwaist, brushed and pressed her black serge skirt, and polished her shoes.

At the breakfast table Lenore found the watch and a small green, paperbound volume titled *The Reach Official American League Base Ball Guide 1907.* She lifted the booklet and found a note.

Lenore,

Sorry that the guide is out of date, but the 1908 issue has not as yet been published. Also, it says American League on its cover but it includes a number of pages about the National League. I could not find a Spalding booklet. I think you will find several things of interest to read while on the subway. Best of luck. You will be most impressive, and you should accept Mr. Pulliam's offer. It is best for you and best for your mother and our household.

Trudie

P.S., I cleaned and pressed a skirt and shirtwaist appropriate for office employment. I wear similar clothing every day. I am sorry I missed you this morning, but the doctor expects me at my desk by 8:00, as you know.

She exited the subway and walked west along a crowded Twenty-Third Street. She had less than fifteen minutes to make her eleven o'clock appointment. The temperature was in the thirties, not too cold to enjoy a stroll. At Madison Avenue she took a path through the park and crossed Fifth Avenue at Twenty-Fourth Street where Broadway meets Fifth. The tall, red-brick St. James Building stood across Broadway on the southwest corner at Twenty-Sixth. She guessed that Mr. Pulliam's office on the fourteenth floor must be near the top.

She found the arched entrance on Broadway, passed through a dark, narrow hallway, and stepped into the lobby. The tiled floor was spotless. A coffered ceiling arched overhead with large stylized blossoms, carved in wood and illuminated with soft-yellow electric light. A wide mural depicting bare-chested Greek goddesses sitting before a temple of wide columns adorned the high wall just below the ceiling. A winding marble staircase led up from the rear of the lobby. A tall Chinese vase of colorful fresh flowers stood in a wall alcove just at the first turn of the steps, and a large clock with roman numerals high on the back wall told her it was five minutes before eleven.

She found the bank of elevators on the left at the rear of the lobby and asked the uniformed operator to take her to the fourteenth floor. As they silently rode up through the building she noted that the top floor was the sixteenth. Stepping off the elevator she found number 1424 at the end of the short hallway to her right. "National League of Professional Base Ball Clubs" was painted in black on the door's pane of pebble glass. A crude sign hung from the doorknob asking visitors to "Please Knock," and so Lenore lightly tapped her knuckles on the glass.

"'Tisn't locked," boomed a deep voice in an English accent.

She turned the knob and entered the office. Late morning light poured into the bay windows that filled the wall opposite the door. The photographs of a dozen or so men, many in base ball uniforms, hung on the walls to the left and right. Doors leading to inner offices, she assumed, stood closed to her immediate left and right. An elderly man with a full white, tangled beard down to his tie sat at a rolltop desk reading a document. He looked up at Lenore as she closed the door.

"Why, Miss Caylor," he said, smiling. "So nice to see you." He rose and stood at the desk. "It must be ten years since last we met. Entirely my fault. How is your mother?"

"Mr. Chadwick? What a pleasant surprise. My mother is doing well, Thank you."

"And you are living here in New York?"

"Yes," said Lenore. "Mother and I have a flat on West 111th Street. Mother's sister lives with us as well."

"Gertrude, yes?"

"You have a wonderful memory, Mr. Chadwick."

"I must call on you soon. That is if you would be so generous as to invite an old, ungrateful laggard."

"Of course. Mother would be very happy." She removed her hat and began to unbutton her coat. "And you, Mr. Chadwick? Do you work for the National League?"

"Oh. You mean that." He flipped the pages of the document. "No. Harry, uh, Mr. Pulliam—you are acquainted with Mr. Pulliam?" She nodded. He smiled. "Harry asked me to come in to review this report." He walked across the office to help her with her coat.

"Then you still live in New York?"

"Brooklyn. Same as always."

Chadwick hung Lenore's coat on a wooden coat stand. "Thank you, Mr. Chadwick. And you still write about base ball?"

"Same as always. Base ball, cricket, billiards, just about anything the *Eagle* sees fit to publish." He pulled a chair away from the wall adjacent to the front door. "Please, sit down." Lenore accepted Chadwick's invitation as he returned to the rolltop desk. "Are you here to see Mr. Pulliam or Mr. Heydler?"

"Mr. Pulliam."

"He should be out shortly. He is speaking on the telephone with someone very important, I should think. He closed his door. He rarely closes his door." He pointed to one of the framed photographs. "You see, Harry has your father in his hall of fame. He was a great friend to O.P." He cleared his throat. "Quaint idea, a hall of fame, don't you think?"

"Very nice." She looked up at her father's portrait and decided she rather liked the simple brown wooden frame.

The door to her right opened and Pulliam entered the office. He looked pale but smiled when he saw Lenore.

"Miss Caylor," he held out his hand. "Thank you so much for coming." Lenore took his hand and began to rise. "No, no. Please, make yourself comfortable. Have you met Mr. Chadwick? The 'Father of Base Ball'?"

"Yes. Mr. Chadwick was one of father's dearest friends."

"Of course," said Pulliam.

"'Father of Base Ball.' Rubbish." Chadwick slapped the document. "But I will tell you one thing. I am more of a father of base ball than this General Doubleday that Spalding and his hirelings mean to force on the American base ball rooter."

"I am not at all surprised by your reaction, Henry. I was just on the telephone with Spalding. He's quite determined to make the Doubleday story the official history of the game."

"We've fought over this issue for years," said Chadwick. "But he never mentioned anyone named Doubleday before. Or that hamlet where he supposedly created the game. Where the devil is Coopersville anyway?"

"Cooperstown," said Pulliam. "Upstate somewhere."

"Rubbish."

Pulliam turned to Lenore. "My apologies, Miss Caylor."

"No need to apologize, Mr. Pulliam. I'm finding the offices of the National League to be quite interesting."

Pulliam laughed. "Henry, how far have you read?"

"Far enough," said Chadwick. "But I have several paragraphs yet to go."

"Very well. I will meet with Miss Caylor while you finish."

Pulliam returned to his door. "Miss Caylor, will you join me in my office?"

"Certainly." She rose and followed him through the door to her right. Inside Pulliam's office a single desk with a matching slatted wooden chair stood near another set of bay windows that looked down onto Broadway. Two more chairs stood to either side of the front of the desk. Pulliam gestured to one of them.

"Please."

"Thank you." She sat in the chair to the left. Pulliam's desktop was neatly organized with file dividers and an in/out tray. A large green, felt blotter, bordered in deep brown leather, covered much of its surface. A photograph of a very pretty young woman in a wedding dress standing in front of a large Victorian house stood framed near a telephone. An electric lamp with a green glass shade was centered toward the rear of the blotter.

Pulliam walked around the desk and sat in his chair, his back to the windows. "Now, Miss Caylor," he began, "have you considered my offer of employment? Actually, I assume you have because otherwise you would not have agreed to meet with me today."

"Yes, sir."

"Goodness," he said, leaning back in his chair. "Please do not call me sir. As a friend of the family I hope that you will be comfortable referring to me as Harry."

"Thank you, Mr. Pulliam."

"Very well."

"I would like to know what my duties would include."

"Your title would be 'stenographer' but that would not be the total extent of your responsibilities."

"But I am not a qualified stenographer."

"The National League, in recognition and gratitude to your father's contributions to the game, will be happy to pay for your instruction in stenography. I believe there is a business school on Twenty-Third Street near Sixth Avenue. Take as long as you need. In the meantime, you will have several other duties that will keep you quite busy if you go to school, say, for an hour or two each day."

"Mr. Pulliam, may I be honest with you?"

"Of course."

"I came here mostly to please my mother and my aunt. They seem very anxious for me to quit my sinful dancing ways and take on honest employment. Quite frankly, I do not believe I qualify for any of the tasks you may have in mind."

"Neither did I when they named me president!" he laughed. "Some say I still don't have what it takes to hold this position. Nonetheless, here I am."

Lenore caught herself nervously wringing her hands and stopped. She placed them, one on top of the other, on her lap. "I don't see how I may help you."

"You still follow the game. You told me so the other night."

"Of course. It's part of our family heritage."

"Then you are qualified. I would like to give you the title of secretary, but Mr. Heydler holds that distinction. Secretary/treasurer, actually. Your most important charge would be to help Mr. Heydler and myself with the day-to-day business of the National League. The details are unimportant. There is also the business of the National Commission which includes myself, Mr. Johnson of the American League, and Mr. Herrmann of Cincinnati. The commission has employed its own secretary, Mr. Bruce, but I will appreciate your assistance with matters directly related to our league."

She stared at the framed photograph as a way to divert her eyes. Pulliam followed her gaze.

"My sister Grace," said Pulliam, picking up the picture. "On her wedding day. The house is her home in Nashville where the wedding took place. She has twin boys one of whom she named for me. Harry Pulliam Cain."

He replaced the photograph. "You haven't asked about your salary. It will be twelve dollars per week, as approved by the league."

Lenore's eyes opened wide. "That's very generous, Mr. Pulliam."

"I believe it's fair. We know you will be well worth our investment."

"I would like to request a day or two to consider your offer."

"Of course. Discuss it with your mother and aunt."

"There is no need to do that. I know how they feel already." She stood. "May I ask one question?"

"Of course."

"Did Mr. Chadwick know I was coming today?"

"No. Why?"

"He recognized me immediately. I haven't seen him since Father died."

Pulliam smiled and nodded. "Remarkable man. At eighty-two, or eighty-three—I'm not sure exactly—he is as keen as ever." He rose to his feet signaling that the interview had ended. "Thank you for coming in, Miss Caylor. I trust you will give our offer of employment serious consideration." He held out his hand.

Lenore stood. "I certainly will, Mr. Pulliam. Thank you." She took his hand for a short moment and quickly released her grasp.

"Take your time. I understand that working for the National League would be a dramatic change from your current career, but I would suggest that for someone like you, someone with base ball in the blood, as it were, a position in our offices would prove very interesting and perhaps quite fulfilling." He walked around his desk. "Let's see how Henry is faring." He opened the door and waited, smiling, for her to precede him into the outer office.

Chadwick sat reading at the rolltop desk. He made no acknowledgement that they had returned from Pulliam's office.

"Henry?" said Pulliam.

"This man Abner Graves, who is he?" asked Chadwick looking up from the document. "And why is the very dubious testimony of this one man enough to determine that Doubleday invented the game whole, as a finished product, apparently out of nothing, one day in Coopersville in 1839?"

"Cooperstown," said Pulliam.

"Rubbish."

"I need to study Mr. Mills' report a bit more thoroughly."

"Do you have another copy, Harry? I'd like to take it home with me. And I'll no doubt need it at the *Eagle.*" Chadwick picked up the pages and tapped them on the desk to align the edges of the individual sheets of paper.

"I can employ a typist to make a copy. The league has an open account with a secretarial service in the building. We can drop it off, go to lunch, and pick it up when we return."

Chadwick pulled a tarnished silver watch out of his vest pocket and flipped it open. "No. Thank you for the offer, but I have a luncheon appointment with Ebbets on Court Street. I must get back to Brooklyn."

"I would be happy to copy your document," said Lenore. She pointed to a typewriter on a side table adjacent to a wide office desk.

"Miss Caylor," said Pulliam, "thank you very much for your very generous offer, but it would be no trouble for me to drop off the report at the secretarial service and then send it to Mr. Chadwick via messenger."

"Mr. Chadwick," said Lenore, "may I use your chair?"

"Then you are accepting our offer of employment?" asked Pulliam.

"I am helping a family friend." She crossed the office, glancing at the portraits in Pulliam's hall of fame. Chadwick rose and guided the chair to the typewriter table.

As she sat, Lenore read aloud the humble paper label glued to the wall under the photograph of a young uniformed ball player with full cheeks, a cleft chin, and slightly wavy hair parted in the middle. "Clarence 'Ginger' Beaumont." She found the player handsome. His hair looked dark in the picture, and she wondered if it was black, brown, or perhaps a deep shade of red.

Pulliam cleared his throat. "Yes. Ginger came to the Pirates in 1899, the same year I moved from Louisville to Pittsburgh with Mr. Dreyfuss. I admit to perhaps some personal bias in my decision to install his photograph as the first, how shall I say this?" He put his fingertips to his forehead. "The first member, or inductee, of the National League Hall of Fame. This was some five years ago."

"But, Harry," said Chadwick, "he doesn't play with the Pittsburghs anymore."

"In my defense, Ginger has led the National League in runs, batting average, and hits over the years. He batted over 200 hits the year I installed that photograph."

Lenore found a supply of blank paper on a shelf near the typewriter. She quickly examined the black Underwood and found it in good working order. As she spooled a sheet into the machine she asked, "Where does Mr. Beaumont play now?"

"In Boston," answered Chadwick.

"Nationals or Americans?" She gathered the pages of a document titled "Mills Commission Report" and placed them to the left of the typewriter.

"Mr. Dovey's Doves," said Pulliam. "If he had deserted to the American League I most certainly would have removed his likeness from these offices."

"Perhaps," said Chadwick, "you should consider waiting until a player retires from the game before you nominate him for your hall of fame." He gestured at another framed portrait. "Like Cap Anson there. You might avoid the problem of shuffling photographs."

Pulliam's face flushed red. "It is not my hall of fame, Henry," he said tersely. "It is the National League of Professional Base Ball Clubs' Hall of Fame. And shall I have the Father of Base Ball telling me how to administer the business of this office, along with the magnates and the teams and the newspapers and..." He stopped himself and grabbed the back of a chair, bracing himself.

Lenore paused and looked up at him.

"I apologize, Harry," said Chadwick, almost whispering. "I did not mean to..."

Pulliam held up his free hand. "No, no, Henry. It is I who needs to apologize." He stood up straight and pulled on the bottom of his vest with both hands. He smiled. "You see how we need you, Miss Caylor? If only to shield myself and Mr. Heydler from the best intentions of our dear friend the Father of Base Ball." He smiled at Chadwick who replied with a hearty laugh. "Now, Henry, perhaps you'll join me in my office so we may leave Miss Caylor to complete the task she so generously volunteered to do for us."

"Of course, Harry." Chadwick strolled past Pulliam toward the inner office. Pulliam smiled and nodded at Lenore as he turned and followed Chadwick.

She paused and inspected the office. A small telephone switchboard was mounted onto the wall to her right, on the other side of the typewriter table. In addition to the rolltop desk and the office desk that she assumed would be hers if she accepted the position, a small conference table with four chairs stood on the other side of the room.

Lenore struggled with the Underwood at first but knew that her high school typing skills would quickly return to something close to full strength. And the report was brief, more like a long business letter, ten paragraphs or so. After wasting two sheets of paper with uncorrectable mistakes, she had a clean copy completed in a quarter of an hour.

New York, December 30, 1907

...While "Father" Chadwick and I have not always agreed...yet I always have had respect for his opinions and admiration for his inflexible honesty of purposes....

In the days when Abner Doubleday attended school in Cooperstown, it was a common thing for two dozen or more of school boys to join in a game of ball....

It is possible that a connection more or less direct can be traced between the diagram drawn by Doubleday in 1839 and that presented to the Knickerbocker club by Wadsworth in 1845....

My deductions from the testimony are:

First: That "Base Ball" had its origin in the United States.

Second: That the first scheme for playing it, according to the best evidence obtainable to date, was devised by Abner Doubleday at Cooperstown, N.Y., in 1839.

Lenore wondered what the evidence might be. It apparently had something to do with the Mr. Graves mentioned by Mr. Chadwick, but she saw no specifics in the short document. And thinking back she could not remember her father ever speaking about a man named Doubleday.

She heard brief but loud laughter coming from Pulliam's office. The door opened. She stood. Chadwick led Pulliam out, all smiles. Pulliam slapped Chadwick on the back.

"Well," said Chadwick, "he's one of my oldest friends yet. We'll get through this splendidly, as we always have."

"I'm certain you're right, Henry. Miss Caylor, it appears you've completed your task."

"Yes. It wasn't very long or difficult."

"Then your office skills haven't diminished during your years on the stage?"

"I'm afraid they have, Mr. Pulliam. But I managed, at the expense of several ruined sheets of the league's foolscap."

"And I'm sure your stenographic ability will return as well." When Lenore scowled Pulliam continued, "Your aunt detailed your qualifications when we spoke on the telephone. However, if you determine it necessary, the offer of classes at a business school still stands."

"The stage?" asked Chadwick.

"Yes," said Pulliam. "Miss Caylor has for these many years danced in the theater."

"Excellent. Mrs. Chadwick and I love a good show with music and dance. Have I seen you perform here in New York?"

"I doubt it, Mr. Chadwick. I'm afraid most of my appearances have been in very small theaters."

Chadwick glanced at his watch. "I really must be going, Harry. I'll take Miss Caylor's copy."

"Please take the original, Henry. You'll need it for the guide. I'll keep the copy."

"Indeed. I'm afraid our friend Mr. Spalding will insist."

"The guide?" asked Lenore.

"Yes," said Chadwick. *Spalding's Official Base Ball Guide for 1908.*"

"Henry is the editor," said Pulliam.

"Guilty as charged, Miss Caylor. The, uh, distinguished Mr. A. G. Spalding, the perpetrator of the nonsense you were kind enough to copy for us, is one of my employers. He will insist on exploiting his popular annual journal to further his personal view of the origins of the game, as articulated by Mr. Mills and his cohorts." He laughed loudly. Lenore brought the two copies of the Mills report to the men, handed the original to Chadwick and the copy to Pulliam. Chadwick set his on a chair while he put on his topcoat. Pulliam went to a shelf and found a large envelope where he placed Chadwick's document.

"Thank you, Harry."

Lenore looked at Pulliam. "If that will be all, I'll leave with Mr. Chadwick."

"Splendid," said Chadwick.

"Of course," said Pulliam. "I'm not your employer yet, after all. And I thank you both for your time this morning. One day soon we will all go to lunch at Café Martin across Broadway."

Lenore put on her coat and hat. "Thank you, Mr. Pulliam. I will call you within a day or two and give you my decision."

"Excellent."

Chadwick took a battered top hat from the coat stand. "What decision, Miss Caylor?" he said. "There is no decision to be made. You could not do better than to work for the game with Mr. Harry Clay Pulliam."

As they rode the elevator to the first floor, Chadwick sighed and straightened his hat. "Harry sincerely needs your help, Miss Caylor. You saw how he lost his temper over a mere trifle. That is not the Harry Pulliam that I know. Not at all. Oh, he could engage a professional service and find a perfectly acceptable office employee, but he would never find a base ball person like yourself. I remember you as a young girl. You had your father's enthusiasm, his appreciation for the finer points of the game. Surely you cannot have lost all of that."

"Perhaps I lost all of that when I lost my father."

Chadwick nodded slightly, steadying his hat with his free hand. "Perhaps. Yes, perhaps. But I am sure it is still there, in your heart." He smiled. "And I'm certain it will come back to you, much as your typing did just now."

The elevator made two stops for additional passengers before arriving at the lobby. Lenore and Chadwick had been gently forced to the back of the car and so waited for the others to exit first, each of whom exchanged a pleasant greeting with the operator.

As they stepped into the lobby Lenore asked, "Mr. Chadwick, what is your personal theory on the origins of base ball?"

Chadwick stopped and faced her, waving the envelope while holding it by a corner as if it were contaminated. "My dear Miss Caylor, it is very simple. Base ball evolved from certain antecedents, most importantly the game of rounders, which I myself played as a lad in England. Rounders is a bat-and-ball game with four bases, over two centuries old at least. A ball is pitched to a batsman who endeavors to strike it into the field of play so that he may safely run the round of the bases in order to score a run. There are differences between the games, of course, but you might as well claim that the language spoken in this country sprang fully formed from the waters of the Hudson River and has no relation to the language of Shakespeare, Byron, or even Dickens. It's preposterous. Nonetheless, I will be forced to publish this," he slapped the envelope, "this drivel, in Spalding's guide for 1908."

He began walking toward the building's entrance. He held the door for Lenore. "Shall we find a cab in Madison Square? Can I drop you somewhere?"

"That won't be necessary. Thank you, Mr. Chadwick. I believe you have an appointment in Brooklyn. I live far uptown on West 111th Street in the opposite direction. I can catch the subway at Fourth Avenue and Twenty-Third Street."

"At least let me drop you there. It is January, after all." He raised his head and glanced toward Madison Square. "The wind has picked up somewhat. There's a damp chill in the air." He extended his hand in the direction of the square where a line of carriages and hansoms stood waiting along the curb for fares, the nostrils of their horses emitting clouds of visible breath. Lenore began to walk in their direction. Chadwick stepped in next to her. As they approached Twenty-Fifth Street Lenore thought she recognized Thomas standing on the sidewalk holding his horse's bridle.

"Any of these carriages will do, I'm sure," said Chadwick.

"Shall we try the man just there?" she pointed. "I'm not certain but I believe he may be Mr. Pulliam's favorite."

"Thomas? Is that Thomas? I believe you might be correct." Chadwick stepped ahead of Lenore. "Thomas? Is that you?"

The driver turned toward them. He hesitated but then recognized both. "Mr. Chadwick." He saluted by lightly touching the brim of his top hat. "Miss Caylor." He bowed slightly.

"Hello, Thomas," said Chadwick. "I need to be driven to the Brooklyn Bridge cable car terminus in Park Row. On the way we will stop at the Fourth Avenue subway station at Twenty-Third Street for Miss Caylor."

"Very well, sir." Thomas went to the hansom door near the curb.

Before she climbed in Lenore said, "Nice to see you again, Thomas."

"Thank you, miss."

Chadwick had walked around the horse and climbed into the cab through the door on the other side. "The bridge cable cars will be gone soon," he said as he settled into his seat. "End of the month. Have you been to Brooklyn recently, Miss Caylor?"

"It's been several years. We live so far uptown."

The cab pulled away from the curb and started down Broadway as trolleys passed in a continuous stream on their left. The Flatiron building loomed tall above the intersection of Broadway, Fifth Avenue, and Twenty-Third Street, silhouetted against the bright gray, midday light of a low sun trying to break through the clouds.

"It's a different city today," he said. "Excuse me. A different 'borough.' But I simply cannot get accustomed to the idea of Brooklyn and New York City as one metropolis, along with the other so-called boroughs. I've lived in Brooklyn since arriving from England seventy years ago and as far as I am concerned it's quite a separate place from the island of Manhattan. And Staten Island? It should have been annexed to New Jersey, not New York City."

The hansom turned left onto Twenty-Third Street. Thomas guided the horse behind a trolley and through the chaos of the three wide avenues coming together. Lines of trolleys, many only a few feet apart and traveling in both directions, dominated the center lanes leaving the outer lanes for horse-drawn vehicles and the occasional automobile.

"Nicely done!" said Chadwick. "This intersection was once identified as one of the most dangerous in the city. The Broadway and Twenty-Third Street trolleys would come within inches of each other, and not always miss."

"But not now?"

"Well, no. They've installed some safeguards, and much of the traffic has moved uptown to Forty-Second Street." He paused. "I have watched the center of this city progress from City Hall to Union Square to Madison Square to Longacre Square."

"Times Square?"

"Of course," he laughed. "And I've watched the game grow, too. From rounders in Brooklyn to the first time I witnessed a base ball game in Elysian Fields across the Hudson, to the new World's Series. I tell you, Miss Caylor, it's an American game, certainly, but it was born of an immigrant parent as so many other things thought of as American. Does that make it any less American? Not at all." He held up the envelope. "Spalding means well. After all, 'Goodwill' is his middle name."

"But is he all good will? He has a business to run. I imagine that declaring base ball purely American will help sales."

"I am quite sincere, Miss Caylor. 'Goodwill' is his middle name. Albert Goodwill Spalding." Lenore quickly put a hand to her mouth to stop herself from laughing too loudly. "Anyway, we are still friends and won't allow a minor disagreement to change that. It's not ultimately important to the game. Not like the problems of gambling and alcohol." He looked up as the hansom came to a stop. "Fourth Avenue. Let me help you step down." He opened his door.

"Mr. Chadwick, please!" shouted Thomas.

Lenore saw that he was climbing out of the hansom on the traffic side, away from the curb. She reached out to stop him but was too late. From her seat she saw Chadwick suddenly raise his arms to his face, the envelope flying out of his grasp and over his head. He fell and disappeared from her view. She heard metal-on-metal grinding, a horse's shrieking neigh, and the dull thud of something soft being struck by something solid.

An automobile had stopped just to the left of the hansom, its driver on the street rushing forward on foot. Thomas appeared in the narrow space between the motorcar and hansom. Lenore climbed out and followed him toward the cab's agitated horse. A small crowd gathered in front of the automobile.

"He came out of nowhere," said the driver, pale and panicking. "I was slowing for Fourth Avenue but couldn't stop." Lenore looked down and saw Chadwick writhing on the pavement below the automobile's radiator. She dropped to one knee and held his shoulders.

"Who's that?" shouted Chadwick. He tried to turn toward Lenore, but groaned in pain and fell back onto the street.

"It's Lenore Caylor, Mr. Chadwick. You've been hurt."

"Please help me up. I must see Ebbets on Court Street."

Lenore looked up and saw Thomas calming the horse and keeping it away from Chadwick. "Thomas, can you help me? We must get him to Bellevue."

"I have room in my motorcar," said the driver.

Chadwick struggled to his knees. "I will not go to Bellevue. I am fine. Thomas, please help me stand."

"Take him to Bellevue," said someone in the crowd. "It's just up the street."

"I will not go to Bellevue. If I go to Bellevue I may never emerge alive."

Another man said, "Let me hold the horse."

Thomas jerked his horse by its bridle to the curb where the man took hold of the leather reins and pulled them taut to the horse's jaw. Thomas went to Chadwick who reached toward him with his right arm. Thomas quickly took hold of the arm as Lenore grasped Chadwick's shoulders firmly.

"You see," said Chadwick, "I am not injured."

The automobile driver took his other arm. Very gradually they brought him to his feet. He winced.

"I am sorry, Mr. Chadwick," said Lenore, "but you are in no shape to meet Mr. Ebbets."

"Then take me home. Will you take me home, Thomas?"

"Certainly, sir." Thomas glanced at the automobile driver. They slowly guided Chadwick to the door of the hansom. Lenore tried to follow him into the cab but Chadwick sprawled across the entire width of the interior.

"The envelope," said Chadwick, out of breath.

"Don't worry about the envelope, Mr. Chadwick," said Lenore. "I will find it and have it sent to you immediately."

"Thank you," said Chadwick. He tried to shift his weight but gave up, groaning. He put a hand to his side.

"I'm sorry, sir," said Thomas, "but can you tell me your address?"

"It's 840 Halsey Street."

"Do you know it, Thomas?" asked Lenore.

"Yes. Off Atlantic Avenue, almost to Broadway."

Thomas climbed up onto his perch at the rear of the hansom. He glanced at Lenore but then snapped a whip over his horse and turned into Fourth Avenue. Lenore looked to her right. The automobile was gone. The crowd had dispersed.

A horseless electric hansom pulled up and stopped behind her. "Hey, lady?" shouted its driver. She turned to face him. "You can't stand in the middle of the street. You have traffic backed up to Tenth Avenue." Lenore could only stare at the man. He knitted his brows. "Say, you okay, lady? Why you standing there in the middle of the lane?"

She stepped onto the sidewalk and looked back onto the street for Mr. Chadwick's envelope. White sheets of paper were strewn and trampled from where the hansom had stood into Fourth Avenue. She turned and briskly walked back toward the St. James Building.

"Mr. Russell no longer resides at the Prince George, sir." The voice at the other end of the line was stiff, mechanical. Pulliam felt a low panic set in.

"When did he move out?"

"Just a moment, sir." He heard the voices of several operators chatting in the background.

He rotated his chair and stared out of the bay windows, over the roof of the Café Martin across Broadway to the barren treetops of Madison Square Park.

The mechanical voice returned. "Mr. Russell vacated his rooms yesterday morning, sir."

"Did he leave any forwarding information?"

"No, sir."

Pulliam heard the outer office door open. "Thank you." He placed the earpiece onto its cradle and stood. John Heydler filled his office doorway. He wore a heavy tweed topcoat and black derby.

"Good afternoon, Harry."

"John. How are you?"

"Fine, Thank you."

"Any improvement in the weather?"

"Not at all. It's still winter."

Pulliam laughed. "How many days until the season begins?"

"Too many, I fear."

"You mean to tell me you're not keeping an exact count? And you the league statistician?"

"It's a scandal, Harry. Actually, I'm keeping track on a calendar in my office. I can run over there and check."

"Ha! Just give me a holler when you sit down."

"Certainly. Top priority." Heydler began to remove his hat and coat.

"I trust your meetings went well."

"Very. I've come to some understanding with both the Superbas and the Giants about our statistical reporting."

"And Brooklyn's financial obligations to the league?"

"I merely informed them of their tardiness. They assured me that payment was being processed through their accounting office and should arrive any day."

"Of course it should." Pulliam sighed audibly. "Thank you. Is there anything else?"

"Mr. Chadwick left me a note about developing a statistic that accounts for batters advancing runners on base."

"Oh yes. Did you know that such a statistic was calculated years ago?"

"I did not."

Pulliam smiled. "Henry calls it 'teamwork at the bat.' The fact that it was quickly abandoned is one of his favorite complaints. I don't disagree, but the players hated it twenty-five years ago and would hate it today."

"Would the fans follow another statistic such as that?"

"Some. Not many. Most fans are very happy with batting averages and earned run averages, don't you think?"

"Of course."

"The most fanatic among them will parse and analyze any numbers we might publish. But they are a small minority."

"I would like to proceed as requested by Mr. Chadwick," said Heydler. "And I would like to draft formal language for the runs-batted-in statistic, which I believe is related to Mr. Chadwick's advancing-the-runner idea. Can't do any harm."

"Certainly. Perhaps you can develop a simple formula for each proposed statistic so the magnates and players will quickly understand both."

The outer office door opened again. Heydler turned. "Yes? May I help you?"

"I must see Mr. Pulliam." Lenore, exhausted from rushing through Madison Square Park and up Broadway, used the door to steady herself.

"Miss Caylor?" said Pulliam. "Please come in." Heydler stepped farther into Pulliam's office. Lenore entered without removing her hat or coat. "Miss Caylor, allow me to introduce Mr. John Heydler, secretary and treasurer of the National League.

"Very pleased to meet you, Miss Caylor." Heydler bowed.

Lenore stared at Pulliam as if she had not heard the introduction.

"Miss Caylor?" said Pulliam. "Is there something wrong?"

"There's been an accident. Mr. Chadwick ..."

"Henry?" said Pulliam. He stood, his two hands firmly on his desk's blotter for support.

"He was struck by an automobile on Twenty-Third Street. I believe he is injured, but not severely."

"Is he at Bellevue then?"

"He refused. Thomas is taking him home. He seems to be tender along one side. Perhaps a broken rib."

Pulliam looked at Heydler and then his watch. "John, please call the *Eagle* and inform them. And try to reach Spalding?"

"Of course," said Heydler.

"I will call Henry's home."

Heydler hurried out of the office. Pulliam motioned for Lenore to sit as he lifted the telephone's earpiece.

"Please, Mr. Pulliam, if you could just give me your copy of the Mills Commission Report, I would like to type another copy for Mr. Chadwick. His was lost on the street."

Pulliam frowned as he opened a desk drawer and retrieved a black book. "Nonsense. Please, Miss Caylor, you must relax. Would you like a glass of water?"

"No, Thank you." She watched as he searched his book for Mr. Chadwick's home telephone number. To her right she saw the report at the edge of the desk. She picked it up and left Pulliam's office, closing the door behind her.

Lenore took the subway from Fourth Avenue and Twenty-Third Street to the City Hall stop, which she knew to be near the Park Row Brooklyn Bridge Cable Car terminus. Crossing the bridge she had a view of downtown Manhattan and the East River to the Upper Bay, and Brooklyn itself to her left. The landscape looked vast, but serene. The midafternoon sun had broken through the clouds and reflected off the water, silhouetting a ferry on the bay. Backlit mist and smoke from the many cargo and passenger ships shrouded the outline of Staten Island in the far distance.

She found the Court Street trolley and made her way to Atlantic Avenue. At 840 Halsey Street, a red-brick row house of three stories, she hesitated but finally proceeded up the walk to the front steps. She tapped the door's brass knocker and waited. A slender woman of late middle age answered, opening the door only enough to peer out at Lenore.

"Yes?"

"Is this the Chadwick residence?"

"Yes."

"I have an envelope for Mr. Henry Chadwick. I work for the National League."

"Oh. I'm Mr. Chadwick's daughter. I'll take it." The woman reached through the half-opened door for the envelope. "I'm sorry to be so abrupt, but my father has had an accident."

"I know. How is he?"

"The doctor says he has a couple of broken ribs, but he'll survive. He's very grumpy just now or I would invite you in."

"Thank you, but I must be going anyway. Please tell your father that Miss Caylor hopes that he will heal quickly, and please convey the best wishes of the National League."

"Thank you. I'll tell my father."

It took over two hours for Lenore to make her way to West 111th Street. When she entered the apartment Trudie hurried to the door, her face ashen with worry.

"Lenore, where have you been, dear? Mr. Pulliam has been calling all afternoon. We thought you were with him at the league offices. He thought you must have returned home hours ago."

Lenore took off her hat and coat, sat on the love seat, and told her story to her concerned aunt and mother.

"I'm so glad," said her mother. "You have a nice job in base ball. Your father would be so happy."

Pulliam considered walking to the gallery on the way home, but decided against it. Ted would be in touch soon, he was certain. No doubt between moving and working on the planned February Macbeth exhibit he was very busy.

He stepped out onto a dark Broadway. The weather had warmed. He walked the short distance along Twenty-Sixth Street between Broadway and Fifth Avenue, passing the Café Martin, very quiet at this early evening hour, and turned uptown. It was just six o'clock. He had a free evening ahead. He purposely did not bring any files or papers with him when he left the league offices because he wanted to clear his mind. No questions of rule changes or banning the spitball or new statistics would clutter his thoughts. And Henry seemed to be in relatively good shape. In ill humor, but physically stable.

He knew the Macbeth Galleries were near Thirty-Ninth Street, but he had never actually visited them. He didn't like American art, the gallery's focus. The Hudson River artists were too dramatic. Those

Americans who followed the French Impressionists appeared too derivative. Why bother with these pretenders when he could visit the beautiful new Metropolitan building in Central Park and see many of the world's finest paintings.

Pulliam recalled when Ted visited him from Louisville in 1903, just after Pulliam had moved to New York from Pittsburgh to begin his post as president of the league. The Metropolitan Museum of Art building had been open for only a year. Ted loved the new American art and so found the museum building offensive. "With all the wonderful twentieth century architecture being designed the Metropolitan Museum chooses to build a façade that is old before completed," he had complained. "Beaux arts," he scoffed. "Nothing 'beau' about it."

He approached Thirty-Third Street and saw the bright electric lights of the Waldorf-Astoria illuminating the avenue. Ted and he had shared a drink there during that first visit. They had discussed everything New York and finally agreed to disagree on most topics.

"You champion your American national pastime," Ted had said. "Allow me to champion the new American art and architecture." Pulliam had laughed and held up his glass for a toast. "To America in the new century." They touched glasses.

He paused outside the hotel and thought, *Why not? I have determined to have a night off, so I'll have a drink at the bar.*

He entered the men's café and stood at the four-sided bar. He ordered a double bourbon and drank it rather quickly as he watched the elite of New York imbibe amid the huge fluted columns and crystal chandeliers. The omnipresent dark woodwork began to oppress him. He left too much money on the bar and hurried out.

At Thirty-Fourth Street he considered turning west toward Herald Square and Broadway, which he could take uptown to Seventh Avenue and his rooms at the Athletic Club, or catch the Sixth Avenue El. But he crossed the street and continued on Fifth Avenue, checking the addresses as he walked. Between Thirty-Eighth and Thirty-Ninth he saw 424 and knew that Macbeth, at 450, would be on the next block.

He crossed the street, continued past Thirty-Ninth and looked back across Fifth Avenue. The Macbeth windows were dark. He crossed again and peered into the gallery. Paintings hung from temporary partitions and along the walls. The traditional style of the art visible at the front of the gallery told him that the show preceding the February exhibition was still on view. He strained to see the rear of the space through the darkness. Perhaps he would see light coming from a back office. But there was no hint of any illumination anywhere in the gallery.

He decided to eat alone at the club. He stepped to the curb and hailed a carriage.

—— WEDNESDAY, JANUARY 15, 1908 ——
NEW YORK, NEW YORK

Lenore found May reading a newspaper at a table near the back of the room. She wore white gloves and gripped the handle of an ornate porcelain coffee cup decorated with tiny pink tea roses. Shanley's second floor ladies restaurant, resplendent in red and green Louis XVI excess, bustled with young women rushing to finish their lunches and return to work. Several tables were occupied by older patrons who lingered over their meals. Bright sunlight filtered in through the tall, narrow windows.

"There you are," said May. "I've got wonderful news for you."

"Hello, May." Lenore sat. "Our second lunch at Shanley's this month. Does the maître d' know you by name yet?"

"Very funny, Lenore. Where else when we have wonderful news to celebrate? Let's order something special to start." She handed Lenore a menu.

"Wonderful news?" She glanced at the long luncheon card.

May lifted her head and searched the room for a waiter and, finding one, delicately waved a hand just above her forehead. The waiter arrived.

"We'll start with two glasses of champagne."

"May!" protested Lenore. "It's only 1:30 in the afternoon."

"Don't be such a prude, Lenore." She turned again to the waiter. "Make it Veuve Clicquot."

Lenore flipped over her menu and read the wine list. "Did you rob a bank, May?"

"And I intend to have more than one."

The waiter bowed slightly. "Then perhaps the mesdames would like a bottle for the table."

"Why not?" said May.

"At four dollars?" laughed Lenore.

"Will that be yellow label or gold label?" asked the waiter.

"Which would you order?" asked May, looking up at the waiter.

"The gold label is the brut, madame."

"Of course. Thank you."

When the waiter left the table May casually picked up her menu and began to scan its contents.

"Oh, May," said Lenore. "Don't be a bother. You must tell me what we are celebrating, for goodness' sake."

May dropped her menu and leaned over the table. "Mr. Ziegfeld himself came to the auditions yesterday up in the Jardin de Paris." She smiled and took Lenore's hand. "I'm to be in the line for this year's *Follies.*"

"No!" said Lenore. "That is indeed wonderful. How exciting! I'm very happy for you."

"But that's not all." She looked around the room as if making sure no one was eavesdropping. "There are still three places to fill and Abby agreed to give you a look."

"I can't believe that." She sat back in her chair and released her hand from May's light grip.

"It's as true as you and me sitting right here. At first, after the New Year's Eve problem, she said she never wanted to see your face again, but then they told her about this president of the National League who you left with and she was very impressed by the title. You know, a president of anything sounds very big indeed, I should think. And so she thought maybe you have something that people like, especially men, even if you've lost a step or two, which is what she says, not me. Why, I'm quite certain that once Mr. Ziegfeld sees you he'll put you in the line right away. And Abby thinks maybe so, too. Oh, he'll like you well enough, that's certain. Not in any untoward way, I don't mean. Word is he's smitten with Lillian, young as she is. Anna stares daggers at him whenever Lillian is in the same room. But I don't think Lillian will be in the line this year. Too many missteps. She needs to watch her drinking, I'm afraid."

"When would I audition?"

"I'm quite certain Mr. Ziegfeld needs to fill in the line as soon as possible so maybe this week. Today is…"

"Wednesday."

"Yes. So maybe Friday? I can check with Abby and call you on the telephone."

Two waiters arrived with the bottle of champagne, two glasses, a silver ice bucket, and a tripod stand. As one set up the bucket, the other set the glasses in front of May and Lenore, removed the foil from the top of the bottle, and silently popped the cork into a spotless white towel. He wrapped the towel around the base of the bottle and poured the wine into Lenore's glass first.

"Lovely," said May. When her glass was full she raised it and held it out to Lenore. "To success," she said. Lenore touched May's glass. They drank. "And so. Tell me. Whatever happened to this president of the league and his offer of employment?"

"It pays well. I was very seriously considering it and actually tried to call him several times this week, but he's been busy or away from his desk. I didn't leave my name."

"And now?"

"I don't know. I would certainly like to audition for Mr. Ziegfeld."

"Of course you would." May picked up the menu. "Let's see here. I think the cream of lettuce soup with croutons sounds lovely. And then fresh mackerel sauté, meu…meu… Can you read that French word, Lenore?"

Lenore sat backstage next to May, waiting to audition in front of Ziegfeld. She would turn twenty-five this year and felt old among the children who would try out with her. Some of the girls could be no more than fifteen. They sat primping and giggling, nervous energy pouring out of them in endless chatter, and for some, sweat.

She looked at her hands. They belonged to a grown woman. She didn't want to be the old lady among the young hopefuls. She was tired of chasing a career that she knew was ending and found herself giving in to the urge to get up and leave. She thought often of Mr. Pulliam and his offer, especially after talking with him on the telephone two days ago. He admitted to being disappointed, but said he understood. He told her not to hesitate to call if she changed her mind—that the immediate needs of the league would be met by a secretarial service.

May spoke to her, but she hardly heard her. "And she'll bring Jack Norworth with her," she said. "They're quite the couple. There's going to be a wedding."

"Who?"

"Nora Bayes," said May, exasperated. "Aren't you listening at all?" She smiled. "Oh, it's all right, Lenore. You're nervous, aren't you, dear? Don't worry. You'll be fine."

"Is Abby out there?"

"Sure. She made good on her promise to give you a chance, you know."

"I almost wish she wasn't here," said Lenore. "It doesn't matter, I guess."

"Doesn't matter? Are you feeling well?"

"Fine. I'm fine. I just want...I just want to leave."

"Now, now." May patted Lenore's knee. She tipped her head down and looked up into Lenore's eyes. A group of girls ran off the stage, panting, heads down, faces anxious. "Come on now," said May. "You're on."

She went through each silly step not caring, oblivious, as she had been when she tripped into that banquet room at Delmonico's. Oblivious to everything except the time. She wanted to get home before Mr.

Pulliam left his office for the day. She would call him and accept his offer of employment.

May met her as she left the stage. "Oh, Lenore! You were just wonderful. I've never seen you dance so smoothly. You made it look very easy indeed."

"Thank you, May. Do you know the time?"

"The time? Who cares?"

Lenore found her hat and coat.

"What's your hurry, Lenore? Don't you want to wait and hear what they thought of your audition? I looked out into the seats and Mr. Ziegfeld, Jack Norworth, Anna Held, and Nora Bayes were all there. I'm certain they loved you."

"It doesn't matter."

"Have you lost your mind?"

"I'm sorry May, but I'm just not interested anymore."

"But Lenore..."

"The *Follies* were a big hit last summer, but there's no guarantee that the next *Follies* will be as successful this year."

"Of course not, but if I had the money to bet on any show next summer it would be Mr. Ziegfeld's."

"Maybe." She pulled on her coat. "But it's not only that. Listen, May. When I was out there dancing I had the distinct impression that I was being sized up like a prize steer. And I know Mr. Ziegfeld's reputation as well as you, and I couldn't help feeling I was auditioning for his office couch as well."

May shrugged. "That's life in the theater."

"Mr. Pulliam never made me feel that way."

"Who's Mr. Pulliam? He's not that banker you used to see."

"No. He's the base ball man."

"Excuse me," called a male voice from behind them. The man stepped forward. "Good afternoon, Miss...?"

She stopped and looked at him, a little alarmed. May stared, eyes wide. "Oh my goodness," she said. "It's Jack Norworth. He writes the songs."

"Well," said Norworth, making a bad attempt to look humble, "actually just the lyrics."

"Jack," came a woman's voice from behind Lenore. Nora Bayes stepped out of the backstage shadows.

"Excuse me. I'm late," said Lenore.

"What's your hurry?" said Jack Norworth.

"Jack," repeated Nora Bayes.

"I have an appointment," replied Lenore.

"What kind of an appointment could be so important?"

"Base ball," said Lenore as she turned toward the stage door. "May, will you telephone me when you get home?"

"I don't know what to say, Lenore. I took a very big risk with Abby for you."

"I'm sorry." Lenore walked between May and Norworth and out the door.

"Base ball?" Jack Norworth turned to Nora. "That's all I ever hear about. All the newsboys. Everyone. The Giants. But it's January. Why is everyone talking about base ball in January?" He shook his head. "Do they get a good audience?"

"They call it a crowd, dear Jack," said Nora, "not an audience. And they draw more than we do. By the way, don't worry about your new friend. She's in the line. You'll have plenty of time to flirt with her." She turned and walked toward the stage.

When Lenore arrived home her mother sat knitting in the living room. Lenore was grateful that Aunt Trudie wasn't home from work. She took off her coat and hat.

"Hello, Mother. I must make a telephone call. Can I get you a cup of tea?"

"How was your day, my dear? And a cup of tea would be nice," said her mother, letting her knitting drop to her lap. "The telephone. That reminds me. A nice young woman called you. She said they accepted your follies. Whatever does that mean, dear? I've never known you to have follies of any kind."

"I don't know, Mother. I believe it was my friend May."

"Yes, I'm certain it was her."

Lenore went to the phone. Her mother had hung the earpiece over the mouthpiece instead of replacing it in its metal cradle. She pressed the cradle down and held it for several seconds as she freed the earpiece. She hesitated, but took her hand off the cradle and asked the operator to connect her with the National League of Professional Base Ball Clubs in the St. James Building.

Lenore assumed the male voice that answered the telephone belonged to John Heydler.

"Hello," she said. "Can you put me through to Mr. Pulliam? This is Lenore Caylor."

"Why, hello, Miss Caylor. John Heydler here. Mr. Pulliam is out of the office. May I help you?"

"If you would be so kind as to leave him a message that I telephoned, I would appreciate it."

"Of course. I don't expect him back today, but I will leave him a note and I am certain he will return your call in the morning."

"Thank you, Mr. Heydler."

She held down the earpiece hook for a moment, let it up, and gave the operator May's number.

A man answered the phone. "State your business."

"Hello, sir. I am trying to reach May."

"May don't live here. Who's asking?"

"My name is Lenore."

"You one of her dancer friends?"

"Yes, sir."

"I guess it's okay then. May has a roommate down near that tall building they call the Flatiron. She moved in with someone from that show. Another dancer, I should think."

"Do you have a telephone number for her?"

"Sure do. It's right here on the wall." He paused. Lenore wondered how May could move in with one of the girls without telling her. "Gramercy 0493."

"Thank you, sir."

"My pleasure." The line was disconnected.

Lenore gave the operator the Gramercy number. A woman answered. Lenore knew the voice.

May had moved in with Abby.

Lenore hung up the earpiece without speaking.

The call came into the Forty-Seventh Street engine house at 2:51 in the morning. Henry was asleep and had to be shaken awake by another fireman. Ladder Company 21 needed assistance at a fire on West Thirtieth Street. A boarding house, mostly young women.

Groggy, Henry pulled on his gear and jumped onto the back of the wagon as it pulled out onto the street. The snow that had begun the previous afternoon now came down in large, heavy flakes that threatened to make the streets difficult to negotiate.

They drove west on Forty-Seventh and turned downtown on Ninth Avenue, encountering only the occasional trotting carriage that would quickly move to the curb to make way for the fire wagon. The snow had collected to several inches deep. He could sense that the wagon's three horses galloped more cautiously than usual, as if unsure of their footing. At Thirty-Fourth Street a horse pulling a hansom slipped and tumbled to its side, legs flailing as it struggled to avoid their wagon. The hansom driver fought in vain to control his cab, losing his top hat as he pulled hard on the reins, straining against the weight of his horse.

He first saw the fire's glow as they approached Thirty-Second Street, the rooftops of tenements silhouetted against an unnatural, pulsing orange horizon, slightly dimmed by the falling snow. He could see it was bad and prayed that the building's tenants had by now escaped. When they turned onto Thirtieth Street his heart sank as he watched a fireman carry a limp form down the building's front steps.

They pulled up and jumped off the wagon. Flames almost completely engulfed the right side of the five-story, red-brick tenement. Two of the firemen pointed toward its top. Henry looked up to see a middle-aged woman leaning out of a window on the fifth floor waving with one hand as she held a white cloth to her nose and mouth with the other. A ladder was propped against the wall, but it stopped at the floor below.

He looked back at the men discussing what to do. He pulled on his gloves and grabbed the pompier hook from his wagon. He slung the short, single-pole ladder over his back and secured the hook on his shoulder. He began climbing. He looked below and saw two firemen with a Browder life net, but there were too few available men to hold it.

At the top of the ladder he took hold of the bottom of the pompier and swung it over his head so the hook cleared the fifth-story window ledge. He pulled on the pole and felt the hook grab onto the sill inside the room. Satisfied that it would hold him, he reached up, hand over hand, and took quick strides up the rungs as the ladder bounced against the outer wall of the building. At the window ledge he somersaulted into the room. A heavyset woman lay crumpled in a ball on the floor.

His best chance was to lift her out through the window and let her down by her arms to another fireman, if one had followed him up the ladder. He looked out. The ladder was gone. Two men had moved it across the façade of the building to another window. He looked behind him. The flames were close, but he quickly scanned the room and located their weakest point, a seam that might afford a path to safety. He remembered that the left half of the building was not completely ablaze. Reaching for the woman, he rolled her onto her back. She was dressed in her nightgown, a cheap cotton fabric. He estimated that she weighed about 150 pounds. He took her wrists and twisted her around onto his back as if she were a large sack of flour. He pulled his helmet off. Getting down on all fours, he let her limp form ride him like a pony, her arms dangling over his shoulders and dragging on the floor and her cheek bouncing on the back of his head. Crawling would be slower, but they needed to stay low to avoid inhaling too much smoke.

He followed the seam in the fire and made it through the thin wall of flames before the woman's nightgown could ignite. He stood, holding onto her wrists and letting her dangle against his back. They entered a short hall that led to her smoldering front door, a sight that would have frightened the woman and sent her back to the window. Henry knew that the fire had weakened the wood. He held her wrists tighter and ran at the door. It gave easily.

The stairs had caught fire, but were useable. He could hear the sounds of other firemen in the building below him. He leaned forward so his back would take the bulk of her weight and took the stairs as fast as he could, balancing his speed and the bulk of the woman's body so their momentum wouldn't topple them.

Standing on the street a few minutes later, watching the medical men revive the woman, his coat charred and smoking, he felt good. Maybe they would get through this one with no fatalities at all.

A fireman from his crew passed him. "Monkey McBride," he said. He patted Henry's arm and continued toward the wagon.

McBride saw that the men were now concentrating on preventing the fire from spreading to adjacent buildings. The captain from Ladder 21 stood talking to an elderly man wrapped in a blanket. He walked over to them.

"Sure?" asked the captain.

"I think so," said the man. "Yes. I saw Martha and Mrs. Belden and everyone from the fourth floor. They all got out."

"Think a minute."

Henry heard a faint scream from the rear of the building. The captain heard it, too. "Damn," he said and pushed the man away. He and others in the crew from 21 ran into the building. Henry followed. They continued through a hallway and found their way to a rear entrance that led into a backyard. A small, young woman, perhaps Maureen's age, knelt on the ledge of a fourth-floor window, dressed only in her nightgown and bedroom slippers, pleading for help. She balanced herself precariously on the sill, silhouetted against the flickering orange and red glow from within. A policeman stood in the yard looking up at her.

The captain from 21 yelled at her not to jump and then rushed with a contingent of his men to fetch a ladder and the life net. Henry started to follow, but one of the men from 21 held him back. "This is our show now," he said. Henry stopped and joined the policeman.

They looked up and watched the young woman. The firemen were within minutes of returning with the equipment, but she could not know that.

The young woman on the window sill looked down and saw a fireman and a policeman staring up at her, doing nothing. One of them, the fireman, waved his arms and screamed something at her, but she could not understand him. The flames singed the hem of her gown. Her side and the soles of her feet burned as if on fire.

It didn't look so far down after all.

The fireman was still waving and pointing at the building. She tried to look along its outer wall but worried she would lose her balance.

The ground below her appeared soft and white and cool. The snow was deep and thick and inviting. And there was no one coming for her.

She jumped.

The girl's gown billowed like wings extended above her. Henry and the policeman instinctively moved toward the spot in the yard where she would land. But two floors from the ground she stopped in midair and flipped 180 degrees so that her nightgown floated over her head, baring her legs, her panties, her torso, and the gray slippers on her feet. One leg had caught on a flapping shutter, breaking her fall. She dangled in the air for a moment, arms flailing, and then fell again, her direction changed by her contact with the shutter. Henry jumped and reached with both arms in her direction, but he was still much too far from her to help.

She landed facedown, impaled on two white, pointed pickets of the yard's fence. Her arms and legs jerked upward, as if she were trying to free herself, but quickly fell limp at her sides. The two men stood motionless for a moment, knowing there was nothing more they could do.

Without looking at each other they assumed their professional roles and walked purposefully to the fence. Henry gathered the young woman's legs as the policeman crossed her arms just above where one of the pickets had run through her abdomen. Henry averted his eyes from the deep-red stains on her gown and the large open wound sticking to the fabric. They slowly lifted her slight, lifeless body and placed it on the ground. Her hair covered her face in a knotted tangle. Henry thought about brushing it to either side, but he did not want to see her face in death. He thought of his Maureen, about the same age as the dead girl in the snow. He forced himself to maintain his poise as a fireman. The other men arrived with a ladder, but the life net's folded metal frame had been too large to fit through the narrow hallway.

When the fire was extinguished, Henry decided to walk through the snow back to the engine house. He would switch shifts with Billy Brennan and take a couple of days off. He needed to forget about what he had seen and spend some time with his girl. He'd take Maureen to a nice restaurant and perhaps a show.

The snow fell faster and heavier. Drifts began to form at the curbs and against the walls of buildings. The few carriages that passed moved slowly.

And it's only January, he thought. Fully three months until real spring and warm weather and base ball. Come April he'd take Maureen to the Polo Grounds to see a game. She had no interest in base ball, but they had made a deal. He would take her to one of those dancing shows in Times Square if she would watch the Giants with him. Seeing Maureen's reaction to the antics of McGraw and the others would be almost as much fun as the game itself. The thought of it helped push the image of the falling young woman to the back of his mind.

Lenore knew when she entered the subway station that she would have no trouble finding a seat. The heavy snow had kept many morning riders home. The walk to the train had been difficult, but she prided herself in being able to handle any sort of weather.

She assumed that the middle cars, normally the most crowded, would be empty, and so she didn't bother walking to the end of the platform as she had the other mornings of her first week of work. When the train pulled in, she found an empty pair of seats two rows in from the door. She sat and pulled her book out of her bag.

Trudie had given her a copy of Elinor Glyn's *Beyond the Rocks* as a congratulatory gift in celebration of her new job. Lenore would have preferred a volume of historical fiction but was grateful to her aunt for the diversion the book would afford her mornings and evenings on the subway. The inside cover was inscribed, "Dearest Lenore, So your travel downtown and back home will give you a modicum of pleasure each day. Best wishes in your new employment. I know you will experience nothing but success. With love, Trudie."

Madame Glyn had wasted no time in establishing the plight of poor, pretty Theodora Fitzgerald. Miserable after agreeing to an arranged marriage with a portly man thirty years her senior, she accepted her doom so her hapless, but charming, father and two elder, and plain, spinster sisters could enjoy the windfall of the considerable wealth of her new husband, Mr. Josiah Brown, whose fortune had been accumulated somewhat by accident in Australia.

Our dear friend Theodora is going to stray, thought Lenore.

At Seventy-Ninth Street a man boarded the train and sat next to her. He looked to be in his late thirties and was well dressed in a heavy, gray woolen topcoat and damp bowler. "Thank goodness for the subway," he said.

Lenore looked up and smiled, but said nothing. She continued reading. His presence next to her made it difficult to concentrate, but she was able to retain that Mr. Josiah Brown was the jealous type and a needy hypochondriac.

The man took a newspaper from his inside coat pocket and scanned the front page. "Nothing about the storm here," he said. "I hope it doesn't turn out to be as bad as the blizzard of '88. I was only ten years old at the time, but I recall it well. You're much too young to remember that one."

"Yes," said Lenore without looking up.

"I'm sorry. I don't mean to annoy you. It's just that the snow is such that I feel like I must say something to somebody."

"I understand."

"I'll leave you alone now."

"Thank you." She found herself hiding the title of her book from his eyes lest he think her silly.

They traveled in silence. As the train approached Twenty-Eighth Street the man rose and made his way to the car's doors. Lenore decided to exit as well. Her usual shortcut through Madison Square Park would be impassable so Twenty-Eighth would be slightly quicker to the St. James Building. She let several passengers fill in behind him before she left her seat. As the small crowd slowly climbed the station's stairs, each in turn dipped his or her head against the strong wind that swirled down through the exit. On the street the snow fell heavier than when Lenore first arrived at the 110th Street station. City workers trudged along the Fourth Avenue curb alongside a parade of a dozen or more horse-drawn carts loaded with sand. Their white uniforms almost disappeared into the high snow drifts. They used short-handled shovels to spread the sand over the street.

Traffic on the avenue was light, and there were no vehicles of any kind to be seen on Twenty-Eighth. Lenore decided to take Fourth Avenue down to Twenty-Seventh and then turn west to take advantage of the shelter of Madison Square Garden's pillared arcade. The snow collected rapidly. Drifts at Twenty-Seventh Street made it difficult to cross the intersection. Lenore stopped and considered walking on the street.

"Let me help you, miss," shouted a voice to her right. She looked up and saw the man from the subway. "Oh," he said. "It's you."

"Oh, it's you," said Lenore. She held out her right elbow. He took her arm and together they fought their way through a drift and across Twenty-Seventh. His hold felt reassuring. She was embarrassed, but the weather was too miserable to worry about such matters for long. The blustery wind cut through the city from the west along the cross-town streets making even the walk under the arcade difficult.

The man said, "I hope you don't have far to go."

"Twenty-Sixth and Broadway."

"I'll see that you get there."

"Please, I do not want you to go out of your way. I can make it."

"Not at all. I work near there myself."

As they turned south the buildings along Madison Avenue cut off the worst of the wind. They turned right at Twenty-Sixth. Several men shoveled the sidewalks between Madison Avenue and Fifth Avenue, but the wind proved to be a greater obstacle than the snow. At the Broadway entrance of the St. James Building he stepped into the lobby with her. They brushed the snow off their shoulders and shook out their hats.

"Thank you," said Lenore. "And I apologize for being less than polite on the subway."

"No need to apologize. I understand perfectly."

"You said you don't have far to go?"

"No. Just over there." He gestured vaguely to his right and behind him. He held out his hand. "Good luck, then," he said. "Let's hope the trip home tonight isn't as difficult."

She took his hand. "Indeed," she said. "Goodbye." He turned to leave. "By the way," she called after him. He stopped and looked back. "Lenore Caylor."

He smiled. "Norman Adams. A pleasure."

"I work," she began, "I work for the National League of Base Ball Clubs on the fourteenth floor."

He nodded and left the building.

"Idiot," she berated herself. "He's probably married."

Pulliam stood at Lenore's desk looking out the windows at the snowbound streets. He turned when he heard the door open and rushed to help Lenore remove her coat. "Miss Caylor," he said. "I tried to telephone you, but you had already left. You should have stayed home."

"Thank you, Mr. Pulliam, but I had no idea the weather would become so severe. Did Mr. Heydler make it in?"

"No. I spoke with him on the telephone. He left his home but could not travel more than a block in his carriage. I talked to your aunt as well."

"Trudie? Then she didn't make it to work?"

"No. Making one's way across town is all but impossible. She told me she relies on the 110th Street trolley but there were none to be had."

"She works for a doctor at Madison Avenue."

"I would insist you return home, but perhaps it would be safer for you to wait out the storm right here."

"And I believe you have the upcoming meetings to discuss with me." She went to her desk and picked up a stenographer's pad. "The National Commission and the question of ineligible players and the O'Rourke Resolution. Also rules thirty-four, thirty-five, and thirty-six. For the National League meetings the order of business includes the

World's Series schedule and several constitutional amendments. The Joint Rule Committee will cover two proposed rules changes."

Pulliam raised his eyebrows. "Excellent, Miss Caylor. Thank you. I'll give you a chance to dry off and settle in. We can begin whenever you're ready."

"Thank you."

"And I believe we'll take lunch right here. I'll order something from Café Martin across the street. Compliments of the National League as an expression of our gratitude for the considerable effort you made to get to the office this morning. You'll find a recent luncheon menu in the bottom drawer of your desk. I'll telephone Louis Martin myself at about, say, eleven thirty."

"That's very generous, Mr. Pulliam."

He smiled and returned to his office. Already hungry, Lenore hesitated only a moment before she opened the drawer and found a brown cardboard folder containing menus for more than a score of local restaurants. The Café Martin card was toward the bottom of the stack. She immediately saw the note explaining that dishes listed as plats du jour and marked with a star were ready to serve. To make ordering simple and inexpensive, but appropriately French, she settled on "Cold Egg à la Estragon" for twenty cents. She had no idea what "Estragon" could mean, but assumed that an egg cooked in any fashion must be safe. She made a note of her choice.

"This will never do," said Pulliam when she handed him the note with her selection. "I've already talked to Monsieur Martin. They are shorthanded because of the storm, but he has offered to prepare whatever we would like himself. I can't very well ask him to cook an egg," he laughed. "Please don't take offense, Miss Caylor. You no doubt wanted to keep things easy and frugal. Do you have the menu handy?"

Lenore said nothing. She felt her face turning warm and red. She handed Pulliam the luncheon card.

"Let's see now," he said. "Do you like chicken and rice?"

She nodded.

"Good. We can share a "Chicken à la Valencienne" and whatever vegetable Louis recommends. How does that sound?"

"Very nice. I won't need to eat dinner."

"We may have to eat the scraps for dinner right here if we're stranded by the storm." He stood. "I'll let Louis know right away, and in a bit I'll dash across the street to pick it up." When Lenore frowned he explained, "That was part of the bargain. He can't spare anyone to bring our meal to us. Apparently the storm doesn't keep local residents from enjoying a good lunch. They expect to be quite busy and understaffed."

He left to pick up lunch forty-five minutes later. Lenore planned to use the time to type up the notes from their morning discussions and to draft proposed agendas for the February meetings.

She was surprised to hear the outer door open only a few minutes after Pulliam left for the restaurant. She looked up to see a very thin, elderly gentleman standing in the hall, supporting himself with two wooden canes. He stared at Lenore and appeared reluctant to step inside.

"Where's Pulliam?" he demanded. He wore a gray suit of expensive cloth that hung loosely from his emaciated form. A pearl tiepin held a muted green silk cravat in place. "You must be Lenore Caylor, Ollie's girl."

"Yes, sir. Mr. Pulliam stepped out for a moment. Won't you please come in? He should be back soon."

"Where'd he go?"

"Across the street to pick up lunch."

"Café Martin? Just what I would expect of Pulliam. Do you know what they allow at Café Martin, Miss Caylor?"

"No, sir. I've never been to Café Martin."

"They allow women to smoke. Anywhere in the restaurant. Why, when I heard they were going to start that kind of scandal on New Year's Eve, I moved my party to Delmonico's." The man put one cane forward and then the other and took a step over the threshold. "I'm Brush. John Brush. I own the New York Giants."

"Very nice to meet you, Mr. Brush."

"No it ain't." He glared at her. "I expect Pulliam has already told you a pack of nasty lies about me."

"I shouldn't think so, sir."

"Then you don't believe they're lies?" He brought a bony fist to his mouth and coughed loudly, wincing with a pain that shook his entire body. He stood and breathed heavily, trying to regain his composure. "Doesn't matter," he said. He reached into a jacket pocket and pulled out a folded sheet of paper. He slapped it onto a small mahogany table to the right of the door, nearly toppling a crystal vase of silk flowers. "See that he gets this and tell him I expect payment out of his own pocket and not the limited resources of the National League."

"I'm sorry, sir?"

"Seems he didn't think I'd check my Delmonico's bill closely enough to notice a mug of coffee and a snort of brandy delivered to his driver on Forty-Fourth Street and billed to my party." He paused, staring at Lenore. "I'm a better businessman than that." He lowered his voice. "Then again, he probably knew damn well I'd notice. Expected me to notice. He did it to get my goat. Never misses a chance." He turned to leave but struggled with his canes.

"Let me help you, Mr. Brush," she said.

He looked back at her over his shoulder. "Ordinarily, I'd tell you to go to blazes, anyone who works for the league. But seeing as you're Ollie's girl, I reckon it will be all right." He tried to stand erect as he waited for her to approach him. She took his left arm. Beneath his suit coat's cloth she felt only bone. Repulsed, she hesitated.

"Don't worry," he said. "I won't fall. Just to the elevator, please. Someone from my office will help me from there."

"Of course, sir."

"You seem quite sure of yourself, Ollie's girl," he said as they made their way down the hall. "And I don't mind saying that you're quite attractive. Now don't get me wrong. I'm speaking in a purely professional sense. You see, my wife, Elsie Lombard—perhaps you've heard of her?—she's an actress and quite accomplished on the stage. Perhaps you would like an audition with Cohan or Ziegfeld? Can you sing?"

"Not very well."

"No matter. Not important. You think about it and then come on down to my office and let me know, and we'll help you get out of that damn league office and away from that invert."

"Thank you, Mr. Brush, but I'm quite pleased with my position."

They arrived at the elevator.

"You won't be for long. Keep it in mind."

The elevator doors opened. The uniformed operator stepped out to help Brush. Safely at the back of the car, Brush smiled weakly and nodded his head. The doors closed. Lenore walked back to the office and picked up the sheet of paper. She was impressed by how beautifully the lettering and figures were written on the page.

Pulliam returned in a jovial mood. "It's quite remarkable outside," he said as he closed the outer door. "Invigorating. And the snow has rendered the city almost completely silent." He set their lunch, a large square package neatly wrapped in wax paper and tied with twine, on Lenore's desk. "You have scissors somewhere I trust?"

She opened a top desk drawer. "Yes, I'm certain I've seen a pair in here somewhere." She rummaged through rulers, a letter opener, pencils, and boxes of pins and clips. "By the way, Mr. Brush stopped in to see you."

Pulliam's face darkened. "Mr. Brush?"

"He said you owe him money based on his New Year's Eve check at Delmonico's." She handed him the sheet of paper and continued looking for scissors.

Pulliam quickly examined the figures and laughed loudly. "It's the coffee and Cognac I ordered for Thomas. Was Mr. Brush upset?"

"Yes."

"Good, good. I'll take care of it this afternoon. I'm surprised he made it into the office today. Actually, I'm surprised that he's in New York and not Indianapolis." He turned toward his office, removing his hat and coat as he went. "I wonder if I should include a percentage for the gratuity." He glanced down at Brush's reckoning. "Beautiful penmanship, don't you think?"

"Very," said Lenore. She located the scissors and snipped the twine.

Pulliam paused, found his coat pocket, and produced a clear bottle of White Rock spring water. He held it up for Lenore to see. "Lest you think I neglected the beverage."

They ate at Lenore's desk. Café Martin had sent the Chicken à la Valencienne in a small, oval Limoges vegetable bowl with matching plates decorated in a pattern of flowing stems and flowers. Pulliam provided crystal goblets for their sparkling water.

"Your dealings with Mr. Brush seem a bit difficult."

Pulliam laughed. "Difficult? I would be the happiest man in base ball if my relationship with Brush was merely difficult."

"But how?"

"You may as well know the worst. It could affect your position with the league. It already has, apparently." Pulliam sipped his water. "He has men follow me. They probably followed us to your home New Year's Eve."

"But why would the owner of the Giants be following you on New Year's Eve?"

"It's quite normal. Several of the team magnates hire detective agencies to follow their players to make sure they are not associating with gamblers or similar types. Mr. Herrmann of Cincinnati is well known for the practice. Mr. Brush has me followed because he and McGraw mean to destroy me. Again, I apologize for making such a strong statement, but it's quite true."

"Destroy you? Why?"

"What are the usual motives? Greed, revenge, power, lust. It's all of those—except lust." He laughed.

"That doesn't tell me why."

He sat back and looked up. "Mr. Brush and I have been at odds for many years. He has tried to take control of the league and the players several times and believes that I stand in his way at every turn, costing him money. That's the deadliest sin in his eyes. The team's manager John McGraw tries to undermine the authority of this office whenever he can. They push, and I push back."

"How?"

"How?" He lowered his eyes to look directly at Lenore. "For example, a few years ago I suspended and fined McGraw for fighting with Fred Clarke of the Pirates. He appeared at the ball park the next day anyway shouting obscenities and insulting Barney Dreyfuss's Jewish heritage."

"The Mr. Dreyfuss you mentioned earlier."

"Yes. The owner of the Pittsburgh team. So, McGraw was expelled from the ball park again. I fined him again and suspended him for an additional fifteen days. His employer, Mr. Brush, took it to court and won an injunction to stay the fine and suspension."

"They took it to court?"

"Yes. The next year I suspended McGraw yet again for harassing an umpire. The next day he arrived at the ball park early and locked out the umpires. He tried to start the game using players as umpires, but the other team, the Cubs, refused to play and protested. I awarded the game to the Cubs as a Giants forfeit. And, as I mentioned before, Brush and McGraw refused to play in the 1904 World's Series mostly because I supported the National Agreement that made the Series possible. The story goes on and on."

"It doesn't help that the Giants are located in the same city as your headquarters."

He laughed again, a dry, cynical snicker. "With offices just downstairs from ours."

Lenore thought a moment. "Downstairs? That explains why he wore no coat or hat." She watched as Pulliam sampled his lunch. "And what could they possibly use against you?"

"Perhaps we don't know each other well enough yet."

"Is there a woman involved? Are you married?"

Pulliam took his gold watch from a vest pocket and flipped open the cover. "I will say one thing, Miss Caylor. You are not timid or retiring. Exactly the kind of help we need in our office. I am convinced you will work out just fine." He flipped the watch closed with a metallic snap and looked directly at her. "If I were married, I would not have very publicly brought you home New Year's Eve." He paused. "There is no woman involved." He looked out the window.

Neither spoke for several minutes until Pulliam noticed the short length of the twine that had secured their lunch. He picked it up and examined it closely.

"Miss Caylor," he said, "have you ever reflected on those things we now take for granted that not so very long ago seemed rare and miraculous?"

"Sir?"

"The telephone, for example. It has become a commonplace household item. Most business concerns will have one for each office, as we have here." He placed his fork on his plate and held the twine with both hands, turning it slowly and focusing on the individual strands that had been twisted together to compose the single length.

"When I was a young boy living on a tobacco farm in Kentucky, we had an old gray barn that leaned quite precariously to the north. My daddy had built a new red barn across the road, but let the old one stand. I guess it was so full of memories that he just couldn't bring himself to tear it down. Kept putting it off. My sister Grace and I loved that old barn.

"One day we heard that the general store in Scottsburg had put in a telephone. It was a wonder to us. You could talk to someone all the way in Nashville or Louisville, or even Cincinnati, if you knew anyone who lived in Cincinnati. Daddy showed us pictures of telephones. Our imaginations just took hold of us and wouldn't let go. We went out to that old barn with a roll of Mama's twine, just like this, and we wired every inch of it for new telephones that we made out of bits of wood and bottles and lead pipe. Every stall, the hayloft, my daddy's workshop. It was a wonderful afternoon. We even ran a wire around to the outhouse." He looked across the desk at Lenore. "Pardon me, Miss Caylor. I do rattle on at times." He placed the bit of twine on the desk.

"Not at all," she said. "You must be close to your sister."

"Yes, but not in proximity. Grace tells me that I keep moving farther and farther away from her. Louisville, Pittsburgh, and now New York. And our brother lives in Wisconsin."

"Do you still have family on the farm?"

"The farm's gone. They breed racehorses on it now. But one evening before he died Daddy sat rocking on our porch when a strong wind rose up out of the south and knocked the old barn down. I'm sure our telephone system was still in there. We were all happy that Daddy was able to see that happen. It seemed to give him a sense of closure."

He stood and lifted his plate and glass. "Miss Caylor, I believe I'll finish my lunch as I work on the agendas for next month."

"Certainly, Mr. Pulliam."

"By the way, have we asked after Mr. Chadwick's health recently?"

"Yes. I talked to his wife yesterday."

"Oh yes. Of course. And he is recovering nicely. Isn't that what you told me?"

"Yes."

"Thank you." He entered his office and closed the door.

He sat staring out at the falling snow. Perhaps the operator at the Prince George had the wrong information. It was not normal or proper to check out of a residential hotel without leaving a forwarding address.

But Ted would do it, he decided. Ted would do it because he knew that Pulliam would try to reach him, and, in spite of insisting that Ted leave New York, Pulliam could not stay away from him for any length of time. Leaving no new address or telephone number would punish Pulliam and make him suffer for presuming that he could dictate where and how Ted should live.

There was a knock on his office door.

"Yes, come in."

The door opened and Lenore entered as he turned back to his desk. "I hope I'm not disturbing you," she said.

"Not at all."

"I thought that I would clean up the lunch dishes." She looked down at his plate. "But you haven't finished. I can come back a little later."

"No, no. It's fine. I've had my fill." He picked up his plate and handed it to her. "Miss Caylor?"

"Yes?"

"Do you enjoy the fine arts?"

"I'm sorry, sir?"

"Painting, sculpture, that sort of thing."

"Yes. Very much. My mother and aunt and I enjoy visiting the art museum on Fifth Avenue."

"Would you, your mother, and your Aunt Gertrude consider visiting an art gallery with me? You see, there's to be a new exhibition of paintings at the Macbeth Galleries."

"I believe I've read something about it, sir."

"Several papers have been covering the event. The artists don't like the way they've been treated by the art establishment and mean to use their art to make some kind of statement about it. I happened to meet a couple of the painters recently. They piqued my curiosity."

"I'm quite certain my mother and aunt would be very pleased to accompany you, Mr. Pulliam. Thank you very much."

"Excellent." He flipped through some papers and then consulted a leather-bound calendar. "The exhibition opens February 3, which is a Monday. It will no doubt be very crowded that night. Would any other evening be more convenient for you and your family?"

"Well, Aunt Trudie works for a doctor."

"And so she is free Wednesdays." He took a pen and circled a date on his calendar. "Then we'll arrange for Thomas to pick up your mother and your aunt and bring them here by five thirty on Wednesday, February the fifth. Thomas will be able to secure a suitable vehicle. We will join them downstairs and proceed up Fifth Avenue to the Macbeth Galleries. I believe an hour or so will be enough time to view the paintings, after which Thomas will bring us back downtown for dinner at Café Martin."

"Mother and Aunt Trudie will be thrilled. Thank you again, Mr. Pulliam. We don't often get an evening out, especially for something as exciting as this." She turned to leave but stopped. "Mr. Pulliam?"

"Yes?"

"I hesitate to ask, but it's been on my mind all afternoon. Mr. Brush is quite obviously unwell. He is unnaturally thin and can only walk with the help of canes."

"He suffers from locomotor ataxia." When Lenore didn't reply, he said, "It's a relatively delicate issue. Your aunt works for a physician. Perhaps she can explain it to you better than I."

"Locomotor...?"

"Ataxia. And Miss Caylor?"

"Yes?"

"The snow doesn't seem to want to stop. I suggest we finish up within the hour and leave for the day. And I don't believe the city will recover until sometime over the weekend, so," he smiled, "I am officially declaring the offices of the National League of Professional Base Ball Clubs closed until Monday."

"Thank you, sir. I'm sure my mother will be relieved. As am I, to be perfectly honest." She took the dishes to the restroom and rinsed them as well as she could. Back in the office she bundled them in newsprint and found a ball of string in her desk to secure the package.

She glanced out the windows and noticed that the snow had slowed. The afternoon light was brighter, but still gray. She leaned on the sill and looked down onto the deserted intersection fourteen stories below. The street, the sidewalks, and the roof of Café Martin across Broadway were covered with a thick, pure white, and, as yet, undisturbed blanket of snow.

The phone rang.

"National League of Professional Base Ball Clubs," said Lenore.

"Miss Caylor?"

"Speaking."

"My name is Norman Adams. We met this morning?"

"Oh, yes, Mr. Adams. How may I help you? I'm afraid we have no 1908 tickets available." She laughed.

"No?" he said. "Not even for the Brooklyn team?" He paused. "Actually, Miss Caylor —uh, it is 'Miss' I trust?"

"Yes."

"Actually, I was wondering if I might help you find your way back to the subway this evening. It's quite bad out there. Perhaps worse than this morning."

"Mr. Adams, that is a very kind offer, but I don't want you to—"

"It's no trouble. I work just across the way."

"Across the way?"

"Yes. The Brunswick Building at 225 Fifth Avenue between Twenty-Sixth and Twenty-Seventh. The large, red-brick building that occupies the entire street frontage."

"I'm very familiar with the Brunswick Building. I can see it from my office windows." Neither spoke for a moment. "We are closing early today because of the weather, so I don't think—"

"I can be there in ten minutes. I'll wait in the lobby."

She thought she should dissuade him but instead said, "How about thirty minutes?" She found herself looking forward to chatting with Mr. Adams.

She rang Pulliam's extension from her desk telephone and told him that an uptown neighbor offered to help her negotiate the walk to the Fourth Avenue subway stop at Twenty-Eighth. She let him know she would be leaving in half an hour and would drop off the dishes at Café Martin on the way.

"Splendid," said Pulliam. "I'll be taking the Sixth Avenue El. I trust the trains have blown the snow off of the elevated tracks."

After Lenore said her goodbye and wished him a pleasant weekend, and he heard the outer door close, he picked up his telephone and asked the operator to connect him to the Macbeth Galleries at 450 Fifth Avenue. He apologized for not knowing the number.

There was no answer at the gallery.

Of course there was no answer. They, like much of Midtown, would be closed by the blizzard. But they had just over a week to prepare for the opening of the exhibition. Ted would certainly be at the gallery for the entire weekend. He would call on Saturday. Or perhaps he would walk to the gallery and pay him a visit on Sunday. It would be a coincidence. But then again, perhaps it would be best to wait until he appeared there during the exhibition in the company of the three ladies. Yes, that would be his strategy.

They had no difficulty finding two seats together on the subway.

"Perhaps we've beaten the rush," said Norman.

"Or perhaps there will be no rush today," said Lenore.

"You're no doubt right. The Brunswick Building seemed quite empty."

"And what do you do in the Brunswick Building?"

"I am a marine underwriter."

"Interesting."

"It's a business like any other. We have a couple of offices and a meeting room."

"Then you sell insurance to boats?"

"My company does. I am responsible for the actual underwriting. But enough about my position, I'd much rather talk about base ball. How long have you worked for Mr. Pulliam?"

"Then you are familiar with Mr. Pulliam? You must follow the game closely."

"I do. And your employer is often in the papers and the base ball guides."

"And what team do you support?"

"The Chicago Nationals."

"The Cubs? But it's very easy to back a winning team, unless you're from Chicago."

"No. Troy, New York, hometown of Johnny Evers who plays second base for the Cubs."

"Then you're acquainted with Mr. Evers?"

He laughed. "My goodness no. I'm just loyal to my hometown. But I have doubtless worn a collar that he made."

"A collar?"

"Troy is known as the 'Collar City' because of the number of men's collars manufactured there. Mr. Evers worked in one of the collar factories before becoming a professional ball player. My second cousin, on my mother's side, had a friend whose sister knew a girl whose brother worked with him. Something like that."

Lenore smiled. "Then perhaps you can get me tickets when the Cubs come to the Polo Grounds."

"No one can get those tickets," he said and shook his head in a mockingly grave manner.

At Forty-Second Street a large number of passengers boarded making the car suddenly crowded. Many stood. Adams, sitting in the aisle seat, shifted his weight closer to Lenore to avoid being almost smothered by a large man wearing a wet woolen topcoat. Lenore did not attempt to inch closer to the window.

"I haven't asked about your stop," said Norman.

"It's 110th Street. And you?"

"I mean to see you to 110th Street and determine how clear the uptown streets are for walking."

She opened her purse and found a nickel. She turned his hand over and pressed it into the palm of his glove. "For your return trip from 110th to Seventy-Ninth Street." He closed his fist around the coin.

The walk to Lenore's building on 111th Street proved less treacherous than fighting the drifts and gusting winds in Midtown.

"I feel much more comfortable walking now," said Lenore as she stopped in front of number 503. "Especially since I'm home. Thank you, Mr. Adams. You have been very kind. Can I invite you in for a cup of tea, or something stronger? I'm certain Mother and my Aunt Trudie would be happy to meet you."

"Thank you, but the sooner I get home the better. Another time perhaps?"

"Of course."

He reached into an inner pocket and produced a business card.

"Norman S. Adams," Lenore read. "Marine Underwriter. Appleton and Cox. 225 Fifth Avenue."

"That's me," he said.

"Well, I don't own a boat," said Lenore. She laughed. "But perhaps we'll meet again on the subway. Good evening."

When Lenore asked Trudie about locomotor ataxia at the dinner table, her aunt blushed and quickly speared a bite of lamb to delay responding.

"It sounds serious," said Lenore's mother.

"I believe it's very serious," said Lenore. "The man I met was quite emaciated and could hardly walk. His name is John T. Brush. Do you remember him, Mother? He seemed to know Father."

"Didn't he have something to do with the Reds? I think he had something to do with the Reds after we left Cincinnati. I remember your father getting into very loud arguments with a Mr. Brush. But then again, your father argued with everyone. It was so sad. I loved Cincinnati and the river and the hills. Mount Adams. I wish we never moved away. We were always moving during those years. Didn't Mr. Brush marry a showgirl? Father said it was quite a scandal at the time. She was much younger. Young enough to be his daughter. And a showgirl?"

"Mother," said Lenore, "I happen to know many so-called showgirls who—"

"Lenore!" said Trudie. "Mother, I need Lenore's help in the kitchen. Please excuse us."

"Well," said Mrs. Caylor, "Father would not have allowed you to leave the table before supper was over."

Trudie paused as she stood at her place. "That was the nineteenth century, Luella," she said. "It's perfectly acceptable in the twentieth."

"Father would not have allowed it."

Trudie pushed her chair back under the table and turned toward the kitchen. Lenore followed. Trudie leaned against the stove and folded her arms. "Why do you answer her when she speaks like that? You know she barely knows what she's saying." Lenore didn't respond. Trudie stood upright and let her arms fall. "Anyway, I don't need a medical book. We see the condition from time to time, although its symptoms are not what one might normally associate with syphilis. In cases such as this, the infection attacks the spinal cord. The poor man is dying a very slow and painful death—although he brought it upon himself in my opinion, unless he contracted it from his wife. No offense intended to you or your theater friends, Lenore."

Lenore shook her head. "Then there is no cure?"

"No."

——— Wednesday, February 5, 1908 ———
New York, New York

Pulliam stood before his open closet for several minutes. He wanted color in his wardrobe this evening. They would be visiting an art gallery where minds should be open, especially during an exhibition of a group of artists who had been quite vocal in their collective determination to snub their noses at the staid and stuffy National Academy of

Design. And he wanted Ted to see him happy and playful. He selected his blue-violet and gold brocade vest with a solid-gold bow tie under his best black suit. He attached his gold pocket watch to a matching double-rope chain with the gold National League medallion fob that Barney Dreyfuss had given him for Christmas one year. A gold silk handkerchief in his jacket's breast pocket finished the look.

When he arrived at the office he was surprised to see Miss Caylor in her standard business attire of a pleated white shirtwaist and dark gray woolen skirt.

"I brought a change of clothes," she explained. "You look wonderful, Mr. Pulliam."

"Thank you, Miss Caylor. I'm looking forward to our outing this evening. And this," he pulled a bright yellow silk rose from the crystal vase, "will be the final touch." He threaded the stem through his jacket's left lapel buttonhole.

Throughout the morning he tried to finalize the agendas for the upcoming meetings but was easily distracted. Was his vest too colorful? His bow tie too bright? Would Ted disapprove or, worse, laugh? Would Ted speak to him? Would he even be there?

He couldn't eat lunch. His nerves had twisted his stomach and upset his system so that he felt an urgent need to use the restroom, but he could not allow Miss Caylor to suspect he was in such a state. He was sweating but could not remove his jacket for fear of visible stains.

What time was it? Ten minutes after three o'clock. Should he take a drink of whiskey to calm his nerves? No. He would rise to his obligation to entertain the Caylor family. He would concentrate on that and on his obligations to the National League.

Ineligible players. The National Agreement, Article viii, section 5. The 1908 World's Series schedule.

Would Brush attend the meetings? He hoped not.

Should the National Commission allow the American Association to field a team in Chicago? No. Base balls discolored intentionally by a player or manager or coach in order to give that team's pitcher an advantage. Ejection? Suspension? Fine?

He checked his watch again. It was 3:40. He rose and went to his window. High drifts remained from the storm, now soiled by coal soot, automobile exhaust, and horse droppings in spite of the best efforts of the white-coated "White Wing Brigade." He looked down onto the roof of Café Martin and hoped he would be able to do justice to his dinner that evening.

At exactly five o'clock he rose from his desk and went into the outer office. Miss Caylor was not there. He wandered to her desk and casually glanced at its surface. In the few weeks she had worked for the league she had arranged active files in order of importance, he assumed, in a rack at one corner. A low, open wooden box of neatly stacked miscellaneous papers and reports sat at the opposite corner near a tidy collection of outgoing mail to be dropped off in the lobby at the end of the day.

Not knowing what to do with himself he turned to Miss Caylor's windows and looked out onto a dark city, street lamps and illuminated office windows creating a pattern of yellow brilliance and deep black void around Madison Square.

The office door opened and Lenore entered.

Pulliam smiled broadly. "You look lovely, Miss Caylor," he said, and meant it. She wore a lilac jacket accented with silver thread and silk braid and a matching ankle-length contoured dress.

She smiled. "Thank you, Mr. Pulliam."

The call from the lobby came just before five thirty. Pulliam put on his topcoat and bowler as Lenore carefully placed a wide-brimmed, black Merry Widow hat trimmed with small white feathers and yellow and baby blue silk ribbon.

He helped her with her coat. "Again, Miss Caylor. Quite lovely."

The hat worn by Mrs. Caylor was not as tasteful, Pulliam noted. Even in the darkness of the carriage interior he could see that silk flowers, ribbons, lace, feathers, and a stuffed bird filled the cabin to its ceiling. Gertrude's hat was not as flamboyant, but neither was it as restrained as Lenore's.

As Thomas closed the carriage door behind him, Pulliam said, "We are going to 450 Fifth Avenue, Thomas. Between Thirty-Ninth and Fortieth."

"Yes, sir," said Thomas. "Mr. Pulliam, would you like me to keep an eye open for other hacks?"

"No need this evening, Thomas. Thank you."

"Very good, sir." He climbed onto his box and steered his horse around to the uptown side of Broadway and then turned an immediate right onto Twenty-Sixth for the short block past Café Martin to Fifth Avenue.

Pulliam pointed to the restaurant, brightly lit from within. "That's where we will be dining later this evening."

"Very exciting, Mr. Pulliam," said Mrs. Caylor. "We can't thank you enough."

"Yes, Thank you," said Trudie. "I've been reading about the exhibition in *Town Topics.*"

"*Town Topics?*" said Pulliam.

"I work in an East Side doctor's office. The doctor subscribes for business reasons. I know it has a scandalous reputation, but nonetheless he has found it useful. And since your very generous invitation I noticed Mr. Stephenson's coverage of the exhibition."

"Have his reviews been favorable?" asked Pulliam.

"Not entirely, but he has made the work sound very interesting and quite an event in the New York art world. I mean to avoid judging until I see the pictures for myself."

As the carriage turned onto Fifth Avenue, Pulliam pointed to the northeast corner and said, "Do you see the building to my right? It's called the Brunswick Building because it replaced the old Brunswick Hotel."

"I remember the Brunswick," said Mrs. Caylor. "Are you certain it was right there? My, my. The city has changed so much. I don't wander below 110th Street often anymore."

"It was one of the most fashionable hotels in New York," said Pulliam. "Hearst would book several suites and rooms at a time when he came here."

"Why would they tear down such a nice hotel?" asked Mrs. Caylor.

"Everything is moving uptown, Luella," said Trudie. "Above Forty-Second Street. The best hotels. The theaters. The restaurants."

At Twenty-Eighth Street Pulliam gestured to his left. "Just down there is where all of the most important music publishers have studios and offices. On a warm day you can walk along Twenty-Eighth between Broadway and Sixth Avenue and hear pianos tinkling away in almost every open window."

"Trudie used to play the piano so beautifully," said Mrs. Caylor. "Why don't you play the piano anymore, Trudie?"

"We sold the piano, Luella. Remember?"

"Such a shame. I guess we're just a base ball family again." She shrugged. "Mr. Pulliam?"

"Yes?"

"Do you remember Cap Anson?"

"Of course."

"Does he still play for the White Stockings? I understand that the White Stockings won the championship a couple of years ago."

"Mother," said Lenore, "that was the Chicago White Sox."

"Did they change their club name?"

"Actually," said Pulliam, "that brings up a very interesting piece of base ball history. Do you know the name of the team that won the very first National League pennant in 1876?"

"My, yes," said Mrs. Caylor. "It was those White Stockings. Father had just begun working for the Cincinnati club in their offices. He kept score for the Reds, too. We had a horrible team. I don't think we won ten games that year. Father and I were very young then."

"You are correct, Mrs. Caylor."

"Of course I am. I was just about Lenore's age at the time. Very, very young."

"I mean," said Pulliam, "about the White Stockings winning the first National League championship."

"Oh that," said Mrs. Caylor. "I wish I could forget it."

"But do you know which club won the very first American League pennant in 1901?"

"Oh my no," said Mrs. Caylor. "We don't follow that league."

"I know," said Trudie. "It was the Chicago White Stockings." Lenore looked at Trudie. "The doctor started following the American

League from the start, even though there was no New York team yet."

"American League?" asked Mrs. Caylor. "Did the White Stockings change leagues? That would be good for our Reds."

"Here's what happened, Mrs. Caylor," said Pulliam. "The Chicago National League ball club changed their name during the 1890s. So when Charles Comiskey was looking for a name for his new American League team, he chose the discarded White Stockings name. And his team won that first pennant seven years ago. So for both the National and American Leagues it was the Chicago White Stockings who won the first-ever championships for their leagues. The American League club has since shortened its name to the White Sox."

"I'm sure," said Mrs. Caylor, "that I don't know what in heaven you're talking about, Mr. Pulliam."

Lenore and Trudie laughed. Lenore said, "It doesn't matter, Mother. But," she turned to Pulliam, "I can assure you I will retell that story whenever the subject of base ball comes up with any of my acquaintances. It will especially annoy the New York rooters of either league."

The carriage stopped and Thomas tapped on the roof to signal their arrival at the gallery. He jumped down from his box and opened the curbside door. A knot of people crowded around the gallery's entrance, and a line extended up the block almost to Fortieth Street. Pulliam looked briefly out of the carriage and turned to his guests. "Please wait here a moment while I confirm our appointment."

A young woman sat at a table just inside the door explaining the situation to a well-dressed, middle-aged couple. "Yes, I understand," she said, "but it's been like this since the opening on Monday."

Pulliam looked into the gallery. Small groups stood before each of the paintings while a larger, very vocal crowd packed the center of the space, chatting.

"Pardon me," he said to the woman at the table. "My guests and I have an appointment with Mr. Russell."

"Mr. Russell? I didn't realize Ted made appointments." She sighed and motioned to a young man dressed as a waiter. "Please tell Ted that his appointment, Mr....Mr.?"

"Pulliam. Harry Pulliam and guests."

"Mr. Harry Pulliam and guests have arrived."

"Thank you." He turned to look out the door. Catching Thomas's eye, he gestured with his hand that the three ladies should be escorted into the gallery.

"If you don't mind," said the woman at the table, "could you step behind the table and out of the doorway?"

"Of course."

He looked more closely at the interior of the gallery. He estimated it to be a bit longer than the distance between bases on a base ball diamond and perhaps thirty feet wide. The wall space had been divided evenly among the eight artists.

Thomas led Lenore and her family through the door. Pulliam motioned that they should join him on the other side of the table.

"Who are they?" asked a woman waiting to get in. "Rockefellers?"

"Wouldn't be surprised," said a man behind her in the queue. "The word is out that a Vanderbilt is here tonight."

"This is very exciting indeed," said Mrs. Caylor as they joined Pulliam. "I've never seen so many people. Except at a ball game, of course."

"This is very kind of you, Mr. Pulliam," said Lenore, "but I must admit to feeling a bit guilty about barging in ahead of all those people waiting outside in the cold."

"Nonsense. From time to time it becomes necessary to use one's connections. If any of those poor souls had a connection such as we, he wouldn't hesitate to take advantage of it."

Pulliam looked into the gallery and saw Ted approaching from the back. He wore a well-tailored black suit, gray vest, and red tie with a tight diamond pattern, and looked quite handsome, Pulliam thought.

"Good evening, Mr. Pulliam. I am very pleased that you and your friends are able to join us this evening."

"Thank you, Mr. Russell. Allow me to introduce you to Mrs. Luella Caylor, her daughter Lenore, and Mrs. Caylor's sister Miss Gertrude Pittenger."

"Charmed," said Ted as he took each woman's hand in turn. "Unfortunately, I am in a meeting just now with several artists and a prospective buyer."

"If you don't mind my asking," said Trudie, "can you tell me which artists? I've been following news of the exhibition in the papers."

"Excellent," said Ted. "Well, right now she's very interested in paintings by Messieurs Henri, Davies, Shinn, Luks, and Lawson."

"Five out of eight," said Lenore. "Very nice."

"And two each by Mr. Henri and Mr. Davies," said Ted, smiling, proud. "Macbeth is very pleased, especially considering the bank panic."

Pulliam nodded. "I imagine money is a bit tight right now, even for the wealthy."

"My goodness," said Mrs. Caylor. "Imagine being able to buy seven pictures."

"Someone said a Vanderbilt was here," laughed Trudie.

"Actually," said Ted, "she's a Vanderbilt Whitney. But I must get back to the meeting. Please, enjoy the exhibition."

"Will we see you after your meeting?" asked Pulliam.

"Of course," said Ted.

"We are dining at Café Martin later. Won't you join us?"

"Please do," said Mrs. Caylor.

"Thank you," said Ted. "It sounds lovely. Very nice to meet you and very nice to see you again, Harry." He turned to go.

"Mr. Russell?" Pulliam called after him.

"Yes?"

"May I have a card?" Ted hesitated but finally took a business card from a vest pocket.

Pulliam, Lenore, and her family strolled through the gallery, politely arguing over the paintings, and then stood in the center of the exhibition comparing favorites. They lingered as Pulliam waited for Ted as long as good manners would allow.

Ted never reappeared, nor did he join them at Café Martin.

Pulliam arrived at the New York Athletic Club at just after ten o'clock. The clerk behind the counter spoke to him as he approached. "Good evening, Mr. Pulliam."

"Good evening, Robert. Any mail today?"

"I'll check, sir." He turned to the mail slots but paused.

"Mr. Pulliam?"

"Yes, Robert?"

"A gentleman is waiting for you in the lobby." He pointed. "He's been here for about thirty minutes."

Pulliam looked into the lobby but saw no one.

"I believe," said Robert, "that he took a chair on the other side of the pillar to the left. If you would like to join him I will be happy to bring your mail to you there."

"Thank you, Robert." He walked into the seating area of the front lobby.

He knew it was Ted when he saw his shoes, well-polished black leather with high olive-green fabric tops, the upper button on each unfastened. One foot rested on the opposite knee while the other tapped on the floor as if its owner listened to a private concert. Pulliam walked around the pillar to the front of the high-back leather chair. Ted sat hidden behind an open copy of the *Sun*.

"Listen to this, Harry," he said without confirming that it was Pulliam who stood before him. "It's written by that dilettante Hunker. 'Any young painter recently returned from Paris or Munich would call the exhibition of the eight painters very interesting but far from revolutionary.'"

"I would agree," said Pulliam. Ted folded the newspaper in half and glared at Pulliam. "I enjoyed the exhibition very much and so it could not possibly be revolutionary."

Ted's gaze softened. He smiled. "Oh, Harry. I'm going to miss you terribly."

Pulliam found a small armchair and placed it directly across from Ted. As he sat he said, "Miss me how, Ted? Miss me in that you are indeed returning to Louisville, or miss me because we will no longer," his eyes scanned the otherwise empty lobby, "...because we will no longer meet as friends."

"Something like that." Ted folded the newspaper again and placed it on a small table next to his chair. "I'll be brief because I am exhausted and tomorrow will be another long day. We see hundreds come through the door every hour, so whether or not you found the exhibition revolutionary, it is certainly a success."

"I assume your meeting with Mrs. Vanderbilt Whitney was a success, too?"

"Yes. She bought all seven. She means to feature them in a new exhibition space in the Village. But that won't be until the paintings return to New York. The artists have decided to send the show on the road and me with it."

"On the road?"

"Philadelphia first. Most of them are from there and have connections at the Pennsylvania Academy. Then Chicago, Toledo, Detroit. Perhaps nine or ten cities in all. The closest I will come to Louisville will be Cincinnati and Indianapolis, but I'm not sure I will bother to visit home from either."

"I thought you hated your job."

"Not the job. I hate Macbeth."

"How long will you be gone?"

"A year. Fifteen months, perhaps. Not all of the painters can attend exhibitions in all of the cities. I know the work well, and I am unattached." He stared at Pulliam. "You wanted me to leave New York. You have your wish."

"Will you stay in touch?"

Ted sighed. "I'll send you postcards."

"You're wrong, you know."

"Wrong?"

"I don't want you to leave New York. It is necessary that you leave."

"Necessary." Ted stood. "Why did I come here? What did I expect? That you would try to talk me out of going? I guess I hoped that by moving out of the St. George and avoiding you that...that perhaps you'd actually miss me. What an idea. You have your game to keep you company. I cannot compete with your game." He turned and began to cross the lobby.

Pulliam remained in his chair. He wanted to jump up and stop Ted, to hold him, to tell him he had changed his mind, but instead he sat and watched his lover leave through the club's front door.

Robert arrived with a small stack of envelopes.

"Thank you," said Pulliam without a glance at his mail.

"Of course, sir. Will there be anything else?"

"No, thank you." Robert turned to go. "On second thought...," Pulliam called after him. Robert stopped and looked back. "A glass of Old Crow rye, water on the side."

"Very good, sir. Will you take your drink in your rooms?"

"No. Right here. I mean to sit right here for the moment."

———— SUNDAY, FEBRUARY 23, 1908 ————
NEW YORK, NEW YORK

Sunday afternoon at the firehouse was very quiet, to Henry McBride's relief. He happily cooked a big dinner of steaks, fried potatoes, and green beans for the crew, after which he escaped to the stables and tried to stay awake while reading *The Reach Official American League Base Ball Guide for 1908.* He skimmed over the many pages of batting and pitching records printed in tiny type, but enjoyed the summaries of the 1907 season and the brief analysis of the problems that plagued the struggling New York Americans. He normally limited himself to Spalding's National League guide, but had to agree with the Reach publishers' preface that "the American League is now so well established as a major league that its permanence is assured."

He remained a Giants rooter, but thought he might make his way up to 165th and Broadway to watch a Highlanders game or two, especially when the Detroit team came to town with their young star Ty Cobb. From everything Henry had read, Cobb was the most exciting player in either league. He had won the 1907 American League batting championship while only twenty years old.

"McBride?" The captain stood in the stables doorway. "Visitor."

"Thank you, sir." Henry rose from his chair and walked out to the front of the station.

Maureen stood smiling at the door. "Good evening, Mr. McBride."

"Maureen? What a nice surprise. What brings you to Forty-Seventh Street?" She looked beautiful bundled up in wool.

"Colleen and I met in Times Square for a coffee. She stopped in the pharmacist's shop so I thought I'd pop in and say hello."

"Hello!"

"And how's your day? Quiet I should hope."

"Oh, yes. Nobody burning down any buildings yet today. Maybe they've all taken Sunday off."

Maureen giggled. "Well thank goodness for that." She glanced down at her hands grasping a blue canvas handbag. "Henry? Do you remember our little agreement about base ball and a show?"

"Sure I do."

"Well, we, Colleen and I, decided to visit the theaters and look at the posters and buy a copy of that magazine all about the shows, you know?"

"Not off the top of my head, darling."

She opened her bag and took out a copy of *The Theatre*. "Here it is," she said and flipped through its pages. "It says here that Mabel Hite is back in New York after almost a year in Chicago, and she's agreed to star in a new show called *The Merry-Go-Round* and it will open in April. Isn't that wonderful? Isn't that when base ball opens as well?"

"Opening Day is early April, yes, Maureen." He paused. "Just a minute here. Did you say Mabel Hite?"

"Yes. Her show will play at the Circle Theater up at Sixtieth Street. We could watch the Giants and then take the El back down to Fifty-Eighth Street, and we'd be right near the show."

"Mabel Hite?"

"Yes, Henry. Mabel Hite."

Henry jumped in the air and hooted in delight. He went to Maureen and held her arms. "That's the best news I've heard all year!"

"You like Mabel Hite then, Henry?"

"Never seen her." He released her arms and began strutting around the firehouse. "Gobble, gobble! Gobble, gobble!" he chirped, tucking his fists under his shoulders and flapping his arms like a pair of wings.

"Henry! What is the matter with you?"

"Don't you see?" He stopped just in front of her and leaned down so their noses almost touched. "Tell me, now who might be Mabel Hite's husband?"

Maureen thought for a moment, biting her lower lip. "I believe she's married to a Mr. Donlin, and...," she paused, "and isn't he a ball player?"

"Yes, but not just any ball player. He's Turkey Mike Donlin, the biggest Giants star of 1905. Hurt in 1906 and in 1907 moved to Chicago with his new wife because he and the Giants couldn't agree on a contract. He played ball with a semi-pro team in Chicago last season because he can't stay away from the game and now his wonderful, beautiful, talented wife returns to New York and that can only mean that Turkey Mike is back, too. And I'll bet a dollar to your dime that he'll be playing for the Giants again in 1908!"

"I suppose that will be good for the Giants."

"Good? Good, Maureen? Good God, girl!"

"Henry! Don't use the Lord's name in such a way."

"Sorry. Good gracious, girl! Turkey Mike is the final piece of the puzzle. We'll have Matty and Moose and now Turkey Mike. The Chicagos had better beware because the Giants are coming!" He resumed his turkey strut. "Gobble, gobble! Gobble, gobble!"

"Now, Henry," said Maureen. "Henry!"

"Maureen, darling," he said, panting and smiling broadly.

"This means you agree? I'll attend a Giants game with you one afternoon after which you will come with me to see *The Merry-Go-Round*? If it's not convenient it doesn't have to be the same day, of course. I'm sure it will depend on when we can get tickets and your shift here at the firehouse."

"Same day or any day, my darling." He wrapped his arms around her and lifted her off her feet. She placed her hands on his shoulders to balance herself.

"If Mabel Hite likes base ball," she said laughing, "it must be fun."

"Fun?" He carefully placed Maureen back on the floor. "I don't believe I've ever thought of following the Giants as fun exactly."

"Then why do you do it?"

"I just have to. That's all. Ever since my dad took me to see them play at the old grounds at 110th Street when they were called the Gothams."

"Well," she said, straightening her coat and hat, "that's a strange way to look at something that you travel all the way to the Harlem River for and pay good money to see. And to see your team lose as often as not."

"Lose? Oh, not this year, my darling Maureen. Not this year. Turkey Mike is back!"

―――― TUESDAY, FEBRUARY 25, 1908 ――――
NEW YORK, NEW YORK

Lenore sensed him standing over her a moment before he spoke.

"Hello. Nice to see you again," he said.

She looked up. He smiled as he held on to one of the subway car's canvas loops. "Mr. Adams," she replied. "Nice to see you as well. It's been, what? Over a month now since the blizzard. How have you been?"

"Very well, thank you. Very busy. I've been going into the office early of late. Have you been taking this train downtown, too? Perhaps we've been on different cars."

"I have to be at the office a bit early this morning."

"Big day?"

"Big week. League meetings, National Commission meetings, Rules Committee meeting."

"Sounds exciting," he said. "Will many of the team magnates be in town?"

"Most all of them."

The car became more crowded as it traveled downtown, but Adams was able to maintain his place next to Lenore.

"Do any ball players attend?" he asked.

"I'm told Mr. Chance of Chicago is expected for the Rules Committee meeting on Thursday."

"Frank Chance?"

"Yes."

"That *is* exciting. The Peerless Leader himself."

"And you, Mr. Adams. What compels you to be on a subway at six thirty on a Tuesday morning?"

"Flying machines," he said. "Do you recall reading about a couple of brothers inventing a motorized machine that has wings and can fly? It was early 1904, or perhaps late 1903."

"Oh, yes. My friends and I talked about it a little," said Lenore. "Some didn't believe it."

"It was true. Happened down in North Carolina."

"Why haven't we heard more about it these four years?"

"You will again soon," said Adams.

"What does your marine business have to do with it?"

"The brothers, name of Wright, contacted our firm from their home in Dayton. They have convinced the army to look at their invention, and the French as well. They mean to make their flying machines much more than a curiosity. They can stay up in the air for more than an hour and travel longer distances. They have commercial plans as well, so they need insurance. They contacted us, several other maritime underwriters, and railroad insurance companies as well, no doubt."

"It still sounds much too fantastic to me."

"People doubted the telephone at first, too. We feel that we must take them seriously. And that's why I'm on the subway so early. I have my regular work plus flying machines now."

The subway slowed. Adams dipped his head to look out of the window behind Lenore. "Grand Central," he said. "Will you be getting off at Twenty-Eighth Street again?"

"Yes, but this time I'll drop you off at your building."

Adams smiled and nodded once.

They walked west on Twenty-Eighth and turned left at Fifth Avenue to walk the block and a half to the Brunswick Building. As they crossed Twenty-Seventh, Adams pointed to the block-long, red-brick building and said, "This is it." They stopped at the building's entrance in the middle of the block. Adams turned to Lenore. "Perhaps...perhaps we can get together for lunch one day. Since, I mean, we work so close to each other."

Lenore turned and faced him. "Now, Mr. Adams, please answer one simple question for me."

"Certainly. Anything."

"Are you married?"

Adams' eyes widened and he stepped back. He looked down at the sidewalk. "I don't understand."

"It's a very simple yes-or-no question. Your hesitation tells me all I need to know." She turned to continue toward Twenty-Sixth Street, but paused. "I'm sorry to be so blunt, but experience has taught me to be cautious."

He looked directly into her eyes. "I understand, Miss Caylor, and I apologize if I in any way implied anything but innocent, what should I say, good cheer."

"Thank you, Mr. Adams. Perhaps we'll meet on the subway again in the future, at which time we can continue the good cheer and leave it at that. Good morning." She walked away.

When she arrived at the National League offices she fumbled her keys and dropped them onto the hallway floor in front of the door. She stared down at them. Mr. Adams's lunch invitation was to her little better than a proposition to join him in a hotel room. Perhaps he didn't mean it to sound that way, but as soon as it had been articulated, a young gentleman who had been polite, helpful, and enjoyable to talk with turned into the same crude, forward, often drunk, and clumsy womanizer she had been fighting off since her first days in the theater.

She retrieved the keys, let herself in, turned on the lights, and tried to put the incident behind her by focusing on preparations for the day's meeting. A large round table and four chairs had been brought into Pulliam's office. She distributed fresh ink bottles, extra pencils and pens, pads of notepaper, ash rays, match holders, and water glasses to each place. She then stacked the appropriate National Commission records, filed in hardcover, leather-bound binders, in the center of the table. Returning to her desk in the reception area she proofread the meeting's agenda one last time and was annoyed to find the word "commission" misspelled.

As she spooled fresh sheets of foolscap and carbon paper into her typewriter, the outer door opened. A short, stocky man entered wearing a bright-blue plaid suit with a yellow carnation in the lapel and a ruby pin in his royal blue tie. He carried a large brown leather case. His black woolen overcoat had been tossed over his arm.

"Good morning," he said, louder than necessary. His dark, close-cropped mustache spread in a wide arc around a generous, almost laughing smile. "Herrmann's the name; base ball's the game. And you must be the lovely Miss Lenore Caylor."

She stood and approached him. "Mr. August Herrmann?"

"Garry to my friends," he laughed. "Short for Garibaldi." He extended his hand.

"Very nice to meet you, Mr. Herrmann."

"Likewise, Miss Caylor, likewise." He placed his case on the floor and removed his black bowler. He hung his coat and hat on the coat stand. His hair was well oiled, combed very flat on his head and parted just to the left of the middle. He smoothed it with a hand bejeweled with a large diamond pinky ring. "I assume I'm the first to arrive." He took a gold watch attached to a gold chain from a vest pocket and opened it.

"Yes, sir," she replied.

"Good, good. I need to finish my breakfast. Is that seat free?" He snapped the watch closed and pointed at a slatted chair pulled up to the rolltop desk.

She extended her open palm toward the desk. "Of course, Mr. Herrmann. Please..."

"Thank you. Thank you." He flopped his case onto the desk as he sat, exhaling loudly as if the effort of lifting it had exhausted him. He unfastened the case's metal latches and opened it. Reaching inside he removed a small parcel wrapped in light brown paper.

"You were born in Cincinnati, were you not, Miss Caylor? I seem to remember your father supplying all of us at City Hall with the best of Cuban cigars to celebrate the occasion. Hell of a...sorry. A fine man. A gentleman, your father."

"Thank you, sir. I was indeed born in Cincinnati, but I don't remember it very well. I've lived most of my life here in New York."

"No matter. You're a Queen City girl in my book. It's in your blood."
He folded back the last corner of the parcel to reveal four long chunks
of cooked meat on thick hooflike bones. Lenore brought a hand to her
mouth and stepped back.

"Ah, perfect," said Herrmann. He rubbed his hands together in two
quick motions. "Can you believe I had to teach the cook at the Waldorf-
Astoria Hotel how to properly prepare pigs' feet? Now, let's see." He
reached into his case and produced a silver fork, a small wood-han-
dled carving knife, and a bottle of beer. "And they call Manhattan civ-
ilized. Bah! Now this is a real breakfast." Two brown eggs completed
Herrmann's morning feast. He rolled one on the table and began to
peel it, dropping the bits of shell onto the butcher paper.

"Would you like a plate, or a glass for your beer?" asked Lenore.

"No thanks. I'm used to this. Never travel without my own provi-
sions. I forgot the kraut, though, and you can't find good kraut anywhere in Manhattan. Nothing that compares to Over the Rhine, that is.
And the pigs' feet? I had to hoof it, so to speak," he chuckled, "all the
way down to Gansevoort Street to find a suitable butcher." He looked
in his case and found a second parcel wrapped in red paper and tied
with twine. "This is for later. Real Thüringer Rostbratwurst from Over
the Rhine. Do you remember Over the Rhine, Miss Caylor?"

"Only from visits to Cincinnati."

"Best sausages and best beer in the world. Although I have to admit that there are a few German areas of Chicago that have excellent
sausage and delicious beer." Picking up the knife and fork he carved
a morsel of meat from one of the pigs' feet. He closed his eyes as he sa-
vored his first bite. He wedged a thumb under the metal collar that
held the beer's cork stopper in place and popped open the bottle. Tilt-
ing his head back he drained half of its contents, looked admiringly
at the bottle, and then finished it. He produced another from his case
and opened it.

"You know, Miss Caylor, we are entering the most progressive, dy-
namic era in base ball history, and do you know why?"

"No, sir."

"Because the great city of Cincinnati is running the game. Look at the

National Commission. There's me, of course, but Johnson of the American League is a Cincinnati man, and your employer is from Kentucky, right across the river. And now we have Miss Lenore Caylor, born in Cincinnati and the daughter of O. P. Caylor who as much as founded my Reds. I'm telling you!" He bit off half of one of the hard-boiled eggs. "Why, when I heard we were to offer you a job in this office, I let everyone know that if they even thought of not hiring you they'd have to deal with me, and Harry Pulliam, too."

"How did you know my father, Mr. Herrmann? Were you with the Reds back then?"

"No. I worked at City Hall at the time, and the Eleventh Ward was mine as well. We knew everyone who was anyone. Your father was a big man around town, first with the newspapers and then in base ball. I was very sad to hear that he had passed." He cut himself another bite of pigs' feet.

Lenore started toward Pulliam's office. "Thank you, Mr. Herrmann. If you'll excuse me, I need to finish preparations for your meeting." She hurried past him, averting her eyes from the sight of his breakfast.

As he approached the St. James Building, Pulliam saw John Brush's large black Hewitt limousine parked along the curb on Twenty-Sixth Street just west of Broadway. The motor was running and Brush's driver stood alongside stomping his feet against the cold early morning air. Pulliam slowed. The driver, bundled to the neck in a bulky brown woolen coat with broad gold epaulettes, noticed Pulliam. He brought his right hand to the brim of his Rough Riders campaign hat and saluted.

"Good morning, sir."

"Good morning, Arthur. Ready for battle I see."

"Mr. Brush would like a word with you."

Arthur opened the automobile's door. Pulliam looked inside and saw Brush lying on his side, his head toward the front of the compartment. Half of the interior had been customized to fit a narrow bed. A black, leather-clad armchair had been mounted into the near half. Brush was wrapped in a thick blanket. He wore a flat gray-flannel cap. He looked so thin to Pulliam that he seemed to meld into the bed.

"Morning, Harry," said Brush. "Like what I had them do to my car? This damned disease makes it mighty hard for me to sit up sometimes." He paused to clear his throat and spit into a cuspidor, out of sight between the bed and the chair. "Those Hewitt folks did a nice job, don't you think? The bed rotates and tilts so come base ball season we'll just park along the outfield rope, open the door, and spin me around to watch the games."

"Very nice, John."

"Come on in. The chair is quite comfortable."

"No thank you. Garry is probably already up in the office."

"Herrmann can wait. He no doubt has his sausages and beer to keep him happy. I need to talk to you."

"Won't you be attending the league meetings?"

"No. I'm catching a train to Indianapolis this morning. That's what I want to talk to you about. Please sit down." Brush tipped his head toward the chair.

"No, thank you."

Brush glared at him. "All right then." He coughed and spat loudly. "I won't be at the Waldorf come Wednesday, and I won't be there Thursday either."

"I understand, John. In your current condition—"

"And I'm not sending Fred Knowles or John McGraw or anyone else from the Giants." Pulliam remained still, standing on the curb, peering down into the Hewitt. "I don't mean to be...," Brush said, pulling himself up onto an elbow and leaning toward Pulliam, "I don't mean to be insulted ever again by the likes of you and your damn Fleischman Resolution."

"I'm sorry if—"

"Sitting there as you proudly proclaim the success of your umpires in ejecting and suspending twice as many Giants as players from any other team."

"You know that's not true, John."

"Twice as many! And now I see you mean to stick the Fleischman thing into the league constitution. Make cheating the Giants the law of the land."

"Our office reviewed each and every case, John, and every ejection and suspension of your players and those of the other clubs were justified based on the reports filed by the umpires."

"Horseshit."

"And if you would spend as much effort controlling the histrionics of your manager as you do opposing the league office at every turn, the ejections and suspensions of your players, and of McGraw himself, would diminish to respectable levels."

"Respectable? Funny word coming from you."

Pulliam pushed himself away from the Hewitt and stood erect. "I'm very disappointed to hear that the Giants will not be represented at the league meetings. It is unprecedented and won't be appreciated in the least by the other owners."

"Damn the other owners to hell. They're all against me, too."

"I will inform the other club representatives at the start of Thursday's meetings."

"You do that, Harry. I'm certain you'll find the right words to put into the meeting notes. Or have your sweet Miss Caylor do it for you."

"How dare you bring her name into this? You have no shame, sir. No honor."

Brush laughed loudly, coughed deeply, and spat again. "Honor? Silly Southern crap." He looked past Pulliam. "Arthur? Arthur!"

"Yes, sir."

"Close the goddamn door and drive me to Grand Central."

"Yes, sir."

"Oh, and Harry," said Brush as Arthur nudged Pulliam away from the door, "congratulations on the success of the 'Eight' exhibition. I know it meant a lot to your little friend from Louisville." He smiled. "Close the door, Arthur."

When she finished rearranging the notebooks, ink wells, pens, and ledgers for the third time, Lenore sat and waited to hear the office's front door open, signaling the arrival of the other members of the National Commission, including Mr. Pulliam. She wasn't sure if it was Mr. Herrmann himself or his pigs' feet that made her feel uneasy, but she could not bring herself to return to the outer office as long as he sat there alone eating and drinking his beer. She felt guilty that she could not be a more congenial hostess but finally decided that it was up to Mr. Herrmann to be more sensitive to the possibility that his eating habits might offend.

She heard a key being inserted into Pulliam's hallway door. She stood, startled. Mr. Pulliam always entered his office through the reception area. The door opened and Pulliam stood and hesitated at its threshold when he saw Lenore. He looked very pale.

"Is anyone here yet?" he whispered.

She nodded. "Mr. Herrmann."

"I see." He entered and closed the door. "Please, continue. You're preparing for the meeting I see."

"Everything is ready, Mr. Pulliam."

He sat at the table, removed his bowler, and ran his hands through his hair. "I need...," he began, but stumbled over his words. "I just need a moment to calm down. I had a confrontation with Mr. Brush on the street just now, and I'm afraid it has made me quite upset."

"Can I help? I can delay the meetings. I can tell them you've been held up by some important business that came in overnight."

"Is there coffee?"

"Café Martin hasn't delivered yet. Shall I call them?"

"Are they late?"

"No. I didn't want the refreshments to sit too long so I arranged for delivery at eight forty-five. I can..."

"No, no. I'll be fine. I'll just sit here and collect myself and then put my hat on and walk out that door and down the hall and come back in through your door and slap Garry on the back and have a good laugh with him over something trivial. Is he eating?"

"Pigs' feet and beer."

He smiled. "Of course." He placed his bowler atop his head and gave it a tap. He stood and bowed at the waist. "Thank you, Miss Caylor.

Thank you for your patience and understanding." He turned to the door and opened it. "Once more unto the breach! I shall imitate the action of the tiger!" He stepped into the hall.

"But sir?" she called after him. Pulliam turned back to Lenore. "The Tigers are in the American League."

He smiled and winked and shut the door behind him.

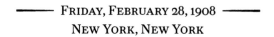

FRIDAY, FEBRUARY 28, 1908
NEW YORK, NEW YORK

Lenore stood at the kitchen counter and mashed potatoes as they waited for Trudie to come home from the doctor's office. Her mother worked at the sink.

"A day off so soon after starting a new job," said Mrs. Caylor as she snapped green beans. "Father would not have approved."

"Then today I suppose I'm happy I work for Mr. Pulliam and not Father."

"Lenore! Such a thing to say about your late father, may the Lord have mercy on his soul."

"I'm sorry, Mother, but it was a very difficult week. The extra day off is most welcome."

"Difficult? I'm sure I don't understand. Just the other day you told me that Mr. Pulliam is a very nice man and quite pleasant to work for."

Lenore jammed her fork into a potato. "He is both of those, Mother. I didn't say that Mr. Pulliam was difficult. I said the week was difficult. With all the meetings and such. The club magnates coming and going. Dinners to be arranged. It was a very stressful week for Mr. Pulliam as well."

"Stressful for Mr. Pulliam?" Trudie stood at the kitchen door removing her gloves, still wearing her coat and hat.

"Why, hello, Trudie," said Mrs. Caylor. "I didn't hear you come in."

"Luella," said Trudie. "Lenore. The lamb smells delicious."

"Aunt Trudie," said Lenore, "how was your day?"

"Much like Mr. Pulliam's week I should think. Would anyone like a glass of sherry?"

"Yes, please," said Lenore.

"Now, girls," said Mrs. Caylor. "You know Father would not approve."

"Luella, please. You are not my mother." Mrs. Caylor opened her mouth to reply, but said nothing. "Lenore, please join me in the parlor."

By the time Lenore removed her apron, washed her hands, and joined her aunt, Trudie had filled two small stemmed glasses almost to the brim with an amber liquid. Her hat and coat were on the arm of a chair. She handed Lenore one of the glasses. They touched rims.

Trudie drained her glass. Lenore took a first sip and coughed.

"I'm sorry," said Trudie. "I should have warned you that I had something stronger than sherry in mind. I couldn't say the word 'whiskey' in front of my sister."

"I need a drink of water."

Trudie reached for a tall clear-glass bottle and poured several inches of water into a goblet. Lenore drank it quickly and breathed deeply.

"Just about the only thing your father bequeathed the family," said Trudie. "Several bottles of fine Kentucky bourbon."

"What's the occasion?"

"No occasion. Any occasion at all. Perhaps just several days during which the medical profession inspired a loathing of the human condition."

"Anything in particular?"

"No." She paused. "Yes. But not now. Perhaps when your mother retires for the night we might return to Kentucky and while away the late hours. But we'd better get back to the kitchen. I shouldn't have been so rude to her."

During supper Mrs. Caylor showed no sign of remembering that Lenore and Trudie had gone off for a drink before dining. By the time she went to bed she no longer remembered what day it was and urged her sister and daughter to get plenty of sleep in order to be ready "for another busy workday tomorrow."

Later, Lenore and Trudie sat side by side on the love seat. Trudie had turned off the electric lamps and lighted four tapers in a brass candelabrum. The bottles of bourbon and water stood on the coffee table, just within reach.

"Feeling better?" asked Lenore.

"Yes, of course. Luella may be having certain...certain difficulties, but her cooking is as marvelous as ever. Always makes me feel better, like an opiate." She poured a small amount of whiskey into glasses and diluted the drinks with water. "So, tell me about Mr. Pulliam's stressful week." She handed one of the glasses to Lenore.

"It's Mr. Brush of the Giants. The meetings themselves went well enough, I suppose. I only sat in on the National League meetings. The National Commission has its own secretary."

"And Mr. Brush disrupted these meetings?"

"Mr. Pulliam had an argument with him on the street outside our building. He refused to attend or send anyone else from the Giants."

"I believe your father knew Mr. Brush when he was connected to the Cincinnati club. Did we meet him back then? I don't recall."

"You would remember him. He's very thin and has a disfigured nose. It looks like it was broken and did not heal well. And he has very large eyes. Abnormally large. Not handsome at all. Somewhat difficult to look at, actually. I imagine his disease would cause much of that."

"Not the broken nose." They laughed and sipped their drinks.

"There's another very curious aspect to the relationship between Mr. Pulliam and Mr. Brush. The first night we met he was certain Mr. Brush was having him followed."

"Followed? To what end?"

"He didn't say exactly except that he believed Mr. Brush means to destroy him. That is how he put it. 'Destroy me,' he said. He told me that teams often have players followed by detectives, as if it were a normal business practice. And Mr. Herrmann of Cincinnati and Mr. Pulliam exchanged words over the status of some minor league team. I believed Mr. Herrmann to be one of Mr. Pulliam's supporters, but there was definitely tension between them."

"I worry about Mr. Pulliam," said Trudie. "He acted distant and preoccupied the evening we attended the exhibition. Especially at Café

Martin. Always checking his watch. Looking at the door every few minutes. He seemed very anxious that the man we met at the gallery..."

"Mr. Russell."

"Yes. I'm sure that he was upset that Mr. Russell didn't join us as promised." She took another drink. "Is Mr. Pulliam married?"

"No."

"Is he associated with any woman? Does he have a fiancée, or someone he calls from the office, or perhaps even someone who visits him at the office? Someone he might have mentioned in casual conversation?" She brought her glass to her lips, hesitated, and then emptied it. "All right, I'll say it. You are more of a sister to me than a niece, and the Lord knows you have seen much during your years on the stage." She set her glass on the table but did not remove her hand from its stem. "Does he have a mistress?"

Lenore sipped her drink. "Mr. Pulliam is a very private man. I know little about his life away from the office, except that he has a sister to whom he is quite devoted. She lives in Nashville and has twin boys, one of whom is named for Mr. Pulliam. He is very proud of his nephew."

Trudie mixed herself another bourbon and water, this time with a higher proportion of whiskey. "About a year ago," she said, "one of our patients came to the office with her son. She was very upset. Her son, a boy of sixteen or seventeen, said nothing. He sat staring at his shoes for most of their visit. He had been caught at school with another boy. The mother was convinced his condition, as she called it, could be treated and cured, like a broken arm."

"And what did the doctor say?"

"I've never known him to turn down a patient. He took the case. The woman is wealthy." She paused. "Last summer the boy disappeared. The family hired a Pinkerton man to find him, to no avail. Yesterday we heard that he was found dead in the Bowery. A gang of boys from the Tenderloin had been out hunting fairies, as they call those cursed with that particular affliction." When Lenore said nothing Trudie continued. "The boy's mother came into the office today. She was hysterical. Why didn't the doctor cure her son? His death was our responsibility. We were murderers, as guilty as the boys from the Tenderloin.

In a way I agreed with her. The doctor never should have agreed to take the boy on as a patient."

"I'm very sorry, Aunt Trudie."

"The killers will not be pursued. Tammany connections. I'm sure they boast openly to their friends. They will no doubt go out hunting fairies again." Trudie looked at Lenore. When her niece said nothing, she continued, "What I want to say is that if someone means to destroy Mr. Pulliam, as you have described Mr. Brush's intentions, he can do it with impunity."

"Your choice of words is much too strong, Trudie. It's only base ball, after all."

"Perhaps. Perhaps the events of the week have influenced my outlook. That and your father's excellent Kentucky whiskey."

"In any case, Mr. Pulliam will have time to calm his nerves. He leaves on an extended trip tomorrow. First Nashville to visit his sister and her family, then up to Louisville, and on to southern Indiana where several clubs train. Then to Cincinnati for the start of the season. I believe he intends to be in Chicago for the Cubs' first home game. He feels he should be there for the raising of their World's Series pennant. I won't see him for more than a month."

"Then you will be in charge at the league office."

Lenore laughed. "Hardly. Mr. Heydler will be there, and we have the telephone and Western Union. I'm happy that he will be able to get out of New York for a while."

"I hope it helps him. I've always been rather fond of Mr. Pulliam." She sipped her drink. "We first met him when I was your age. He was in his late twenties, handsome, charming, entertaining, polite, kind, and somewhat ambitious. The perfect catch. I was perhaps a bit too... too forward, I thought, and put him off. Plus I wasn't as pretty as you. Anyway, now I don't believe that was the problem. It's something of a relief. Perhaps there is hope for me yet."

"Then your arranging for Mr. Pulliam to rescue me from the evils of the theater was for yourself as much as to protect me?"

Trudie smiled. "I must admit I was excited at the prospect of seeing him again. But everything turned out well, don't you think? You are happy in your new life, your new employment. And I...I have extinguished my torch with no further damage to my self-confidence. I am at the perfect age to pursue a rich widower or confirmed bachelor that needs to be convinced otherwise." She reached for the bottle and put its cork back in the top. "And you?"

Lenore shrugged. "I'm in no hurry, and I intend to be very, very careful."

Pulliam sat in his armchair listening to the distant rattle of the Sixth Avenue El. He felt happy to be done with the meetings and looked forward to a month of travel. The days and nights on trains would afford him pure escape. No telephone, no telegraph, no messengers, no mail. And then the season would begin and the magnates would have their clubs to worry about instead of the politics of the league.

He would have the game. The artistry of the game. The 1908 season promised to be as exciting as any in memory with the improved Giants and the always solid Pirates ready to challenge Chicago's two-year reign. The hours spent at ball parks around the league would make everything worthwhile. And the game would help him put Ted Russell out of his mind.

He stood and crossed the room to the closet and took out his suitcase.

———— WEDNESDAY, MARCH 4, 1908 ————
NEW YORK, NEW YORK

Lenore arrived at the St. James Building a quarter of an hour early. She collected the morning's mail in the lobby and flipped through it on the elevator. She came across a small white envelope of fine linen paper addressed to her with no return address. The handwriting was neat and clean, if perhaps a bit old-fashioned. She immediately thought of Henry Chadwick. She put the league correspondence aside and opened it first.

My dear Miss Caylor,

First let me apologize for my unforgiveable behavior Tuesday morning last. Although I sincerely meant no harm, I failed to behave as a proper gentleman and so deserved your response. Indeed, I compliment you on maintaining your dignity so thoroughly where others may have been justifiably incensed and reacted in a less polite manner. I certainly merited no politeness.

To answer your very reasonable question, yes, I am married, as you so quickly surmised. However, my wife is in the process of suing for divorce. I prefer not to go into her reasons at this time. At the present I live alone not far from the Seventy-Ninth Street subway stop. We have no children.

My personal situation in no way excuses my clumsy, forward behavior toward you. I only hope you will forgive me and if I am fortunate enough to meet you by chance on the subway or perhaps on a street in the vicinity of Madison Square, you might acknowledge a casual greeting from myself as nothing more than a sincere expression of friendship.

Finally, I apologize for writing to you in care of the National League, but I failed to note your home address the evening of the blizzard.

Sincerely,
Norman S. Adams

PART II

John Heydler arrived at the office mid-morning. Lenore looked up from her typewriter as he entered the reception area from the outer hall.

"Good morning, Mr. Heydler."

"Good morning, Miss Caylor. Big day today."

"Yes, sir. Opening Day. Will you attend the game in Brooklyn?"

He shook his head. "Not possible. I have to be ready to collect the results of all of the Opening Day games simultaneously. There will certainly be problems. I want to have everything under control as the season gets underway. And I'm sure Mr. Pulliam will be in contact with me from Cincinnati. I've just been down in the Giants' office confirming our communication methods and timing."

"How can I help you?"

"I'm sorry, Miss Caylor, but I'm so used to doing this myself that I have given no consideration to dividing the tasks."

"I understand, sir. Should something come up I plan to be here all day."

She turned to go to her desk, but Heydler lifted his head. "Miss Caylor?"

She stopped. "Yes, sir?"

"There is something you can do. Would you be at all interested in going to Washington Park this afternoon since neither I nor Mr. Pulliam will be able to be there?"

"If you believe it necessary."

"I received a call from Mrs. Jane Chadwick. She's worried about Henry."

"He hasn't recovered from his injuries?"

"It's not that. He attended an exhibition game in inclement weather a few days ago and caught a chill. And now he insists that he must attend the first Brooklyn game today. Can you call Mrs. Chadwick and offer your services to either talk him out of it, which will be next to impossible, or to accompany him to the game? As an official representative of the National League? I understand you are a friend of the family."

"Certainly. I'll telephone her immediately."

Mrs. Chadwick answered after the first ring. "Hello? Chadwick residence."

"Mrs. Chadwick?"

"Speaking."

"Good morning. Mr. Heydler of the National League asked me to call. I'm Lenore Caylor."

"Oh yes, Miss Caylor. Henry has spoken of you. We knew your father well. We might have met when you were a child."

"I'm certain we did, Mrs. Chadwick." She paused. "Mr. Heydler tells me that your husband isn't feeling well but will be going to the game at Washington Park today."

"He's been coughing and sneezing for days. I'm very worried. It's rather chilly today. The *Eagle* says it won't get up to fifty degrees, too cold to be sitting in that drafty old ball park for two hours. But he insists on going to the game, it being Opening Day and all. He thinks he's still thirty-five years old. He'll catch his death."

"Won't you be going along with him?"

"He won't have me. Says it's work and he can't be worrying about me while he's trying to cover the game."

"Well, perhaps I can offer to accompany him. Let me think a minute."

"That would be wonderful, Miss Caylor."

"Perhaps I can ask him to help me cover the game for the league office."

"Yes. Excellent. You can appeal to the chivalry in him."

"Then if he seems to be getting worse or the weather turns nasty..."

"You can claim that it's you who needs to leave. Yes. A perfectly wonderful idea. Thank you, Miss Caylor."

"Then we'll hang up now and I'll call back in a few minutes and ask for Mr. Chadwick as if I never talked to you today at all."

"Yes. Let's do that. Goodbye, Miss Caylor. I can't thank you enough."

Lenore hung up the earpiece and returned to John Heydler's office.

"Mr. Heydler, do we have tickets for the Brooklyn game?"

"Yes. Right here." He opened the top right drawer of his desk and pulled out a business envelope. "Then you'll be going with Mr. Chadwick?"

"I think so. It's not certain. I still need to speak with him directly."

He handed the envelope to Lenore. "There's a note in here from Mr. Ebbets. They've remodeled the ball park and have reconfigured the entrances, so tell Henry and Thomas you'll be going in at the main entrance on Fourth Avenue at Third Street. It's in the note."

"Yes, sir."

Heydler opened another drawer and took out a small gray metal strong box. He spun a combination on its dial and lifted its lid. "And this should cover expenses, including Thomas. Please, no subways or trolleys." He handed Lenore five dollars. "There should be enough there for a box of Cracker Jack, too." He smiled.

"Thank you, Mr. Heydler."

"The game is scheduled for three, but Opening Day ceremonies will no doubt delay the start. Nonetheless, give yourself plenty of time to get to the Chadwick residence and then to the ball park."

"I'll telephone Mr. Chadwick now and make arrangements."

———— MONDAY AND TUESDAY, APRIL 20 AND 21, 1908 ————
CHICAGO, ILLINOIS

Ban Johnson and Charles "Commy" Comiskey lingered at the table much too long as far as Pulliam was concerned. They never tired of discussing the subtleties of the business end of base ball. He found the young newspaper man Ring Lardner much more entertaining. He reminded Pulliam of himself at the beginning of his years as a base ball writer at the Louisville *Commercial*.

Comiskey had hosted Pulliam and Johnson at the White Sox game at South Side Park that afternoon. Although Pulliam had pleaded fatigue, Comiskey insisted on dinner. He had made reservations at the Tip Top Inn on the ninth floor of the Pullman Palace Car Building. Johnson had mentioned that Comiskey loved to entertain the press and might invite a writer or two to join them .

"He believes in cultivating their good opinion of him," said Johnson. "Keeps them drunk and happy so they'll write nice things about his team. And about him."

They had arrived in time to admire the view of the palatial Art Institute with its verdigris lions below, illuminated in a soft yellow glow as the sun set. Deep blue and placid Lake Michigan extended beyond to the eastern horizon.

The Art Institute made Pulliam think of Ted. The museum was to host the "Eight" exhibition later in the year. Perhaps he would plan a return visit to Chicago to coincide with its opening.

"They tell me," said Lardner, "that Mike Donlin had to cut a deal with John Brush about his, how shall I put it, love affair with the bottle."

Pulliam smiled. "I understand he wanted a six hundred dollar bonus to stay sober last year and Brush refused. That's one reason he came here with his wife and sat out the season."

"I saw him play with the Logan Squares. A vicious natural hitter."

"Yes, but the drink will kill that, and him, too, sooner or later. It's a pity and a waste of talent," said Pulliam.

"I'd take the sonofabitch in a heartbeat," said Comiskey. "And I'd keep him sober without paying him to do it."

"Anyway, Commy," said Johnson, "he's in their league. Let Harry here worry about it. We have problems enough of our own. I'd rather take Hans Wagner off the National League's hands."

"He's back with Pittsburgh," said Lardner. "And with his help they lost three in a row to the Cincinnatis."

They laughed. Comiskey drained the last of the brandy in his snifter and slapped his two hands on the table. "Time for me to get along. Nan will be wondering where the hell I am."

"That's a good one," said Johnson. "If you walk through the door before midnight she'll worry you've come down with something. Or someone died."

They laughed again. Comiskey stood. "Well, nonetheless, I'm on my way home. You boys feel free to have another round or two and add it to my bill."

Johnson rose. "Thank you, Commy, but I've had my fill for the evening. I'll walk out with you."

Pulliam and Lardner stood and said thank you to Comiskey and good night to both executives.

"Perhaps I'll see you again before I return to New York," said Pulliam.

"Could be," said Johnson. "I may try to make it to the Cubs' pennant-raising party before the game on Wednesday."

"I don't think I'll make an appearance at that," said Comiskey. "Now, Ring, take good care of our National League friend here. Stay away from the Levee."

More laughter as the two men left. Pulliam and Lardner looked at each other, shrugged, and sat back down. They ordered one glass each of the Tip Top Room's best Kentucky bourbon.

"Are you familiar with the Levee?" asked Lardner.

"By reputation only," said Pulliam.

"A man has to be very careful down there. Might end up dead. Then again, you might have the best night of your life."

Pulliam wanted nothing more than to excuse himself and walk the two blocks to his room at the Palmer House Hotel. But Lardner was a newspaper man. He wrote about base ball. Newspaper men who wrote about base ball talked. To turn down an invitation to partake of the pleasures of the Levee District would be another mark against his manliness, especially if word of his hesitation made it back to Brush.

When Pulliam didn't respond Lardner motioned for the waiter. "Do you have a telephone that will reach this table?"

"Of course, sir. Right away, sir." He turned and went to a small alcove where he opened a cabinet. He removed a telephone and brought it to the table, uncurling its cord as he approached.

Lardner lifted the earpiece. "Calumet four-twelve, please." He paused. "Yes, Calumet four-one-two ."

He waited a moment and then said, "Hello, Minna, please. Oh, hello Minna. Ring. Tell me, how's it looking down there this evening? How about the Copper Room? The Gold Room then? Fine. Yes. I'll be bringing a friend. See you in thirty minutes."

"Minna?" asked Pulliam.

"Minna Everleigh. She and her sister Ada run the Everleigh Club."

A line of carriages and hansoms stood waiting along Adams Street. The doorman motioned for the next in the queue. Pulliam climbed in ahead of Lardner. They drove along South Michigan Avenue, a very dark Grant Park to their left and the wall of tall office buildings, concert halls, private clubs, hotels, and a large automobile showroom to their right, bright warm light spilling out of doorways and windows and onto the sidewalk and street. Beyond the Auditorium Annex Hotel at Congress, the commercial avenue became more residential with elegant town houses and apartment buildings that had thus far survived the expansion of Chicago's business district. At Twelfth Street Pulliam looked up to his left at Central Station's illuminated clock tower and saw that it was five minutes after eleven. He longed for his bed at the Palmer House.

"It's somewhat ironic," said Lardner, "that the robber barons of our fair city built their mansions within blocks of one of the most notorious vice districts in the world. But maybe that's why they've almost all moved north of the river. Too late for Marshall Field's son, though."

"I recall the story," said Pulliam. "Tragic. Killed himself a couple of years ago while cleaning a gun. His home is nearby?"

"On Prairie Avenue. Maybe half a mile from here." Lardner chuckled. "Killed himself you say? That's the story the family put out, and most of the papers went along with it. A friend of mine saw the whole thing."

"And what did your friend see?"

"Field Junior had arranged to throw a party for his mistress at the Everleigh Club. Imagine holding a party for your girlfriend in a resort of such ill repute? Well, as you would expect there was heavy drinking. They argued and the girlfriend shot him with a derringer. He was severely injured but conscious and asked to be sent to his home a few blocks away." Ring gestured to his left. "Guess he didn't want his wife to find out he'd been visiting a bordello. He died in his mansion, which had been given to him and his bride as a wedding gift from the old man. If you ask the sisters about it, they won't tell you a thing. Their employees are not supposed to discuss it either, but one night my friend had a little too much champagne."

"What happened to the girlfriend?"

"The old man paid her a lot of money to blow town. The family couldn't have a trial with all the publicity that would come with it."

"Of course."

"Field had him buried in Graceland Cemetery on the North Side. He bought close to half an acre for the family plot. Hired a famous sculptor to build a monument that sits in front of a reflecting pool. Field himself is there now, too. Died the next year. The girlfriend's derringer killed them both, if you ask me."

In the near distance Pulliam heard loud clanging bells. He smelled the acrid stench of painted wood burning. "Seems there might be a fire nearby," he said.

"Wouldn't be surprised. You'll see a fair number of wooden structures down here. We are south of where the fire of 1871 burned its path, so there are buildings that predate the new codes. Fires are common."

They turned west on Cullerton and within a block Pulliam noticed crowds of people from all levels of society strolling the sidewalks. Well-dressed gentlemen wearing expensive bowlers and boaters, as well as the down-and-out, moved slowly along littered sidewalks in front of shabby two-story, wood-frame houses, dilapidated limestone and red-brick flats, cheap hotels, and taverns advertising drinks for pennies. Young women walked the streets alone or in groups of two or three. Older women sat on stoops or stood in front of building doors hawking the pleasures to be had within.

They turned south on Dearborn Street and passed establishments Lardner identified as "Dago Frank's," "Madam Ann's," "French Em's," and "Vic Shaw's."

"Poor Vic," said Lardner. "She was Queen of the Levee until the Everleigh sisters opened up. She's never forgiven them for stealing her thunder—and clientele. She even tried to frame them for the Field murder."

"And?"

"And it didn't work. The sisters got wind of the plot. One of their own girls was in on it."

"What did they do to her?"

"Forgave her. Put her back to work. Name of Nellie." Lardner paused. "Then she treated them ill again and had to go. She eventually jumped off a bridge. They fished her out of the south branch, not far from here. She left a note behind for whoever found her to call the Everleighs because they were the only ones she could trust to give her a nice funeral."

"And?"

"And they gave her a nice funeral. She might be in Graceland, too." Lardner laughed and looked out of the cab. "Here's Sappho's. The Everleigh Club is next door."

"Sappho's?"

"Women who prefer women."

The cab pulled up to a residential three-story building that, along with a mirror-image building next door, stood out as clean and well maintained, two elegant stone and brick façades in the midst of the busy squalor.

"Here we are," said Lardner. He climbed down from the carriage before Pulliam. "Looks like the Reverend Bell is hard at work."

Pulliam joined him on the sidewalk. A small crowd stood at the curb in front of the buildings. One of their group, a slender, hatless man with a heavy, drooping mustache and receding hairline, stood taller than the rest. On a soapbox, Pulliam assumed. He appeared to be in his early forties. The man raised a hand holding a black book above his head.

"It is the word of God," he said to the approval of his listeners. "Men in gilded coaches driven to the very gates of hell." He stared at Pulliam and Lardner and gestured at the buildings with the book. "Enter and die a thousand deaths. Enter and murder the innocent prey of the white slaver. Enter and feel the blood of sixty thousand dead and diseased sisters and daughters of the fruited plain of America. Feel their blood as it drips from your fingers. Enter and curse thyself. Curse thyself. Curse thyself and your hopeless, helpless young victims.

"No! Sixty thousand times no! Instead, walk with me, brothers! Turn away from the house of the harlot and the white slaver! Onward! March!"

The group broke into song. "Onward Christian soldiers. Marching as to war!"

Lardner smiled. "They're known as Reverend Ernest A. Bell's Midnight Mission. They had some success at Custom House Place so now they've set their aims on the Levee and the Everleigh sisters in particular. They're here about every night."

"And what do the Everleigh sisters do about it?"

"Nothing. Business couldn't be better. And why they picked the Everleighs is beyond my limited understanding. The sisters never buy girls from procurers. They don't need to. There's a mile-long waiting list of girls who want to work here. It's a class house that treats its people well. But what do I know about reformers?" He turned his attention away from the group at the curb. "Shall we go in?" He led the way up a dozen stone steps to the arched entrance. He rang a bell and waited a moment for one of the heavy wooden double doors to slowly open.

A woman of perhaps thirty-five stood smiling as she held the door for the two men. She was dressed well enough to be the daughter of one of Chicago's Prairie Avenue industrialists. "Good evening, Mr. Lardner," she said. "Miss Everleigh is expecting you."

"Thank you, Gladys." Ring led Pulliam into the front lobby, a narrow room of mahogany paneling, Persian rugs, silk drapery, fine art in gilded frames, gold cuspidors, and a crystal chandelier. Pulliam heard faint music, violins and a piano, Brahms, he thought, wafting into the lobby from somewhere within the house. A short but full palm plant stood in a gold pot on a golden pedestal in front of the thickly carpeted staircase. Pulliam looked up at a deeply coffered ceiling. It reminded him of the St. James Building lobby.

Lardner gestured to one of several hand-carved and gold-trimmed divans with thick red silk, gold-tasseled cushions. "Have a seat. Minna will be right with us." They sat, glancing at several other men on similar benches along the wall, each well-dressed and barbered and holding an expensive bowler. They appeared to be a group of some kind, whispering to each other and stifling laughter. Pulliam looked to his right and admired a tall ceramic urn decorated with a flowing arrangement of hand-painted flowers.

Lardner watched him. "French porcelain, I believe. Eighteenth century. Minna says it once belonged to a count. It was looted during the Revolution and found its way here after the fire of 1871."

"If you don't mind my asking, Ring, how can you afford such a place?"

"Minna loves the gentlemen of the press. I'm not sure why. Perhaps her sister, Ada, believes it's good business to keep us happy. Like Comiskey." He laughed. "No need to have the papers screaming that the Levee should be shut down any more than they already do." He looked around the lobby. "Funny," he said, "I usually see a few of the boys here." He turned to the woman who had opened the door. "Gladys? No other newspapermen this evening?"

"Oh yes, Mr. Lardner. There's a couple upstairs. But a call came in about a fire up on Wabash at Eighteenth? So most of the others ran out."

"I see." He turned to Pulliam. "Must have been what we heard and smelled on the way down here. We leave the Everleigh telephone number with the boy who holds down the desk during the night. If something big comes in he calls here because he knows he'll find at least a few newspaper men available to cover the story."

A slight woman in her mid-forties, her dark hair pulled back tightly and held in place by diamond-studded pins, struggled down the staircase caressing the railing and smiling thinly with closed lips. Her red silk kimono-like brocade dress flowed before and behind her. Her gown, her neck, her fingers, and her wrist sparkled with jewels of every color and cut. Pulliam soon realized that her slow progress was meant to hide her natural gait, a kind of jerky, stop-and-roll forward motion. "Ring, my boy," she said in a light Southern accent. Pulliam tried to place it and decided on the East, not the Deep South. Virginia or southern Maryland. "How are you? Nice to see you again. It's been a few weeks, hasn't it?"

Ring and Pulliam stood. "Hello, Minna," said Ring. "I was out of town covering a story in Joliet."

"Oh my," said the woman as she reached the bottom of the stairs and held out her hand to Pulliam. "And whatever could possibly happen in Joliet?" When Pulliam put his hand in hers, she held on lightly but did not release him. He was surprised at how short she was, perhaps less than five feet tall.

"You'd be surprised," said Ring.

"I see you brought your big brother with you this evening. He may be even more handsome than you, Ring, my boy."

"Actually, Minna, this is Mr. Harry Pulliam, president of the National League of Professional Base Ball Clubs."

"President? Impressive," said Minna. "Then he is not your brother? You look enough alike."

"I'm afraid," said Pulliam, "that I am almost old enough to be Ring's father."

"Nonsense," said Minna. "You would have had to father him at age ten. Although I've seen stranger things in my time."

"Harry," said Ring, "this is Miss Minna Everleigh."

"Charmed," said Pulliam.

"Equally," said Minna. She released his hand. "Shall we proceed on to the Gold Room? I believe that's what we discussed on the telephone. Am I correct, Ring, my boy?"

"Indeed you are, Minna."

As she led them through the building she turned briefly to Pulliam. "We see some of your colleagues here from time to time. Not the ball players, the poor dears. Their bosses, the mag...mag... What do the papers call them, Ring, my boy?"

"Magnates."

"Yes. Magnets. All very attractive," she laughed.

"Magnates, Minna," said Lardner. "Not magnets."

"Maggots? Sounds like a species of insect. Of course, I cannot tell you which of these insects has graced our home. I don't remember."

"I'm sure," said Pulliam, "that I'd rather not know."

"I understand," said Minna.

"Most of them, if not all, are married men. Unlike myself."

"Then you are quite an unusual guest, Mr. Pulliam. As is my boy

Ring." She stopped at heavy wooden double doors in the middle of the hallway. "Here we are."

She turned the two brass knobs at once and pushed the doors open. Pulliam stepped into a room that almost blinded him with its abundance of gold. Gold-painted paneling. Gold andirons at a gold-trimmed fireplace. Golden light fixtures. Gold-rimmed porcelains on every golden surface. Gold-thread tapestries and large erotic oil paintings in gilded frames hung on the walls. Dominating the space at the far end of the room stood what appeared to be a solid gold baby grand piano played by a thin man with long flowing hair, impeccably dressed in a black tuxedo. A quartet and a harpist accompanied him. The full-size harp was gold. They played the Brahms that Pulliam had heard in the lobby, and not particularly well, he thought.

"Please, make yourself at home." Minna gestured to a pair of golden thronelike armchairs. As they sat she pressed a button on a nearby wall. Within moments, a man dressed in traditional butler livery appeared with a golden ice bucket containing a bottle of champagne topped with gold foil. He carried two gold-rimmed, ornately cut crystal glasses. A shorter man followed dressed in a spotless, perfectly fitted waiter's uniform. He held a tray of caviar, biscuits, medallions of beef, sliced duck, oysters, and a small gold bowl containing a dark sauce.

The butler poured champagne into the two glasses and handed them to Pulliam and Lardner.

"Will that be all, Miss Everleigh?" he asked as he placed the bottle in the ice bucket.

"Yes, Edmund. Thank you."

He nodded. "A pleasure to see you again, Mr. Lardner."

"Thank you, Edmund."

The butler and waiter exited through the double doors.

"Please," said Minna, "help yourselves. I shall return shortly with a pair of beautiful butterflies to brighten our evening." She left the room.

Pulliam sipped his champagne and immediately appreciated it as one of the finest vintages he had ever tasted.

"We must sample Minna's little meal," said Ring. "Her kitchen is one of the best in Chicago, if not the best. She'll be very disappointed if we don't." Pulliam nodded and followed Lardner to the table. He filled his gold-rimmed plate with a sample of each of the choices. He assumed the sauce to be a red wine reduction of some kind, prepared to complement the duck.

They nibbled and listened to the music that segued from Brahms to a Dvorak piano quintet. Pulliam drank his champagne too quickly and began to feel a bit drunk. The musicians sounded more skilled than earlier.

Lardner paused between bites. "If you prefer something a little livelier, a ragtime tune or something by Cohan or Von Tilzer, I'm quite certain my friend Van Van will be able to oblige. They are very versatile."

"No. This is very nice. I'm enjoying it." He took the champagne from the ice bucket and poured himself and Lardner another glass and was surprised that they had finished the bottle. "Van Van?"

"The piano player. Mr. Vanderpool Vanderpool."

Pulliam finished his glass of champagne. Lardner filled his glass. He didn't recall seeing Edmund return with a new bottle. He decided he was drinking much too quickly and resolved to slow down.

The doors opened and Minna entered with two very elegantly dressed young women. They were introduced as Bessie and Belle. More glasses appeared and Lardner poured champagne for the three women. They toasted each other. Pulliam felt as though he may have spilled some of his drink, but no one noticed. The women joked and laughed. At Lardner's request Van Van and his quartet played a slightly bawdy rag. The young women danced and held out hands for the men to join them.

The room whirled as Pulliam tried to keep up with one of the young women. He gave up, but slapped his thighs and laughed at his own lack of coordination. He looked for Minna, but she had left without his noticing. Soon he was being led out to the hall by one of the women. He wasn't sure if she was Bessie or Belle. She took him to a room that he would later remember as being very blue. He sat in a chair. The woman stood before him and began to undress.

"Please," he said, "don't do that."

"Of course, sir. I'm sorry, sir." She sat on a brass double bed covered with frilly lace linens. She picked up a blue telephone and removed its earpiece. "Yes. Tell Minna she was right." She paused. "Yes. Yes, I understand." She replaced the earpiece and put the telephone back on the bedside table.

Pulliam felt his head clearing, but his stomach tightening. He didn't know how to proceed. "I'm the one who should be sorry," he said.

"We meet men like you from time to time," she said. Pulliam noticed that she had let down her long blond hair so that it flowed over her shoulders. "The sisters aim to please their customers, but we can't have that kind of thing in our house."

"Yes, I understand. I'll leave now."

"No need for that. Miss Everleigh will be here in a moment."

They sat looking at each other for what seemed to Pulliam to be a long time. The woman smiled at him and wound her curls around her fingers.

Minna entered the room and stood next to the bed. "Please leave us, Bessie." The young woman rose from the bed and left the room, gently closing the door behind her.

"My boy Ring won't be ready to leave for a little while now," said Minna, "and we can't have you returning to the parlor or the front this quickly. It wouldn't do for you or for our house."

"Then we sit and wait until...until it's proper?" Pulliam thought his use of the term "proper" rather humorous.

"If you like. But we intend to satisfy our customers, so this is what we offer men like you. Keep in mind, we make no judgments. We tell no tales. My boy Ring has brought you here to make you happy." She sighed. "There is a hotel across the alley. Edmund will guide you down the backstairs. You will meet someone in our yard. If he's to your liking he will take you to the hotel. I'm sorry the Marlborough is no Palmer House, but it's convenient. Later, he will bring you back and you will return to the lobby via this hallway. Ring will be waiting for you there. Your reputation will be intact."

"Am I that obvious?"

Minna shook her head and smiled. "Not at all. But we are professionals and know men well. All types of men." She started toward the door.

Pulliam thought of Ted, but the promise of physical companionship heightened his need to satisfy a longing he had fought for weeks. He followed Minna.

He awoke the next morning fully dressed and sprawled across his hotel bed. At first he didn't remember where he was. Then the memory of the previous evening flooded his thoughts. He had enjoyed himself but felt sickened that he had drunk too much and let a young man take him to a dingy room in a cheap hotel in the Levee District of Chicago. He turned to the small table next to the bed to check the time. A telegram lay under his watch. He didn't recall reading it. He picked it up.

WESTERN UNION

1908 APR 20 PM 2 04

H PULLIAM

PALMER HOUSE CHICAGO

HENRY CHADWICK PASSED TODAY. FUNERAL APR 23. PLEASE ADVISE.

L CAYLOR

He felt physically ill and stood to calm himself. He waited a few moments until the nausea subsided. He picked up the telephone and called the front desk.

"Yes, Mr. Pulliam."

"First, I need to be booked on the next train to New York City. The Twentieth Century."

"The next train leaves LaSalle Street Station at 2:40. You would arrive at Grand Central Terminal at approximately 11:40 tomorrow morning."

"Please book a sleeper."

"Yes, sir."

"And please send the following telegrams. There will be two. First to Miss L. Caylor. C, not T, A-Y-L-O-R. National League of Professional Base Ball Clubs. St. James Building. New York City. Fourteenth floor."

"Yes, sir."

"Taking train express to New York. Arrive tomorrow morning late. Will telephone later today. Pulliam."

"Very good, sir."

"Second. Charles Murphy. Chicago National League Base Ball Club. Chicago.

"Henry Chadwick passed. Must return to New York immediately. Funeral April 23. Regret missing opening ceremony and raising pennant. Congratulations again. Pulliam."

—— WEDNESDAY, APRIL 22, 1908 ——
NEW YORK, NEW YORK

Lenore walked to the Ninth Avenue El Station at 110th Street to catch the train to the Polo Grounds. The cars were crowded, so she stood all the way to 155th Street.

Mr. Pulliam insisted that she not bother to come into the office in the morning. Since she lived on 111th Street, it would be much more convenient to go directly to the ball park that afternoon, if she so chose. He understood perfectly, he had said, if her sorrow over Mr. Chadwick's death prevented her from going at all. They would meet at the office the next day and travel together to his funeral in Brooklyn. In the meantime, the game went on. No contests were cancelled, and Pulliam felt obligated, since he had rushed back to New York from Chicago upon hearing of the tragedy, to attend the Giants' first home game with Mr. Heydler.

"And the game," he had said to her, "can often supply just the right tonic to soothe any pain."

She agreed with him. Escape to the ball park could help her get through the next few days.

The streets around the Polo Grounds reminded her of Times Square on New Year's Eve. Lines for tickets stretched far down the street. There was excitement in the air, but it was different from opening night on the stage. No snooty "prove it to me" attitude that so many of the swells cultivated as they milled around the theaters, wondering just how they would denigrate the entertainment they had just spent as much as $2.50 to see. These base ball "fanatics" had no idea what they were about to see, but there was a spirit of confident hope in the bits of conversation she overheard.

The Brooklyn team, whom the Giants would play for their first home game of the season, had given Pulliam only two tickets. Brush claimed he had only outfield standing tickets left for anyone else from the fourteenth floor.

"That's where I'll be," he had said. "If the rope is good enough for me, it's too good for the National League office."

Lenore happily accepted two tickets and looked forward to standing behind the outfield rope because she wanted to avoid the drunken fan club members stumbling into the grandstand entrances. Pulliam made her promise she would attend the game accompanied by a suitable male companion. She assured him that a cousin, one of her mother's nephews, would be with her, but she was determined to attend alone. She wanted no obligation to be pleasant company to anyone else.

She entered through a gate near the elevated tracks that stood just beyond the left and center field bleachers. Making her way to the low, white outfield rope she noticed a few other women arriving alone. Suffragettes, she laughed to herself. It made her think of Mr. Pulliam and his claim to have marched for women's right to vote.

The excitement and anticipation thrilled her. Spectators took every available spot in and around the field. She looked up over the grandstands behind home plate and saw that the steep, rocky slope of Coogan's Bluff behind the ball park was covered with fans straining for a view over the low roof of the upper level. She found a nice spot in left center field and, not wanting to stand the whole game, decided to step over the rope and sit on the outfield grass. But she felt pressed more and more as the crowd inched farther into the outfield, her own space shrinking. She pulled up her knees and held them with her arms.

She looked to her left and saw a section in center field protected from fans by a squadron of security officers in gray uniforms. Ten minutes before the game was to begin, a large black Hewitt limousine pulled up. The uniformed driver and one of the officers opened the rear door and worked in the interior for several minutes. When they turned away Lenore could barely see a kind of cot tilted and protruding slightly from the automobile, a pair of shoes just visible at the bottom.

The talk she heard around her was about Big Six, Christy Mathewson, and the return of Turkey Mike. Across the field, at the Giants' bench, she could see the little tank of a man who waved his chunky arms and threw his cap and kicked the dirt. She thought she could hear his high, whining voice all the way across the field and above the screaming throng. John McGraw loudly protested every call and every play that didn't go his way.

The talk came back, again and again, to a team that wasn't on the field. To a team that had won the pennant two years running, and one World's Series, and threatened to do it again. The hated Chicago Cubs. Random player names bounced through the crowd. Tinker, Chance, Pfiester, Evers, and someone with only three fingers. She heard talk about the Pittsburgh Pirates, too, and Honus Wagner, who had finally decided to return to the game.

Going into the bottom half of the last inning, the Giants were behind two runs to one. The crowd screamed and cheered, demanding that their team score a run to at least tie the game. Those who had been sitting on the outfield grass now stood. Rooters across the field pushed their way to the foul lines so that it appeared almost impossible for a hitter to run to first base.

A lanky kid named Merkle pinch batted for the pitcher Mathewson and hit a double into the crowd standing in the outfield. Lenore couldn't see what happened after that as rooters stood and blocked her view, but with two out the Giants had hope with a runner on second. The player called Turkey Mike came to the plate next and connected for a home run into the right field bleachers to win the game for the Giants, three to two. At that moment the field disappeared completely as rooters stormed the diamond in wild celebration. Hats, seat cushions, newspapers, and other debris flew through the air. Lenore struggled against the surging crowd as she made her way to the nearest exit.

She wanted to take the El home, but when she finally made it outside the ball park it looked as though half of the day's attendance had the same idea. The line stretched from the exit to the station two blocks away, but there was no real alternative so she inched her way along, listening to the talk.

The victory had reassured most that this would be the Giants' year. Others countered that the Cubs had started out the year just like the Giants—they were tied for first with five wins and one loss each. "Six and one for the Giants," said one fan as if the rest of the crowd had forgotten what they had just seen. "And if the Cubs lose today, that would put the Giants in first place all alone."

"With only 147 games left to play," said another, "it's a cinch." Many around Lenore laughed and agreed with the man's cynicism. Lenore found herself laughing, too, and enjoying the buoyant mood in the line. But she knew that if the player named Turkey Mike had not hit the home run but had made an out, the crowd would have been despondent instead of hysterical in their joy. It came down to that, to the last play of the game.

In the theater, you knew opening night how every performance thereafter would be received, if you lasted beyond opening night. You loved the applause each time, but you also came to expect it if you were lucky enough to dance in a hit show. There were no surprises. In fact, you worked very hard to avoid surprises. But in base ball, the extreme swing from anticipated victory to the knowledge of defeat treated the fans harshly. She could see it on the faces of the Brooklyn fans in the crowd. One minute they reveled in the prospect of ruining their borough rivals' first home game, and with the next pitch they knew they had a long, depressing trek back across the East River.

"Lenore? Lenore is that you?" came a woman's voice from across the street. Lenore turned and saw a row of carriages and one motorcar lined up along the opposite curb. A cheerful face peered out of the automobile. "Hello, Lenore!" An arm reached out of the narrow window and a gloved hand waved frantically. "It's me! Mabel!" she called.

"It's Mabel Hite!" a woman cried. Breathless murmurs of "Where?" and "No!" and "Is it really?" responded.

They had met during the three week run of *A Venetian Romance* at the Knickerbocker Theater in 1904, one of Lenore's first shows. Mabel had been kind to her, the newcomer, when others would have just as soon tripped her on the stage. They became friends but after the show closed rarely ran into each other.

"Oh, damn, Lenore," said the woman. "Now they've seen me. Hurry over." The face retreated as a crowd approached the automobile. Mabel must have told her driver to help because somehow a path was cleared and Lenore found herself at an open door. She climbed in and sat next to Mabel. The driver returned to his post in the front seat.

"Base ball rooters are beasts, aren't they?" laughed Mabel. "They'll tear you apart if you give them the chance."

"It appears so," replied Lenore.

"At the stage door they crowd around you and push little booklets in your face, but you never feel threatened, do you, Lenore?" Lenore didn't know because no one had ever asked for her autograph. Mabel didn't wait for a reply. "How are you? And what have you been doing? Any shows?"

"No. I've given up the theater."

"No! Whatever for?"

"I felt it was time. And I was offered a very comfortable position. How about you, Mabel? Did I hear that you were to open at the Circle?"

"Yes, in *The Merry-Go-Round.* A nice part. Tomorrow I'm bringing the whole chorus line here for the game. A little treat before we open."

"When's that?"

"The next day. Can you believe it? It's so exciting. And the Giants are going to win the World's Series. I can feel it. It's going to be a grand year."

Lenore looked out the window. "Why are you waiting here, Mabel?"

"I'm waiting for my husband."

"Of course. You married a ball player a couple of years ago, didn't you? Does he play for the Giants or the Brooklyn team?"

Mabel nodded and smiled. "The Giants."

Several young men bolted from one of the ball park gates. One of them fought off fans and jumped into the automobile and onto Lenore's lap.

"Whoa!" he cried. "I'm sorry, ma'am. Mabel, what the hell?"

The car started up, pushing the man more closely into Lenore.

"Don't have too much fun, Mike," laughed Mabel. "She's an old friend."

"Doesn't look too old to me," he said, his eyes less than a foot from Lenore's own.

"This is Mike, Lenore," said Mabel, pushing herself into a corner of the back seat to give her husband room. "Mike, Lenore. I was in a show with Lenore, what? four years ago?"

"Just about," said Lenore, pushing the man off her toward the small open space between her and Mabel.

"Where to, Lenore?" asked Mabel.

"She's coming with us," said Mike.

"Where to, Lenore?" repeated Mabel.

"You can drop me at a 111th and Amsterdam. Thank you very much."

"Is it nice there? We need to find an apartment. I'm tired of living in hotels."

"Why go home?" said Mike. "We're going to have a good time tonight. Did you see the game?"

"As much as I could," said Lenore. "It didn't look good for the Giants until that player named 'Turkey' hit the home run. But I barely saw that for the crowd."

"The player named Turkey," mimicked Mike. "That's swell." Mabel laughed into her fist.

"That's all I know," said Lenore. "I saw the ball fly out toward right field and then the fans yelled for Turkey Mike." She blushed. "Turkey Mike. That's you, isn't it?"

"Damn right it's me. But let's forget the 'Turkey' part. And just because you're so quick and clever you're coming with us tonight."

Mabel leaned forward. "Driver? Please, 111th and Amsterdam."

"Thank you, Mabel," said Lenore. "And this way you'll be able to see where I live. It's a very nice street."

"Excellent. Say, Lenore, we should get together after a show sometime. Catch up on old times."

A man wearing a brown bowler sat on the El, very glum. He had left the game after the bottom of the eighth inning in order to get a jump on the crowd, convinced that the Giants would not come back and even tie the game, let alone win it. While waiting in line he heard the insanely glorious cheer from the crowd inside the ball park and knew that he had missed something. He learned later that Turkey Mike Donlin had won it in the ninth with a home run, with two outs and two strikes on him. So he had missed one of the best endings in anyone's memory. He vowed then and there never to leave another game early, be the score two to one or twelve to nothing.

Worse, he owed Rube Hanson five more dollars. He had taken the Giants, but had to give Rube three runs and the Giants won by one. He wasn't sure how much his total with Rube was, and he had no idea how he would find the money to pay him.

Charlie Ebbets rushed to Pulliam's box and confronted him before the last player left the field.

"Harry, you gotta do something about that cheap sonofabitch Brush," screamed Ebbets over the noise of the celebrating crowd. He would have been screaming anyway, thought Pulliam. His team had just dropped a close game in the bottom of the ninth. "Did you see the hit by that rookie Merkle?"

"Yes, Charlie, I saw it."

"Ground-rule double? Not possible!"

"Those are the rules, Charlie."

"Look, Harry. You're always so damn worried about the integrity of the game. Any other day that's a routine fly out. But Brush doesn't know how to say no to a dollar, or a goddamn nickel for that matter, so he keeps letting people in and pushing them onto the outfield grass and between the seats and the foul lines until there's almost no field to play on. That ain't right, Harry. You gotta control that bastard. It ain't right for the fans in the lower seats, neither. How the hell are they supposed to see the game with all those drunken bums standing in front of them? I could hardly see the game myself. I don't think you really saw it."

"Are you going to protest the game?"

"And what about that so called security force? What does Brush pay them to do? Maybe he doesn't pay them. Maybe that's why they let the fans push them around."

"It's a private security company."

"Yeah. The Sherlock Holmes Security something-or-other. Doctor Watson could do a better job." Pulliam chuckled. "It ain't funny, Harry," said Ebbets. "You gotta make Brush get real cops in here. They got real cops at ball parks in every other city in the league. But not here. Oh no. Too much to ask. Or too much money is more like it."

"Charlie, I agree with you. The field of play should not shift based on any given day's attendance. Nor should the ground rules. But it's the way it's been done for as long as anyone can remember, and those things are sometimes very difficult to change."

"It's dangerous, Harry," said Ebbets. "My outfielders could get killed out there, surrounded by all those insane Giants rooters."

"I suppose Superba fans are more refined?"

"That's not the point, Harry. What'll it take to get some action on this?"

"Build a bigger ball park, maybe."

"Yeah sure. With what money?"

"Barney Dreyfuss is planning one for the Pirates."

"He needs a new park. It's like playing in a swamp over there."

"He's looking at land away from the river, up in the Oakland neighborhood. And he's looking at concrete and steel instead of wood."

"Concrete and steel. Good for him. No more floods and no more fires. But what do we do here in New York in the meantime, Harry? Maybe talk to the city about some kind of crowd limit ordinance."

"Do you know anyone in City Hall?"

"Tammany Hall, you mean. Of course not. You're right. Never mind. I'd have to sell my soul. Anyway, Brush is hooked in with Tammany and you know it." Ebbets looked out onto the field. "I guess we're all going to have to look at building new ball parks. We need more seats. I don't want to turn people away any more than Brush." He paused. "You hear what they're drawing in Chicago? Nationals and Americans?"

"Yes. Both teams will be in the pennant race at the end of the year.

Just like 1906. They're already talking about a repeat of their city World's Series."

"Yeah." Ebbets turned to go. "Harry, you know I'm on your side. But it's getting rough out there. Brush has Herrmann lined up against you again. He's lost five straight to Chicago and is mad as hell. Not that it's your fault his team can't play base ball, but he's reconsidering his support of the league office."

Pulliam turned and looked out at the field. "Thank you, Charlie. Have a nice evening."

"Not too likely, Harry. But tomorrow's another game, if Brush can get the field back in shape."

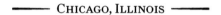

CHICAGO, ILLINOIS

Johnny Evers watched as Joe Tinker walked down the hall of the Auditorium Annex Hotel. Tinker needed to make a telephone call and had asked that Evers hail a cab to take them home. Tinker would get out first and pay back the fare tomorrow. He was a little short after celebrating the Cubs' sixth win out of their first seven games of the 1908 season. They had met some of their friends on the Cincinnati Reds, whom the Cubs had beat four out of four so far, and Tinker insisted on buying a few rounds. First at Joe Biggios's across from the ball park, next at the Berghoff downtown, and then at the Reds' hotel.

Screw him, Evers thought. *Damn Tinker is always short.* And Evers didn't want company for his ride home either, least of all Tinker. He was sick of hearing him talk about their supposedly famous double-play combination. Wouldn't be worth spit without the pitching and the hitting. *Let him walk home, all the way to Oak Park. Serve him right.*

Evers took the stairs down to the tunnel that connected the hotel under Congress Street to the Auditorium Hotel. He emerged near the lobby, walked quickly to the South Michigan Avenue exit, grabbed a cab, and went home. They had another game with the Reds tomorrow and he was mad as hell at how drunk the Cubs got that evening. A team of goddamn kraut eaters—Steinfeldt, Hofman, Reulbach, Zimmerman, Schulte, Kling, and the rest—who could never say no to just one more stein of beer.

Tinker returned to the lobby of the Annex and, finding Evers gone, vowed to throw the ball at his ear the first ground-ball, double-play chance that came his way.

——— Sunday, May 10, 1908 ———
New York, New York

Lenore turned from the 110th Street news kiosk and opened the *Herald* to the base ball columns. She began to read the coverage of Saturday's Giants game on the Polo Grounds. It had been a very wet day, and she had wondered if the game would be played at all.

"Good morning, Miss Caylor." She folded her newspaper over to see Mr. Adams standing between her and the Broadway curb, dressed in a light suit and wearing a bright white boater hat. "Very nice to see you again."

She smiled. "Good morning, Mr. Adams. What brings you up to 110th Street?"

"Oh, nothing in particular. My usual Sunday stroll. I almost didn't recognize you without your winter coat and scarf." Lenore felt herself blush. Adams shifted his weight from one foot to the other. "I mean... I didn't mean...I mean it's been since winter that we have..."

"Then you walk up here each Sunday?"

"Not every week. Sometimes I stroll downtown. Sometimes to the Central Park. Sometimes to the Riverside Park, although it is not as pleasant when the trains roll through."

"Yes."

Adams cleared his throat. "Checking on yesterday's base ball games I trust?"

She nodded.

"And how did the Giants get on?"

"I was just reading about their game." She reopened the newspaper. "Let me see...the Giants won over the Bostons seven to three. Mr. Mathewson pitched."

"Big Six has been unstoppable this year. He'll win thirty, maybe thirty-five games."

"He will need to the way the Chicagos are playing." She spooled the newspaper through her hands to the bottom of the page. "Let me see... the Cubs are still in first by two games. Pittsburgh and New York are very close for second place. Then Boston, Philadelphia, the Reds, Mr. Ebbets's club, and St. Louis." She refolded the paper, looked at Adams, and waited for him to respond. He shuffled his feet and removed his straw hat. "In which direction were you walking, Mr. Adams?"

He looked at her. "Oh. Uh...I was going to take 110th Street to the top of the park and then back down its west side."

"Then I shall accompany you until Amsterdam Avenue." She folded the newspaper and began walking.

He followed her and then stepped up next to her as she turned the corner onto 110th Street. "With all the rain," he said, "they must have considered postponing the game."

"Did you hear about Mr. Dreyfuss's contraption in Pittsburgh?"

"Contraption? No."

"He attached a huge tarpaulin to a truck that pulls it over the infield to protect it from rain. Very clever."

"I understand it rains often in Pittsburgh. They need some kind of protection for the field."

"Mr. Pulliam is very pleased. The other magnates have all heard about it and will purchase their own tarpaulins soon. Let's say a game is in the fourth inning and it starts to rain. If they can quickly pull the tarpaulin over the field and perhaps save it from the worst of the weather, they can resume playing later because the infield will be dry."

"It might work at that."

"I think it will," said Lenore. "And how is your maritime underwriting business?"

"Very strong, thank you. Premiums much better than claims just now. And with the bank crisis behind us, our investments seem to be safe. We're seeing signs that the economic contraction will ease soon and... but I'm boring you. My business isn't quite as colorful as base ball."

"And it's Sunday today, is it not?"

"Yes it is. And I mean to relax and enjoy it."

Lenore stopped. "And I hope you do, Mr. Adams."

He stopped and looked around. "Oh, Amsterdam Avenue. Can I walk you to 111th Street?"

"No, thank you." She smiled at him.

"Then, perhaps we'll..."

"Mr. Adams?"

"Yes?"

"Excuse me for being frank, but do you have any other news?"

He sighed. "No, Miss Caylor. The legal proceedings are moving slowly."

"I see." She held out her hand. "Then sometime soon we may meet again on the subway or perhaps at the news kiosk on a Sunday when you choose to stroll uptown."

"I sincerely hope so."

"Good day, Mr. Adams."

"Good day, Miss Caylor." He tipped his hat as she turned onto Amsterdam Avenue. He watched until she disappeared onto 111th Street, and then he continued east toward the park, a little spring in his step and a gentle smile on his face. She had asked about his divorce.

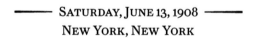

SATURDAY, JUNE 13, 1908
NEW YORK, NEW YORK

The Cincinnati team was in town for the first time this season, so Lenore decided that this warm Saturday in June would be the perfect day for her family to attend a game at the Polo Grounds. They began the morning by strolling to Broadway for a late breakfast. They bought a copy of the *American* at a newsstand and entered Lenore's favorite café at the corner of 110th Street. They chose a table by the window. Settling in, Lenore went right to the sports page to read about Friday's game and to check the standings.

"Lenore," said her mother, "I would expect you already know all about everything that happened in your base ball world yesterday."

"Lenore leaves work before the games are over, Luella," said Trudie. "They don't begin until three o'clock, and in the Midwest that means four o'clock our time."

"Let's see," said Lenore, scanning the sports page. She frowned. "Our Reds lost to Mr. Dovey's Bostons one to nothing."

"That's terrible," said Mrs. Caylor. "They couldn't even score a single run? And who is this Mr. Dovey?"

Lenore continued looking over the paper as she replied to her mother. "A very nice man who owns the Boston Nationals. That's why they call themselves the 'Doves.'"

Trudie laughed. "Not a name to instill fear in its opponent."

"Why Lenore," said a voice behind her, "I didn't know you were a fan."

Lenore turned to see Helen, her usual waitress, holding a pot of coffee and reading over her shoulder. "Good morning, Helen."

"How have you been? We haven't seen you here for quite a while. And who are the two lovely ladies having breakfast with you this morning?"

Lenore introduced her mother and aunt to Helen.

Helen gestured at the newspaper. "And what is this about base ball?"

"I haven't followed it too closely for the past couple of years, but I'm interested in a professional way now."

"Professional?"

"Lenore works for Mr. Pulliam of the National League," said Mrs. Caylor.

"You don't say. Who's Mr. Pulliam?"

"President of the league. I work in the league offices."

Helen turned three cups over and poured coffee. "I don't know why I follow the teams. Heaven knows the Highlanders won't amount to much, and the Giants can't even beat the St. Louis team. Those damn, excuse me, Chicagos will win it again this year, like they always do. I can't stand them."

Lenore laughed. "I hate the Cubs, too, Helen, but not for the same reason."

"What do you mean by that?"

"We're from Cincinnati. We've hated the Cubs since base ball began, when they were called the White Stockings. And Chicagoans hate the Reds right back."

"Well then you gotta pull for the Giants this year, don't you?"

"Maybe, but not today."

"How did the Giants do yesterday, by the way?"

"Let me see." Lenore looked up to the top of the page. "According to Mr. Kirk they lost to the Pittsburghs four to nothing." She cleared her throat and read: "About six thousand fans came to see the Giants win the final game of the series, and after the dust had settled about six thousand grouches plodded wearily homeward."

"Humph," grunted Helen.

"Only six thousand," said Trudie. "That means we should have no trouble buying tickets for today's game."

Helen shrugged. "I guess it's okay if you root for Cincinnati, but just until your Reds leave town." Helen turned away from Lenore's table, but then paused. "You eating today?"

"How about two fried eggs with toast and ham?"

"You got it. I'm throwing in potatoes, too. No charge. Mrs. Caylor? Miss Pittenger?"

"That sounds lovely," said Mrs. Caylor. "Make that two orders."

"Same," said Trudie.

"You got it," said Helen as she walked toward the kitchen.

Lenore looked back at the newspaper. "It seems the Giants' catcher Roger Bresnahan sprained an ankle. That means Mr. Needham will be behind home plate this afternoon."

She read aloud again:

The accident to Bresnahan is a calamity indeed. Needham is a good, steady catcher, but he cannot infuse ginger into the local lads with anything like the skill shown by Bresnahan, and if there's anything we need now it is ginger. We had about as much ginger yesterday as a bowl of cold custard.

She looked across the page at the standings.

"Chicago is in first, three games ahead of both the Reds and Pittsburgh. Then Philadelphia and the Giants are tied for fourth."

"Chicago, Chicago, and Chicago again," said Mrs. Caylor.

"Oh, Luella," said Trudie. "I recall very well that you rooted for the Chicago Nationals when we were growing up in Iowa. I was sure you would marry Cap Anson some day."

"Well I didn't, did I? I married a Cincinnati man and so a Cincinnati woman I became."

Helen returned with their orders. "Here you go, ladies."

"Looks wonderful, Helen," said Lenore. "Thank you."

"Sure." Helen didn't leave her table right away. "So you like base ball. Work for a base ball league."

"We all love base ball. My father was a base ball man."

"And you're planning to go to the Polo Grounds today?" asked Helen. Lenore nodded.

"See your Reds beat the stinking Giants?"

Swallowing, Lenore replied, "All three of us are going."

"You got tickets?"

"No. We're going to buy them at the ball park."

"Where you sit?"

"Wherever we can afford," said Lenore.

"You should have nice seats, being base ball people and all." Helen turned and left the table. They watched as she walked to the back of the café and talked to a middle-aged man sitting alone at a table against the wall.

"What is she doing, Lenore?" asked Mrs. Caylor.

"I don't know."

The man reached into his jacket pocket, took something out, and handed it to Helen. She smiled at him and walked back toward their table.

"It appears to me," said Trudie, "that your friend Helen has some kind of connection."

"Connection?" said Mrs. Caylor. "Whatever do you mean?"

"For tickets," said Trudie.

"Here you go," said Helen. Three tickets landed on the table.

"What's this?" asked Lenore.

"They're tickets for today's game. Upper deck. Great view. You can see everything from home plate to the El tracks to the river to the Bronx."

"But..."

"Guy back there," Helen jerked a thumb over her shoulder. "He had the tickets but can't use them. He always has tickets." Lenore looked across the room at the man. He smiled at her. She nodded. "Don't worry. You don't gotta meet him, unless you want to."

The man rose and approached their table.

"We can't accept these," said Lenore, watching him.

"Sure you can," said Helen.

"But they cost a lot of money."

The man arrived at the table. "Enjoy the game," he said. He was a handsome man, Lenore thought, thin and clean shaven and well dressed in a black suit.

"It's very kind of you, sir," said Mrs. Caylor, "but we can't accept this."

"Gregory's the name, Miss...?"

"You must at least let us pay for them," said Trudie.

"Lenore," interrupted Helen, "this is Gregory Mason. Friend of my brother. Gregory, this is Miss Lenore Caylor, her mother Mrs. Caylor, and aunt, Miss Gertrude Pittenger. Did I get that right?"

"Yes, Helen," said Lenore.

"It is my pleasure to meet you all." He bowed. "And don't think a minute about the tickets. They were given to me by a business associate. I didn't pay a thing for them, and I can't use them. First thing I said to Helen when I came in this morning was, 'Helen, know anyone who wants to see the Giants lose this afternoon because I have tickets I can't use?' And she said to me that she didn't know but would ask around, and then it turned out that you were going to the game but didn't have tickets yet."

"Thank you, Mr. Mason," said Lenore. "It's very generous of you."

"Not at all. I've seen you in here before, and now we can at least say good morning and exchange civilities about base ball—if there were anything at all civil about the way McGraw plays the game." He laughed and put a black bowler on his head. "Well, as I said, enjoy the game." He turned from the table. "Helen? As always the perfect beginning to the day. Best pancakes in town." He strolled toward the door.

"Thank you again," Mrs. Caylor said to his back. He lifted a hand and waved. He opened the door and went out onto the street, tipping his hat as he passed their window.

"Well, Helen," said Lenore. "I should thank you, too. I'm looking forward to the game more than ever now." She thought to herself that it was a real pity that she would never see Helen again as she would definitely have to stay away from not only the café but the entire block in order to avoid seeing Gregory Mason.

"My pleasure," said Helen. "Like I said, that guy, he always has tickets. People throw them at him."

"Why?"

"He puts advertisements in the newspapers for one of those big stores down on the Ladies' Mile. All them newspapers got tickets, so they give them to him hoping he'll put some advertisements in their pages." Helen placed the check on the table. "Have fun."

They arrived at the Polo Grounds and climbed the stairs to the upper deck. But as they stood in the aisle just behind their section, tickets in hand, Lenore saw Gregory Mason sitting in the fourth row with three empty seats to his right. Lenore wanted to leave, hoping she could exchange their tickets for three of equal value, but then Mason, looking for them, glanced over his shoulder. He caught her eye and waved.

"Oh," said Mrs. Caylor. "It's that nice young man who gave us the tickets."

Lenore and Trudie glanced at each other.

"There you are," he said with pleasure when they arrived at the row. He stood. "As it happened, my meeting was cancelled and I had another ticket. They always give me two or four, and I couldn't let you ladies watch the game alone, could I?"

"So the newspapers always give you two or four," said Lenore with little emotion.

"Oh, Helen told you. Yes, it's a great little extra that comes with my position at the store." Lenore remained standing. "Please, these three seats are for you." He walked to the aisle and gestured with his arm for them to sit.

"Mother," said Lenore, "you first."

"Why, thank you, Lenore. Mr. Masonry."

"Mason."

Mrs. Caylor went to the last of the four seats.

Lenore turned to Mason. "Why don't you sit next to Mother, Mr. Mason? I'm sure she will enjoy your company."

"Certainly." He bowed and took the next seat. Lenore and Trudie hesitated for a moment. When it became clear that Lenore had no desire to sit next to Mason, Trudie entered the row and Lenore took the seat at the aisle.

"Oh no," said a gravelly voice from the next row. Mason turned and looked at the man sitting directly behind Lenore. "Come on, friend," said the man. "A little help with the hats."

"What's wrong?" asked Trudie.

"I'm afraid it's your hats," said Mason.

"Our hats?"

"They're blocking the view of the gentlemen behind us."

"I'm sorry." Lenore reached above her head and began removing the pins that held her hat in place. Her aunt and mother watched.

"Remove my hat?" said Mrs. Caylor. "Why, I never heard of such a thing. We are outdoors, after all."

Trudie began removing the pins from her own hat. "It's all right, Luella. We have a roof above us so the sun won't bother you. It's the polite thing to do."

"Polite? I don't recall removing my hat when I went to games in Cincinnati with Father."

"Perhaps the hats weren't as large back then."

"Well," said Mrs. Caylor, "I wore a cute little rimmed hat that looked like a boater. It was very easy and comfortable."

"And small," said Trudie.

"Those were the days," said the man sitting behind them.

Mrs. Caylor removed her hat.

"That's very kind of you," said Mason to Trudie and Lenore. "It's become something of a controversy here this year. Some ladies refuse to remove their hats, and it seems the bigger the bonnet the stronger the refusal. Yours aren't too bad, but the size of these new designs is getting a little out of hand. My art department has to draw them for our advertisements. With all the lace and ribbons and feathers and even birds, it takes hours."

"And which store do you work for?" asked Trudie.

"B. Altman on Sixth Avenue."

"I hope the style changes soon," said Lenore. "They weigh much too much, and they don't stay in place." She put her hat under her seat. A cheer went up from the spectators behind her.

"Now there's a real lady," said the man. "Can I buy you a hot dog or a soda, ma'am?"

"A hot dog?" asked Lenore.

"It's a sausage in a long roll," said Mason. "One of the base ball writers started calling them hot dogs in the newspaper and it kind of caught on." He turned to the man. "Our pleasure, sir. No need to buy us a thing."

Lenore looked out over the field and for the first time appreciated the view from their upper deck seats above home plate. The grass was brilliant green. She could see the elevated tracks and train yard beyond the outfield bleachers. A light mist hung in the air above the Harlem River, obscuring but not completely hiding the apartment houses rising in the Bronx at the far end of the iron trestle bridge. The crowd was a sea of black suits and white boaters and black bowlers. In the outfield, spectators stood two deep behind the low, white outfield rope. She looked for the Hewitt between the rope and the bleachers, but apparently Mr. Brush chose not to attend today's game.

"I believe there are many more than six thousand fans here," she said.

"It looks almost full," said Trudie.

"I think," said Mason, "that it will be full by the second inning. Always some late arrivals."

The Giants took the field. Their reception was loud, but not as enthusiastic as the first game she attended. A reflection of their current slump, she thought.

When the three women clapped for the third Giant out in the bottom of the first inning, Mason asked Trudie, "Are you Cincinnati rooters or do you just hate the Giants?"

"Cincinnati fans."

"Well, lately you've had more to cheer about than us. But excuse me if I say that it has more to do with the Giants playing down to Cincinnati's level than the other way around."

"I don't know about that, Mr. Mason," said Lenore. "The Reds have been playing very well. Give them some credit. Is it normal for New York fans to emphasize the negative over the positive? If they're losing does it always have to be the Giants' poor play and not something the other team might be doing right?"

"I'm sure Father would be pleased," said Mrs. Caylor.

"Call me Gregory, and I think I have a very positive outlook."

"How's that?" said Trudie.

"I'm certain that we will all have a wonderful afternoon at the old ball park."

Trudie turned and looked at him. "A positive outlook, I guess. But not realistic. One of the two teams must lose."

An error by Giants second baseman Larry Doyle put a man on first to begin a two-run Cincinnati rally in the top of the second inning. Lenore looked down and saw John McGraw pacing back and forth in front of the New York bench. In the Giants' half of the inning Spike Shannon was called out on strikes, which sent McGraw running to home plate to confront the umpire.

"Here he comes!" said Mason as the crowd cheered in anticipation.

"It looked like a strike to me," said Lenore.

Mason glanced across Trudie to Lenore and frowned, and then he turned his attention back to the field. McGraw waved his arms and stomped his feet and kept his face within inches of the umpire's own, continuously jawing and gesturing. Mason and most of the rest of the crowd stood and jeered. When McGraw was ejected from the game, about half applauded the entertainment while the other half loudly protested the injustice with boos and shouted opinions of the umpire's intelligence, eyesight, and heritage. The three women remained seated and silent.

As Mason sat he turned to Lenore. "I wonder if your boss will suspend him again," he said.

"My boss?"

"Helen told me that you work in the National League offices."

"Yes, I do."

"Then you must work for Harry Pulliam."

"Yes."

"Pulliam has suspended McGraw so many times I can't count that high. He hates McGraw and the Giants."

"I am aware of Mr. McGraw's record, and if what I just saw is any indication, he deserves whatever judgment the umpires and the league have brought down upon him."

"I couldn't agree more," said Trudie.

"Maybe," said Mason. "I wonder if he's here."

"Who?" asked Trudie.

"Pulliam. He comes often. But I'm sure you're already aware of that. He sits right over there." Mason stood on his toes and stretched his neck. "There. He's there. See?" He pointed to their left. Lenore and Trudie stood and looked.

Mrs. Caylor remained seated. "He reminds me of Father in a way."

"Mr. Pulliam?" asked Mason.

"Land sakes no. That little man who was yelling at the umpire. Father had a temper, too."

Trudie turned to Mason. "I don't see him. Mr. Pulliam, I mean."

"He's the tall man standing in the lower box seats. About the only one not booing or cheering."

Lenore saw Garry Herrmann sitting next to Pulliam. She felt depressed. The incident would probably mean another confrontation with Brush, unless Pulliam decided to let the umpire's ejection be punishment enough for McGraw.

"Well, it looks like your employer will have to suspend McGraw for certain this time," said Mason. "He witnessed the whole thing himself."

Mason sat morose and quiet for most of the rest of the game. The score didn't change. Some Giants fans left, but Lenore was impressed that most had remained for a losing cause.

Turkey Mike Donlin hit safely in the bottom of the ninth. Lenore wondered if Mabel Hite had made it to the game, but decided she was probably scheduled for a matinee. Donlin scored on a bad throw to third after Art Devlin singled.

Mason's mood, and that of the crowd, improved markedly. He turned to Trudie as Devlin stood on third with the tying run. "Anything can happen now," he shouted over the rising din of the crowd.

"Of course," said Lenore. "It's base ball."

A Reds error allowed the run to score, and before Lenore could react, the crowd, Mason included, stood and cheered as loudly as the ninth inning of the Opening Day game when Mike Donlin hit the winning home run.

The Giants won on a bases-loaded single by Devlin in the tenth inning. For the second time Lenore watched as the New York "bugs" swarmed the playing field celebrating a comeback win. Mason clapped for a short while but then just stood quietly watching the chaos on the field.

The women accepted Mason's offer to drive them home, which put him in an even better mood. To refuse would have been an insult to someone who had given them free tickets, Lenore knew.

As they arrived at his shiny black automobile, she waited as he opened a rear door for her mother. Before she could decide whether to take the other back seat or the seat next to Mason, Trudie climbed into the front passenger seat.

"This is my first ride in a motorcar," said Trudie. "I want you to tell me all about how it works."

"I'll be happy to," said Mason, smiling.

"What was that fucker's name?" screamed McGraw as he threw a bat at a clubhouse wall.

"Rudderham," Donlin answered. "Rookie ump."

"Well the fairy boy president is going to hear about this one from me. Things are bad enough without some shit rookie umpire throwing my ass out of a game after he makes the worst fucking call of the year so far."

"A lot Pulliam'll do about it. You know how he is about his umpires. And anyway, we won. Take it easy."

"This fucker a girlfriend of his?" McGraw sat down on a bench. "I'm not going to sit by and let myself get suspended over this horseshit." He reached for another bat and pounded it on the floor. Christy Mathewson approached and held his arm. McGraw stopped and looked up at him. "And that cheap sonofabitch Brush is going to have to make some deals," he said in a lower voice so only Mathewson could hear him. "We didn't win today, the Reds gave it to us on a goddamn platter."

"Come on, John," said Mathewson. "He brought in Tenney and Bridwell from the Doves."

"You know what I mean, Matty. We need another pitcher. You can't go out to the slab every damn game."

On the way home on the El, Henry turned to Maureen and apologized. "For what, Henry?" she asked. "It was grand."

"The language, Maureen," said Henry. "Not fit for a lady. Especially when the ump threw McGraw out of the game. You shouldn't have to hear things like that. I mean, the Giants won and all, and in the tenth inning so you saw a great game, but the language, Maureen. The language. I wouldn't blame you if you never wanted to set foot in a ball park again."

"Don't be silly. I hear that and worse on Tenth Avenue every day." She put her arm through his and pulled him close. "Can we go again soon?"

"What? Are you kidding me, Maureen?"

"Not at all. If I go, the Giants will win again, I'm sure. I think I'm good luck for them. They just need to get more hits and runs than the other team, like they did today." She squeezed his arm. "And I won't make you go to another show neither."

"I'm sorry about the Mabel Hite show," said Henry. "It's been horrible hard to get tickets. But I'll get them sure. You'll see. I just found a connection through one of the men at the engine house. He knows a fellow who works with the inspector, and he can get us a couple of seats."

"Lovely, Henry. Lovely."

"And I have a day and night coming to me so there won't be no trouble with the captain."

"That will be grand." She squeezed his arm again. "Henry?"

"Yes, Maureen?"

"Do you think we might, once we get back downtown, do you think we might stop for an ice cream?"

"Surely, my dear. And we'll go to one of them fancy places in Longacre Square."

"Times Square, Henry."

He laughed. "Times Square."

Pulliam sat in Thomas's cab feeling horrible—but relieved that Herrmann went to the clubhouse to join his team instead of riding downtown with him. Another good game spoiled by the antics of McGraw. *Ironic though,* he thought. *The rookie ump made a terrible call.* Nonetheless, that was no reason for McGraw to react so violently. There was no place in base ball for that kind of behavior. A suspension was definitely in order.

He made a mental note to keep close track of Rudderham. It was difficult enough backing up an umpire when his call was right. He wouldn't tolerate one who wasn't doing his job. He had let McGraw get to him, Pulliam surmised. Not tough enough.

Brush called late in the day. "Pulliam what is this crap about the games today? You better do something about that umpire Johnstone or we will take it up with the National League Board of Directors."

"There was a downpour," said Pulliam. "Mr. Johnstone called the games because of rain. There is nothing unusual about that."

"Not at all. Only that he just happened to call off the doubleheader in the fourth inning when the Giants had the lead. One more inning and the game would have been official. But Johnstone couldn't have that, could he? He wouldn't miss a chance to take one away from us, would he?"

"It's up to the umpire once the game starts to decide whether or not weather conditions should prompt the suspension or postponement of play. Perhaps if you had invested in a tarpaulin as Mr. Dreyfuss has done, the game could have been resumed later in the day."

"Shut up, Pulliam. Don't give me any horseshit about your Jew friend in Pittsburgh and his silly quilt."

"Mr. Brush, I must demand that you—"

"I know the rule and I know that game should have been stopped two innings before when it was raining even harder than it was in the fourth. But the Reds were winning then. That pile of cowshit you call an umpire would have let them play in Noah's flood if the Reds kept the lead."

"Mr. Brush, I will listen to your protest but not your profanity or your disrespect for this office. If you continue in this vein I will hang up the phone."

"You hang up on me and I'll be in your office before the earpiece stops shaking on the hook."

"The doors of the league office are always open to rational discussions with representatives of member teams."

"Rational? You call Johnstone rational? He's still holding a grudge from that little scuffle last year, isn't he? He blames the Giants and McGraw for everything."

"I'll expect a written protest from your office."

"Written protest? Horseshit. You'd use it for toilet paper." Brush started coughing. Pulliam heard the muffled sound of his hand over the mouthpiece. "And speaking of which, how's life been treating you, Harry? I don't think you're quite yourself these days. Suspending Mc-Graw like that over a harmless little comment on the field. And it was Johnstone who was kicking about it again, wasn't it? Even though it was his partner who called that pitch a strike. A pitch that was so far off the plate the third baseman could have caught it. What's got into you, Harry? Or maybe it's that nothing has got into you since your friend left town. Is that it, Harry?"

"Mr. Brush, I will not listen to this."

"You should look into finding a good woman, Harry. You must be lonely. I know that your little friend hasn't been too lonely lately. We check up on him from time to time. He's found some new friends, did you know that?"

Pulliam hung up the phone. He ran out of his office and to the men's room down the hall. He just made it into a stall before throwing up.

Lenore had to admit that she enjoyed opening night. The audience loved the show and loved the chorus line. The numbers had been mostly tasteful, if you got past the phallic imagery of a group of showgirls bursting out of a "tube" in the "Mosquito" number, or the unsubtle, blinking "For Hire" signs on their taxicab costumes. Backstage, after the final curtain call, everyone hugged and laughed and congratulated each other in the knowledge that they would be employed for the next three months.

May wrapped her arms around Lenore. "The *Follies* will be the biggest show in town. This could be the start of something wonderful for all of us. I wish you were in the line."

"It's great, May," said Lenore. "You were the best dancer on the stage. You stole the show. And thanks again for the ticket. I enjoyed myself."

"Will you be coming to the party, Lenore? Mr. Norworth said it was fine with him. He remembers you. He's asked about you."

The last thing she wanted to do was attend an event with Jack Norworth and Nora Bayes. "I need to get home, May. And I'm sorry if I caused you any trouble after that audition."

May smiled. "Don't matter now. You'll stay in touch?"

"I will. You, too."

She kissed each of the other girls and bade them good night, turning down another invitation to a party for the line. In the hall outside the dressing rooms, she shouldered her way through the crush of well-wishers, production staff, and cast members, mouthing "congratulations" and smiling at each. The stairs were less crowded so she made good time down to the ground floor.

She opened the stage door and welcomed the fresh air, though it was a close, warm summer evening. The streets glistened and steamed from an early evening downpour. Theater fans crowded the alley waiting for a glimpse of Jack and Nora or Flo and Anna. They stared at her wondering if they should recognize her.

"Are you in the show?" asked a teenage girl.

"Prompter," she replied. Disappointed, the crowd left her alone. She continued through the alley to the street.

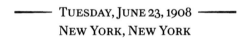

TUESDAY, JUNE 23, 1908
NEW YORK, NEW YORK

John McGraw's Giants were in fourth place, four and a half games behind Chicago, but he knew it was too early in the season to draw any conclusions about the rest of the year. Mathewson rolled along but needed help from the other pitchers, and the Giants had to do better than the one game over five hundred they had struggled to accomplish in May. But they had just beaten the Cubs two out of three with one more to play today, so he wasn't too worried. It was Brush that was getting to him. And Pulliam. One didn't care about the game, and the other cared too goddamn much about it.

Bring the rooters in, he thought, get them drunk and bring them back again and Brush is happy, the syphilitic bastard. But Pulliam, the cock-eating dandy, thought there was something special about "the game." Like goddamn Sunday mass with his umpires as priests.

Like so many times before, he was just coming off a suspension at the hands of Pulliam. How many had there been? These days he could feel them coming. Give the umpire a red-blooded curse or two to keep him honest, and before you know it he's in your face with a thumb. And Pulliam always backed them up. Suspended two days here, three days there.

His pool halls in Herald Square were doing well, though. All the ball players from all the teams, National League or the junior American League, came by when they were in town. It was easy money, plus a few bucks more won with cards and dice. But he would rather be back in Baltimore, spending his afternoons playing the horses at Pimlico. This year, though, base ball was everything. The fans couldn't get enough. It was bigger than Broadway, bigger than the presidential election. William Howard Taft Jennings Bryan—who the hell cares?

——— CHICAGO, ILLINOIS ———

Johnny Evers got the word from Charlie Murphy, president of the Cubs, who was none too pleased. "Evers you are a dumb shit," he said. "Couldn't you hold it in? Pulliam's gonna back up his umpires again, and not only that," he said as he spat on the locker-room floor, "if there's any way to get the goddamn New York press off his back by giving hell to a Cub instead of McGraw, he'll do it. Life is shit for him at Broadway and Twenty-Sixth. You know that."

Evers knew that Murphy was mad because the Cubs had just lost three out of four to the Giants in New York. But he didn't care if he was mad or not. He didn't like Murphy and he didn't like Klem, the umpire who had taken issue with his complaints and thrown him out of the game a couple of days ago. Now he had three days off—suspended by the league office. He'd study the rule book and figure out just how he'd been abused. He'd been right when he complained to Klem, and he would be right more times than not and they all knew it.

The league was on notice, not him. And they would listen to him. They'd hate his guts, but in the end they'd listen to him. Especially Pulliam. Because he, Johnny Evers, knew the game like he knew his own fingers, and Pulliam stayed true to the game. Evers had never seen anything like it. Everything Pulliam did, he did for the game. Not for the players. Not for the owners. Not for the umpires and not for the fans. And certainly not for himself. God knows life would be much easier for him if he went with the flow. But, no, it was all about the integrity of the game.

So from now on Johnny Evers would be on Pulliam's side. Or rather, he would be on the side of the game. He would make sure that every goddamn play and every goddamn call would be as pure and correct as a swing and a miss.

———— THURSDAY, JULY 2, 1908 ————
NEW YORK, NEW YORK

Jack Norworth decided to leave the theater early. He had arrived at the Jardin de Paris at noon determined to work out the final bugs of "You Will Have to Sing an Irish Song." There was something off in the orchestration still, after almost three weeks of performances. That done, he decided to work at the music publishing house for the rest of the day. He walked east on Forty-Fourth to Sixth Avenue and turned right.

It was too hot to walk the fourteen blocks to Twenty-Eighth Street so he climbed the steps of the El station at Forty-Second Street and waited for a downtown train. He paced back and forth on the platform, reviewing the troubled song's arrangement in his mind.

A poster caught his eye. Large block letters proclaimed:

Base ball again, he thought. *The damn game won't leave me alone no matter where I go. Not even a flesh and blood rival but a crude game played by coarse men. And it has captured the heart of the entire city.*

He heard the girls in the line talk about it. The men in the *Follies* audience would chat about base ball during intermission when he strolled the lobby to gauge reaction to an evening's show. The waiters, cooks, bartenders, and customers argued about it in the restaurants and saloons of Manhattan. He had once overheard two men walking along the street discussing the merits of some Chicago club and whether or not they could "do it again." Do what again? Even Nora had said that ball games drew larger "crowds" than their *Follies,* with their chorus line of pretty girls in scanty costumes.

The station platform began to vibrate as a train approached. Turning away from the poster he stretched and then shook his shoulders as if trying to drive base ball out of his mind forever. How could such a vile pastime be more popular than his songs?

But as he watched the train slow to a stop he thought, why get upset? Perhaps there was something there. Von Tilzer had been pressuring him to pen a new hit to follow up on the success of "Shine On Harvest Moon." Well, ten or fifteen or twenty thousand fanatics gathered every day at ball parks across the country. One day's attendance at the Polo Grounds could eclipse the total audience numbers for all the shows on Broadway any given evening. Had anyone written a successful song about the game? Not in his memory. Sure, there was "Uncle Josh at a Base Ball Game" and other ditties, but nothing he would call popular, as in "Harvest Moon" popular.

As he boarded the train he reached into his jacket pocket and took out a small black notebook and a pencil. He sat on the closest available seat. Opening the notebook, he found a blank page and wrote "The Base Ball Game Song."

"Take me to a base ball game." No, not quite right. It should be more like

*a date. "Take me out to a base ball game." No. "Take me out to a ball game."
No. "Take me out to the ball game." Yes. Then, a repeated phrase. "Take me
out to...," what? "The teams?" "The field?" "The rooters?" No. Use "root" as
a verb somewhere. What did Nora call the audience? Yes. "Take me out to
the crowd." Not quite. "Take me out with the crowd."*

He looked up to see the train pull into Twenty-Eighth Street. He
jumped out of his seat, stepped off the car, and ran down the stairs.
He walked quickly east along Twenty-Eighth, the tinkling of dozens
of pianos filtering out of open windows on both sides of the street. Not
quite to Broadway he stopped, opened the door at 40 West, and took
the narrow stairs two at a time to the offices of Al Von Tilzer's York
Music Publishing Company.

He knocked once on the pebble glass window of the door and entered the outer office. Five young men sat rigidly in chairs in the waiting area, leather cases on their laps. A woman sat behind a wooden
desk talking on the telephone, her black hair disheveled with a pencil stuck in the tangle above one ear. "That's right," she said into the
mouthpiece as she looked up at Norworth and smiled. "We got six new
tunes we want you to do for Maxine Elliot." She nodded and gestured
to him with her thumb that he could go on back. Von Tilzer was in his
office. "Yeah. New theater. Yeah. Thirty-Ninth Street. Today."

Norworth entered a hall behind the woman and found Von Tilzer's office door open. The composer sat hunched over sheet music at
his cluttered desk, jacket off, tie loosened, and stiff white collar askew.
The walls were crowded with framed copies of sheet music cover art,
not all of them his own songs, or even York Music songs. A few fea-
tured George Cohan songs, a competitor in his own building. An upright piano sat in the corner opposite the desk.

"Al, you busy?" He took off his hat and hung it on a brass coat stand.

"No," answered Albert Von Tilzer, a dark-haired, trim man of thirty.
"I'm taking a long Fourth of July weekend sweating like a pig in this
inferno going over this proof of your goddamn song which is gonna
stink like a turd in the East River."

"Forget about that song," said Norworth.

"You don't even know which one it is," said Von Tilzer, looking up.

"It doesn't matter. I have a new one."

"You always got a new one."

"This one can't miss, if you can get the tune right."

"Likely."

"Listen to me, Al. It's a natural." Norworth sat on the piano bench. "Tell me. What's the most popular thing going in the entertainment world?"

"Cohan."

"No. It's not music."

"I don't know and get lost, will you? I actually do want to have a long holiday weekend."

"You ever been to a ball game?"

"A ball game? You mean base ball?"

"Yeah."

"I can't go to the ball game today." He hunched back over the sheet music.

"I don't want you to go to the game today."

"Why not? You don't like me?"

Norworth sighed. "Listen to me, will you?" He stood and walked to where Von Tilzer sat at the desk. "They have base ball in Indianapolis, don't they?"

"Yeah, they used to have a National League team, but I never went."

"Not even when you lived in Chicago?"

"No."

"Me neither," said Norworth. He returned to the piano bench. "Everybody else in America seems to go."

"So what?"

"So that makes base ball a good subject for a song."

"Why? Everybody pukes from time to time, but I haven't heard of any songs about throwing up."

"Come on, Al."

Von Tilzer looked up from his desk and turned to face Norworth. "Okay," he said. "Sorry, Jack. Come to think of it, that's all anyone around here talks about these days. You wouldn't think it was an election year with all the gab about the Giants."

"That's what I'm trying to tell you." Norworth took his notebook out and found the right page. " 'The Base Ball Game Song.' That's the title."

"It stinks."

"We'll change it. But here are the first two lines of the chorus. I wrote them on the El coming down here." He cleared his throat. "Take me out to the ball game. Take me out with the crowd."

"That's it?"

"So far. That's about all I know about it, except I want this to be about a girl."

"A girl base ball player?"

"No. It's about a girl who's base ball mad. The verses. You know. All she wants to do is go to ball games."

"Girls go to ball games?"

"I can vouch for it." Norworth stood and began pacing. "Anyway, she's base ball mad and just wants to go to the ball game and never come back." He jotted down a note in his booklet. "But I don't want it too lively."

"Okay, Jack. You get the rest of the words down and we'll make your base ball song." Von Tilzer turned back to his desk. "Have a nice Fourth."

"I'll finish it now."

"You do that."

Norworth left Von Tilzer's office and returned to the reception area. The woman was still on the telephone, or on the telephone again, and the same five men sat in their chairs.

"Hello, boys," he said and smiled broadly. "I'm, uh, doing a little research for a song and I need some help." They stared blankly. "Anyone ever been to a ball game?" More stares. "Let me start over." He looked down a moment and then back up, smiling more widely. "My name is Jack Norworth." All five sat up and cleared their throats or coughed or murmured to themselves. "And I was wondering if any of you has ever been to a ball game?"

"Sure thing, Mr. Norworth."

"I go all the time."

"Lots of times."

"I love the Giants."

"I'm from Brooklyn. I've been to Washington Park a hundred times."

The receptionist hung up the phone and turned to Norworth. "I was just at a game last week, Jack," she said. "What do you need to know?"

"No kidding, Christine," said Norworth. "That's great. You go with your husband?" Christine nodded. "That's great. And when you're there, is there anything special you do? Or maybe something your husband does to make it a fun outing?"

"He buys me things."

"Like what?"

"Cracker Jack."

"Or hot dogs," volunteered one of the men.

"Hot dogs?" asked Norworth.

"Or peanuts," said another man.

By three that afternoon, Jack Norworth had his chorus completed. By four-thirty he had roughed out his verses.

> Katie Casey was base ball mad,
> Had the fever and had it bad.
> Just to root for the home town crew,
> Ev'ry sou Katie blew.
> On a Saturday her young beau
> Called to see if she'd like to go
> To see a show, but Miss Kate said
> "No, I'll tell you what you can do:
>
> Take me out to the ball game.
> Take me out with the crowd.
> Buy me some peanuts and Cracker Jack.
> I don't care if I never get back.
> Let me root, root, root for the home team.
> If they don't win it's a shame.
> For it's one, two, three strikes, you're OUT.
> At the old ball game."

Katie Casey saw all the games,
Knew the players by their first names.
Told the umpire he was wrong,
All along, good and strong.
When the score was just two to two,
Katie Casey knew what to do,
Just to cheer up the boys she knew,
She made the gang sing this song:

Take me out to the ball game.
Take me out with the crowd.
Buy me some peanuts and Cracker Jack.
I don't care if I never get back.
Let me root, root, root for the home team.
If they don't win it's a shame.
For it's one, two, three strikes, you're OUT.
At the old ball game.

Von Tilzer slapped the sheet of paper. "I don't like it. It's about a dame. I don't care what you tell me, we could go up to the Polo Grounds right now and all we'd see are bowlers and boaters."

"Trust me on this one, Al," said Norworth. "If a dame, as you put it, is base ball mad, the whole country is as well. Get the tune right and it could be the next 'Harvest Moon.'"

Von Tilzer hesitated. "Okay. You win. But I ain't spending more than fifteen minutes on it. You want it should be a Sousa march or something like that?"

"No, no, no. Nothing like that. More like a drinking song. In three-four time."

Joe Rupp stood in left field looking out at Lake Michigan from the ball field at the south end of Lincoln Park. It was getting dark and like most of the players on both teams, he wanted to get the game over and go home. He had to pack before leaving for Michigan for summer vacation. He couldn't wait to roll down the dunes and lounge on the beach on the other side of the lake. His team, sponsored by a Clark Street hardware store, and their rivals from a Division Street bar had even agreed to delay the usual beer spoils for the victors in the interest of getting out of Chicago for the holiday weekend as fast as possible.

The game was tied with two out in the bottom of the last inning. His friend Mike Machac stood on third. Rupp returned his attention to the game in time to see the big, fat captain of the bar's team, whose name he didn't know, crack a solid single over the shortstop and straight at him. He fielded the rolling ball as Mike trotted home from third base with the winning run. But the overweight ox of a batter didn't bother to run out his hit. He never made it to first base. He lumbered directly to the bench to accept the congratulations of his teammates.

Rupp's team trotted off the diamond. But something about the fat man's arrogance and blustery celebration annoyed him. He ran across the infield and stepped on first base. Ball in hand, he pointed at the bar team's bench and yelled, "Batter's out at first. Run don't count. We're up."

Rupp was sure of the rules. The ox hadn't touched first so the ball was still live and he forced him out. But no one wanted to hear about it, on either team. He walked home mad, but he would prove himself right. And so, with his wife angry over his delay in getting ready to leave for Michigan, he composed a letter to a column that he enjoyed reading in the *Tribune* called "Inquisitive Fans."

Sports Editor of the *Tribune*:
In the last half of the ninth, with the score tied, two men out and a runner on third, the batter hits to left and the runner scores. The batter, seeing the runner score, stops between home and first, thinking the game over. The ball is thrown to the first baseman, who steps

on his base and claims he forced the hitter out. Can runner score
on this? Joseph Rupp, Chicago

He changed the details a little because he didn't want the readers of
the *Tribune* to think him an idiot for describing a player who ran all
the way from left field to first base to force a runner. Basically, though,
he thought it clear enough. He folded the letter, sealed it in an envelope
and dropped it in a mailbox on North Avenue on their way out of town.

—— SATURDAY, JULY 18, 1908 ——
NEW YORK, NEW YORK

At eleven fifteen Pulliam came out of his office and, smiling, approached
Lenore's desk. "Thank you for coming in today, Miss Caylor," he said.
"I assure you that I won't ask you to work too many Saturdays, and
none at all after the season."

"I don't mind," said Lenore. "I'm used to working weekends, you know."

"Of course. Your busiest days on the stage, weren't they?"

"Well, it didn't make a lot of difference, Tuesday or Thursday or Saturday. It was the same routine every night."

"But don't you think there's something special about Saturday night
at the theater? People dress just a little nicer. The noise in the lobby
has an extra level of, I don't know...anticipation?"

"Yes, you're right. But it also usually meant a later night for me. There
were always private parties or dinners after Saturday night shows."
She looked down at her desktop and blushed, realizing too late what
her description of late Saturday nights might imply.

"It can be the same in base ball," he said quickly. "I go to a game, then
dinner with a visiting magnate perhaps." He laughed. "One night not
too long ago, when the Cubs were in town, Mike Donlin invited everyone to see a show after the game. His wife's show. I don't recall the
name of it just now."

"The Merry-Go-Round," said Lenore. "His wife is Mabel Hite."

"Yes, that's it. But of course you would know." She nodded. "Right. Anyway, everyone went to see the show, Cubs, Giants, McGraw, Murphy. I was at the game and so Turkey Mike invited me as well."

"I thought the Cubs and Giants hated each other."

"Not really. They're all ball players. They've played against each other for years, and many of them have played on the same team in the past, and may play together again someday. They leave their fights on the diamond. It's the exception when they don't. I've seen home teams fight their own fans to protect visiting clubs."

"And in this case they invited the visiting team to a show."

"Yes. It was really quite enjoyable. But after the show and a couple of drinks, I went home and got a good night's sleep. Others went off to other places, but for me, I did my job and represented the league professionally, I hope."

She smiled at him, grateful for his making the conversation easy for her. She would have made it worse if she had tried to explain away the after-theater dinners. "Yes. I know exactly what you mean," she said. There was a moment of awkward silence. "How did you like Mabel's show?"

"Fine, fine. Very entertaining."

The outer door opened. They turned to look and saw no one at first, but then heard the gurgling cough of John T. Brush. Lenore looked up at Pulliam and saw his face pale. He walked to the door.

"Good morning, John," he said. "Let me help you." He reached over the threshold to assist Brush.

"Don't touch me, Pulliam. Get out of my way."

Pulliam backed off. "What can I do for you, John?"

Brush grasped onto the doorframe and pulled himself into the office. He looked at Lenore. "Miss Caylor."

"Good morning, Mr. Brush."

"I'll tell you what you can do for me, Pulliam." Brush glanced at Lenore. "You can get that man Murphy drummed out of the league, that's what you can do."

"Charlie Murphy?"

"You know who I mean. Do you know what that sonofabitch did?"

"Mr. Brush," Pulliam interrupted, "please conduct yourself properly in this office."

"Do you know what he pulled in Chicago the other night?"

"I've heard of nothing happening in Chicago except several well-played games between your Giants and the Cubs, the first two of which were won by the Giants."

"Crap. The first game was eleven to nothing and over before it started. But it's the third one I'm talking about, Pulliam."

"If I'm not mistaken it was a pitchers' game won by the Cubs one to nothing. Isn't that right, Miss Caylor?"

Lenore, who had been staring at Brush, looked up at Pulliam. "Yes, sir. One to nothing."

Brush turned on Lenore. "And who pitched that game for the Giants, Ollie's girl?" Lenore rolled back in her chair in self-defense, bumping into the switchboard console.

"Mr. Brush," said Pulliam, "I insist that you act correctly. You know as well as I that Mr. Caylor hated the nickname Ollie and to use it here gives offense to his daughter. Please show some respect."

"Respect, Harry-boy? What do you know about respect?"

"If you wish to discuss a matter of base ball with me, please come into my office." Pulliam went to his door, turned, and waited.

Brush made his way through the outer office by using chairbacks to pull his emaciated form along. He reached Lenore's desk, slapped his hands on its surface, and shifted his weight onto his outstretched arms. He leaned toward her, his face red and his lips damp with spittle.

She noticed his hands most of all. Gray and bony, freckled with age spots, and lined with bulging blue veins, they grasped the surface of her desk like claws.

"Miss Caylor," he said. "Ollie's girl." He turned to Pulliam. "She's pretty, too, Harry. Did you notice?"

Pulliam stepped toward Brush. "I must insist that you stop this."

"Did you know, Harry, that I offered to set up an audition for Miss Caylor here with Cohan or Ziegfeld and she turned me down?"

"Miss Caylor has already worked in the theater and was offered a place in this year's *Follies*. She chose to work here instead."

Brush jerked his head to stare at Pulliam, then slowly turned back to Lenore. "So, Lenore Caylor, too good to dance for Ziegfeld. You're so smart with your one to nothing score, tell me something. Have you ever heard of a Chicago man named Barnes?" Lenore shook her head. "No? Well, let me tell you about Mr. Barnes. You see, when my boys are in Chicago, ol' Chubby Murphy is always willing to demonstrate Cubs hospitality by taking some of the weaker-willed players to the Levee, maybe to see Vic Shaw, or even the Everleighs. Maybe get them a little tired out and sleepy so they ain't on their best game the next day. But he could never get to Matty. You know who Matty is, Ollie's girl?"

"Yes, sir. Christy Mathewson. He pitched yesterday."

"That's right. He pitched for my Giants yesterday. Now, everyone in base ball knows that Matty is as straight as they come and can't be tempted by the evils of the flesh. But Chubby, he's a smart one. He knows Matty's one weakness."

"Mr. Brush, please. Come into my office and we'll discuss this in a dignified manner."

Brush ignored him. "Do you know what that weakness is, Ollie's girl?"

"No, sir."

"Few do. But Chubby found out." He stood up straight, wobbling back and forth like a drunk. "I don't think your boss here knows what it is either." He turned his head and glared at Pulliam.

"And what would that be?" asked Lenore.

Brushed looked back at her. "What'd you say?"

"What is Mr. Matthewson's one weakness?"

"Checkers!" yelled Brush.

"What?" said Pulliam.

"That's right. Checkers."

"Checkers?" Pulliam brought his hand to his mouth to hide a nervous laugh.

"He thinks it's funny," said Brush, staring at Lenore. "But what's so funny about sending a checkers shark named Barnes to the team hotel and tempting Matty with a friendly game, knowing all the time that Matty can't stand to lose and making sure he's up all night because he'll never beat this Barnes, this checkers hustler, the night before he's to pitch a big game against the Cubs? It ain't funny. It's a cheap trick." Brush coughed, leaning over and covering his mouth with his fist. He tried vainly to control it but couldn't stop the gagging deep in his chest. Pulliam went into his office and returned with a cuspidor. He held it near Brush's head. Brush turned and spat and then reached into his jacket pocket and produced a soiled handkerchief. He wiped his chin, bunched the handkerchief, and returned it to his jacket pocket.

"John," said Pulliam. "Please come into my office and sit down."

Brush glanced back at Lenore. "What do you think of that, Ollie's girl?"

"I think," said Lenore, "that Mr. Mathewson pitched a brilliant game, giving up only one run, which is lower than his earned run average. I also think that perhaps you should be discussing this with Mr. Mc-Graw instead of Mr. Pulliam. If McGraw's hitters had scored some runs, one Cub run wouldn't have been enough to win."

"What did you say?"

"And I think that a man in your fragile health should avoid working Saturdays. You appear to need your rest."

Brush and Pulliam stared at Lenore. Brush's mouth twitched. Then he smiled and started to laugh. "My God, Harry-boy," he said, struggling to get the words out, "you've got a real prize here. I like you, Ollie's girl. You've got spunk. A lot like your father." Pulliam took Brush's elbow with his free hand and led him into his office. "She's a keeper, Harry-boy," said Brush as Pulliam closed the door.

Lenore returned to her work, typing a letter from Pulliam to Ban Johnson. Now and then she heard raised voices coming from the inner office. As she finished typing, she looked up to check the time on the wall clock and started slightly when she saw a man standing a few feet from her desk. He was young and thin with light wavy hair parted in the middle. His tan suit was a little rumpled, and he held a worn black fedora at his side. He looked tired.

"It's 12:20 and he was supposed to be done at noon," he said.

"Pardon me?" said Lenore. "I'm sorry. I didn't hear you come in."

"The door was open," he said and paused. "I've been waiting across the street."

"Did you have an appointment?"

"You might say that."

"With Mr. Pulliam or Mr. Heydler?"

"With Harry."

The sound of Brush's angry voice came from inside Pulliam's office.

"I can hear that he's busy," said the man.

"He's with Mr. Brush of the Giants."

"Oh. Him. The sick one."

"You say Mr. Pulliam is expecting you?"

The man looked at the closed office door and sighed. "Not really," he said. "I was going to surprise him." His eyes returned to Lenore. "I left him a note saying that I was Barney Dreyfuss, and I would meet him for lunch at noon at Café Martin. But I'm not Barney Dreyfuss."

"I see." She stared at him. There was something familiar about his voice.

"Still, I hate being stood up." He put a hand in his trousers pocket and took out a key. He set it on Lenore's desk.

"Mr. Brush wasn't expected."

"I suppose." He put his hat on. "Tell Harry that Barney Dreyfuss is really Theodore from Louisville and that I'm waiting for him in my hotel room. That's a duplicate key."

"Of course. You're Mr. Russell. We met at the Macbeth Galleries during an exhibition."

"Oh, yes. You were there with your mother and sister, I think."

"My mother and my aunt."

"Your aunt. Yes. Very nice to see you again." He put his hat on. "Tell Harry I'll be there all afternoon."

"Which hotel?"

"The Prince George." He gestured at the window behind Lenore. "He knows it." He turned and left, closing the door behind him.

Lenore pulled the sheet of paper out of the typewriter. She replaced it with an envelope and typed the American League's Chicago headquarters address. She then put the letter and envelope at the corner of her desk where Pulliam signed correspondence.

She sat and stared at the outer door. She turned to the shelves along the wall and saw the statistics ledger. She decided to review Friday's attendance figures and compile the week's totals and have the report ready for Mr. Pulliam a day early. The numbers were good, better than the same week in 1907. The report would please him and maybe end his work week on a good note instead of the sourness of Brush's visit. She opened the large, leather-bound volume and worked with the ball park names and numbers for about a quarter of an hour until Pulliam's office door opened again. Brush came out and stumbled for the door. Just before leaving he turned to Lenore. "Nice to see you again, Miss Caylor." He didn't wait for an answer but opened the door, pulled himself through, and slammed it closed.

Pulliam stood at his door watching. When Brush was gone he went to Lenore's desk, glanced at the letter to Johnson, and took a pen from a holder. "You should have been gone for the day by now, Miss Caylor," he said as he signed the letter. He spoke with quiet resignation. "It's Saturday."

"Someone came to see you just now," she said. "He said you had a lunch appointment."

"Oh yes," he replied, glancing at the clock. "Barney. But why didn't he stay and wait for me?"

"It wasn't Mr. Dreyfuss."

"Not Barney?"

"No. It was Mr. Russell from the art gallery."

Pulliam tensed and looked down at Lenore. "Ted?"

"He said he wanted to surprise you so he used Mr. Dreyfuss's name. He left this." She pointed to the key on her desk. "He's at the Prince George."

Pulliam dropped the pen on the desk and picked up the key. He turned it in his hand as if he had never seen a key before. The pen rolled off the desk and onto the floor. Placing the key in his jacket pocket, he walked to the outer door. Lenore thought of telling him that he forgot his hat, or of running to his coat stand and getting it for him, but instead she sat and watched as he left the office.

Her hand shaking slightly, she picked up the pen and placed it in its holder.

Johnny Evers couldn't play because of a bum leg, so he got out of bed a little late, dressed, and hobbled to the corner for the morning papers. He opened the *Tribune* and turned to the sports page and "Inquisitive Fans," his favorite column. A letter from Joseph Rupp of Chicago interested him, as did the editor's answer: "Run cannot score when third out is made before reaching first base."

Evers opened his rule book. Flipping through its pages, he found the section on scoring runs and read the rule, a rule he knew was violated by every team in both leagues, but ignored by every umpire.

Rule 59

If a runner reaches home on or during a play in which the third man is forced out, a run shall not count.

Not just the batter forced out at first, as Rupp had asked, a force-out at any base that ended an inning canceled a run scored from third. He couldn't count how many times he'd seen runners stop between bases when they thought the winning run crossed the plate in the ninth inning, or an extra inning. He'd done it himself. But the ball was still technically live and in play until all runners safely reached the next base. A runner could be forced out no matter where the ball landed and then that winning run would not count. The game would go on.

He would remember that rule. Some runner, someday, wouldn't bother to touch first or second on a base hit that drove in a winning run in the last inning. And when it happened, he would be ready with Rule 59.

McGraw was glad to get out of St. Louis. The last-place Cardinals had handled his Giants, beating them three out of four. And the fans were more brutal than his own Giants rooters.

But he did not relish stopping in Springfield, Illinois, for an exhibition game. He had followed the newspaper accounts of the race riots that had ravaged the city over the weekend. First, he didn't like being upstaged by the excitement of the looting and burning. Second, the minor league Springfield Senators would be all hopped up, still a mob. He didn't want to play against any mob.

He smelled Springfield before he saw it. The lingering stench of smoke drifted in the train's open windows as they rolled along between endless rows of head-high cornstalks. By the time they arrived at the city's train station it overpowered him. He wanted to continue on to Cincinnati and regretted agreeing to the game. But several of his boys were from the area and wanted to show off a little to the home folks, plus he had told Brush he would take a close look at the Senators' star pitcher Forrest More with an eye to bolstering the Giants' pitching staff for the last month of the season.

Outside the station an Army battalion patrolled the street. A small delegation led by a tall, lanky man of about thirty welcomed the Giants. "Mr. McGraw," said the man, "in the name of the Springfield Chamber of Commerce, I'd like to welcome you to the capital of the great state of Illinois, the Land of Lincoln."

"Mighty fine to be here," said McGraw.

"Kelly's the name. Bart Kelly. The mayor and the governor pay their respects and wish they could be here to greet you personally, but we had a little trouble in town over the weekend so they're kind of busy just now."

"I read about it in the St. Louis papers. A sad thing."

"Well, I suppose. But every now and then you gotta put the niggers in their place, don't you?"

McGraw smiled but remained silent.

"Tell you what," said Kelly, "there's plenty of time before the game. Would you like to take a little tour of the city and see where it all happened?"

McGraw agreed. He told Mathewson to see that the players found their hotel and made it to the ball park on time.

Kelly laughed. "Ain't no danger of them finding themselves a cathouse no more, if that's what's worrying you. We torched the Badlands sure enough. Most of the nigger whores left town, and the white ones are laying low afraid the niggers will rape them next."

"That's fine, but can you keep the local bookies away from my players?" quipped McGraw.

Kelly laughed again.

"I'm serious," said McGraw.

McGraw took a seat in the open front carriage. He looked behind him and saw three carriages of laughing, drinking men following them.

They began their tour at the destroyed restaurant of a man who had helped the sheriff protect the black man accused of raping a white woman. Farther on, the reek of the burned-out Levee district was so strong that McGraw had to cover his mouth and nose with a handkerchief. Passing block after block of torched homes, they paused outside the remains of a saloon. A blackened, truncated tree stood in front of the gutted building.

"Now this here tree," said Kelly, "is where they hung the first nigger, though he was already shot dead."

McGraw wished he was at the hotel with his team.

A block past the state capitol the entourage stopped and Bart Kelly jumped out. "Right there is where the other nigger lived," he said, pointing at a house with a broken dining room window. "They took him across the street," Kelly continued, whirling around with his arm extended, "and hung him from that there tree in the school yard."

"What'd he do?" asked McGraw.

"White woman," he said with finality.

"Rape?"

"He was married to her. Just as bad."

A teenage boy ran up to the carriage holding a small wooden box.

The men from the other carriages climbed down and gathered in a circle around Kelly and McGraw. Kelly took the box and held it out to McGraw. "Right here," he began, clearing his throat, "we'd like to present you with a little souvenir of your visit to our fair city. Our small way of saying thank you for stopping in Springfield during this busy, fretful base ball season." McGraw took the box and opened it. A two-inch section of thick rope lay on a coarse, gray cloth. "That there is a piece of the actual rope that hung the nigger Donnegan from that tree over yonder."

"Well, thank you one and all," said McGraw. "And seeing as I don't have a lucky charm for this season yet, which could be why we're in second place instead of first, this little token will take the place of a rabbit's foot for the Giants."

The tour finally over, the procession ended at the hotel, where McGraw thanked his hosts. Later that afternoon, he felt good enough to play second base for two innings, giving Larry Doyle a much needed break.

NEW YORK, NEW YORK

"Look at this, Henry," said Maureen as she read the sports page. "The Cubs lost again. Soon it'll be a race between the Giants and the Pirates."

"Don't count the Cubs out," he replied. "Evers was hurt awhile. There's lots of games to be played yet."

"Yes, but the Giants will play most of them on the Polo Grounds, and we'll be at all of them, won't we, Henry?"

"I still have a job, you know, Maureen."

"So you'll sign up for the early morning shift at the firehouse which will leave us every afternoon free to go to the ball games."

"Won't be easy to get in."

"Then we'll go to the Gotham and watch the game on the big board. It's almost as much fun."

Fun? he thought, *nothing fun about it.* It was serious business. The pennant race was up for grabs. He'd thought about taking Maureen to see the Highlanders at Hilltop Park, but decided against it. The ball park was a dump, in spite of its view of the Hudson River and New Jersey beyond, and the Highlanders were terrible and no fun to watch. And he didn't want her to get a look at Hal Chase, the Highlander's star first baseman, whose reputation with the ladies from downtown to the Harlem River to Brooklyn to Jersey was legendary. More accurately, he didn't want Chase to get a look at his pretty Maureen.

"Sure thing," he said. "The Gotham will be fine. It's close enough to the ball park."

"Can we get married on the Polo Grounds do you think?"

"I don't think your parents or Father Donovan would like that too much."

———— FRIDAY, SEPTEMBER 4, 1908 ————
PITTSBURGH, PENNSYLVANIA

Honus Wagner stepped up to the plate. Johnny Evers wished that the Flying Dutchman had retired, as he had threatened before the start of the season. Now he was hitting around .350 and was bound to put the ball in play.

The steep hills to the west of the junction of the Monongahela and Allegheny Rivers threw broad, long shadows over the playing field of Pittsburgh's Exposition Park. The light, dimmed by clouds of black smoke pouring out of the tall, steel mill chimney stacks across the river, was going fast. It was the bottom of the tenth inning of a nothing-to-nothing tie, and Evers knew that the game would be suspended for darkness before many more innings could be played. And the outcome of any single game could mean the difference between going to the World's Series or going home for the winter. The Cubs, Giants, and Pirates were all within reach of each other at the top of the National League with a month to go in the season.

Pirate left fielder and manager Fred Clarke stood on second base representing the winning run. There was one out. Clarke was as mean a bastard as Evers himself and would do anything, use any trick, to gain an edge and win this game.

Wagner connected, driving a hard ground ball toward right field. Evers dove for it and knocked it down, preventing it from rolling out of the infield. Clarke had to stop at third base. But Wagner stood safe at first.

Standing on the mound, Mordecai Centennial "Three Finger" "Miner" Brown looked at Wagner, looked at Clarke, and looked at Evers. A Tinker to Evers to Chance double play would end the inning. *Get the ground ball,* he told himself. The grip of his mangled, three-fingered hand gave him the sharpest curve in base ball and resulted in, more often than not, ground ball outs—if the hitter hit the ball at all. And against the next batter, rookie first baseman Warren Gill, the hook broke beautifully. But right into his leg. Gill was awarded first base and Wagner moved on to second.

The bases were loaded with one out. Brown, angry with himself for letting a youngster like Gill reach first in such a crucial game, got Ed Abbaticchio on strikes. That brought up Owen "Chief" Wilson, another rookie fresh up from the minor leagues.

Another kid, thought Evers. "He can't hit the curve, Miner," he yelled to Brown. "Go get him." But hit the curve he did, on the line into center field for a single. Clarke trotted home with the winning run. Disgusted, Evers looked at Gill running from first to second. The rookie had stopped half way, jumped up and down once in celebration, and ran off in the direction of the Pirates' clubhouse.

Rule 59, thought Evers. Joseph Rupp and "Inquisitive Fans." He ran to second and screamed at Jimmy Slagle in center field, "Throw me the ball! Throw me the ball!" Slagle threw the ball. Evers caught it and stepped on second base. "The runner from first is out," he yelled. "The run don't count. We're going on to the eleventh inning."

But he made his protest only to other Cubs. Hank O'Day, the lone umpire working that game, was on his way off the field and didn't see the play. When pressed by Evers, he refused to nullify the winning run.

"It's worth a try," said Cubs President Charlie Murphy when Evers explained the rule to him in the clubhouse. "But that pantywaist invert Pulliam will rule with his umpire. He does every time."

"Goddamn right it's worth a try," answered Evers. "Fucker Gill never touched second. I forced him out. That run don't count."

Evers changed into his street clothes. He and Murphy left the ball park and found a Western Union office just across the Allegheny River in downtown Pittsburgh. Murphy composed his telegram to Pulliam.

Chicago claims Gill should have touched second base before he ran to the clubhouse and will prove by affidavits of a number of persons that he failed to do so.

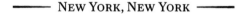

NEW YORK, NEW YORK

The Western Union delivery boy arrived at the National League offices in the St. James Building at a few minutes past six thirty. Lenore had just put on her hat to leave for the night, hoping that Mr. Pulliam had gone directly home from the Superbas-Doves game in Brooklyn. He often stopped by the office on his way from Washington Park to his rooms at the New York Athletic Club on Fifty-Ninth. When he did, he stayed too late.

She paid the boy with petty cash, adding a tip, and took the receipt. Looking at the cover envelope she saw that it was from Charles Murphy of the Cubs, wiring from Pittsburgh. *What on earth was so important that it warranted a telegram?* she wondered. *Another protest from the Cubs, no doubt.* As the season went into its last month, the complaints and protests grew more frequent, especially from the Cubs, Giants, and Pirates as they battled each other for the pennant. The pressure was beginning to take its toll on Mr. Pulliam.

He had given her permission to open any correspondence that came across her desk, but she hesitated. The lateness of the hour, and the fact that it was from Murphy, meant it would be a problem. She decided to give Mr. Pulliam until seven o'clock. Then she would close up the office and let the telegram wait until morning.

She took a file from her "active" rack and began reviewing batting averages. She became so involved in the task that when Pulliam opened the outer door at 7:20, she had no idea what time it was.

"Miss Caylor," he said, "why are you still here?"

"Good evening, Mr. Pulliam," she said. "I was about to leave but a Western Union delivery boy brought a telegram. I thought I should wait for you." She picked up the envelope and held it out over her desk. He approached.

"The days are getting shorter, Miss Caylor," he said as he took the telegram. "I don't want you staying here this late. It's not safe." He opened the envelope and read. She watched his face and knew that her instincts had been correct. "Miss Caylor, will you join me in my office," he said.

"Certainly, Mr. Pulliam." She picked up her notepad and a pencil and followed him through his door.

He handed her the telegram. She took it and read it. "Does the runner have to touch second on a hit that wins the game?" she asked.

"The rule states that he can be forced out. But that's not how the game has been played. Ever. The run has always been conceded and the game declared over. Forever. Always. I've never heard of this kind of protest before. It's Evers of the Cubs. I would bet money he memorized the rule book."

"But from what you're saying, he's right."

"Of course he's right. He's always right. On a hit like that, when it's the winning hit, the ball is live until all runners are safely on a base or across the plate."

Pulliam stood and turned to the window. He looked down onto the intersection of Broadway and Twenty-Sixth Street. "It was a lovely day, Miss Caylor," he said softly. "A beautiful day for a base ball game."

"Yes, sir. How was the game?"

"Fine. A good game. Boston won three to two. You would never have known that neither team is still in the pennant race. They played hard."

"Big crowd?"

"No. Not at all." He turned and looked at Lenore. "I'm sorry you stayed so late Miss Caylor. I had no idea you'd still be here. I sat with Charlie Ebbets. We stopped at a place on Union Street after the game."

"Now I'm sorry, Mr. Pulliam. I really wouldn't have been here except for the telegram. I had my hat on my head."

He smiled. "Thank you for waiting for me."

She gestured at the telegram. "Would you like to respond to Mr. Murphy tonight?"

"Can you get O'Day on the phone for me? Do you have his hotel on record?"

"Yes, sir."

A few minutes later she knocked on his door.

"Come in, Miss Caylor."

She opened his door. "I have Mr. O'Day. Shall I connect him to your phone?"

Pulliam stood and rushed past Lenore to her desk. He picked up her telephone. "O'Day? Pulliam here. Are you aware of the protest filed by the Cubs?" He listened for a moment. "Good. Please tell me your version of the events of this afternoon."

The conversation was remarkably short, from Lenore's point of view. He hung up the earpiece. "Can you bring your notebook into my office? I'll send you home in a carriage as soon as we're done here."

He dictated quickly. "The umpire in this case, by allowing the winning run, ruled that there was no force at second, because if there had been the run could not have been scored. The protest is denied."

When he finished the document he looked at Lenore and said, "Evers is indeed behind this. But I agree with him. The rule is clear. But it is also clear that Mr. O'Day did not see Gill forced out at second. The umpire's decision is final. We can rule no other way."

"I'm sure the umpires will pay closer attention from now on," said Lenore.

"O'Day will, that's certain. As for the rest? Do you think anyone will actually read the League's ruling on this?" He stood and took his hat from the coat rack. "I hope Thomas is still down there somewhere.

We'll stop at Western Union and send this to the Pirates, the Cubs, both at their Chicago office and at their hotel in Pittsburgh, and to the other teams' offices. And send it to the appropriate newspapers. Then Thomas and I will see you home."

"That's unnecessary, sir. The Western Union office on Twenty-Third is on the way to the subway."

"Miss Caylor, you are not taking the subway home at this hour."

Thomas waited on Twenty-Sixth Street, facing east. He jumped down from his seat when he saw them exit the St. James building.

"Good evening, Miss Caylor."

"Hello, Thomas. How are you?"

"Just fine, thank you." He opened the carriage door.

"Thomas," said Pulliam, "let's head uptown on Fifth Avenue. Keep your eyes open for a Western Union office."

"Isn't Fifth Avenue a little out of the way?" asked Lenore. "We could go straight up Broadway and get there much more quickly."

"I'd like to avoid Herald Square and Times Square. They're always so congested with trolleys and carriages. Especially now." He pulled his gold watch out of his vest pocket and flipped open its cover. "It's almost time for curtains to go up in theaters from here to Columbus Circle. Broadway will be impassable."

Thomas guided his horse into Fifth Avenue heading uptown. They passed the Brunswick Building on their right and then Thomas pulled over in the middle of the next block. He jumped down and opened the curbside door. Both Lenore and Pulliam stepped down and went into a storefront telegraph office where Lenore handed the clerk the league ruling on the Gill play and the addresses of the recipients.

Back on the street Pulliam said, "Miss Caylor, you must be famished. I know a little place at Forty-Fourth Street. It's on the way."

"So that's why you wanted to take Fifth Avenue," she said. "But Mr. Pulliam, I cannot go to Delmonico's dressed like this. Thank you very much just the same. And you've already eaten."

"That was just a snack," he said. "And you look beautiful."

She smiled. "Thank you very much, sir, but even if that were true, this dress is not appropriate for Delmonico's."

"Very well," he replied. "I know a wonderful little place on Seventh Avenue."

"Please, Mr. Pulliam. If you insist on dinner then I know a place where I'll feel comfortable."

"I do insist. Name it and we're as good as there."

"It's a café at Broadway and 110th Street and well known on the Upper West Side."

"Excellent." He stepped to the carriage and took the door handle from Thomas. "Did you hear, Thomas? Do you know the café?"

"Yes, sir," said Thomas, climbing onto the driver's seat. "Broadway at 110th Street. I've eaten there myself."

"You have?" said Pulliam. "Well then, it seems that I must keep better track of Manhattan's finer restaurants." Lenore stepped into the carriage and Pulliam followed, closing the door behind him. As Thomas edged the hansom into traffic Pulliam asked, "How well do you know Fifth Avenue?"

"A little," said Lenore. "I used to go to restaurants closer to Seventh. The farther east we went, the less we were welcome. But I've danced for private parties in most of the Fifth Avenue hotels."

"The Holland House?" he asked as they passed it on their left, at Thirtieth Street.

"No, not that one."

"The *Duchess of Devonshire* stayed there, you know."

"I'm certain she would stay at the very best hotels in town."

Pulliam laughed. "You see, the *Duchess of Devonshire* is a painting by Gainsborough that was stolen in London in 1878 by a famous thief named Adam Worth. He became smitten by the lady and couldn't bear to fence her. So he kept the painting for more than twenty years until he decided he needed the money more. In 1901 he made a deal with the Pinkerton Detective Agency and exchanged it in Chicago for $25,000. The *Duchess* spent a night at the Holland House on her way back to London."

"Did Mr. Worth go to jail?"

"Several times, I should think, but never for that particular crime."

As they traveled uptown, he continued with a running history of the landmarks of Fifth Avenue until they turned left at Fifty-Ninth Street. At Seventh Avenue he pointed out the New York Athletic Club where he lived. They took Columbus Circle around to Broadway.

"I'm curious," said Lenore.

"I hope not about this part of town," he replied. "Once we get up here I don't know the history very well. It's too new."

"No," she said. "I'm curious about you. You're not from here. Why do you know all this New York history?"

"I guess it's the newspaper man in me," he said. "I like the stories."

"I've thoroughly enjoyed the tour," said Lenore. "Thank you."

Thomas pulled up in front of the café. "Are we here?" asked Pulliam, looking out the carriage window. He opened the door, hopped down onto the sidewalk, and held a hand out for Lenore.

She took Pulliam's hand, stepped down, and walked to the café door. "It's humble, but I can vouch for the food. And you can loosen your tie."

Pulliam looked over the exterior and pronounced it "perfect."

Lenore ordered pot roast with boiled potatoes and green beans. Pulliam took the oyster stew. "Can't get fresh oysters in Louisville," he said to Lenore. "The menu says that these came right out of Long Island Sound today."

As they waited for their food, Lenore asked, "I realize that the Cubs, the Giants and the Pirates all have a chance to win the pennant, and so they need every game. But this protest seemed to mean more than just making a decision based on the rule book." Pulliam looked down at his hands and hesitated. "I'm sorry," said Lenore. "Maybe we've had enough base ball for the day."

"No, no," said Pulliam. "It's all right. It's just difficult to explain." He took a sip of water. "I would say," he began, "that since the turn of the century at least, and maybe before, the game of base ball has been trying to...how should I put this? The game of base ball has been trying to mature. To grow up. There has been so much about the game that has been accepted without question for no other reason than that's the way it's always been. The fans standing and sitting on the field for instance. That's a holdover from the days when people went to a park on Saturday afternoon with a picnic basket and watched the local teams while sitting on a blanket in the grass. Charlie Ebbets is campaigning to keep spectators off the field entirely, and I support him. But others see it as a loss of revenue."

"Others like Mr. Brush?"

"You've worked for the league for many months now. You can draw your own conclusions." He buttered a piece of bread. "This Gill incident. Do you think if a similar play had happened between the Superbas and the Doves today that anyone would have called for the ball, as Evers did, and claimed to have forced a runner who didn't bother to run all the way to second base?"

"No," said Lenore. "Probably not. The game at Washington Park today had no influence on the standings at all. No player would have bothered."

"And if he had, no one would have paid any attention," said Pulliam. "But to Murphy it means money won or lost. And if the pennant race comes down to the last game of the year and the Cubs lose, he will never let me forget the Gill play. It would not just be the difference between winning the pennant and not winning. It would have nothing to do with pride or the recognition of the press, of the fans, and of one's peers. It would be a question of whether or not World's Series revenue is included in the profit and loss statement. That is all I see when we get a telegram such as the one we received today. Or when Mr. Brush pays us a visit. It's always about dollars and cents, no matter what the issue seems to be."

"Perhaps nothing more will come of it."

"I hope not. But is that what my job has been reduced to? Hoping that the Cubs win the pennant so I don't have to face Murphy later? And if the Cubs do win, you can bet I'll have to face Brush and McGraw, no matter how fairly the pennant was gained. Do you remember Mr. Brush's tirade about checkers and Christy Mathewson?"

"Yes. He was completely irrational."

"Can you imagine what he might do if the Giants lose more than just a one-run game? If he loses the pennant he will find a way to blame our office for his lost revenue."

"But if they lose, there's nothing you can do about it."

"Not according to Brush. Or Murphy. Or even Barney Dreyfuss lately —and he's an old friend." He sighed. "The game is better than that. Deserves better than that."

Their food arrived. Lenore regretted bringing up the Gill play.

"I believe my Aunt Trudie has a beau," she said.

"That's nice." Pulliam kept his eyes on his meal and picked at his food.

"Have you heard from your sister and your nephew lately?"

"No, I must call them."

Lenore ate her pot roast and said nothing more.

After a few more bites, Pulliam put his fork on the table, used his napkin, and consulted his watch. "I really must get you home, Miss Caylor." He turned and signaled for the check.

———— Saturday, September 5, 1908 ————
Pittsburgh, Pennsylvania

Hank O'Day sat on the edge of his hotel bed reading the decision. He didn't like it, although Pulliam had supported his call on the Gill play. Touching second, or any base, when a winning run scored was a formality. A technicality. Everyone knew the runner could make it safely and would just continue on to the clubhouse from there, so why bother? There were other plays that were allowed but did not strictly follow the rule book. And speaking of second base, what about the "phantom" step on the base during a double play? *There was no better practitioner of that maneuver than Johnny Evers himself,* thought O'Day. *The sonofabitching, troublemaking bastard.* He wished a photographer could freeze the moment when Evers caught a throw from Joe Tinker and was supposed to step on second base for the force before throwing to

Frank Chance to complete the double play. Such a photograph would show, O'Day was certain, that his foot was inches if not feet from the bag. But he and every umpire in both leagues called the runner out every time—and probably would for as long as base ball was played.

He read the key line of Pulliam's decision again, "...there was no force at second, because if there had been the run could not have been scored." A thinly veiled reprimand of himself, he was sure, for not staying on the field to see the entire play. Fine. He would call it strictly by the book from now on. He just hoped that everyone in the league, from owners down to batboys, understood what Pulliam, and Evers, had just done to the game. And he prayed that every bush-league bum on every goddamn team would touch second, or first or third, on game-winning hits.

—— MONDAY, SEPTEMBER 7, 1908 ——
NEW YORK, NEW YORK

The switchboard telephone rang at a few minutes past ten. Lenore connected the line. An operator said, "I have Chicago on the line. A Mr. Murphy for a Mr. Pulliam."

"Put him through." She waited.

"Hello, Pulliam?" said Murphy.

"Good morning, Mr. Murphy. I'm sorry but Mr. Pulliam is not in the office just now."

"Where the hell is he?"

"He is in Brooklyn."

"Well, what's he going to do about the umpire problem?"

"I'm sorry, Mr. Murphy?"

"He needs to hire more umpires. This thing in Pittsburgh proved that once and for all."

"I'm certain this is something that will come up during the league meetings."

"League meetings? They aren't until February. We need more umpires now. At least two per game, every game," he said, raising his voice. "But more for important games, and every game in September is going to be mighty important."

"I'm certain," she said, "that Mr. Pulliam will do everything he can."

"How can the league," continued Murphy as if she had said nothing, "with the Pirates and Cubs and Giants trading places at the top of the standings about every day, and staying within a couple of damn percentage points of each other, how can the league send only one poor bastard of an umpire to a series between the Cubs and the Pirates? It proves that you folks in the league office don't know what the hell you're doing. And that...that incompetence," he stumbled over the word, "must be laid squarely on Pulliam's own desk. What the hell else does the league office do that's worth a damn but schedule and supervise umpires?"

"Mr. Murphy," said Lenore, "first, there is no need to use profane language with me, and second—"

"You tell your boss, missy—"

"Don't call me missy."

"You tell your boss that Brush and Herrmann are already lined up against him and much as I hate to side with Brush on anything, I may have to join them, and then who's gonna be left on his side? Maybe his kike friend in Pittsburgh, which was, by the way, sure as I'm sitting here, the real reason Pulliam ruled for the Pirates on that Gill play."

She broke the connection, wishing she had done so sooner. Just hearing Murphy's voice made her skin crawl. The only silver lining of this latest dark black cloud was the fact that it had nothing to do with Brush or McGraw. They had been very quiet the last few days, happy to be in first place and beating up on the Brooklyn Superbas, winning four in a row against them with one scheduled for Saturday and a sixth on Monday. In fact, since losing three in a row to the Cubs to close out the month of August, the Giants had won ten out of their last eleven. And after each game Mr. Pulliam looked visibly relieved. He no longer seemed as excited about the pennant race; the accomplishments of Christy Mathewson of the Giants and of the entire Cubs pitching staff; the huge crowds attending games in Chicago, Pittsburgh, and New York; or the fact that base ball had totally captivated the imagination of the entire country. He had to work at his enthusiasm. If he showed any real energy at all it was in confronting Brush or McGraw before whom he could show no weakness.

———— SATURDAY, SEPTEMBER 12, 1908 ————
NEW YORK, NEW YORK

At the 110th Street newspaper stand Lenore selected the day's *Times*. She paid the boy and started to return home, but paused. She looked down Broadway wondering if, perhaps, Mr. Adams might be in the neighborhood. She quickly admonished herself for being silly and hurried home.

She opened the front door to see her aunt standing in the hall clutching an envelope. "Good morning, Aunt Trudie."

"Lenore, Mr. Mason stopped by with this note."

Lenore held out her hand for the envelope.

"Oh, it's not for you. It's addressed to me. He's invited me to another ball game, but says that you and Luella are welcome if you're available but if not the two of us would have a swell time and maybe stop after the game for a cup of coffee or a light dinner at the café."

"That sounds very nice for you, Aunt Trudie. If you think it's nice, I mean."

"Yes, of course, but I can't accompany Mr. Mason alone."

"When is the game? This week? I'm normally in the office during games."

"This afternoon."

"Today? My goodness. That is very short notice. I had planned on some errands and—"

"I know it might be difficult, Lenore, but it's a big game and should be very exciting."

"Did you talk to Mother?"

"Not yet, and to be perfectly honest I would rather Luella not join us. She will judge every action and every word spoken by either me or Mr. Mason." She looked down at her hands. "I swear she thinks she's my mother." She raised her head. "But I cannot go alone, and I want to go. I haven't been alone with Mr. Mason yet. I think it's too soon."

Lenore reached out and took Trudie's arm. "Of course I'll go with you. It will be fun."

"Thank you, Lenore," said Trudie. She embraced her niece. "I know I'm being a silly old maid, but I rather like Mr. Mason and..."

"You are not an old maid, Aunt Trudie."

Trudie smiled as she released her niece. "Mr. Mason will pick us up at two. His note said something about our seats being quite unique."

"Unique?"

"That's what it said. Whatever could that mean?" Trudie shrugged and turned toward the kitchen. "I'll put the kettle on. I'd like a cup of tea. Would you like to join me?"

"No, thank you. I need to get ready." She went to her room, took a sponge bath, and dressed quickly, choosing her lightest, most comfortable cotton skirt and white shirtwaist. She reviewed her collection of hats and decided not to bother with one at all. She would only have to place it under her seat where it would be vulnerable to peanut shells and spilled beer.

Gregory Mason rang their bell just before two o'clock. Lenore agreed with Trudie that it would be better to meet him at the outer door to avoid an extended chat with her mother. Lenore waited as Trudie pinned her subdued Merry Widow hat to her hair.

"I don't want to bother anyone sitting behind us," said Trudie. She glanced at Lenore. "What about your hat, Lenore? Mr. Mason is waiting."

"I'm not going to wear one."

"Not going to wear one?" Trudie laughed. "How modern of you. I don't have the courage to do that, and besides, Mr. Mason seems to be a very traditional gentleman."

"Then he'll be very pleased with the way you look."

"Do you think so?"

Lenore nodded. "Of course."

Mason smiled broadly when he saw Trudie, and bowed deeply to them both before leading them to his motorcar. Trudie sat next to Mason, Lenore in the back.

As they drove up Eighth Avenue Lenore leaned forward. "Mr. Mason will you be so kind as to explain the unique experience you mentioned in your note to my aunt?"

"Did I write that?"

Trudie took the note from her small handbag and held it up. "You certainly did. Would you like me to read it back to you?"

Mason grinned and said, "Oh yes. I recall now. I think you're going to enjoy these very special seats, but I don't want to spoil the surprise. Let's wait until we get there. Now, Miss Caylor, tell me. What's going on in the base ball world?"

"Mr. Mason," said Lenore, "I believe you're changing the subject. And anyway, I see your copy of the *Herald* back here, opened to the sports page. I would wager you know more than I do about the standings."

"If Lenore wagered, that is," said Trudie. "Which of course she doesn't."

Mason leaned back and laughed. "Okay. You win, Miss Caylor. Let me see. The Pirates beat your Reds yesterday and are now eighty-one and fifty. The Cubs beat the St. Louis Cardinals and are eighty-one and fifty-one, half a game behind the Pirates. The Giants continue to humiliate the poor Superbas, winning yesterday six to one, and are in first place with eighty wins and forty-six losses, but have played many fewer games than the other two. Now, do you want the bad news about the rest of the league? Or perhaps the Americans?"

"That's quite enough for me," said Trudie. "I'm not sure I understand what you've already said. I don't need to hear more."

"Miss Caylor," said Mason. "Can you tell me anything about the incident in Pittsburgh the other day? The play involving Evers of the Chicagos and the Pittsburgh rookie."

"There isn't anything of note to tell you, Mr. Mason. The umpire, Mr. O'Day, ruled that the run counted and the Pirates won the game. Mr. Pulliam supported that ruling."

"But it's a very interesting argument made by Evers, don't you think? If indeed the Pittsburgher failed to touch second then he could be forced out and the final run would not count."

"That's the rule," said Lenore.

"I've never seen it done. Have you, Miss Pittenger?"

"I'm quite sure I don't know what you're talking about," said Trudie.

"It's not important, Trudie," said Lenore. "A rather boring little technicality."

"But," said Mason, "it could be the difference between the Pirates going to the World's Series or the Cubs."

"Highly unlikely," said Lenore. "There are still a number of games to be played." She looked up through the front window and saw they were approaching the ball park. On either side of Eighth Avenue streams of rooters lined the sidewalks walking quickly toward the Polo Grounds.

When they arrived the grandstands were empty except for a few hundred fanatics who crowded around the fences near the Giants' and Brooklyn Superbas' benches. Members of both teams stretched along the foul lines and sprinted through the outfield. A few players tossed balls back and forth. A sprinkling of fans strolled in the open area in front of the bleachers. One carriage had pulled up to the rope, its horse reaching for a taste of outfield grass. Lenore looked for Brush's special motorcar but it was not in its usual location. Elevated trains came and went at the El station and in the railroad yards on the other side of the left and center field walls. All was oddly calm, thought Lenore, in the midst of this crazy pennant race.

Mason led them to a section of the grandstands that had been separated from the rest of the seats by a barrier of rough vertical planks. A security guard in a faded gray suit sat dozing near an opening in the crude wall. Gregory reached into his inside coat pocket and pulled out two small sheets of paper. "Here we are," he said. "After you, Miss Caylor. Miss Pittenger." He gestured at the opening.

"But what's this?" asked Trudie.

"It's the press box."

The guard woke and looked at them through lids so close together that even in the daylight Lenore couldn't see his eyes. "Hold on there, folks. Press only."

"I have these," said Gregory, handing the papers to the guard.

He looked them over and said, "Mercer's gonna love this." He glanced up at Lenore and Trudie. "And dames to boot." He chuckled. "Go ahead in."

They stepped past the guard into a section with a low, wooden counter nailed onto a railing at its front. Notebooks, ledgers, newspapers, pencils, and ashtrays—mostly empty—were scattered across its surface. A lone Smith Premier typewriter sat at one end. Battered and dirty, it was one of the older models that had separate keys for upper and lower case, Lenore noticed. She had used a similar machine in school a decade ago.

Mason turned back to the guard. "Where is everybody?" he asked.

"On the field. Talking to players."

"Where should we sit?"

The guard stood and peered into the press box. "Oh, right where you're standing should be just fine." He grinned and pulled a thin black cigar from his pocket. A stick match appeared in his right hand. He struck it against the outer wall of the press box and lit his smoke.

"Thank you," said Mason.

"I feel distinctly out of place," said Lenore. "How did you get permission to sit here?"

"From the vice president of my department. We advertise in the *American* so somebody in Hearst's office gave him several press passes. You see, usually there are reporters covering both teams here. You know, from New York and the visiting team's city. But since today it's the Superbas against the Giants, they don't need to send both Brooklyn and New York base ball writers to cover it. That makes room for guests like us."

They sat and looked out onto the field. She picked out a few men with notebooks and pencils in their hands. One by one they flipped their pads closed and headed back into the grandstands.

"Who the hell is that, Morrie?" came a voice from just outside the box. Lenore, Trudie, and Mason turned to see a tall, rather thin man with an open collar under a worn black suit. "And a couple of dames? Judas priest."

Morrie, the guard, looked up at the man and grinned. "They got passes, Sid. From Hearst."

"Well Hearst ain't my boss. And that mug is in my chair. Who the hell are you, pal?" he said looking at Mason.

Rising awkwardly to his feet, Mason replied, "Uh, my name is Gregory Mason. I work in the advertising department at B. Altman and—"

"Advertising!" shouted the man named Sid. "You gotta be kidding me. So one of those thieving ad salesmen at the *American* said that Hearst said that it was perfectly okay for you to take my seat?" He stepped into the press box and threw his notebook at Gregory, who ducked allowing the flapping pad to hit Lenore on the side of her head. "I work at the *Globe,* pal, and that's a *Globe* chair."

A group of men behind the man named Sid laughed. "Jesus, Sid," said one. "Now look what you done. You struck a lady."

Gregory turned to Lenore. "Oh my God, Lenore. Are you all right?" He looked back at the man named Sid. "Look here, sir. This is uncalled for."

Lenore, her face hidden by a hand rubbing the side of her head, slowly stood and faced the man named Sid. "Hello, Mr. Mercer," she said. "Nice throw."

Sid Mercer's face blanched. "Miss Caylor? What are you doing here?"

Mason looked at Lenore and then turned and stared at Sid Mercer. "You two know each other?"

"It's Lenore," said another of the sportswriters. They jostled one another to be the first to attend to her well-being.

"Are you all right, Miss Caylor," said one.

"Can I get you a drink of water? A soda?"

"A beer?"

"I have a flask of brandy," said another.

"Lenore," said Trudie, "you know these men?"

"Yes," said Lenore. "I know these gentlemen well. I work for Mr. Pulliam, don't forget. We talk to the press often."

Mason shook his head. "Of course. I should have known."

"Miss Caylor," said Sid Mercer, "I'm awful sorry. I meant to hit your advertising friend here."

"It's all right, Mr. Mercer. Fortunately," she said reaching down to retrieve the notebook, "there's not much weight to what you write."

The other writers laughed loudly.

"Oh I know that," said Mercer. "That's why I'm a base ball writer like the rest of these illiterates."

"Very well put, Mr. Mercer," said Lenore laughing. "Mr. Mason, Aunt Trudie, allow me to introduce you to some of my journalist friends."

"Journalists? Flattery will get you everywhere," said one of the men.

"Thank you, Mr. Fullerton. And this is Mr. Gregory Mason and my aunt Miss Gertrude Pittenger." Hugh Fullerton, a small man with a high forehead, short tousled hair sticking out from under a pushed back bowler, and wide, round spectacles, extended his hand. "Mr. Mason, this is Mr. Hugh Fullerton of the," she paused and stared at Fullerton for a moment. "But Mr. Fullerton, you're with the Chicago *Examiner*. What are you still doing here in New York?"

"Good question," said Mercer.

She looked at Mason. "Mr. Fullerton was at the office yesterday to talk to Mr. Pulliam about that Pittsburgh play."

"Cubs go to Boston next," said Fullerton. "The paper sent me here to talk to Pulliam and then head up there. So I had a free day or two in New York. Thought I'd take in a game with my friends here."

"And shoot pool at McGraw's joint," said one of the writers.

"Maybe," said Fullerton.

"What else is new?" said Mercer. "And what did Pulliam have to say about the Pittsburgh play? No, don't tell me. I already know. Pulliam always supports his umpires, no matter how bad the call."

"And you didn't hear about John Rudderham?" asked Lenore.

Mercer scratched his temple with a pencil. "Wasn't he the rookie ump who made that bad call in the Cincinnati game last June? Got McGraw suspended?"

"Mr. Pulliam dismissed him last week," said Lenore.

"Only took him three months to do it," said Mercer.

Lenore smiled and gestured at Mason. "This is Sid Mercer of the *Globe.*" They shook hands. "You're in his seat, it seems."

Mason stood.

"No problem, Miss Caylor," said Mercer. "There's room today."

"And this is Mr. Gym Bagley of the *Evening Mail,* and Mr. Ernest Lanigan of the *Press.*"

"Ernie," said Lanigan. "Pleased to meet you."

"Mr. Sam Crane of the *Evening Journal,*" continued Lenore.

"Here, Miss Caylor," said Fullerton. "Why don't you sit next to me? Do you know how to keep score?" He pulled out a chair.

"I've seen some scorecards," she said, sitting in the seat held by Fullerton. "Mr. Heydler keeps those records."

Fullerton sat next to Lenore and flipped open a ledger. "Well, this is a scorebook. Better than the scorecards they sell around here."

Lenore looked at the open pages, the scribbled record of a recent game. "How do you decipher this?" she asked. "It's quite different from the scorekeeping I've seen at the office." The pages resembled a bookkeeper's ledger. The names of players were listed in spaces along the far left column, with a thin space to the right to enter each player's position, coded by number. Next to each name were rows of boxes imprinted with little diamonds. The headings across the top corresponded to the innings, one through eleven to accommodate extra innings if the game ended tied in the ninth. A group of totals columns crowded the right margin with abbreviations like AB, R, IB, SB, PO, A, and E, for keeping track of other game details for each player. In the little boxes Fullerton had scrawled a web of codes including numbers, letters, symbols, and a variety of squiggly lines.

"You'll learn as the game plays out," said Fullerton. "It's my own system. I'll explain everything."

Mason watched from the end of the booth where he stood next to Trudie. Mercer looked at him and shook his head in disgust. "Hey, Mason," he said.

"Yeah?"

"Sit down already. You and Aunt Gertrude can have my seat and the one next to it for the day."

Mason glanced at Lenore and sat back down in Sid Mercer's chair. The reporter took the seat next to him.

"Thank you, Mr. Mercer," said Trudie. "Tell me, is there a ladies' room nearby?"

"Sure," said Mercer. "Back up the aisle and to your left and then down under the seats."

"Thank you." She stood.

"Shall I accompany you, Miss Pittenger?" said Mason.

"Nonsense," said Trudie. "I'm perfectly capable. I shall return shortly."

When Trudie left the press box Mercer moved closer to Mason and lowered his voice. "You close to Lenore and her aunt?" he asked.

"What do you mean?"

"I mean are you engaged to one of them or related or neighbors or what?"

"That's getting a little personal," said Mason.

"So's sitting in my favorite chair," said Mercer. "Okay. I get it. You'd like to be a little closer to Miss Pittenger, but maybe she don't seem so interested yet so maybe you try to impress her and her niece who works for the league by getting these passes to the press box." Mason didn't reply. "Okay, okay. I get it."

"I'm sorry if we've upset your routine," said Mason. "I didn't mean any harm. I'd leave you alone, but it seems," he glanced beyond Mercer to Lenore, "that at least Miss Caylor is enjoying herself. I would expect she means to remain for the duration of the game."

"And you sure don't want her to leave the ball park with the likes of one of us." When Mason didn't reply, Mercer continued. "Like I said, it's okay. Enjoy the game. I may ask your opinion from time to time. It may give me a new point of view."

"You'd trust the opinion of an evil advertising man?"

"Hell, you ain't no worse than some of them players."

"I appreciate the compliment."

"And if Lenore likes you enough to come to a game with you and her aunt, you can't be all bad."

"Thank you."

"But I gotta tell you something. It ain't your fault, but we gotta do something about visitors to the press box."

"Why? Is it a problem?"

"This year worse than ever. With this nutty pennant race, everybody and his uncle wants to get into the games. There ain't enough seats. You ever see the people on Coogan's Bluff? On the El platform? Or behind the outfield rope?"

"Yes, I've seen them."

"Believe me, anybody who thinks he's somebody will use a connection to get in here. The ball players send their mothers to us. It's a mess. Anyway, I've talked to Hughie about it and we're thinking of starting a base ball writers' organization of some kind, with rules about entry into the press box and other things. Hughie mentioned it to Pulliam yesterday."

"Sounds reasonable," said Mason.

"Yeah. And you know what? Pulliam likes the idea. We kind of thought he might, being an old sports scribe himself. And if he helps us on this thing, we'll love him like a brother, fairy or no fairy."

"Fairy?"

Mercer turned and looked at Mason. "You didn't know? Lenore didn't tell you?"

"No. I don't know her well enough to discuss..."

"Maybe she don't know about Pulliam herself." He looked down the counter to where Lenore and Hugh Fullerton sat huddled over Fullerton's scorebook. "Well, everybody leaves him alone, know what I mean? He don't let it get in the way of doing his job. We wouldn't even know it except..."

"Except?"

"You cover base ball in this town you find out things about guys. Players, owners, managers, league presidents."

"I see," said Mason. He looked out at the grandstands and saw John Brush struggling down an aisle toward a seat in the front row. "And Brush. What about him? He have an accident of some kind? I knew he was ill. Nobody that thin can be healthy."

Mercer sighed. "I've said enough." He looked down at Brush. "He must be feeling better today. He usually watches from his Hewitt out there." He gestured toward the outfield.

"What's wrong with him?" said Gregory.

"Okay. I'll tell you because Lenore and her family seem to like you and because maybe you'll take it as a cautionary tale about the evils of the flesh."

Gregory stared at him a moment and then said, "The flesh? But the symptoms aren't..."

Mercer nodded. "Yeah. It ain't affecting his mind like what happens to a lot of guys. He's as sharp a bastard as ever. It's eating away at his spine. That's why he can't walk so good. And it's getting worse."

Gregory looked onto the field, the bright sunshine bleaching his vision. The Giants ran out from their bench and took their positions.

"It's play ball time," said Mercer. "I gotta go to work."

Trudie returned to the press box as the second batter walked up to home plate.

—— WEDNESDAY, SEPTEMBER 23, 1908 ——
NEW YORK, NEW YORK

Lenore sat at her desk half asleep. She had met May and Lillian after the previous night's performance of the *Follies* and stayed out too late. She had enjoyed herself, but nothing about being at the theater made her the least bit nostalgic. She was glad she had a steady job. With four performances to go, few of the showgirls knew what they would do next. Lenore didn't worry so much about May. She was determined to make a career of it, and she had Abby on her side. But Lillian got by on her looks, and those would fade, especially if she stayed out late every night. The new fall season would be opening soon and she had not yet landed a new show. She said she had her eye on Ziegfeld himself, but what chance did she have with Anna Held very much the attentive wife and very much a star?

The telephone rang. Lenore sat up straight, startled. She realized she had dozed off for a moment. Confused, she swiveled in her chair and faced the switchboard console. She inserted a plug and fumbled for the mouthpiece and earphone.

"Hello? Hello?" a man said at the other end of the line. She recognized Ted's voice. He had been calling often lately, and each time Mr. Pulliam took the call in his office with the door closed.

"Hello? Is someone there?"

"Yes," she finally said. "I'm sorry. National League of Professional Base Ball Clubs. Can I help you?"

"I know who you are," he said. "I need to talk to Harry."

"Mr. Pulliam? One moment please. Who should I say is calling?" she asked, knowing what the reply would be.

"Please, Lenore," he said and then sighed loudly in exasperation. "A friend. Please connect me."

"One moment please."

"You already said that. Please put me through. I'm calling long distance."

"Yes, certainly." She pulled a cord out of the console and plugged it into an input jack. But she knew she did something wrong. She had connected outside calls to Mr. Pulliam's office a hundred times, but this time it felt different.

The wrong cord? The wrong jack? That was it. She had plugged it into an office party line. Hearing Ted's voice had thrown her off. She reached for the line to disconnect and redirect it to Mr. Pulliam's private line, but she was too late. She heard a light click as a receiver was lifted and then, "Harry Pulliam" in her earpiece. Her fingers on the plug of the cord, she stopped before disconnecting. She didn't want him to know that she had crossed the wires. She muffled the mouthpiece with her right hand.

"Harry it's me," said the distant voice, mildly distorted by the crackling of hundreds of miles of phone lines.

"Hello."

"I'm sorry to call you at work again, but I can never get you at the club. Did you leave instructions there not to put me through?"

"No, Ted. Of course not."

There was a pause. All she could hear was the static on the line. She hoped they had been disconnected.

"You gotta let me come back, Harry. I have a couple of weeks before I need to be in Toledo. I don't want to go to Louisville."

"You know we can't do that until after the season."

"My family is on my back every goddamn day. They took the train up here and came to the Art Institute and almost made a scene. I'm not living up to my mother's expectations. My father is convinced I'm one of 'those' men. What am I doing working for artists? That's not a man's job. Do you know what he said to me?"

"I'm sorry, Ted, but—"

"He said, 'Teddy, I know what you're about. You just keep it private. Keep the family out of it and don't ask me to meet your boyfriends.' Can you imagine it? Keep it to myself? He should talk with all his little girlfriends on the side."

"That's why you must stay away from New York for now. They were following me. You. Us."

"But it was New York, Harry. Nobody cares in New York."

"It's the National Base Ball League, Ted. How many times do I have to tell you this? Brush and McGraw and Herrmann will drum me out of base ball. They would have me sent to prison if they could."

"Then why don't you quit?"

"Why do you ask me to do that? You know I can't quit base ball."

Ted's voice grew louder. "But you can send me into exile, can't you? If it wasn't for the exhibition I'd be stuck in Louisville. But that's all right, isn't it? I can suffer and be alone with those Kentucky blueblood hypocrites. But you? Nothing can come between you and the true love of your life. That goddamn game played by a collection of hillbillies."

"Please, Ted."

"And corn huskers. I bet the Giants wouldn't have a full set of teeth if you combined the yaps of the whole fucking team."

"Ted, please."

"And you, Harry. You think you're going to force dignity on that lot? I know your tastes, too, don't forget."

A click sounded at their end of the line.

"Do you hear me?" A pause. "Do you hear me, Harry? Did you disconnect, Harry? Oh, Harry." Lenore thought she heard a sob. "Oh, Harry." The man coughed and the line went dead. Lenore quickly disconnected the cords.

Pulliam's door opened. He stood just inside his office, his hand on the doorknob. He looked pale and exhausted. He attempted a smile.

"Good morning, Miss Caylor. I didn't hear you come in."

"Good morning, Mr. Pulliam."

"But of course you came in because you connected that call." She flushed and felt her heart jump into her throat. "How are you today?" he asked. "How was the show last night?"

"It went well. The audience seemed to like it even more than opening night."

"Better than Ziegfeld's show last year, isn't it?"

"So I've heard."

"You look tired, Miss Caylor."

"I'm fine, sir."

"Well, nonetheless, you look positively spent today." He turned and looked out the window. "A beautiful day today. A beautiful day for a base ball game." He approached her desk. "Mr. Heydler will be meeting us there with George Dovey."

"Thank you for the invitation, but I have a lot of work to get done."

"This is not an invitation, Miss Caylor." He smiled again. "It's an order. You'll learn how to keep score for the league. John is taking on more responsibility, and his role as statistician has become more difficult for him lately."

"I know how to keep score, Mr. Pulliam."

"You do?"

"Yes. Mr. Hugh Fullerton taught me."

"Fullerton? Excellent. Well then, it's settled. You will come to the game and be official scorer for the National League. Can you arrange to have Thomas waiting for us downstairs at one o'clock?"

"Yes, sir."

"And please, stop calling me 'sir.'"

"Yes, Mr. Pulliam."

"Oh, it's hopeless." He returned to his office. He left his door open.

She stood to leave, putting on her hat as she walked around her desk. Heydler's office door opened and the league secretary came out hat in hand. "Hello, Miss Caylor," he said, smiling. "Half day today?"

"Very funny," she replied. "Mr. Pulliam has asked that I accompany him to the game."

Heydler scowled and looked at Pulliam's office door. "I see."

"I'm just going out to find Thomas. Can we give you a ride to the game?"

"No, thank you," said Heydler, smiling again. "I'm meeting George Dovey in front of the Waldorf. We're going to have a quick bite to eat at my club and then go to the game. I'd invite you and Mr. Pulliam, but, you know, it's men only."

"Thank you just the same," said Lenore. "Will you ride down the elevator with me?"

"Of course."

At one thirty Lenore and Pulliam exited the St. James Building onto Broadway at Twenty-Sixth. The streets were crowded with carriages, trolleys, and a few automobiles. Pulliam looked to his left and then his right. "There he is. Wait here a minute, Miss Caylor." He walked off toward Madison Square.

A moment later Thomas guided a large carriage to the front of the building, Pulliam walking with it along the curb. When it stopped, Pulliam opened the door. "Here we go, Miss Caylor. I expected to be driving Mr. Heydler and Mr. Dovey as well, so Thomas arranged for this wonderful carriage. We shall be very comfortable."

She approached the carriage. "Hello, Thomas," she said looking up. "Beautiful day, isn't it?"

"Afternoon, Miss Caylor," said Thomas, touching the brim of his tall black top hat with his index and second fingers. "Yes, it's a fine day."

"A beautiful day for a base ball game," said Pulliam as he helped Lenore into the carriage.

"Yes, sir. Gonna be a lot of folks heading there today," said Thomas. "Big game."

"Yes, indeed," answered Pulliam. "And if you get us there in under an hour, there's a ticket to the game in it for you. And please charge us for the half hour you've been waiting."

Pulliam sat next to Lenore in the carriage. Above them Thomas snapped his whip. They pulled away from the curb.

"You see, Miss Caylor?" said Pulliam. "Base ball is the talk of the town. Ten years ago it was little better than a downtown rat fight."

"It's been a great year," said Lenore. "They've been getting twenty thousand a game here and in Chicago and Pittsburgh."

"And the new league is doing well, too. Their race is as tight as ours. The Naps are right there with the Tigers and the White Sox."

"In Chicago they're talking more than ever about a repeat of the 1906 World's Series between the Cubs and the White Sox."

"Yes," said Pulliam. "And the Cubs would love to get their revenge on the White Sox. That's the kind of thing that makes our game exciting."

"Not all of the magnates see it quite that way."

"There are a few who need to be convinced that in the long term our ideas will be much more profitable for them than their narrow, short-term concerns."

"And the players?"

"They're doing better and better. Frank Chance has a wonderful contract. There are problems, certainly, but some of the players can be problems themselves. Ban Johnson is going to have to do something about Cobb in Detroit. He's bad for the game. And the Highlanders are lucky Hal Chase quit and went back to California. He's no good either."

"As a player?"

"No. He's the best first baseman I've ever seen. But as a man he is dishonorable. He's notorious for lying down."

"Excuse me?"

"Throwing games. Gamblers get to him. So a virtuoso of the game, a man who can turn the most difficult play into a graceful display of physical skill, makes the easiest plays look impossible. It's a shame. But our own league is wild enough this year."

"Losing the doubleheader to the Cubs yesterday certainly hurt the Giants," she said. "I wouldn't have expected that to happen this late in the season on the Polo Grounds."

"The Giants have to win one of the next two games against the Cubs to stay in first." Pulliam smiled. "It's anyone's pennant—the Cubs, the Giants, or the Pirates. Look outside the cab. The traffic uptown is much heavier than downtown. This game is the biggest thing in New York today. Much bigger than Mr. Ziegfeld's show. No offense."

"None taken. And bigger than the election. Not that I can vote."

Pulliam laughed. "Who's running? Oh yes. Taft for the Republicans and Bryan for the Democrats." He paused and thought a moment. "I have a good tale about the election. Murphy of the Cubs told it to me. It happened that the chairman of the Democratic National Committee, a gentleman named Norman Mack, was in Chicago earlier this month trying to put together a schedule for his candidate. He met with two aldermen named 'Bathhouse John' Coughlin and 'Hinky Dink' Mike Kenna."

"Bathhouse John and Hinky Dink?" laughed Lenore.

"Laugh if you will but they are the two most powerful men in the city, according to Murphy. They control the Levee. Anyway, when Mr. Mack asked them when would be a good week for Bryan to stop in Chicago, they told him not until late October. 'October?' he complained. 'But that would be too close to the election and Bryan would be halfway across the country.' They explained to him that there was nothing to be done about it. Base ball had the entire city in its spell. If the Cubs weren't in town, the White Sox were and you couldn't fill a closet with the men who would miss a game to hear a politician. Just about then the ward office started filling up with party regulars. 'What about these boys?' asked Mack. 'Hell,'...uh, excuse me Miss Caylor.'"

Lenore nodded.

"Anyway," he said, "Hinky Dink waved his arm and said, 'Why these boys are here for the game. We have our own Western Union wire.' And with that Mack gave up and joined them for the afternoon's game. 'Atta boy,' said Bathhouse John, 'you don't have to worry about the vote in Chicago anyway. We'll see to the election for you.'" Pulliam laughed heartily, and Lenore joined him.

"Sounds very much like Cincinnati politics," said Lenore.

"Or Tammany Hall," said Pulliam.

"Very colorful, they say."

"Yes. Unfortunately, the word 'colorful' is too often a euphemism for corrupt." Pulliam frowned. "It's the same in base ball."

The man sat on the El train watching the city speed by. He held his not-so-new brown bowler on his lap. The car was packed with fans, more crowding on at each stop. He was thankful that he and his brother had gotten on the train at Christopher Street, early enough in the uptown run to get a seat.

"This is it," said his brother.

The man with the brown bowler shifted in his seat and faced him. "What do you mean 'this is it'?"

His brother, a wiry man wearing a black suit and bowler, shrugged. "This is it. If the Giants don't beat the Cubs today they're out of it."

"But they'll only be a half game out. There's a week left. Anything can happen."

"Sure, sure. But I'm telling you that this is it. That's all I know. If they lose today, Chicago will take the pennant, sure as I'm your brother."

"What about the Pittsburghs?"

"Okay. I'll give you that. It will be either the Cubs or the Pirates, but not the Giants."

A man sitting in front of them turned. "Shut up, my friend. If you don't like the Giants keep it to yourself."

The brother leaned forward. "Listen, mac, I love the Giants more than you or anyone with a ticket for this game, or anyone without a ticket for that matter. I'm just being realistic about it. You think the Chicagos are going to lie down for McGraw's boys? They've won it two years in a row and they know how to do it again."

Several fans near them turned on the brother. "Shut up, you shit," said one.

"What kind of a rooter do you call yourself?" said the man in front of them.

"Let me give him a taste of a Giants rooter's left hook," said a third man.

"Now look what you done," said the man with the brown bowler. He waved his arms at the angry passengers. "It's all right. It's all right. He don't mean it. He lost a bet on the doubleheader yesterday, and he's a little mad, is all."

"Tell him he'll win his money back today and tell him to shut up or he'll have to get off this train at the next stop," said the man in front of them.

"And we'll help him off the train by sending him through the window and it might be between stations," said the other.

"And we'll send you out with him," said the third man.

The man with the brown bowler put his arm around his brother. "C'mon. Snap out of it. We'll win it all back today." He smiled up at the scowling passengers, who finally turned away. "Where are those seats now? I know they're good ones. Rube never lets us down."

His brother reached into his jacket and pulled out the two tickets. "Behind third base. Four rows up."

"There. You see? The best seats in the house for the biggest game of the year. What could be better?"

"The Giants could be better, that's what."

"Sure. They can always be better, can't they?" The man in the brown bowler sat back in his seat. "And today they'll be plenty good enough to beat the Chicagos."

He wished he believed it himself.

Henry and Maureen sat in their left-center-field bleacher seats, near the top, just to the left of the "Sam Thompson Pure Rye" billboard. The field looked to be miles away, but at least they could see over the heads of the throngs who stood behind the rope and spilled onto the field.

"It's the best I could do," said Henry.

"It's swell," replied Maureen.

"No place for a lady. Not no way."

"Still not as bad as Tenth Avenue can be, Henry. Calm down."

The Cubs ran out from the center field clubhouse and onto the field to warm up before the game. The fans stood and shouted at the visiting team.

"You scum, Evers!"

"I'll ram a bat up your arse, Chance!"

"Back to Chicago with you, you shits!"

"You cheaters! You thieves! You sonofabitch bastard cowards!"

Henry shook his head. "They're already drunk," he said.

"I love it," said Maureen.

Thomas stopped under El tracks next to the Polo Grounds. Fans packed the entire area, striding quickly back and forth in a jumble of dark suits, black hats, and clicking heels. The air was thick with cigar smoke and the excited voices of fans talking base ball. Pulliam opened the carriage door. "I'll have to get a ticket for Thomas here," he said, "and then we'll walk around the ball park to our seats." He closed the door and looked up at Thomas. "Wait here a minute, Thomas. I'm sure I can get you something."

Lenore remained inside the cab, watching the crowd. Pulliam returned quickly.

"We can get in through the office here, at the players' entrance." He reached up and handed something to Thomas. "Here you go. Not bad. Upper level behind the plate."

"Best seat I've ever had, sir. Thank you. No fare required today, sir."

"Of course we'll pay your fare, Thomas. And, we'll meet you here after the game."

"Yes, sir," said Thomas. "I'll be here."

Pulliam opened the carriage door and held out a hand to help Lenore. They made their way across the sidewalk and entered through a narrow gate. Pulliam nodded to a small man wearing a threadbare, black three-piece suit and a black bowler. "Thanks, Freddy."

"No problem, Mr. Pulliam," said the man. He bowed to Lenore. "Enjoy the game." He jammed the end of a short cigar between his teeth.

They made their way around the field through the crowd that had filled the area between the rope and the bleachers. As they turned at the left field corner she noticed piles of timber and the superstructure of an unfinished new section of bleachers. A few fans had climbed onto the bare beams to get a better view of the field.

"Mr. Brush works quickly," said Lenore. "I was here just ten days ago. I didn't notice any new seats being built."

"I'm glad to see this," said Pulliam nodding at the construction. "But it won't solve the problem of fans on the field." Lenore looked out and saw that with a quarter of an hour to go before the first pitch, fans had spilled into the outfield from behind the rope and were taking up at least ten feet between the seats and the foul line. "The pitchers will have to be on their best game today," he said. "Less room to catch foul flies, and any long fly ball will be a ground rule double."

Pulliam led Lenore through the crowd that had gathered between third base and home plate in foul territory. Spectators in the low boxes yelled at the fans on the field to sit or kneel so everyone could see. Pulliam opened a gate in the low grandstand fence. They walked up an aisle toward their box. Pulliam nodded to their left and said in a low voice, "The mayor." Then a little farther up he nodded to the right and whispered, "The archbishop." Lenore glanced where Pulliam gestured and saw a man in a black suit and ecclesiastic collar smoking a cigar and reading a newspaper. Two rows behind the archbishop sat a distinguished looking gentleman wearing a three-piece gray tweed suit and dark gray fedora, and a woman in a fluffy white dress and white hat flowing with feathers and lace and a large white gardenia.

"Florenz Ziegfeld and Anna Held," she said.

"Ah," said Pulliam. "The Cubs will have at least one rooter. He's from Chicago."

As they took their seats between home plate and third base Lenore removed her hat and placed it under her chair. "These are wonderful seats. I've never been so close," she said.

"Then you come to the ball park often?"

"Oh yes. I wasn't kidding." She opened her handbag and took out her scorebook.

"A true fan."

"A true Reds fan," she answered, "which means I will be neutral today."

"I'm sorry about the Cincinnatis."

She shrugged. "With a little luck they may only lose a hundred games this year."

"Don't worry. The Reds will have their day. The Cubs can't win forever. Nor can the Giants."

"Why not, Harry?" John Brush stood behind them, his hands on the back of the seat next to Pulliam. He stood awkwardly, stooped to one side, relying on the support of the chair to remain on his feet. His tan suit coat wrapped around his thin body like a small blanket. He wore a dark blue cravat of the old style, folded and fluffed under his vest, a pearl pin centered just under the knot. He slapped Pulliam on the back.

Pulliam grimaced and turned back to face the field.

"Mr. Brush," said Lenore. "Nice to see you again."

"Miss Caylor. You look beautiful today, Ollie's girl." Brush laughed and produced a handkerchief to wipe his mouth. "You two make a handsome couple, Harry. But you don't need to explain yourself to me. I see you here with a beautiful woman and I know there's no way there can be anything going on between you two."

Pulliam turned to confront Brush, but Lenore quickly spoke. "And who will Mr. McGraw send to the slab for your Giants today? Mr. Mathewson should be rested."

"Why, Miss Caylor," said Brush, turning to Lenore, "you sound like a base ball writer." He looked out at the field. "Well, we could have used Matty yesterday. Losing two to the Cubs made the race a little too close."

Pulliam said, "Less than a full game now. The Cubs could jump ahead of your Giants this afternoon."

"Matty will stop them."

"I'm sure it will be Pfiester for the Cubs today," said Lenore. "They call him the Giant Killer."

"So what?" said Brush? "Everybody has a bad day once in a while. Right, Harry? Today could be Pfiester's bad day." He leaned forward and whispered something into Pulliam's ear. Pulliam paled, his body tensing.

Brush tipped his hat and turned to leave. "Enjoy the game, Ollie's girl." He stepped out to the aisle and struggled up the steps, grasping seatbacks to pull himself along.

When he was out of earshot, Lenore turned to Pulliam, "Mr. Pulliam, I..."

"Miss Caylor, you already know that Mr. Brush and I agree on almost nothing. He seems to feel that I am in his way. He has an investment. He needs to make money. We all do." He paused and looked down at his hands. "Most of us understand that the public will not buy a product it doesn't trust." He turned to Lenore. "But if you showcase the skill of a Christy Mathewson, or the athletic elegance of a Tinker to Evers to Chance double play, the public will come back again and again." He sat up in his seat and straightened his tie. "Miss Caylor, the game could run a little late. Would you do me the honor of joining me for dinner tonight? Have you been to the Delmonico's at Forty-Fourth Street?"

"Mr. Pulliam?"

He frowned at her and then remembered. "Of course. New Year's Eve. I'm sorry. It's just that I don't associate the Miss Lenore Caylor I've come to know with the dancer I first saw in that ballroom."

"Well, I've never eaten there. If I may stop at home on our way downtown, I'd like to change into something more suitable."

John Heydler and George Dovey arrived breathlessly, running down the steps of the aisle. Dovey was shorter and stockier than Heydler, but sharply dressed in a brown suit with white linen vest. He wore a flat woolen cap that matched his suit.

Pulliam leaned toward Lenore and whispered, "Then it's settled."

"Just made it," said Dovey.

"Hello, George. John. How are things at the office?"

"Fine, sir, I hope. I left before you."

"So you did," said Pulliam. He twisted around in his seat to see Dovey. "And how are things in Boston? How are your Doves doing, George? You've met Miss Caylor I think?"

"Hello again, Miss Caylor." Dovey smiled at Lenore and nudged Pulliam. "Season's over for us, Harry. You know that. Don't rub it in."

"A pleasure to see you again, Mr. Dovey," said Lenore.

A boisterous cheer went up and the crowd stood as the Giants ran onto the field to take their positions.

"Looks like Buck Herzog at second today instead of Doyle," said Pulliam.

"And who's that at first base?" asked Dovey. "Where's Tenney?"

"That's not Tenney?" asked Heydler.

"Heck no," said Dovey. "And I should know Tenney when I see him. I was the idiot who traded him to the Giants just in time for him to have the best year of his career."

"He's been a top-notch leadoff man all season," said Pulliam.

"He's right at the top of the league for walks," said Heydler.

"Who's the kid?" asked Dovey.

"Not playing Tenney in a game as important as this?" said Heydler. "He must be near death or McGraw would send him out on crutches."

Lenore took a notebook out of her bag and flipped through its pages. "His substitute is Fred Merkle."

"Oh yeah," said Dovey. "Our scouts looked at him. Good strong kid."

"He's nineteen," said Lenore. "From Wisconsin. This is his first start."

"What a game to choose for the kid's first start," said Dovey.

On the field, umpire Hank O'Day stood behind the plate watching Christy Mathewson warm up, hoping for a lopsided game no matter who won. And with luck whoever was going to win would jump out to a big early lead. He had never seen a race this close, not just between two teams but among three, and with only a week to go. He didn't need the aggravation of McGraw or Chance or Evers or the twenty thousand misfits surrounding him in the stands and on the field, bitching and moaning over every call. If the Giants scored big right away, the fans would leave him alone and just keep drinking and celebrating all afternoon, harassing the Cubs and throwing their garbage at them instead of at him. If the Cubs went out in front by, say, half a dozen runs, then they'd find someone on the Giants to blame. Not Mathewson, of course, the sainted Big Six. The tall blond pitcher could commit no sin in their eyes. They should see him with a checkerboard and a pile of cash on the table after the game, he thought. As sick a gambler as he had ever met.

But if the score stayed close, they'd all point to some call he made as the reason their Giants didn't win, if they lost as they did twice yesterday. They wouldn't blame Bob Emslie, the other umpire for the series. Of all the umpires in the league he thought Emslie most qualified and almost as cantankerous as himself, a necessary quality for the job. They enjoyed hunting trips together between base ball seasons. But when he was behind the plate, O'Day preferred to call the game alone.

"Play ball!" he shouted, and pulled on his mask.

By the fifth inning, Maureen was completely confused, but not by the game, which she appreciated as a tight pitchers' duel between the Giants' Christy Mathewson and the Cubs' Jack Pfiester. What she didn't understand was all the chatter among the fans in her section, and the constant passing of money back and forth.

A man with blue tie and black bowler stood and proclaimed, "Six to five nobody reaches. What do you say? I got a buck."

"Henry, what are they gabbing on about?" she asked. "I've been watching and listening to them all day and still don't get it."

"They're betting," said Henry.

"I kind of figured that, but on what?"

"On everything." He listened as the standing man repeated his offer. "He's looking for a bet, or a lot of bets, to cover his dollar that no Cubs get on base this inning—that nobody 'reaches,' know what I mean?"

"Okay, but what are the numbers?"

A voice came from a few seats to their right. "I'll take two bits."

Henry jerked his thumb in the direction of the voice. "This boy over here agrees to bet, but only for a quarter. The six to five means the drunk will pay thirty cents to the other guy's twenty-five. Know what I mean?"

"So then if someone takes fifty cents of the man's dollar, he wins sixty cents?"

"That's it."

Another man shouted, "I've got two bucks that say nothing out of the infield this half. Two to one."

Henry looked in the direction of the shout. "That guy is betting that the Cubs won't hit the ball past the infield this inning."

"I'll take that," said a man sitting next to Maureen. She turned to look at him. "That's an easy one," he said to her. "Guy must be drunk, or nuts. Chance is due up and he's had Matty's number all year."

"Can I get a piece of that?" came another shout from several rows down.

"I want half a buck of that," said another.

"You got it."

"Even money somebody fans," said another.

"I got you for two bits."

"I'll take another two bits."

Maureen thought for a moment. Henry watched her. "Get it?" he asked.

"I think so," she said and stood up. "I want fifty cents of that dollar."

The crowd in the immediate vicinity turned to see the woman who joined the gamers.

"What are you doing?" Henry reached up and tried to pull her back down onto the bleacher bench.

The drunk laughed. "Too late, my boy. Your lady has a piece of me now."

A voice from below him bellowed, "I'd like a piece of her instead." The crowd of men snickered and roared in agreement.

"We have to leave, Maureen. This is getting out of control."

"Not on your life. I have fifty cents riding on this inning."

"But I don't have fifty cents to cover it."

"I do." She folded her arms and sat.

Frank Chance stood in the batter's box. The man next to Maureen nudged her. "Here we go, miss. Chance is going to make us both a couple of dimes." She watched anxiously as Chance swung and connected, sending the ball over the second baseman's head for a hit. She jumped up and down, cheering. Henry covered his face in his hands. The man on the other side of her pulled on her dress. "Uh, missy. I'm as happy as you that we're a few cents richer, but it won't do to cheer about it, especially since it's the Chicagos what got the hit." He pointed to the field. The ball had rolled through the outfield to the ropes where Turkey Mike Donlin made a vain attempt to retrieve it from the midst of the crowd on the outfield grass. Chance was past second. He rounded third and raced for home, scoring the first run of the game.

"You jinxed us, Maureen," said Henry. "If you gotta bet, don't bet against the Giants."

"See that?" said the man's brother. "Told you, didn't I? The Giants are falling apart."

"It's only the fifth inning," said the man in the brown bowler. "The Giants got five more at bats, if they need five. It's only one to nothing. Shut up and watch the game. You never had better seats, and at a better game, am I right? Big Six's fadeaway is working like a charm."

"Big Six's fadeaway didn't fade so much against Chance, did it?"

The man in the brown bowler cuffed his brother's shoulder. "What's the matter with you? Chance didn't hit Mathewson's fadeaway, he hit a straight pitch that got too much of the plate." He reached in his pocket and took out a pint bottle. "Here. Have another snort."

Maureen sat quietly for another inning, saying nothing to Henry because she had nothing to say that wouldn't make him mad. She wasn't quite sure why he was so upset with her for winning the bet, but she knew that she was mad at him for being such a bore on such a fun afternoon. By the bottom of the sixth inning, she was about to say something to him about it, but before she could speak the drunk with the six-to-five odds stood and pointed at her.

"Little lady, little lady," said the drunk. "You gotta give us a chance to win back some of our money."

"Shut up, buddy," said Henry. "She'll do no such thing."

The drunk scowled. "Is that a fact? Well, I'll show you no such thing!" He started clawing over fans between them. Henry stood ready to have at him, but he got no farther than two rows closer when another fan stopped him.

"It's too early for a fight, isn't it?" said the fan. "You'll have plenty of time later, and I'll be happy to take either side, but it's only the sixth and you don't want to be arrested and miss the rest of the game, do you?"

Maureen pulled on Henry's coat. "Henry, sit down," she said. "The man's right, after all. I can't just take their money and smile and go home, can I?" She stood. "All right, my man. Double or nothing that the Giants..." She thought a moment. She couldn't make a game bet that the Giants would win because that would force the drunk to cheer for the Cubs for the rest of the game. He wouldn't take that bet. The Cubs' pitcher Pfiester looked good, too, so she didn't want to bet on the Giants taking the lead any time soon, either.

"Please, Maureen," said Henry. "This can only lead to more trouble."

"Double or nothing that the Giants at least tie the game by the end of the seventh."

"You mean," said the drunk, extricating himself from the grasp of the other fan, "that we have to wait until the seventh inning for your bet to play out? What kind of a wager is that?"

"A dame's wager," someone shouted.

The drunk stared at her, wobbling as he stood. "A dame's wager? Well that's fine then. I will oblige the lady and accept her challenge." The crowd cheered. "Now, I've got even money that says the Giants reach in the sixth. Who's in?"

The wagers continued as a Cub error put Herzog on second base. Maureen cheered loudly as the runner took third on a sacrifice. Then Turkey Mike Donlin stepped up to the plate and even Henry got back into the excitement of the game. He didn't want Maureen to know it, but he was praying that she would win this bet, too. Every dime helped their wedding budget.

Lenore wondered if Mabel Hite was at the game. She felt bad for her and Mike Donlin when Frank Chance scored in the fifth. The fans let

Donlin know that maybe he should have reached for the ball with his mitt instead of trying to stop it with his foot. And now he was up to bat with perhaps the game and the entire season hanging in the balance.

Pfiester looked at Herzog on third base and looked back at Cubs' catcher Johnny Kling. He set himself and delivered a fastball. Donlin made contact with a sharp crack of the bat. The fans jumped to their feet as the ball lined over Johnny Evers into right center field for a base hit. Herzog trotted home with the tying run.

"That's it!" cheered Pulliam, making Lenore wonder for a moment if he weren't indeed rooting for the Giants. "This is the heart of base ball. A struggle between two great pitchers and a game tied with a sacrifice and a clean base hit. The inside game. Look around! The fans are enthralled. They have completely lost themselves."

"If the Giants don't win they won't be so enthralled," said Dovey. "They'll turn real ugly real fast."

By the top of the ninth O'Day was depressed, his worst fears realized. A one-to-one tie with an inning to play. And Emslie had botched a play at second base. Luckily it had done no damage, but the Cubs were in a foul temper, especially Evers, the unholy bastard of base ball. O'Day hated Evers more than McGraw. The Giants' manager complained about this and that, swore and threatened, and kicked a lot and mostly made an ass of himself. But Evers? The wiry, scheming little shit was always looking for new ways to humiliate the umpires. And there he stood, just to the right of second base, not watching the batter, or the pitcher, but staring at him, O'Day, challenging him with every spew of tobacco juice to make a wrong call against the Cubs.

The fans were now completely drunk. He prayed for a quick and decisive resolution of the game.

Harry Pulliam hoped for the game to go one way or the other in the ninth, too. The days grew short in late September. There wouldn't be enough light left for more than a couple extra innings.

The man wearing the brown bowler was sick of his brother who sounded more like a Chicago rooter with his negative comments. A tie game, for Christ's sake, with the Giants at home and Big Six at the slab. Everything was in their favor. Have another belt of rye.

When the Cubs failed to score in the top of the ninth, the drunk stood and looked at Maureen. "You got a pile of my money, lady. What do you say to one more play?"

Henry had given up trying to control her. He looked the other way as she replied, "Double or nothing on everything I've won from you that the Giants win it in the ninth."

"Then I pray to Jesus, Mary, and Joseph and all the angels and saints in Heaven above that they wait until the tenth to do it. You have a bet."

Johnny Evers stood at his position to the right field side of second base worrying about Cubs pitcher Jack Pfiester. By the seventh inning he had developed a lump on his pitching arm the size of his thumb. It looked as if the muscles, ligaments, and tendons of his forearm had tied themselves into one big knot. But Pfiester convinced Chance that he could handle the Giants with fastballs by mixing up his angle of delivery. It was the curve that hurt, he claimed, and he would only throw curves to Turkey Mike Donlin whom he couldn't get out with a fastball. Chance didn't like it, but with catcher Johnny Kling's heated assurance, he left him in the game.

At the end of the eighth, Pfiester was in so much pain that Tinker had to help him off the mound. They tried to disguise it, but Evers could see it.

"You want to give it to the fucking New Yorkers?" he screamed at Chance on the bench. "Why don't you just walk over there and tell McGraw he can have the game and kiss his big fat ass while you're at it."

"Step over here a minute, Johnny," said Chance. "I'd like to properly convince you to mind your own fucking business." He balled his two fists and stood.

"Fine," said Evers. "You keep Miner on the bench and risk the whole season on this boy's arm that has a growth on it the size of a base ball."

"Shut up, you fucking weasel," shouted Tinker. He lunged at Evers but Kling came between them.

"Jesus," said Kling. "We have a game to win. There's a week to go in the damn season. Then the two of you can kill each other as far as I'm concerned."

Chance stared at Evers. "Jack stays in," he said.

Evers spat a long stream of tobacco juice and looked out at the field.

In the bottom of the ninth, the score tied, Pfiester would have to keep the ball on the ground in spite of the fact that he could throw no low curves. "Angle Seymour low and outside," Evers told him. "We'll play him around to right instead of guarding against the pulled ball. We'll play the others as they come, but we need to keep it down and away."

He watched and marveled at Pfiester's determination. He reared back and placed the straight balls right where he wanted. Sure enough, Cy Seymour obliged by grounding out sharply to Evers himself. But Jack missed his spot with Devlin who singled, putting the winning run on first base with one out. Both balls had been hit well.

Evers looked at Chance who took his position at the first base bag holding Devlin close. *Why wasn't he doing anything about Pfiester? No one's warming up. What's he thinking? This ain't April. It's the last week of September, for God's sake.* Not that Chance would be able to hear anything he said to him anyway. The crowd noise had become deafening.

Moose McCormick stepped up to the plate. Chance signaled to catcher Kling who relayed the sign back to Pfiester. They would pitch him like Seymour and go for a double play to end the inning. *Now you're using your brain, oh Peerless Leader,* thought Evers. *One pitch, Jack, that's all. Put that one pitch where Moose will fish for it and send it on the ground to me.*

And he did. McCormick swung and hit the second hard ground ball of the inning to Evers. He scooped it up and tossed it to Joe Tinker for the force on Devlin, and Tinker no sooner had the ball than he pulled back to relay it to Chance at first. But it didn't feel right to Evers. It wasn't smooth. Was it his fielding of the ball or his throw to second or maybe Tinker's digging the throw out of his mitt to send it to Chance at first? He didn't know for sure, but the result was that Moose McCormick stood safe at first base instead of the second out of a double play, and the third out of the inning.

The crowd, which had groaned at the sight of McCormick's ground ball, now stood cheering wildly. Evers knew that the game was as good as lost. That pitch to McCormick was all Pfiester had left.

The rookie Merkle came up to bat. To Evers it didn't matter if it was Merkle or a twelve-year-old kid swinging a broom handle or Honus Wagner himself at the plate. Pfiester had nothing. And sure enough the kid lined a hit to right field. Evers watched helplessly as McCormick rounded second for third. He was surprised that Merkle didn't extend his single into a double. The ball went far enough down the line, and the Cubs would not have risked a play at second base for fear of McCormick scoring the winning run on the throw.

Evers returned to his position waiting for the inevitable. But then, something about the situation looked familiar to him. He glanced at Chance, who replied with a shallow nod. He looked at the outfielders. The three fielders gestured their understanding by lifting a mitt, pulling on the bill of a cap, or spitting.

The entire Cub team tensed. They all knew that the batter, Al Bridwell, would connect. Pfiester was lobbing balloons up to the plate.

Johnny Evers stared down at umpire Hank O'Day.

O'Day wanted to throw up. He stood behind the Cubs' catcher watching Evers. He knew what he was thinking. And he knew that Evers knew that he knew. They had been there together before, not three weeks ago in Pittsburgh. Two out. Winning run on third base. Some rookie kid standing on first base, happy as can be that he just delivered a key hit in a clutch situation and oblivious to what a sonofabitch like Evers might be thinking.

He wanted to call time and tell McGraw to make sure the poor kid knew about Gill and Evers and Pittsburgh and Rule 59. He wanted to call time and tell goddamn Frank Chance to get a pitcher in there who could throw the ball. If Pfiester couldn't get Merkle out, he sure wasn't going to get Bridwell.

Merkle took a big leadoff. O'Day waited as Bridwell stepped out of the batter's box and glared at Merkle, telling him with a violent nod to get the hell back to the bag. Why risk getting picked off for the third out when his run didn't matter?

"C'mon, batter," said O'Day. "It's getting dark."

Bridwell turned sharply and scowled at him in reply, but stepped back in.

O'Day watched Pfiester's fastball float in looking as big as a barge and just about as slow. Bridwell had no trouble getting all of it and sending it over Evers's head into right center field for a hit. As Bridwell trotted to first, and McCormick danced home with the winning run, arms waving wildly over his head, and as the crowd, in a frenzy of anticipation, exploded into delirium and rushed onto the field in celebration, O'Day stared out at the base path between first and second base, watching Fred Merkle. He knew that Evers was doing the exact same thing.

Harry Pulliam jumped to his feet before anyone else. "That's it!" he cried. "That's how the game is played." He watched as celebrating fans stormed the field even before McCormick crossed the plate with the winning run. Lenore, Heydler, and Dovey laughed and cheered at the exciting finish.

"What a game," cried Lenore. She turned to Pulliam. She would have embraced him, but when she looked at him she saw his exhilaration fade. He didn't move a muscle, nor did his expression change, but suddenly a broad smile became a grimace. She tried to follow his gaze onto the field but saw only celebrating, inebriated fans swirling in a chaotic victory dance around the infield. He stepped to his right into the aisle, his eyes fixed, and walked mechanically to the gate that opened onto the field. Lenore followed.

"Mr. Pulliam," she said. "What's wrong?"

"Pittsburgh," he said, and looked at her. Then he turned and looked for Heydler. "John! Get Miss Caylor out of here!" he shouted.

From somewhere behind her she heard Heydler's voice. "Certainly. Yes, sir." She didn't want to go, but Heydler pulled her up the aisle away from Pulliam.

"Pulliam!" The familiar voice stood out even among the screaming fans. She turned and saw John Brush fighting through the crowd, making his way down the aisle by hopping from step to step, grabbing the backs of seats, and then letting himself free-fall to the next row. "Pulliam! Pulliam, you sonofabitch! If this shows up in your office you better call it just like Pittsburgh! You hear me, Pulliam?"

Brush stumbled. Heydler released his grip on Lenore and jumped over rows of seats to come to Brush's aid. Dovey followed. They helped him back to his feet and guided him to a seat away from the aisle.

"Mr. Brush, come on," said Heydler. "You can't go down there."

Brush shook them off. "Pulliam! Listen to me you sissy bastard! Pulliam! This game is over, Pulliam! Fuck that prick Evers! Listen to me, Pulliam!"

Lenore looked back at Pulliam. He didn't seem to hear Brush as he stepped onto the field. She stood alone in the aisle just above him. Heydler and Dovey were preoccupied trying to protect Brush and paid no further attention to her. She stepped down to the gate and followed Pulliam.

Brush grabbed the lapels of Heydler's coat. "You see those seats I'm building, Heydler?" He pointed to the unfinished grandstands beyond third base. "They are for the goddamn World's Series. And I mean the World's Series of 1908. I don't intend to wait until next year to fill them. You hear me, Heydler?" He released Heydler's coat. His face red and his mouth sprinkled with spittle, he watched as Pulliam made his way through the mob on the field. "I mean to have those seats return my money this year. Tell your boss that if he does anything to hurt my investment I'll hang his lily-white Kentucky ass from the upper deck." He leaned forward, shouting at the field. "You hear that, Pulliam? You won't be able to walk the streets in this town when I get through with you! You hear me, Pulliam? I'll run you out of here so fast. I'll ship you back to Louisville, you and your downtown sweetheart!" He lost his voice, coughing uncontrollably, and fell back into a seat, gagging and spitting on himself. Heydler and Dovey helped him back onto his feet and up the aisle steps.

The man in the brown bowler and his brother made their way into shallow left field. They shouted and hugged and slapped the backs of any and all Giants fans within their reach.

"I told you I told you I told you," yelled the man in the brown bowler at his brother. He tilted his head back and shouted, "Giants!" as loud as he could. That's when he saw the ball flying toward him, silhouetted black against the light gray evening sky. He could see that its arc would take it directly over his head, within reach. He lifted his hands, cupped them, and caught the ball, feeling its rough leather hide hitting his palms. He brought it back down and inspected it, rolling it in his hand and noting the yellow-green grass stains, the worn red stitches, and the gnashes and dents inflicted by Chicago and New York bats.

"Is that...?" said his brother, gasping. "Sweet Jesus you have the game ball."

"I think I do," said the man. He looked up as if searching for the source of this glorious gift, for someone to thank. Instead he saw three Cubs pushing and punching their way through the crowd, heading straight for him.

Cub first baseman and manager Frank Chance quickly hooked his mitt onto his belt. This was going to be a bad one, he knew. Giants fanatics surrounded him. Their mood was on the edge between euphoria and drunken dementia. So far they tolerated the Cubs' continued presence on the field, but if they took the time to notice Johnny Evers at second base, and notice that umpire Hank O'Day stood at the top of the pitcher's mound watching him, there would be a riot. He watched as the ball sailed in from center, over Evers' head. "Shit," he said to no one.

The clubhouse in center field looked a mile away, blocked by thousands of Giants fans dancing and pushing and howling. Several surrounded Fred Merkle, patting him on the back and shaking his hand. He hadn't made it too far from where he had turned off the base path between first and second.

Chance stood at the edge of the infield when he felt the first shove from behind. He turned and instinctively took a pugilist's stance, balancing right and left legs. He looked into the enraged, bloodshot eyes of a large man who had spilled some sticky liquid down the front of his tie and vest. He wore a black bowler missing a section of its brim as if someone had taken a bite out of it. The man pulled back his right shoulder and cocked his elbow as he balled his hand into a fist. Chance didn't wait to find out if he was serious about swinging at him. He raised his own right fist to protect his chin as he shot his left out in a jab that caught the fan in the jaw, snapping his head around over his right shoulder and sending a foul stream of saliva, blood, and beer through the air. The man stumbled backward and tripped. When other fans in the immediate area realized what had happened, they charged Chance. Backing up, he lashed out with jab after jab, feeling the crunch of bone, the giving way of teeth, and the tearing of the skin over his own knuckles. But he knew that he could not keep the mob at bay for long.

He glanced at second again and saw the ball arcing toward Evers from somewhere near third. Satisfied, he began to fight his way through the outfield toward the clubhouse.

Lenore reached the field and paused near the third base line, searching for Pulliam in the swarming chaos. She finally saw him in the infield struggling with a large man in a long gray coat. The fan knocked Pulliam's hat off his head. He turned to retrieve it and saw Lenore. Alarmed, he fought his way back across the infield toward her.

"Miss Caylor, what are you doing? You have to—" A fan pushed him from behind. He fell into her shoulder. She reached around his back and pulled him close to her as they tumbled to the ground.

As fans rushed the field from the bleachers, the drunk slowly pushed his way up the aisle to where Henry and Maureen waited. "You married to her?" he asked Henry. "Because if you're not, I'll marry her." He reached into his pocket, took out a fistful of coins and counted out Maureen's winnings.

"We're engaged," said Henry.

The drunk shook his head. "Too bad," he said, handing the money to Maureen. "We could rule the Polo Grounds, the two of us. And when the Giants are on the road, we'd rule Hilltop Park. Or Washington Park in Brooklyn. With your luck and my savvy?" He shook his head again.

"Thank you very much," said Maureen.

"My pleasure," said the drunk. "Can you buy me a drink? I'd offer to pay for it myself but I'm a little short."

"Uh, we'd like to," said Henry, "but I've got to get back to the firehouse. My shift starts pretty soon."

"Fireman, eh? A noble profession. Noble profession." He looked out onto the chaos on the field. "Well, if the Giants keep this up, I'll have the World's Series to make up my losses. Goodbye and good luck to you both, although you," he bowed to Maureen, "need no luck."

"Goodbye," said Maureen. The man made his way down the aisle, mumbling to himself and swaying from side to side. "She bets on Chicago, she wins. She bets on the Giants, she wins. No justice."

Pulliam pushed himself up and helped Lenore stand. He pulled her close to protect her. Looking around, not knowing which way to turn, he saw a phalanx of police working their way toward the clubhouse, billy clubs swinging, several Cubs and both umpires following in the protection of their flying wedge. "Lenore, are you all right?" he asked, his lips less than an inch from her ear.

"Yes, I'm fine."

"Come on. This way." Holding Lenore around her shoulders, he pushed through the mob to the protection of the police. They fell in with the players and umpires and stumbled toward the clubhouse.

Johnny Evers made his way through center field in the first line behind the police. He held his flabby, brown-leather mitt on his head as protection against the debris that rained on him from outside the police lines. He grasped the ball against his chest. He looked to his right and saw O'Day.

"You saw the play, Hank," he shouted, showing the umpire the ball. "I know you did. The kid is out at second."

"Shut up, Evers. I don't need no help from you."

Evers jammed the ball deep into his mitt's pocket and sprinted for the clubhouse in center field. Head down, he pushed fans out of his way with his free hand, ignoring the oaths and threats and knocking men and boys over before they could see that a Cub was among them.

As Pulliam led Lenore into the Cubs' clubhouse she knew that she had entered a realm normally forbidden to women. The odor of male sweat mingled with stale tobacco, clogged urinals, and mildew. The locker room was a barren space of brick walls with rows of narrow, shallow wooden dressing stalls hung with the players' street clothes. Crude benches ran the length of the stalls a couple of feet out. Some players sat on the benches, but most remained standing.

The crowd outside grew louder.

Frank Chance took off his cap, wiped his brow, and looked at Pulliam and Lenore. "Not often we have the pleasure of a lady in the clubhouse," he said. "Maybe never. Sorry about the disturbance out there, ma'am."

Pulliam glanced at Lenore and then at Chance. "Miss Lenore Caylor, allow me to introduce Mr. Frank Chance, manager and first baseman for the Chicago Cubs. Mr. Chance, this is Miss Lenore Caylor, league stenographer."

"A pleasure to see you again, ma'am. We met during the league meetings in February. I hope you didn't get hurt out there."

"Thank you, Mr. Chance. I'm all right."

Pulliam looked around the locker room. "I thought the umpires were with us. Where can we find them?"

"Their dressing room is down the hall and around under the grandstand," said Chance, gesturing to a door at the other end of the room. "But there ain't no question about this one, Mr. Pulliam. O'Day saw everything."

"Please come with me, Miss Caylor." Pulliam began to make his way through the players, clearing a path for Lenore as he went. When he came to the end of a bench near the door, Johnny Evers, sitting with his cap on his lap, reached up with a dirty, grass-stained hand and grabbed Pulliam's forearm, stopping him.

"You listen to Frank, Mr. Pulliam," said Evers. He spat tobacco juice on the floor. "O'Day saw the play. This ain't like Pittsburgh."

"I'll talk to Mr. O'Day about that, Mr. Evers," said Pulliam, pulling his arm free.

Cubs president Charles Murphy approached. "And that ain't all, Harry," he said. "The Giants couldn't make the field playable, so we couldn't go on to the tenth inning. Therefore the Giants forfeit. And they owe us money as a penalty for that forfeit."

"There's your real issue," said Evers. "There's money to be had and ol' Chubby just can't resist the chance to pick somebody's pocket. You can be damn sure none of us will ever see any of that money." Murphy glared at Evers. Evers stared him down and spat again.

"Thank you, Mr. Murphy," said Pulliam. "I will, as I said, discuss this with the umpires." Pulliam took Lenore's arm and led her toward the door.

"Evers," said Murphy, "as soon as the lady is gone, let me tell you what I really think of you."

"Don't bother," replied Evers. "I already know." He stood and pushed past Murphy.

Pulliam and Lenore walked down a dimly lit hall and out a side door that opened to a walkway under the bleachers. At the right field corner they turned right and continued under the grandstand until they came to a weathered blue door with the word "UMPIRES" stenciled in fading black paint. Pulliam knocked and then quickly opened it.

Hank O'Day and Bob Emslie sat on a bench in a small room with a few hooks nailed to the plain walls. They looked up and, surprised, quickly stood.

"Mr. O'Day, Mr. Emslie," said Pulliam, "this is Miss Lenore Caylor, league stenographer. I'll be brief. How did you call the play, Mr. Emslie?"

"You asking how I called the last play?" asked Emslie.

"That's right. The Cubs claim they forced Merkle at second, nullifying the last run. The Giants will claim the run counts. You were the field umpire. How did you call the play?"

"I thought the game was over."

"Then you saw Merkle touch second?"

"I didn't say that. Based on what I saw, I assumed the game was over. Bridwell got the hit. McCormick crossed the plate."

Pulliam protested, "But you just said—"

"Excuse me, Mr. Pulliam. I know what I said. I didn't see Evers catch the ball and force Merkle at second. The hit came straight at my head so I had to hit the ground to avoid the ball. I heard about all that just now from Hank. He's the one you want to talk to. Not me."

The room fell quiet. The two umpires sat.

"Mr. O'Day?" said Pulliam.

O'Day pulled a stained rag out of his jacket and wiped his forehead and neck. "I saw the play," he said as he carefully folded the rag and put it back in his pocket. "The rule says if a runner is forced for the third out, the inning is over and no run can score."

"Where was Merkle?" asked Pulliam.

"I don't know. I didn't see him after he stopped between first and second and lit out for the clubhouse. He sure didn't touch second base. I saw Evers standing there but no Merkle."

O'Day paused, brought the rag back out, and repeated his ritual of wiping his forehead and neck. He took a deep breath and looked back up at Pulliam.

"If the Giants complain that we didn't call the play on the field," he said, "I say that their fans wouldn't let us. Would you, Mr. Pulliam, in the face of that mob who just a minute before believed that their team had as much as clinched the pennant, would you raise your arm and make that call?"

"What is your call, Mr. O'Day?"

O'Day sat up straight. "It's not my call to make," he said. "Bob here was the field umpire. It's up to him to make the call."

"But," said Pulliam, "he did not see the play. This is Pittsburgh all over again. We will have to go with the call on the field that the run scored and the game was over. The Giants win."

O'Day stared at Pulliam. "I never called McCormick safe at home."

Pulliam put his hand on his forehead and squeezed the front of his skull. "Then," he said, "you and Mr. Emslie have discussed the play, am I right?"

"Yes," said O'Day.

"What is your call?"

"Based on my consultation with Mr. O'Day," said Emslie, "Merkle is out at second."

"The run from third," said O'Day, "does not count. The game could not be resumed. The score is tied one to one. The rest," he said, looking from Lenore to Pulliam, "is up to you, Mr. Pulliam."

Outside a bottle shattered on pavement. The walls and floor vibrated as an El train rumbled overhead.

"I'll want your statements tonight," said Pulliam. "I live at the New York Athletic Club. Meet me there at..." He took his watch out of his vest pocket and opened it.

"Tonight?" asked Emslie. "I've got a dinner engagement."

"So do I, Mr. Emslie," said Pulliam. "We'll both have to break them, won't we?" Lenore looked at Pulliam, but quickly turned away. "Nine thirty. Do you know where the New York Athletic Club is located?"

"I know it," said O'Day. "We'll be there."

Pulliam closed his watch and tucked it into his vest pocket. "Now," he said, "how do we get to the Giants' clubhouse?"

"Center field," said O'Day. "You'll hear them."

Pulliam gently took Lenore's elbow and led her out. They returned to the area behind center field where Pulliam knocked on another blue door. Upbeat male voices, laughing and talking loudly, could be heard on the other side.

The door opened. Lenore recognized Freddy, the Giants' ticket manager, holding the doorknob, blocking the view inside the Giants' clubhouse. He had shed his jacket. A yellowing shirttail hung down under his vest. He smoked a short black cigar.

"Why it's Mr. Pulliam," he said. "And the lady. What can I do for you two? I'd invite you in but some of the boys ain't exactly decent, if you know what I mean."

"Is Mr. Brush here, Freddy?" asked Pulliam.

"He ain't."

"Then I'll talk to McGraw."

Freddy nodded once, turned, and shouted. "Hey, McGraw! You got visitors!" He smiled as the Giants' manager approached behind him. Lenore was surprised at how short and stocky McGraw looked up close. He wore his rumpled Giants uniform, but was hatless, his graying hair pushed back and up and sticking out in different directions. He frowned when he saw Pulliam.

"Well, well," he sneered. "It's the boy president. What do you want?"

"Please come out into the hall."

"What's this horseshit?" McGraw stepped out of the clubhouse and pulled the door closed. He noticed Lenore and gave her a quick head-to-toe inspection. "Who's she? What's she doing here?"

"Mr. McGraw," said Pulliam, ignoring his question, "I'm here to inform you that umpire Emslie called Merkle out at second base. McCormick's run in the bottom of the ninth inning..."

McGraw's eyes widened. "What the—"

"...did not count."

"Like hell," shouted McGraw, his face turning red. He took a threatening step toward Pulliam.

"The game could not be resumed," continued Pulliam, not flinching.

"Resumed? The goddamn game is over."

"The game is therefore ruled a tie. I assume the Giants will file a protest."

"I'm protesting right now."

"Please tell Mr. Brush that I'll see him, you, and Mr. Merkle in my office at 8:30 tomorrow morning."

"You listen to me, pretty boy. Nobody is stealing this game from my Giants. You got that? And I ain't going all the way downtown at 8:30 in the morning for more of your horsecrap."

"I will see you in my office tomorrow. I'm sorry for the inconvenience. I'm sure it will be no problem for Mr. Brush." Pulliam took Lenore's arm. They turned to go back down the hall toward the Cubs' clubhouse.

"Don't you walk away from me, Pulliam," McGraw yelled at their backs. "I know all about Pittsburgh, and I know what that sonofabitch Evers is up to. It didn't work there and it won't work here."

Pulliam paused and looked back at McGraw. "If you knew about Pittsburgh, Mr. McGraw, then perhaps you would have better served your team by warning your rookie Merkle what that sonofabitch Evers might be up to if the same thing happened here."

McGraw stormed back into the clubhouse and slammed the door. Pulliam and Lenore continued down the hall. They arrived back at the Cubs' clubhouse. Pulliam pushed the door open and held it for Lenore. She hesitated for a moment, wondering about the possible state of undress of some of the players, but then walked in. Murphy and Chance sat on a bench between the rows of stalls hung with street clothes. They stood when they saw Lenore and Pulliam enter.

Chance spoke first, holding an arm out in front of Murphy indicating that he should wait his turn. "What's the ruling, Mr. Pulliam?" he said in a low voice, almost whispering. The rest of the clubhouse grew silent, the muted shouts and oaths of the crowd outside providing a low, ominous background hum.

Pulliam looked around the room at the expectant players. "Merkle is out at second," he said. The clubhouse erupted in throaty cheers and shrill whistles. Some players clapped, others snapped towels or pounded the walls of their locker stalls. Solly Hofman slapped Evers on the back. "But the Giants will protest," said Pulliam over the din. "The incident must be investigated through the proper channels."

Murphy shouldered Chance aside and approached Pulliam. "Not good enough, Pulliam," he said.

A window shattered, its glass shards spraying into the room. The players scattered, ducking and raising their arms to protect their heads. The crowd outside could now be heard clearly through the broken window.

"Sounds like the word is out," said Chance.

Pulliam turned and looked at Lenore. "Miss Caylor, we need to leave at once. Thomas is waiting with our carriage."

"If you can get out alive," said Chance.

"What about the police?"

Johnny Evers spit loudly. "Shit. Police? I got hit more by them cops than by any fans. Excuse the language, miss."

Murphy stepped to within a foot of Pulliam. "Now just a minute, Harry," he said. "We've got a few things to settle here."

Pulliam's eyes flared. "Mr. Murphy, I'm not about to listen to you complain about a game that was handed to you as a gift. Be in my office tomorrow at nine. You can speak your mind then. I'll want to talk to Tinker, Evers, and Chance, too."

Murphy stared at him without blinking. He reached into his inside jacket pocket and took out a long cigar, bit the end off, and spit it on the floor at Pulliam's feet. "We'll be there at nine," he said, grinding his teeth and barely moving his lips.

Joe Tinker entered the row of stalls. He was smartly dressed in a well-tailored, light brown suit with dark brown vest and mustard-yellow tie with a diamond pin. He wore a deep brown fedora with a crease through the middle of the crown. He nodded at Frank Chance.

"Well, Mr. Pulliam," said Chance, "it's like this. Usually we leave together, so the fans know we're ball players. But if we leave one at a time in our street clothes?"

Murphy scoffed. "They're not that stupid. They'll see you leave through the players' entrance and know who you are."

"Not if we leave through the office," said Chance. "Then it's a short walk to the El station." He turned to Tinker. "How about it, Joe? You game?"

Tinker reached into a coat pocket and pulled out a revolver. He flipped open the cylinder to make sure it was loaded, snapped it back in place, and nodded. "You're the boss. I'm ready."

"Mr. Tinker," said Pulliam, "there can be no violence."

"Excuse me, Mr. Pulliam," interrupted Chance, "but it seems to me that there's already been plenty of violence."

"And," said Tinker, "I carry this gun legally. Ain't nothing to do with base ball at all, and once I walk out that door, you got no say over me. Now, do you want me to help all of you get the hell out of here in one piece or not?"

Pulliam looked from Chance to Tinker to Lenore.

"And what about us?" All eyes in the room shifted to the door where Hank O'Day stood with Bob Emslie. "We aren't about to win any popularity contests out there," said O'Day. "And we come to the game in our uniforms. We have no street clothes to change into. They'll spot us in a second."

"What are you doing in here?" said Murphy.

"We couldn't exactly ask the Giants for protection, now could we, Chubby?" answered O'Day.

"All right," said Pulliam. "We can fit four in our carriage."

"Thank you. Wouldn't do to be seen with Cubs anyway," said O'Day. "No offense, boys."

"None taken," said Chance. "I don't like to be seen with Cubs neither."

Evers spit. Several players laughed. Pulliam turned to Chance and nodded. Chance led Tinker, Pulliam, Lenore, O'Day, and Emslie out of the locker room and into the hallway. They walked single file to a door half way to the Giants' clubhouse. Chance turned the doorknob. They entered a small office with two wooden desks at either end. The door to the street had a four-paned window with a stained yellow shade not quite completely rolled up at its top. Dim, blue-gray evening light provided the only illumination in the office. The crowd noise had diminished. Few pedestrians were visible on the street just outside.

"Looks like they're still waiting for us at the players' entrance," said Chance.

Tinker walked purposefully to the door and slowly opened it. He looked both ways, stepped outside, and strolled toward the El station. Dozens of fans continued to mill around the players' gate ten yards away. Police on foot kept the crowd contained by selective prodding with billy clubs, helped by a dozen mounted police guarding the perimeter. More fans hurried toward the mob, bottles in hand, anxious to be part of the excitement, loudly cursing the Cubs and the umpires.

They passed Tinker without noticing him. He disappeared into the crowd filing toward the El station.

"That sonofabitch Tinker." Evers had followed the group into the office and had watched Tinker's progress. "Guess I'll change and be on my way."

"Mr. Pulliam," said Chance, "I think you and Miss Caylor will be safe. Just stroll out of here like you're a happily married couple without a care in the world. Nobody's gonna bother you."

Pulliam looked at O'Day. "You two wait here. We'll get the carriage and pull up to the door."

"What about me?" said Murphy, appearing at the door to the hallway. "I don't wear a uniform. They're going to know me."

"Don't flatter yourself, Chubby," said Evers. "And you're blocking the door. Let me through." Murphy scowled at Evers but stepped into the office allowing him to exit.

Pulliam nodded at Chance who opened the street door.

"Miss Caylor?" said Pulliam as he cocked his elbow toward her.

Lenore took his arm. They walked out the door and onto the street without a glance in the direction of the mob. No one noticed them. Pulliam looked past the crowd and saw Thomas standing next to his horse, trying to keep the animal calm as he scanned the street looking for Pulliam and Lenore.

"Thomas! Over here, Thomas!" Pulliam waved an arm over his head.

Thomas looked in their direction. Pulliam and Lenore hurried to the carriage.

"Sir. Glad to see you're all right. When you didn't come to the carriage right after the game I was a little worried, I have to admit, sir."

"We had a little business to attend to, but we're fine."

"Hello, Thomas," said Lenore. "You don't know how glad I am to see you." Thomas tipped his hat.

"We'll have two more, Thomas," said Pulliam. "Can you pull up to the office door?"

"Yes, sir. No problem at all."

"Then we'll take Miss Caylor home first. My guests and I will go on to the club."

Lenore held out her hand. Pulliam helped her into the carriage and followed her. Thomas closed the door and climbed up to the driver's bench. He directed the horse toward the office.

Pulliam looked out the carriage window at the exterior of the ball park and then up at Thomas. "You see the door, Thomas? Pull over as close as you can."

Thomas made a U-turn and pulled up to the curb in front of the office. The door opened. First O'Day and then Emslie stepped out onto the sidewalk and walked briskly toward the carriage.

Two young men walked toward the umpires. One stopped and grabbed his companion's arm, stopping him, too. "Hey!" he said. "That's them fucking umps what gave the game to the Cubs."

They ran at the umpires. O'Day saw them and darted for the carriage. Emslie paused to look at the source of his colleague's panic allowing the drunken fans to catch up with him before he could make it into the carriage. He cried out as one of the men gripped the back of his jacket. Hearing the cry, Thomas stood at his seat and snapped his buggy whip repeatedly at the two fans.

"Hey, fucker," yelled one, shielding his face with his arms and moving back.

Thomas turned on the other, cracking his whip more violently and popping the youth's hat off his head, revealing a prematurely balding and much more visible target. But the man didn't stop. He yanked harder on Emslie's jacket, pulling him down onto the sidewalk. Thomas snapped the whip again, but the man waved at it as if shooing a mosquito. Thomas lowered the angle of his weapon and curved a snap that hit the man in his right eye. He screamed in pain and released Emslie as he covered his face with his hands. Emslie scrambled into the carriage as the man knelt on the pavement wailing, "My eye, my eye. I can't see. Oh God, I can't see."

Thomas shifted his attention to his horse. They took off at a gallop down the street, the two umpires sitting opposite Pulliam and Lenore. "Mr. Pulliam," said O'Day, "either you get more police protection or tomorrow's game will not be played. That's a promise."

"Mr. Brush and Mr. McGraw will personally guarantee your safety," said Pulliam, "or they will forfeit." The three men looked back and forth at each other. Satisfied, O'Day directed a shallow nod at Pulliam.

The carriage rolled up to the top of Coogan's Bluff and on to Broadway. The four sat silently trying to avoid meeting each other's eyes. The ride to 111th Street was mercifully brief, and they soon pulled up in front of Lenore's building. Thomas jumped down and opened the carriage door. Pulliam hopped out and extended his hand to Lenore. She took it and stepped out. He walked her to the door.

"I'm afraid my keys are in my bag," she said as they stopped and faced each other. "Somewhere near third base."

"I'm sorry, Miss Caylor. It's my fault. I will reimburse you for its value and its contents."

Lenore rang the doorbell. "Please, Mr. Pulliam. There's really no need to worry about it."

They waited silently. A door opened in the building and Trudie approached. She opened the door. "Lenore? Good evening, Mr. Pulliam." She brought a hand to her mouth. "My goodness, Lenore, what happened?"

"Good evening, Miss Pittenger," said Pulliam. "Through no fault of her own, Miss Caylor has lost her keys. And I assure you that Miss Caylor's appearance is the result of her coming to my personal assistance during a very difficult situation on the Polo Grounds."

"Polo Grounds? Good God! You look like you slid into home plate yourself, Lenore." Pulliam and Lenore laughed.

"Very close to it, Miss Pittenger," said Pulliam. "Miss Caylor, please have your clothes professionally cleaned. Send the bill to me."

Lenore looked up at Pulliam. "Then it's good night, Mr. Pulliam. Thank you for seeing me home."

"It is I who must thank you," he said. He grasped Lenore's hand very lightly and very briefly, turned, and walked toward the carriage.

"And Mr. Pulliam?" He stopped and looked back. "You still owe me dinner at Delmonico's."

"Of course. Good night, Miss Caylor." He bowed and continued on to the carriage.

Henry sat just inside the open firehouse door, nodding off and waking back up as the yellow-orange morning light filled Forty-Seventh Street. His shift almost over, he debated going directly home or up a block on Eighth Avenue for coffee and eggs and the morning paper. He was anxious to read the coverage of the Giants' win the day before. He dozed again.

He saw Maureen running toward him, waving, but he couldn't stand up to greet her. She opened her mouth as if calling to him, but he heard nothing. Her hair was on fire, flames trailing behind her as she ran. He wanted to reach out to help her, to extinguish the flames, but he could not move.

Then someone held him and shook him. I'm trying I'm trying I'm trying, he wanted to scream, but he had no voice. He looked up and saw Maureen standing over him, her hair ablaze. He tried to get up from his seat, but the weight of his sleep paralyzed his arms and legs.

"Henry! Henry!" she pleaded. "Wake up! It's horrible!"

He opened his eyes wide, now fully awake, and saw Maureen, her hair aglow in the morning sunlight behind her. "Maureen? What's wrong? Are you all right? What's wrong?"

"Look at this." She handed him a folded copy of one of the morning newspapers.

"Umpires Steal Game from Giants" read the headline on the sports page. "Run erased in base running dispute," said the line under it.

"They say that the runner on first," began Maureen, "you know, that kid Merkle or whatever his name is, he didn't run to second on Bridwell's hit in the ninth inning. So the Cubs threw to second and forced him out. The umpires say the winning run don't count, and the game's a tie."

"I don't believe this," said Henry, reading. "I never heard of nothing like this before. They're cheating."

"It's horrible. A disaster."

"You ain't kidding. The Giants needed that game bad."

"No, Henry. Not that." He looked up at her. "It's the money."

"Money? What money, Maureen?"

"The money I won from that man."

"What about it?"

"I have to give it back."

"Give it back?" He felt a dull, thick dread hit the pit of his stomach as he read the coverage of the game.

"I didn't win the bet after all," she said. She folded her arms and looked out at the sunlit street.

"Sure you did. Bridwell got the single and the Giants won it in the ninth. I don't care what them papers say." Henry stood and joined her on the sidewalk, shading his eyes from the sun.

"It's not up to us to decide, Henry."

"But," Henry started, searching his brain for a good reason, or any reason, to keep the money.

"But nothing. I can't keep the money."

"Why not? He didn't win the bet, did he?" He scratched his head. "He bet the Giants would win in the tenth, and the paper said the game was called because of all the fans running around on the field. So the tenth was never played and so he didn't win the bet, and if he didn't win the bet then he lost the bet and you won the bet."

"Thanks for trying, Henry, but it's no good. The bet was double or nothing that the Giants would win the game by scoring a run in the bottom of the ninth. Very simple. Did they score a run or not?" She took a deep breath. "They did not, according to the umpire. So I lost the bet. I have to give that man his money back, and my money, too."

"But you can't. You can't because you can't find him. You'll never find him again. And, truth be told, if he wants his money back, he should find you, and he'll never find you."

"I will not listen to any argument that suggests that I steal that man's money."

"You're not stealing it, Maureen."

"Of course I'm stealing it. If you have any doubt about that maybe me and you should stroll over to the convent and ask Sister Loretta Claire about it."

The thought of voluntarily going to the convent and asking to see Sister Loretta Claire caused him enough panic to win him over to Maureen's side of the argument, at least in principle. But he refused to give up all hope of hanging onto the money. He reread the story in the paper.

"We'll just have to go back to the ball park today and find him," said Maureen. "I'm sure he'll be there. He looked as though he lived there, like Uncle Connor at the racetrack. And I'm sure it'll be quite a game again today."

"Can't go," said Henry, distracted by the news story. "I switched shifts with Billy to go yesterday. I gotta be here at the... Hey! Take a look at this." He slapped the newsprint. "It says here that the National League office will review the situation today. So you haven't lost the bet yet."

"Really?"

"Not at all. The league could reverse the umpire's call and give the game to the Giants."

"How long will that take?"

Henry paused and calculated. "Well, there ain't much time. Only about a week or so left in the season. With the race this close, they gotta settle it quick."

"That's good. But if it goes against the Giants, promise me you'll take me back to the Polo Grounds to find that man so I can pay him back."

"Sure, Maureen. 'Course." He smiled and put his hands on her shoulders. "I wouldn't want to have to go to confession with this sin on my conscience would I?" His mind, however, continued to calculate. How many more home games were there? Would they even have the chance to find the drunken gambler this year? He didn't think so. With any luck at all they would keep the money by default.

"Thank you, Henry." She leaned forward and pecked him on his lips. "We'll both feel better. You and me both know what Sister Loretta Claire would have said."

"Sure, sure," he said.

"She would've scolded us for gambling and told us to give the money to the Church, which I'll have to do anyway if we don't find him."

Lenore stopped at the newsstand on Broadway before boarding the downtown subway. She bought all of the morning papers. She didn't notice the weather, the traffic on Broadway, or other pedestrians on the sidewalk. She opened the first paper in her stack, the *Times,* to sports on page seven and read as she descended the stairs to the train platform.

BLUNDER COSTS GIANTS VICTORY
Merkle Rushes Off Baseline Before Winning
Run is Scored and is Declared Out

CONFUSION ON BALL FIELD
Chance Asserts That McCormick's
Run Does Not Count—
Crowd Breaks Up Game

UMPIRE DECLARES IT A TIE
Singular Occurrence on Polo Grounds
Reported to President Pulliam,
Who Will Decide Case

So far, so good, she thought.

Censurable stupidity on the part of player Merkle in yesterday's game at the Polo Grounds between the Giants and Chicagos placed the New York team's chances of winning the pennant in jeopardy.

She looked up and found herself standing in front of the open door of a crowded subway, not remembering having paid her fare or hearing the train arrive. She hopped on, running into a large, heavy man who blocked most of the space just inside the car. He didn't move, his face buried in a newspaper. She found a couple inches to grab along the back of a seat and held on as the train lurched forward.

The account in the *Times* was fair enough. She was encouraged that any Giants protest would be a formality and that Mr. Pulliam's decision of the night before would stand, although she did not relish the upcoming meeting with McGraw and Brush, or even Murphy of the Cubs. Buried in paragraph three she read what she thought would be the teams' positions in the case. "Merkle said that he had touched second base, and the Chicago players were equally positive that he had not done so." That was it in a nutshell. Neither would argue the rule; both would argue the legitimacy of invoking it.

Toward the end of the article, the *Times* recalled Merkle's ninth-inning base hit, the play that set the stage for the controversy, as Mc-Cormick stood on first with two out.

> Merkle, who failed us the day before in an emergency, is at bat, and we pray of him that he mend his ways. If he will only single we will ignore any errors he may make in the rest of his natural life.

Lenore hoped this would be the case, for Merkle's sake, for she was certain that Mr. Pulliam would rule that Merkle had blundered far worse than failing to hit safely in a clutch situation.

The other papers reported the events of the disputed game roughly the same, with some variations concerning whether O'Day actually saw the play at second or not. McGraw was quoted in both the *World* and the *Sun* as saying that the game was either a forfeit or a Giants win, not a "no game." And he claimed that Merkle did touch second base. The *Herald* described how the controversy might change base ball.

> An enormous base ball custom has had it from time immemorial that as soon as the winning run has crossed the plate everyone adjourns as hastily and yet nicely as possible to the clubhouse and exits.

But it also wrote of Merkle in a tone that did not bode well for the young player's future popularity with New York fans.

> Our boys did rather well if Fred Merkle could gather the idea into his noodle that base ball custom does not permit a runner to take a shower and some light lunch in the clubhouse on the way to second.

Lenore closed the *Herald* and looked out the window as the subway pulled into a station. She was at Twenty-Third Street. One more paper and she would have missed her stop. She gathered her things, jumped out of her seat, and, hugging her bundle of newsprint, made her way to the door of the car.

Head down and skirt gathered in her free hand, she hurried along Twenty-Third and cut through Madison Square Park. She looked up to watch for traffic as she approached Fifth Avenue and stopped. Mounted police closed off Broadway where it joined Fifth Avenue at Twenty-Fourth Street. She crossed, dodging the horse-drawn carriages, trolleys, and automobiles, all pointed in random directions and clogging the square. Looking up Fifth Avenue, she saw mounted police at the Twenty-Fifth and Twenty-Sixth Street intersections.

A crowd of several hundred jammed Broadway from the front of the St. James Building at Broadway and Twenty-Sixth Street down to Twenty-Fifth, and spilled through the crosstown streets to Fifth Avenue. Lenore approached and stopped at the edge of the mob. She looked for an opening that would allow her to shoulder her way through to the door, but the men stood arm to arm, pressing to get closer to the building.

"Can I help you, little lady?" She turned to see a mounted policeman reining his horse a few feet away. "Dangerous in there."

"Oh," she replied, lifting her left hand to shield her eyes from the morning sun. "Yes, thank you. I need to get into the St. James Building."

"And why is that?"

"I work there."

The cop frowned and leaned down maintaining his balance by resting his forearm on his thigh. "You work in there? And who do you work for, if you don't mind my asking?"

Lenore hesitated. The cop was probably a Giants fan and might be more helpful if she stretched the truth a little. "I work for the Giants," she said. "They have offices in the building."

"The Giants?"

Well, she thought, if she worked for the league she worked for all of the teams, including the Giants. "And," she continued, "there is a meeting at eight thirty in the league offices. The Giants will protest last night's ruling and I need to be there. I'm the stenographer."

The cop sat up straight and looked out over the crowd. He scratched his chin. "Can't have a protest meeting without a stenographer, can we? Especially this protest. Can you ride?"

"Pardon me?"

"A horse. Can you ride a horse?"

She looked at the officer's mount. "Certainly."

"Ma'am, to get you to the door of that building we may have to fight some Indians." He jumped out of his saddle, landing on the pavement with the thud of his two black leather boots. He cupped his hands to give her a leg up. She stepped into them, placed a hand on his shoulder and lifted herself as he boosted her up onto the horse. She landed sitting sidesaddle, both legs dangling against the horse's left flank. The cop then grabbed the underside of the saddle's seat and pulled himself up behind Lenore.

"Hand me the reins," he said. Lenore located the leather straps and lifted the ends over her head. He grasped them, pulling one down on either side of her. He held them close to her sides. He clucked his tongue and the horse walked toward the backs of the men in the last row of the mob. "Go on, Marty, go on. Right on through these bugs." Marty dipped his head and forced his wet black nose between two of the fans, knocking them forward into the men in front of them.

"What the hell?" protested one.

"Get off!" said the other.

"Out of the way," commanded the officer. "Police business." He gathered the reins into one hand and pulled his billy club out of a holster on the side of the saddle. "Move out. You there! Out of the way."

Lenore watched as the crowd, who had squeezed into every square inch of the street and sidewalk with no pavement or air to spare, parted before the horse. The policeman hit a couple of uncooperative men with his club. A few tumbled to the ground, and many more protested.

"Fucking copper!"

"Bet you're a Chicago fan, you shit!"

Most of the rest of the yelling was directed at Mr. Pulliam and indirectly at the Cubs. She saw one sign, its message crudely scrawled in coal on cardboard. "FORCE OUT PULLIAM NOT MERKLE!"

"Now, ma'am," the cop whispered loudly right into her right ear as they neared the building's front doors. "I'll get you safely inside, but I'd like a little favor in return."

"Yes?"

"I'm off duty at noon, and one of my fellow officers and I had talked about how we'd kind of like to see today's game. Last game of the Chicago series, you know. Should be a dandy. Maybe you could put in a good word to Brush or McGraw and meet me back down here when your meeting's over. What do you say, dear?"

"Of course," she replied. She had to get into the building and would say anything. She'd deal with the ticket problem later. "They're hard to come by, but we usually have a couple available on the day of the game."

"You're a sweetheart," he said and pulled his head back. "You there! Out of the way!" They reached the door. He hopped off his horse and held out his hands to help Lenore. She jumped into his arms, and he gently set her on the sidewalk.

"Thank you, officer," she said.

"My pleasure, ma'am," he replied. "I'll see you right here at about a quarter to twelve."

"I'll be here," she said as she entered the building.

When she arrived at the National League offices, Frank Chance, Johnny Evers, and Joe Tinker sat in the waiting area, neatly dressed in suits and ties, their hats on their laps. Cubs president Charles Murphy paced back and forth chewing on the stub of an unlit cigar. "Good morning, Mr. Murphy," she said. "Mr. Tinker, Mr. Evers, Mr. Chance."

"Miss Caylor, how are you?" asked Chance.

"Fine, Mr. Chance. Does Mr. Pulliam know you're here?"

"He knows," said Murphy.

The door to the inner office opened and Pulliam came out, looked around the waiting area, and smiled when he saw Lenore. Murphy yanked the cigar out of his mouth and confronted him. "Now you listen to me, Pulliam," he said, "this is cut and dried. The game ended in a—"

"Miss Caylor, how are you today?" asked Pulliam.

"Very well. Thank you, sir."

Murphy stepped toward Pulliam. "I'm talking to you, Harry," he said.

"Good morning, Charlie," replied Pulliam cheerfully. "Frank, Johnny, Joe. Beautiful day for a ball game, isn't it?"

"You mean two ball games," said Murphy. "Last night I checked the rule book, and the rules clearly state that—"

"I know the rules, Charlie," said Pulliam. He then turned to Lenore. "Miss Caylor, please come into my office."

"I'll be right in, Mr. Pulliam." Pulliam turned and reentered his office. Lenore dropped the newspapers on her desk and removed her hat and hung it on the coat rack. Brushing a stray strand of hair out of her face, she opened a desk drawer and removed a pad of paper and a pencil. She noticed two sheets of New York Athletic Club stationary on her desk. A rough scrawl covered the pages. Clipped to the pages was a note from Pulliam. "Please type up earliest."

She picked up the sheets of paper and read.

New York Sept 23/08

Harry C. Pulliam, Esq.

Pres. Nat League

Dear Sir:

In the game to-day at New York between New York and the Chicago Club. In the last half of the 9th inning the score was a tie 1 to 1. New York was at the Bat, with two Men out, McCormick of N. York on 3rd Base and Merkle of N. York on 1st Base; Bridwell was at the Bat and hit a clean single Base-Hit to Center Field. Merkle did not run the Ball out; he started toward 2nd Base, but on getting half way there he turned and ran down the Field toward the Club House. The Ball was fielded in to 2nd Base for a Chgo Man to make the play, when McGinnity ran from the Coacher's Box out in the Field to 2nd Base and interfered with the Play being made. Emslie, who said he did not watch Merkle, asked me if Merkle touched 2nd Base. I said he did not. Then Emslie called Merkle out, and I would not allow McCormick's Run to score. The Game at the end of the 9th inning was 1 to 1. The People ran out on the Field. I did not ask to have the Field cleared, as it was too dark to continue play. Yours Respt, Henry O'Day.

Lenore put the pages in the drawer, closed it, and went to Pulliam's office door. She paused, collected herself, and knocked lightly, sensing the eyes of the players drilling her back.

"Make sure he gets it right," said Murphy.

She looked at Murphy and smiled, turned the knob, and opened the door.

Pulliam stood behind his desk. Christy Mathewson and Fred Merkle sat on a couch against a wall. John McGraw, similar to Murphy on the other side of the door, paced back and forth. John Brush sat in a chair near the desk. The shouts of the crowd on the street could be heard through the closed windows. Lenore hoped that the mob would disperse soon so they could open those windows. The offices would get warm and stuffy very soon.

"Come in, Miss Caylor," said Pulliam. "Mr. McGraw and Mr. Brush, you both know Miss Lenore Caylor."

"Good morning, Ollie's girl," said Brush.

"Miss Caylor," said McGraw.

"This," Pulliam gestured toward the couch, "is Mr. Christy Mathewson and Mr. Fred Merkle."

Mathewson saluted from his seat. "Pleasure," he said and smiled a broad, toothy grin. His sandy hair was brushed back and perfectly neat. He wore a conservative, blue three-piece suit with a black tie under a stiff, high collar.

Merkle stood, hat in hand, and dipped his head. "Pleased to meet you, ma'am." He looked young and bewildered, especially next to Mathewson and McGraw. His cheap gray suit was too large for his slender, slightly hunched form.

Lenore closed the door behind her. "Nice to meet you, Mr. Merkle. Mr. Mathewson." She crossed the office and sat in a chair behind a small table next to the desk. She set the notepad down and looked up. "I'm ready, Mr. Pulliam," she said.

"Say, Harry," said Brush looking at Lenore, "are you sure about this? Recording our little talk I mean? If this goes wrong it could be real bad for you. Support for you in the league is slipping away, you know." He looked jaundiced and exhausted, his eyes milky and his lips gray.

"Miss Caylor," said Pulliam, "please prepare to transcribe this interview," he said, looking directly at Brush. Lenore took pencil in hand and sat poised to begin.

"Okay, Harry-boy," said Brush. "Just looking out for you. You ain't been looking too good lately."

"Miss Caylor," said Pulliam, staring at Brush, "please record that Mr. Brush is worried about my health."

Lenore wrote a couple of lines in her notebook. Brush scowled at her. "Harry," he said, "you get this wrong and you can book a one-way ticket back to Louisville."

Lenore continued to write.

"Your threat is duly noted," said Pulliam. "Shall we read it back to you?"

"No need, Harry-boy. No need."

McGraw approached Pulliam's desk and pounded on it with his fist. "You can't do this to me, Pulliam," he said, twisting his mouth. "You've suspended me, forfeited my games, and tried everything you can to keep us out of the World's Series, but you're not going to do this." He pointed at the window. "You hear that mob out there?"

Pulliam glared at McGraw. "When the day comes that a base ball decision is made based on the feelings of any one team's supporters, that will be the day base ball dies."

Brush spoke up. "I'll decide when base ball dies in New York, Pulliam. This is my town and you have to live in it. Don't ever forget that."

Pulliam looked past Brush and McGraw. "Mr. Merkle?"

Merkle stood and looked at McGraw, Brush, and Pulliam, continually fingering the brim of his hat. "Yes, sir?"

"Mr. Merkle, please relate the events of yesterday as well as you can remember them."

Exasperated, McGraw retreated from the desk and sat in a chair against the far wall. "Go ahead, Fred," he said.

"Well, sir, Mr. McGraw told me that I was to start at first, which made me mighty pleased seeing as I hadn't started a game all year."

"Mr. Merkle," interrupted Pulliam, "please proceed to the bottom of the ninth, when you were on first base."

"Yes, sir. Sorry, sir. Well, I'm on first thinking I should be on second. My hit went down the line and I could have stretched it easy. But they held me at first. They didn't want to risk me getting throwed out at second when my run don't matter. It's McCormick we wanted to get home with the winning run." He glanced down and noticed that he was ruining his hat. He looked around for a place to put it, but he was too shy to move his feet and so, resigned, continued nervously fingering the brim. "Well, I'm on first just itching to go, so I take a big lead-off. Bridwell, he's at the plate, and he stares at me like I just shit..." He turned to Lenore and quickly turned away, again studying the brim of his hat, blushing. "Spit. Like I spit on his shoes. Hell—uh—heck! I think to myself. Uh, heck, I don't mean nothing out here and it's as if I weren't on base at all. So I shorten my lead and relax. Then, on the first pitch, Al hits it clean into right center, so I take off for second." Merkle stopped. No one spoke for a moment.

"Yes?" said Pulliam. "Please continue, Mr. Merkle."

"Yes, sir."

"Well? Did you make it to second?"

"Mr. Pulliam, I have to tell you, I've done it a hundred times in every league I've played in since I was nine years old. We all do it. I mean, when the runner scores from third on a hit like that, to end the game, I mean, it's like I said. The runner on first don't mean nothing. No one cares a lick if I touch second or drop dead on the base path."

"Did you touch second base?"

Merkle looked nervously from McGraw to Mathewson to Brush.

"It's a simple question," said Pulliam. "When Bridwell's hit went into right center field and McCormick scored from third..."

McGraw jumped up from his chair causing it to tumble onto its side. "You said it, Pulliam!" he almost shouted. "Did you get that, miss? The president of the National League has stated for the record that McCormick scored from third base."

"Did you touch second base, Fred?" asked Pulliam, his voice lowered but tensed.

"He touched second base." All turned to the source of the definitive statement. Christy Mathewson, his legs crossed and his arm casually slung over the back of the couch, continued. "I was there with him."

"Then why won't he tell me that himself?" asked Pulliam. "For the record."

"Because, just like yesterday, the kid's scared. He stopped between first and second and he's stopped talking now because this whole thing has him so spooked he doesn't know first from second or one from two. Isn't that right, Fred?"

"That's right, Matty."

"I can tell you what happened." Mathewson stood and stepped to the center of the office, leaving his hat on the couch. McGraw returned to his toppled chair, righted it, and sat.

Pulliam, relieved to have some distance between himself and Mc-Graw, nodded in Mathewson's direction. "Go ahead, Mr. Mathewson," he said.

"Thank you, Mr. Pulliam. But let me begin by saying that if this game goes to Chicago by any trick of argument, you can take it from me that if we lose the pennant hereby, I will never play professional base ball again."

No one spoke at first, all eyes staring at Mathewson. Lenore sat perfectly still, her pencil hovering over her pad. Finally, Pulliam glanced at her and she recorded Mathewson's statement. He turned back to Mathewson. "Mr. Mathewson, the National League and the entire base ball community would be greatly saddened by your premature retirement. Nonetheless, your career decisions are your own. At this time the National League only wishes to hear your account of the events of yesterday, starting with Bridwell's hit in the bottom of the ninth inning."

Mathewson looked around, took a deep breath, and folded his arms. "I was on the bench. My arm was sore, so I was worried about whether I could face the Cubs for one more inning if the game stayed tied. I wasn't even sure I could face one more batter. Then I heard Bridwell's hit."

"You 'heard' Bridwell's hit?" said Pulliam.

"Yes, sir. I know the sound well."

"Not as well as most, Matty," said McGraw. Merkle laughed nervously.

"Nonetheless, when I heard that ball hit the sweet part of the bat, I knew we had the game." He paused, looking from Pulliam to Merkle to McGraw and back to Pulliam. "I ran out to slap Bridwell on the back. Then I wanted to get to the clubhouse as quick as possible, just like Fred here, to get away from those crazy rooters. But I heard Evers screaming about the ball. I looked out and saw Fred running for the clubhouse. Well, I knew about what the Cubs tried in Pittsburgh, so I took off after Fred. But then he stopped."

"He stopped?" asked Pulliam.

"He sure did," said Mathewson. "He stopped at the edge of the infield and looked at Evers. He heard him calling for the ball same as me. Then Hofman threw the ball to Evers, but he overthrew it. That gave Fred his chance."

"His chance?"

"Yes, sir, Mr. Pulliam. Right then he saw what the Chicagos were up to, and so he ran to second base and touched the bag while the Cubs were trying to recover the ball."

"Mr. Mathewson, you are stating that Merkle touched second base before the ball got to Evers for the force."

"That's right," said Mathewson. "Right about then I got there and took Fred by the arm and said we should go on to the clubhouse."

"Mr. Merkle," asked Pulliam, "is this consistent with your memory?"

Merkle turned to Brush and then McGraw. They glared at him. "Just what Matty says," he replied. "You can believe Matty."

"And what I say is this. I had Fred by the arm and we looked at Emslie and he said that there was no problem with the play. He would not allow the Cubs' claim."

"Then you are stating that Merkle touched second base?" asked Pulliam.

"He touched the bag. I saw him do it." Matthewson approached Pulliam's desk. He took a folded sheet of paper from his inside coat pocket and held it out for Pulliam. "This is my signed affidavit that confirms what I did and saw yesterday during the ninth inning."

Pulliam took the sheet of paper and placed it on his desk. "Thank you, Mr. Mathewson."

Brush screwed up his face and said, "Thank you, Mr. Mathewson," imitating Pulliam's voice with an exaggerated lilt. "There's only one call here, Pulliam. The game was over when McCormick crossed the plate. Chicago may claim the ball was still live, but it was a dead ball as soon as it hit the ground and McCormick touched home. You're so goddamn worried about the so-called integrity of the game. Integrity in base ball means a base hit scores the runner from third. That's the way the game's been played since you were writing poems in Louisville."

"I will advise you of the league's ruling," said Pulliam calmly, looking down at Mathewson's affidavit.

Brush struggled to his feet and leaned on the front of Pulliam's desk for support. "You are not the league."

"Thank you, gentlemen," said Pulliam. He turned to the window.

Brush raised his voice, his throat vibrating with a crackling gargle, his face a bright rosy pink. "You are not the league."

"John," said McGraw. "Don't bother. You can't talk to this boy."

Pulliam turned from the window and stepped toward Brush. Mathewson, McGraw, and Merkle walked to the office door.

Brush remained at Pulliam's desk, grasping its front edge. "You never got over losing your precious Louisville Colonels, did you? You've always blamed me for that, and rightly so. But you deserved to fail. You know nothing about running a base ball team and less about running this league." He extended his neck so his head pitched closer to Pulliam. He hissed between clenched teeth. "You're not going to do this to me, you inverted fairy. Do you hear me? You just remember Louisville. What do you think the league would say about why you had to leave town for Pittsburgh, and who left town with you?"

"Do you think you can blackmail me? You dare to threaten me?" Pulliam now spoke in a stiff whisper. "I recognize the symptoms of locomotor ataxia, Mr. Brush, and I know its cause. Is Mrs. Brush as well informed?"

Brush laughed derisively, his laugh deteriorating into a deep cough. He struggled to regain control, bending over from the strain. He balanced himself on one arm and took out his handkerchief with the other. He spat into the gray linen, crumpled it up, and put it in a jacket pocket. He stood erect. "You can't play my game, Pulliam. Don't try. And you ask about Mrs. Brush? How do you think I caught my disease?" His face contorted into a twisted smile, he started to laugh but stopped himself as he gagged on his own saliva.

The door opened. McGraw, Mathewson, and Merkle stood poised to leave the office. Brush looked at Lenore. "I'm sure, Mr. Pulliam, that your judgment will be the correct one." He turned and limped toward the office door. McGraw waited and took Brush's arm, helping him the rest of the way out of the office.

In the waiting area, the three Cub players stood. As McGraw passed Murphy he stopped, tightening his grip on Brush's arm, and poked a finger in the Cubs president's chest. "I ain't about to let you swipe this one, Chubby."

Murphy grabbed McGraw's hand and pulled it hard to one side. The players closed in on each other. "Not swiping anything, Mugsy. The kid gave it to us. You're the manager. Teach him the rules."

"That is one festering pile of cow shit and you know it. Merkle did nothing that ain't been done a thousand times by every team in both leagues. Even by your own boys. I've seen them do it."

"Ain't talking about my boys here."

"And we'll see it happen a thousand times more."

"Doubt it," said Evers. Merkle lunged at him. Mathewson jumped between the two men, restraining Merkle. Evers calmly took out a pouch of chewing tobacco and filled his mouth with a fresh wad, his eyes never leaving Merkle.

"For Christ's sake, knock it off," said Brush. "Chubby, Frank, boys, how are you today? Ready to take a licking this afternoon?"

Murphy smiled. "Don't forget to bring your checkbook to the ball park, John. Forfeits cost a grand. And don't forget the police protection or you'll forfeit another game, and there ain't much time left to make up the ground."

"Don't know about any forfeits, Chubby," said Brush, "but you can rest assured we'll take good care of you and your boys."

Murphy scoffed. "You always do," he said. "C'mon, boys." He led his players into Pulliam's office. Mathewson released Merkle. They watched as someone closed the door after the last Cub, Frank Chance, had passed over its threshold.

Chance sat in the middle of the couch, Evers and Tinker taking seats on either side. Murphy approached Pulliam's desk, but Pulliam spoke first. "Good morning, gentlemen. You all met Miss Lenore Caylor last evening. She will transcribe our interview."

Lenore looked up at Pulliam. They had gone through the introductions and hellos in the outer office. She looked at his face for signs of stress. Pulliam kept his body moving, arranging papers on his desk, neck twisting as he looked this way and that at nothing specific.

"Sure, sure," said Murphy. "We're best of friends. But you listen to me, Pulliam. This is all very simple. Emslie called Merkle out at second. The force nullified McCormick's run. The Giants couldn't protect my team or their own field from their drunken fans, so the game was stopped with the score tied. The rules state, and, as I said, I read the rules last night..." He suddenly turned his head and looked at Lenore. "Are you getting all this, Miss Caylor, because I can slow down."

Lenore smiled and scanned her notepad. "I would prefer it if you hurried a little, Mr. Murphy. There's a game this afternoon."

Straightening his tie Murphy continued. "Okay, I'll hurry because we got two games to play. Which brings me to my next point. The rules state that the game must be made up on the earliest possible date. And seeing as this is the last day this year both teams will be together, today is your only choice. The game, by the rules, must be made up today." He turned and walked toward the couch, gesturing casually at his players. "The Cubs will be ready to play two games today. If the Giants ain't ready for two, they forfeit nine to zero and pay us a penalty of one thousand dollars. You can't decide this any other way."

"Thank you, Mr. Murphy," said Pulliam. "At this time, however, the league is conducting an investigation initiated by a protest filed by the New York Giants."

"Emslie called the play. What's to investigate?"

"Before we can determine if or when there will be a makeup game, we must go through the correct procedures as demanded by the protest system as described in the league charter."

"Damn your protest system. Stand by your umpire, just like you did in Pittsburgh."

"Mr. Evers?" said Pulliam, looking past Murphy.

Johnny Evers stood. "Yes, sir?"

"Please give the league your description of the events of yesterday."

Murphy protested. "You don't need his description of nothing. I shouldn't have agreed to bring these boys here today. They have a game, I mean two games, to play this afternoon."

Pulliam ignored him. "Mr. Evers?" he repeated.

Murphy threw up his hands, returned to the back of the office, and leaned against the wall, folding his arms in disgust. Evers looked around the room while rotating the wad of chewing tobacco in his mouth. Smiling, he calmly walked past Pulliam's desk to the window and opened it. Unruly crowd noises filled the room from the street. Evers peered out the window, glanced back at Pulliam, and then spat a long stream of brown tobacco juice onto the crowd below. Satisfied with himself, he slammed the window sash back down. Evers returned to the couch but remained standing.

Pulliam picked up a newspaper and went around his desk, unfolding the newsprint as he approached Evers. He held the paper open as if holding the handles of a basket. Evers leaned over, opened his mouth, and let the wad of chewing tobacco plop onto the newspaper. Pulliam rolled it up as he returned to his desk, and dropped it into a wastebasket behind his chair. He looked back at Evers and nodded. "Go ahead," he said.

"I got the ball," said Evers, "and forced Merkle out at second. So the run don't count." He sat back down.

Pulliam frowned. "Mr. Evers, please. The details."

"You want details?"

"Please be as detailed as you can."

Evers cleared his throat. "All right. Details." He stood. "Well, I knew from the crack of the bat that Bridwell hit it good. I was playing back with two out, but, even so, it was past me like a shot. I jumped at it but it was way out of reach. I watched it land in right center field and heard them Giants rooters start hollering and screaming and carrying on. Made me nervous because I knew they'd be on the field in no time. I wanted to get to the clubhouse as bad as anyone, know what I mean? Them Giants fans hold no love for us Cubs. It was gonna get dangerous out there real quick.

"But then I looked back toward the infield and saw McCormick trot across the plate waving his arms like he was flagging the last cab on Manhattan Island. Shoot, I didn't blame him, of course, but I didn't have to like it much." He rolled his tongue in his cheek searching for his lost chaw of tobacco.

"I'm a second baseman, so even on the last play of the inning I'd drifted toward the bag, kind of like an instinct, you know? And then I checked the runner at first, that rookie kid Merkle, and I didn't see him in the base path. I checked short right center and there he was, running for dear life for the clubhouse."

"Did he touch second base first?" asked Pulliam. "Before he left the field for the clubhouse?"

"Merkle made it halfway to second, no farther than that. He would have had to run me over to get to the second base bag."

Frank Chance spoke up from his seat on the couch. "He didn't get far at all. Not a third of the way. He stopped dead and saw all those drunken bugs running all over the field, and he turned and ran as fast as he could through the outfield."

"That's what I thought, too," said Evers. "But now I'm thinking about Pittsburgh and the Gill play. Gill stopped short of second with two out in the tenth. They got me the ball and I forced him out. But you gave that game to the Pirates, Mr. Pulliam."

"Mr. O'Day had left the field," said Pulliam. "He didn't see whether Gill touched second or not. And he didn't see you get the ball and step on second. He let the play stand. I supported his call."

"That's right, Mr. Pulliam. You gotta support your umpires. But by doing that you as much as admitted that the runner on first has gotta make it to second or he can be forced out, base hit or no base hit, because the ball is live until he touches the bag. And if he's forced out, the run don't count. That's the rule and I know the rules as good as anybody."

"Better," said Chance.

"I reviewed the rule in my statement concerning the Gill play," said Pulliam.

"You surely did," said Evers. "Now, I also remembered that O'Day was the umpire for that Pittsburgh game. So I took a good long look at him, and he saw me and started walking to the mound. I almost lost him in the middle of all those fans swarming around the field, celebrating and throwing all manner of...," he glanced at Lenore, "things and stuff up in the air. But then I saw him above the heads of the bugs, standing on the slab so he could see good. At that point I turned to find Solly Hofman who was the one what fielded the base hit. I raised my arms and started yelling for him to get me the ball. I looked to my right and saw Frank standing on the outfield grass and he was hollering at Solly, too. So I knew we were all together on this. We all remembered Pittsburgh.

"So I screamed louder. He finally saw me and reared back and threw the ball. But Solly ain't the best outfielder in the league—we like to use him to spot me or Tinker in the infield, but yesterday we needed him in center. So it wasn't no surprise that he sailed the damn ball over my head. He never was much good at hitting the cutoff man. So I looked over my head and maybe cursed a little and then watched the ball land in the middle of the infield, right between second and the mound.

"Now Iron Joe..."

Pulliam interrupted. "You refer to Joe McGinnity of the Giants."

"Yes, sir. McGinnity. He was coaching third yesterday and at this point was on his way across the infield toward his own bench. And didn't the ball roll right up to his spikes. He quite naturally reached down and picked it up. At first I thought maybe he just wanted the game ball to give to Bridwell or McCormick or even Merkle. Not for a minute did I think that Iron Joe would ever interfere with a play on purpose."

The other Cubs laughed. "Not Joe," said Chance.

"Next thing I know," continued Evers, "a few of our boys, Tinker,

Steinfeldt, and Kroh it was, ran at Iron Joe and jumped on him and got into one unholy scuffle for the ball. So I know that Iron Joe was thinking about the Gill play now if he wasn't before. And he's a tough enough bird—they don't call him Iron Joe for nothing—and so he put up a good fight against our boys for a time. But then I saw his head, without his cap mind you, and his arm rise out of the middle of that brawl and the middle of all those crazy fans, and I saw him flip the ball into the crowd over 'round third base, or just behind it in short left field. Some bug caught the thing, and then Kroh and Steinfeldt took off after him.

"Right about then I looked around to check on O'Day. He was still standing there, watching the whole thing from the mound." Evers paused and looked back at the couch. "Now, from that point, from when Iron Joe threw the ball into the crowd, I'm not the right boy. Oh Peerless Leader," he said to Chance, "could you respectfully request that your so-called shortstop pick up the story from here?"

Tinker stood and sneered at Evers. "It's okay, Frank," he said. "In spite of what your so-called second baseman thinks, I am in the room and heard him just fine."

Pulliam looked at Chance, then at Lenore. "There's a rumor around the league," she said, "that Mr. Tinker and Mr. Evers do not speak to each other. Something about a cab in Chicago."

"Ain't no rumor," said Tinker. "But we didn't come down here to discuss that sonofabitch's lack of manners, excuse me, ma'am."

"Please proceed, Mr. Tinker," said Pulliam.

"Yes, sir. Well, you see, I remembered Pittsburgh, too. Hell, we all did on account of being robbed a game in a close pennant race. So I know what Evers is thinking. He may be a rude cuss and not fit to live with off the field, but on the field he's the smartest base ball man around and a rude cuss on top of that—and being a rude cuss on the field ain't no bad thing."

"Horse crap," said Evers under his breath.

"Anyway," continued Tinker, "I see Evers waving his arms toward the outfield. Then I see Hofman cock his arm back to throw the ball and I move in to back up second, just like I'm supposed to. But next thing

I know, McGinnity picks up the ball. So me and Steinfeldt and Kroh run at him and at first we try to convince him that the game isn't over yet and could he please give us the ball. But of course he's not about to agree with that so we think maybe we gotta apply a little force.

"Like Evers said, McGinnity's a tough one. He won't give up the ball and decides it would be better to lose it in the crowd than give it to us. So he tosses it away, kind of weakly because we got him off balance. I watch the ball and see where it goes. I see these two arms reach up and catch it, and then I see who belongs to those arms and see that it's a kind of tall bug wearing a brown bowler. So I let go of McGinnity and concentrate on that bowler and take off pushing my way through the crowd. Steinfeldt and Kroh see what happened and follow me. Then I make eye contact with the fella and he looks at me and I can see he's a little scared. He turns and runs—or tries to run. It was tough for anyone to get through that mob. Like rowing upstream.

"But there's three of us and so we get through a little quicker than him and don't bother asking him politely for the ball but just tackle him before he can get much farther along. And you know something? He was about as tough as McGinnity. Maybe tougher. Maybe he never had a major league ball in his hand before, much less what he thought was the game-winning ball, and so this would be his once-in-a-lifetime chance to get hisself a souvenir."

Tinker shrugged, caught his breath, and continued. "He just won't give up, holding onto that ball like it was the last nickel between him and death. Finally, I pound his bowler down over his eyes, and don't you know that's all it took? He drops the ball so he can get his hat off his face. Right then Floyd Kroh drops to the ground and starts crawling after it, tripping fans, and knocking them over here and there, the ball getting kicked around a bit. But he stays with it and finally gets ahold of it. Then Steinfeldt gets there and reaches down for it and Kroh hands the ball up to him."

Tinker shifted his weight. "Evers here, he's standing on the bag at second base with his mitt hand in the air. Now, I'm a bit closer to him than Steinfeldt so he shovels the ball to me and I relay it to second."

Evers picked up the story. "Tinker here, I guess he was worried some bug would reach up and snag it so he threw it a little high, but I could reach it. I jumped and felt it hit the pocket of my mitt. I brought it down and covered it with my free hand, but then I stumbled a little on the bag and fell backward but stayed on my feet. I looked over at O'Day and he was standing there just staring at me. So I stepped back up on the bag and jumped up and down on it a couple of times and held the ball high so he could see it, and I screamed at whoever wanted to hear that the runner was out, that Merkle was out at second base and the run don't count.

"Maybe I shouldn't have been so loud about it, though, because some of them Giants rooters saw me and heard me and they turned ugly. I looked over toward first and saw Frank all squared up in his boxing stance—Frank was quite the fighter in his day, you know—just a poking one rooter after another with jab after jab and generally taking pretty good care of himself, but I knew the crowd was going to get the better of him soon. Then I saw O'Day get knocked a couple of times. And then we all lit out for the clubhouse, fighting and pushing the rooters away as best we could until them cops got there. About then I saw you and Miss Caylor here and thought to myself that this one was about as crazy as they come."

"I saw a fan push O'Day," said Tinker. "By that time I'd made my way back between second and the mound. That fan was a big fellow and he jams the palm of his hand into O'Day's shoulder and gets his red, screaming face right in O'Day's saying 'What are you doing out here, you blind bastard? The game is over! Go home! You can't steal this one from the Giants!' and things like that."

"So," said Evers, "that's a long way of saying what I said before. O'Day called Merkle out at second."

"O'Day called him out?" asked Pulliam. "Did Mr. O'Day call Merkle out at second while he, Mr. O'Day, was on the field?"

"You were there," said Chance. "You came into the clubhouse and told us that Merkle was out and the run don't count."

"But this question will come up again if and when this case goes to the National League Board of Directors," said Pulliam. "I would like

Mr. Evers, or any of you, to state for the record whether you heard O'Day or Emslie call Merkle out while on the field."

"He saw me catch the ball and step on the base," said Evers.

"Again, did you see or hear Mr. O'Day call Merkle out at second?"

"No, sir. With all the excitement, I can't say as I did. But here's the difference, Mr. Pulliam, here's the difference. He didn't see the play in Pittsburgh, but he was looking right at me yesterday, same as you're looking at me right now. He saw the play and he knows Merkle was out. I don't care if he called it right then or if he calls it next week. The fair and honest end of that inning came when I caught that ball and stepped on second base."

"Mr. Tinker, Mr. Chance, do either of you have anything to add to this testimony?"

"Testimony?" interrupted Murphy. "This ain't no court and you ain't no judge, Pulliam." He approached the desk, lifted his right hand, and jabbed his index finger at Pulliam. "You was there, Pulliam. You know what's right. Don't you let that syphilitic bastard Brush make you do what's wrong. I know his ways. He'd shoot his own mother to save a thousand dollars."

"I will make the final decision regarding this issue, Mr. Murphy. You and your team have stated your case. Now, if you will excuse us, we have work to do."

"Come on, boys," said Chance. "We're done here."

"Listen, Pulliam," said Murphy. "You remember that this ain't just about the end of that game. You can't follow the rules on that and just stop there. I swear to you that if this season ends with the Cubs down a game, or even two games, you'll hear about this from me until the day you quit the league, or the day you drop dead, whichever comes first and right now either would be just fine with me."

Pulliam and Murphy glared at each other. The three players walked to the door. Chance paused as he turned the knob. "Mr. Murphy?" he said. "We need to get to the Polo Grounds so we can collect your thousand dollars." He put his hat on. Evers and Tinker put their hats on. Murphy turned and looked at his players, put his own hat on, and followed them out the door. When the door closed, Pulliam picked up

Mathewson's document, unfolded it, read it, and held it out to Lenore. "Miss Caylor, please read this," he said.

She stood, went around her table to the front of Pulliam's desk, and took the affidavit from him.

"But this isn't what Mr. Mathewson said just now," she said as she read.

"No, it isn't."

"Why would he tell you that Merkle touched second base, but sign a statement swearing that he didn't?"

"Because Matty the ball player had to support his teammate in public. But he knows that this affidavit will remain confidential. In the end, Christy Mathewson, the man, could not sign his name to anything that wasn't the truth."

"That seems too easy to me," said Lenore. "He gets to have it both ways."

"It's a difficult situation for all of us."

"For all of us? I'm sorry, Mr. Pulliam, but Mr. Mathewson can go back to the clubhouse now and play checkers with his teammates. No matter what you decide, it will be wrong to someone, either the Cubs or the Giants. Maybe both. That is much more than just a difficult situation. Especially for Fred Merkle."

"Then you will understand, Miss Caylor, that from my point of view this affidavit is the best thing that has happened to the league thus far."

"What about you? How does it make it any better for you?"

Pulliam said nothing for a moment and then turned to the window, his arms hanging limp at his sides. The muted taunts of the mob sounded louder than ever in the silent office. "Thank you, Miss Caylor."

Lenore returned to her table, picked up her notebook, and left the office to transcribe her notes. Later that morning she would type up Pulliam's official statement. She spent half an hour calling the newspapers and scheduling a press conference for early afternoon. They would announce the league's decision and leave the writers plenty of time to get to the Polo Grounds for the afternoon game. Sid Mercer of the *Globe* wanted her to read it over the phone right then so he'd be sure to make it to the game on time. She knew very well that he in fact wanted to scoop the other papers with an extra edition covering the decision while his competitors waited in the league office.

She wondered whether Mr. Pulliam would be going to the game himself, which reminded her of the mounted policeman. She picked up the phone and gave the operator the Giants' office number.

"New York Giants," a woman's voice said at the other end of the line.

"May I speak to Mr. Brush," said Lenore.

"Who's calling?"

"Lenore Caylor of the National League office."

"One moment please." The line went dead for a moment and then clicked back live with the sound of someone fumbling with a desk telephone.

"Hello? Yes? Miss Lenore Caylor, is that you?" She recognized Brush's voice. "What do you have to tell me? What's Pulliam's decision?"

"Hello, Mr. Brush. I'm not calling about that, although I can tell you that we will send you a copy of the decision at about twelve fifteen."

"Then what are you bothering me about?"

"I need two tickets for today's game."

"You called me about tickets? You know you have the league's seats available for every game."

"Those have been spoken for. I promised someone else."

"Who? You got a boyfriend who wants to go?"

"No, sir. It's a policeman. Rather two policemen."

"Ollie's girl, you are a treasure, you know that? After what you saw this morning you call me as cool as can be and ask me for tickets." He laughed. She heard the muffled sound of a hand covering a mouthpiece as Brush cleared his throat. "I'm telling you, Ollie's girl, that if you ever decide to quit working for the boy president, you let me know and I'll hire you as general manager." He laughed again, not quite as hard. "It had to be cops. Always got their hands out for something. Tell me, is this personal or for the league?"

"It's personal, Mr. Brush. I can pay for the tickets."

"Nonsense. You'll have two of the best seats in the house in your hands in five minutes."

"Thank you, Mr. Brush."

"My pleasure, Ollie's girl." She heard him chuckle as he disconnected.

Ten minutes later a young woman arrived and handed Lenore an envelope with the Giants' logo in the upper left-hand corner.

Perfect, thought Lenore. The envelope would cover her lie. She rushed to the elevator. The officer stood waiting at the front door as promised. He thanked her and wished success for "your Giants, ma'am."

By twelve fifteen the waiting area was full of smoking reporters and a dense gray haze. The door to Pulliam's office opened. He entered holding a sheet of paper, followed by John Heydler and Lenore. Pulliam stood behind Lenore's desk, Lenore and Heydler behind either shoulder. Pulliam looked down at his official statement, ready to read, but the newspapermen couldn't wait.

"The fans in New York think you're going to steal this game from the Giants, Pulliam," shouted Sid Mercer from near the door. "What're you going to tell them?"

Hugh Fullerton, standing to their left, chimed in, "The fans in Chicago think you're going to steal this game from the Cubs. What're you going to tell them?"

The room erupted in laughter. "Where's the ball now, Pulliam?" asked Ernie Lanigan. More laughter.

"Has Merkle reached second yet?"

Pulliam scanned the room and held up a hand trying to quiet the reporters. "You will each be given a copy of this statement," he said, and then repeated himself, speaking more loudly. The chuckles and murmurs died away. He lifted the sheet of paper and began to read.

"The umpires in charge of the contest filed their reports after the game, stating that the game resulted in a tie score. The report was accepted in the usual manner without prejudice to the rights of either club."

"So Merkle was called out?" shouted Mercer over the excited chatter of the others.

"Yes."

"What does a tie mean to the pennant race?" asked Fullerton. "There ain't many games left to play."

"A tie is a tie," answered Pulliam.

"And what about the Cubs' claim that the game should be either replayed today or forfeited?" asked Fullerton

"No forfeit will be declared."

"That'll get Chubby's goat."

Lanigan added, "And the tie will get McGraw and Brush's goat."

"Mr. Pulliam, do you think your ruling will anger both teams?" asked Sam Crane.

"Hey, Pulliam, we all know you hate McGraw and Brush and they hate you right back. Did that have anything to do with your decision?" asked a reporter that Lenore didn't recognize.

Pulliam looked back down at his official statement. "Much as I deplore the unfortunate ending of a brilliantly played game as well as the subsequent controversy, I have no alternative than to be guided by the rules. I believe in sportsmanship, but would it be good sportsmanship to repudiate my umpires simply to condone the undisputed blunder of a player?"

"Will the game be replayed?" asked Crane.

"In the unlikely event that the season ends with the Cubs and Giants tied for first place, the game will be replayed."

"In New York or Chicago?" asked Fullerton.

"On the Polo Grounds."

"Is this decision final, Mr. Pulliam?" asked Mercer.

"It is subject to review by the National League Board of Directors. That is all. Thank you." Pulliam turned and retreated to his office. Lenore didn't know what to do at first and so looked to Heydler for guidance, but he quickly returned to his own office. She remained behind her desk.

"Miss Caylor, remember me?" asked Fullerton.

"Of course, Mr. Fullerton," she replied.

"What can you tell us about this? Were you in there for the statements of the players and umpires?"

"Yeah," said Crane. "You were there for the statements, weren't you? As league stenographer? Who was here? Who talked?"

"Would you like some coffee?" said Lenore.

"Aw, come on, Miss Caylor," said Lanigan.

"Coffee? Got anything stronger?" joked the one she didn't know. "What's your name? Caylor? Can I quote you in my paper?"

Lenore smiled. "Would you like some water? That's the strongest drink we have."

"Who was here?"

"What did McGraw say?"

"How well do you know Pulliam?" asked the one she didn't know, raising his eyebrows.

"And what's your name, sir?" asked Lenore.

"Aulick. *Times.*"

"I'm surprised a distasteful question like that would come from the *Times.*"

Lenore stared at them. The sportswriters fired question after question. She said nothing and waited for their frustration and concern about meeting deadlines to drive them out of the office.

When the door closed on the last reporter, Lenore took her notebook and pencil and knocked on Pulliam's door.

"Come in, Miss Caylor," said Pulliam. She turned the knob and went into his office. Pulliam stood looking out the window. Lenore walked directly to his desk and flipped open her notebook.

"You wanted to see me after the press conference, Mr. Pulliam?"

"The mob is gone." He took out his watch and checked the time. "They're on their way to the game."

"Will we be going?" asked Lenore.

"We? Miss Caylor, I order you to go home for the rest of the afternoon. You've had a very trying couple of days."

"I'm fine. I need to prepare the report for the board of directors."

"You need to go home. You can start on the report tomorrow." He turned and looked at her. His hair was a bit disheveled and his tie askew. He sat down in the chair behind his desk.

"Mr. Pulliam, please don't take offense, but perhaps it is you who should rest."

"Rest? No. I have a ball game to attend. Thomas is waiting for you downstairs. He'll take you home."

She knew that the last thing he needed was to feel obligated to protect her. "Very well," she said. "Thank you, sir. Is there anything else you need before I go?"

He hesitated. "One thing, maybe."

"Yes, sir?"

"Can you get me the long distance operator? I would like to call Chicago."

"Certainly, sir."

He rotated his chair and looked out the window again. "Beautiful day for a ball game."

"Enjoy the game," she said as she left his office, knowing that Brush, McGraw, Murphy, and Evers had made that impossible.

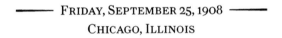

FRIDAY, SEPTEMBER 25, 1908
CHICAGO, ILLINOIS

The noon crowd jammed the sidewalks at the intersection of State and Madison. Joe Rupp struggled to reach the curb. In the street, horse-drawn delivery wagons blocked the progress of trolleys, hansoms, carriages, and automobiles, each pointed in what appeared to be random directions. Screaming teamsters, bellowing horses, clanking bells, and bleating horns made it almost impossible for Rupp to hear himself think. He considered returning to his office on Wabash and skipping lunch with Mike Machac.

He felt a tug on his sleeve. He turned his head to see Machac smiling and holding a copy of a newspaper. "Forget the Berghoff," shouted Machac. "Let's just get a sandwich." Rupp nodded.

They turned and pushed their way east on Madison to the door of a narrow lunch room. They ordered sandwiches over a high glass display and found room to stand at a counter that ran along the back wall.

"So," said Machac, "did you see the morning *Trib?*"

"No," said Rupp, "but somebody at the office told me the Cubs lost five to four, so New York is back in first place."

"Yeah, but only by a few percentage points. Still a lot of games left." Machac opened the paper to page twelve and showed it to Rupp.

"Very funny," said Rupp as he looked at a large cartoon of a ragged but happy Cub player crossing the Brooklyn Bridge with a suitcase, New York "bugs" peering out from behind bars, and the two presidential candidates being asked how they would rule in the Merkle case if elected.

"Very," said Machac. "Now look down column one to right about here." He poked the newspaper. "Read me what Dryden wrote about the Merkle game decision."

"Let's see here...," said Rupp. " 'Following a sleepless night of agony throughout the length and breadth of Manhattan haggard bugs waited—' "

"Farther down."

"Uh, 'the game will be recorded as reported—namely, a tie score.' "

"So you was right. My run didn't count that day in Lincoln Park."

"I already knew that. The 'Inquisitive Fans' guy said I was right."

"Yeah, but now the National League office says it, too. This president guy, what's his name?"

"Let me see here." Rupp scanned the column. "Pulliam. It says, 'War scribes from far and near assembled in Pulliam's outer office.' "

"Yeah, Pulliam. So this Pulliam makes you out to be a real base ball scholar."

"I'm honored. I just hope his decision means the Cubs have a better chance of winning the pennant, that's all. Except," he looked at Machac, "I hope the next time that big ox on your team decides not to run out a game-winning hit, you'll support me when I force him out and nullify the run."

"Like hell. I don't want him coming after me with a bat in his hand."

Jack Norworth and Al Von Tilzer stood in the wings of the New York Theatre watching Nora Bayes take her final bows. The audience stood and cheered. They would demand an encore from Nora, the men knew, especially since this was the last performance of the *Follies of 1908*.

"Here we go," said Norworth, grinning. He grasped Von Tilzer's arm.

Von Tilzer nodded, but did not smile.

Early sales of "Take Me Out to the Ball Game" sheet music had been light. Von Tilzer wanted to cut their losses and drop the song from the York Music Company catalog. Norworth had insisted that they give it another chance.

"No real exposure," he had said in Von Tilzer's office. He promised to convince Flo Ziegfeld and Nora to feature the song as an encore after a performance of the *Follies*. Neither liked the idea, but Nora could not disappoint her new husband Jack, and together they convinced Ziegfeld. He would allow Nora to perform the song closing night. "That way," he had said, "you can't do any damage to my show. And you don't want to do it in the Jardin de Paris anyway. The sound is shit. We're moving downstairs to the New York for a few weeks and closing the show there. You'll be better off."

Bayes stood bowing as ushers collected bouquets tossed onto the stage. She glanced at Jack. He winked at her. She took a step forward and raised an arm to silence the audience.

"Thank you! Thank you! I know what you want now."

The audience applauded its approval.

"Usually I repeat one of the songs from the show. But tonight...tonight I have something very special for you. And I dedicate it to the New York Giants base ball club!"

Deafening cheers rang out through the hall.

"Okay, Fred," she said and motioned to the orchestra pit. The opening theme, taken from the end of the song's chorus, silenced the audience.

"They don't like it," said Von Tilzer.

"They don't know it yet. Give it a chance," said Norworth. He looked out past the stage. Most sat listening politely. Others frowned.

"I don't care if I never get back," sang Bayes. "For it's root, root, root for the Giants!"

The audience roared its approval. At "one, two, three strikes you're out" Bayes held up her right hand and counted the strikes with her fingers. More cheers.

When she repeated the chorus after the second verse, several in the audience screamed "Giants!" at the right moment. A moment later Norworth and Von Tilzer watched as a dozen or more arms shot up throughout the hall as the strikes were counted again. Norworth ran to the edge of the orchestra pit to catch conductor Fred Solomon's attention. He shouted, "Repeat the chorus! Repeat the chorus!" When the orchestra, instead of ending the song as they had rehearsed, played several measures of the chorus as a transition, Bayes picked up on it immediately. The audience stood. Although they hadn't memorized all of the lyrics, they shouted "Giants" and "one, two, three, strikes, you're out" with raucous enthusiasm.

"The audience," said Norworth, "has become a base ball crowd."

When the song ended, Bayes bowed to the cheers. The orchestra started up again and did one more chorus to end the evening.

"Okay," said Von Tilzer. "We'll give it everything. We'll round up the best singers in town and promise we'll imprint their pictures on the music if they work it into their acts. Five hundred copies minimum. We sell them wholesale to the music halls where they appear; they can add whatever margin they want."

"Sam Williams will do it," said Norworth.

"Henry Fink, Trixie Friganza, even Baby Florence. Her mother owes me."

"Baby Florence?"

"Sure. You and Nora get covers, too." Von Tilzer smiled.

"For the music shops."

Von Tilzer nodded. "And I know that vaudeville guy who records for Edison."

"Meeker?" asked Norworth. "Ed Meeker, right?"

"That's him. He has a big voice. Perfect for an Edison cylinder. Perfect for this song."

"Piano rolls?"

"You bet."

Bayes exited the stage, running directly into Norworth's arms.

"Too bad the season is almost over," said Von Tilzer. "But we'll be ready for next year."

———— SUNDAY, OCTOBER 4, 1908 ————
NEW YORK, NEW YORK

The man in the brown bowler sat at the bar on Eighteenth Street. He ordered a shot of rye and draught of beer and waited for Rube Hanson. The bar was crowded for a Sunday evening, with everyone talking base ball. His drinks came. He threw back the shot and drained half his stein of beer. He swiveled on his seat to watch the door and saw two couples vacate one of the high-backed wooden booths that lined the narrow room opposite the bar. He caught the eye of the bartender. "Tommy, give me another round and I'll have it in that booth." Tommy gave him the "okay" sign and reached for a bottle on the counter behind him. The man in the brown bowler stepped across to the booth, setting his stein on its table as if he were staking a claim.

"Hey, buddy-boy," said Rube when he walked into the bar. "Them Cubs came through today, didn't they?"

"Rube, my man," said the man with the bowler. He looked to the bar and caught Tommy's eye. He held up two fingers and then twirled his hand signaling another round, this time for two.

"Never thought I'd root for the Cubs," said the man.

"Me neither," said Rube. "But what the hell? Without them beating Pittsburgh our season would be over. Now it's all up to the Giants to take three from Boston. And they'll be playing on the Polo Grounds. The odds'll be good so put your money on the Giants."

"Rube, that's what I'd like to talk to you about."

Rube Hanson frowned. "You don't need another loan, do you?"

"No, no. Nothing like that. I got some good news is all. Listen to this."

"Good news?"

"I was with my Tammany guy, you know?"

"You mean Quigley?"

"Yeah. That's him. We was watching the wire at the Western Union office in Union Square, and when the Cubs won we passed the bottle around and slapped shoulders and all that kind of shit."

"Sure, sure."

"And then I says that the Giants still have to take three straight and Quigley lets something slip out. You know, in all the excitement and all the whiskey."

"Slip out?"

The bartender arrived at their booth with two shot glasses wedged between the fingers of his left hand and two steins of beer grasped through their handles by the fingers of his right hand. He placed them on the coarse wooden table, spilling not a drop of rye, but letting the foamy heads of the beers slosh and run down the sides of the steins.

"Yeah," said the man with the bowler. "But I didn't let him leave it at that, even though he tried to laugh it off and pretend he didn't say nothing."

"So?"

"So he looks around a little and then whispers that maybe we should step outside and take in a breath of fresh air. So I say okay and we leave the telegraph office and walk around Union Square a bit."

Rube Hanson picked up his shot glass and tossed back his rye. He grimaced as he picked up his beer and gulped a few swallows to chase the whiskey. "C'mon already. What's your point?" he said. He took another sip of beer.

"Okay, okay," said the man, taking off his brown bowler and placing it on his lap. "The long and the short of it is that someone from the Giants and someone from Tammany, they been working on members of the Boston organization while the Pirates have been playing the Cubs."

"Boston organization? Who, organization?"

"Players. Important guys."

"You got names?"

"No. But my Tammany guy—"

"Quigley."

"Yeah, Quigley. Quigley promises me that the Giants will win three against Boston. They've already paid some money up front and they know that the players are hungry for the payoff at the end of the series. What do they care? They ain't gonna get World's Series money. And they'll all be placing their own bets." The man took his bowler from his lap and put it on the table.

Rube Hanson pulled on his beer. "What about the pennant money? What about that? There's a lot of talk downtown that the Cubs can't be touched."

"No, no, no," said the man with the bowler. "That's the other thing. My Tammany guy—"

"Quigley."

"Yeah, Quigley." The man with the bowler stared at Rube Hanson for a moment, and then tossed back his own shot. "Quigley says they got a man in Cincinnati."

"Cincinnati?"

"Yeah, where the National League Board of something or other is gonna decide on the Merkle game. He tells me they're going to give it to the Giants. So you got the Merkle game and the three Boston games and the Giants end the year with ninety-nine wins and take the pennant, and you take home your pennant money."

"So where you putting your money?" asked Rube Hanson.

"Well," replied the man with the brown bowler, "that's the thing. You know I'm between things here."

"Uh huh."

"But this is as sure a bet as there is, Rube, and it was me what got you the line on it and so I figure maybe you can help me out a little."

Rube Hanson leaned back against the high wooden slats of the booth. "Let me get this straight. You want me to risk everything and then pay you off too? Shit. You ain't been worth a fuck for months."

"This is good, Rube. This is from Tammany. Quigley got it from

Brennan who got it straight from Sullivan." The man took a long drink from his stein. "I'm giving you this up-front, out of respect for you. All I'm asking is some consideration for the information when you collect on your bets. And you'll collect sure as we're sitting here tonight drinking rye and beer. A few points is all I ask."

Rube Hanson finished his beer. "Here's what I'll do for you. If the Giants win all three games against the Doves, like you guarantee me, I'll give you two and a half percent." The man began to protest, but Rube Hanson raised a hand to silence him. "Then if the Giants win the pennant, whether by something the league says or by beating the Cubs in that replay game they're talking about, I'll pay you another two and a half. If the Giants somehow don't win the pennant, you gotta cover my investment. You understand?"

The man with the brown bowler said nothing.

"Good," said Rube Hanson. "Then we have a deal. I'll check with my own sources about your friend Quigley. If it sounds up and up, I'll make the bets."

"How much?"

Rube Hanson laughed. "How much? Fuck, man. This is the biggest game in town. Shit." He pointed his finger at the man's nose. "If your information is good, you'll make enough to stay drunk 'til spring training."

The man in the brown bowler smiled.

—— CINCINNATI, OHIO ——

Pulliam arrived in Cincinnati late that evening. He rose from his seat, found his luggage in a rack near the door, and stepped off the train. He walked to the street and took a cab to the Stinton Hotel. He went straight to bed but could not sleep. The next morning he would face the Board of Directors of the National League, Garry Herrmann and Charlie Murphy—both now against him—as well as erstwhile friends

Barney Dreyfuss, Charlie Ebbets, and George Dovey. And he would have to face Brush.

As chairman, he would call the meeting to order and then step down. It was, after all, his decision about the Merkle game that was the subject of their meeting. He would also ask Murphy, as president of the Cubs, and Barney Dreyfuss of the Pirates, to excuse themselves because the final decision of the board would directly affect both of their pennant-contending teams. But he would have to argue his case and then listen to Brush's rebuttals and phony evidence and Murphy's bluster and unreasonable demands.

Ted would be in Toledo, a short train ride away, almost due north. He picked up the telephone and asked to be connected to Ted's hotel.

—— MONDAY, OCTOBER 5, 1908 ——
CINCINNATI, OHIO

He awoke with the first glow of dawn, his room turning deep blue with the lightening sky. Best to get up and review his case with his attorney before the ten o'clock hearing. It was actually better, he told himself, than other trips to Cincinnati. Herrmann, the man's man, reveled in dragging them downriver to the Laughery Club or to the Rathskeller in the basement of the Stinton, for endless beer and spirits. He was sure the others had been down there last night, deciding the Merkle case at the bar, talking too loud, and snickering about his private life. By the end of the night the bartender would probably know more about the upcoming decision than the board members themselves.

At the morning session Brush had even more evidence than he had imagined, piling affidavit after affidavit onto the conference table and barking his protests until his cough took over and he had to sit to regain control of his muscles. Murphy continued to scream for a forfeit. There was nothing said that he hadn't heard before in the Polo Grounds clubhouse or in his office.

Emslie was visibly upset. "I would never have believed that men could swear to such statements as were made by the New York club," he said to the press waiting in the lobby of the hotel.

The meetings went on until ten thirty that night. The board of directors retired to the Rathskeller for further deliberation, while Pulliam, excusing himself, left through a rear door and walked to the Palace Hotel at Sixth and Vine.

"There you are, Harry," said Ted when Pulliam entered the hotel lounge. He stood at the end of the bar. Pulliam thought he had lost weight, perhaps because of his travel with "The Eight" exhibition. His hair was longer, too, and beginning to curl at the ends around his ears. *He isn't taking care of himself,* thought Pulliam. He recalled the first time they met, at a gallery in Louisville. Ted had looked a bit disheveled, his tie knot and collar off-center. Pulliam had thought him vulnerable then, and he worried that Ted was again becoming defenseless while on the road and alone.

"How long have you been here?" asked Pulliam.

"It's late," said Ted. "You're late. Another extra inning game?"

"Maybe we should start over." Pulliam said as he lifted a hand to signal the bartender. "Hello, Ted. It's great to see you."

Ted stared into his drink. "It's good to see you, too."

The bartender arrived. "I'll have a bourbon," said Pulliam. The bartender nodded and went to fix the drink. "I'm sorry I'm late. The meetings just ended."

"I meant that," said Ted.

"You meant which?"

Ted looked at Pulliam. "I meant what I said when I said it's good to see you." He shifted his head a little closer to Pulliam and whispered, "I miss you."

"I feel the same," said Pulliam.

"Can't you say it? Just say it. Right here. It's okay to whisper."

Pulliam looked down at the bartender who was busy pouring a glass of water to go with the bourbon. "I miss you, too."

Ted smiled. "Was that so hard?" Pulliam shook his head once. The bartender arrived with his drink.

"Put it on my bill," said Ted.

"Yes, sir," said the bartender. He turned and walked to the other end of the bar where a man and a woman sat very close, laughing and touching.

"How's Toledo?" asked Pulliam.

"It's not New York. It's not Chicago. The exhibition opens on the fifteenth so right now I'm very busy. I shouldn't have taken today and tomorrow off. I'll have to work next weekend."

"Have you been following the sports pages? Do you know why I'm in Cincinnati?"

"Vaguely," said Ted. "Some controversy over a player who didn't touch second and was called out."

"It's not just a controversy," said Pulliam. "The pennant and the World's Series could be at stake."

Ted repositioned himself on his chair. "I know it's important."

"Thank you for that."

"I didn't say it just for you."

"What do you mean?"

"I think," said Ted, "that there has been someone following me. It reminds me of those men and hansoms in the Village."

Pulliam wondered for a moment if he should feign surprise and shock, but he couldn't. He was too tired. "It's Brush and maybe Murphy. They want me out. They followed us in New York, and they've hired someone to follow you. Did you notice anything in Chicago?"

"I think so. Maybe. I'm not sure. Why don't they just confront you with it and get it over with?"

"I think they're waiting for something. To use it to their best advantage."

"Then why don't you get out before that happens?"

"Ted, we've been over this before."

"Oh my God, don't start going on about the beauty of the game again. Please."

"It's not that. Most of the owners are still on my side. They hired me and expect something from me. I agreed to take this job and do my best, and I must honor my word. My commitment to them."

Ted laughed. "Now you sound just like a real Southern gentleman.

Chest out, saber in hand and ready to charge into the Yankee cannon, and leave the loved ones behind to grieve and carry on."

"I have an obligation and I will fulfill it."

"But where does it end, Harry? At what point do you accomplish what you set out to accomplish and feel satisfied enough about the job you did to walk away? Make me a priority again."

Pulliam lifted his glass and downed its contents. "I have to see this through. I can't pass on the responsibility for the Merkle decision to Heydler or someone else. I have to see this through."

Ted caught the bartender's eye and nodded.

"No," said Pulliam. "Not for me. I have a busy day tomorrow."

"Does that mean you'll be staying in your own hotel tonight?" asked Ted.

Pulliam looked at him. "We probably shouldn't even be in this bar together."

The bartender arrived. "Just one more of these," said Ted, raising his glass.

"Look," said Pulliam when the bartender left, "maybe I can get away before the World's Series starts. The first game is in Detroit, close enough to Toledo. There may be a day or two after these meetings."

"Will you come to me in Toledo?" asked Ted.

"No, it's not safe." Pulliam lifted his glass and sipped the last clinging drops of his drink. "Can you meet me in Dayton? Or Columbus?"

Ted smiled. "Sure. Anywhere."

"Okay. I'll see to it. I promise you. We'll have a day. Maybe two. In Dayton."

"Or Columbus," said Ted.

"Yes."

"Okay, Harry. We'll meet in Columbus."

Pulliam stood. He extended his hand. They shook and held onto to each other's hand for just a moment longer than they should.

Ebbets was the holdout. The other two, Dovey and Herrmann, were ready to give the game to the Giants, but league rules demanded a unanimous decision. After two days of deliberation, Dovey asked that the room be cleared. As Pulliam rose to leave, he turned to the three magnates and said, "You have heard hours of testimony and reviewed volumes of affidavits. All who testified for the Cubs say one thing, and all who spoke for the Giants say the opposite. I would ask you to consider two things. First, Rule 59. And second, the signed affidavit of Christy Mathewson."

The three owners looked at each other. "Mathewson's affidavit?" said Herrmann. "We only have the record of his testimony in your office where he clearly states that he saw Merkle touch second base."

Pulliam felt his stomach go hollow. "Excuse me," he said, "but a copy was in the file that I submitted with the other written statements I received at the National League office. It was to be reviewed in preparation for this meeting."

"We saw no such document," said Dovey.

Pulliam looked from man to man, wondering if they were conspiring against him. He returned to the table, opened his case, and began rifling through his papers.

"Harry, are you all right?" asked Dovey.

"It's here," said Pulliam. He found the sheet of paper in question in a manila envelope. "Here," he said, handing it to Ebbets. "Read this. It is the truth. I tell you that Christy Mathewson may say one thing, or anything, in front of Brush and McGraw and the press, but when he signs his name to a legal document, you can believe it as gospel."

"Harry," said Ebbets, looking over the document, "please leave us to review this new piece of evidence."

"I'm sorry. It's my only copy. It is the property of the National League office. I will stand here while each of you reads it, and then I will take it and put it back in my file and leave the room."

Herrmann began to protest, but stopped when he saw the determined look on Pulliam's face. Each in turn read the affidavit. Dovey handed it back to Pulliam. "Thank you, Harry," he said softly. Pulliam left the room.

He checked his watch. Half past noon. Ted would be on the train to Columbus. Pulliam found an empty hotel conference room and waited alone for the board's decision.

At a little before three o'clock, a bellboy entered with an envelope. He opened it and removed its contents. A small handwritten note fell out of a larger sheet of typed paper. Pulliam read the note first: "Harry, we would like you to join us in the meeting room as soon as you've reviewed the enclosed. George."

Pulliam unfolded the larger sheet.

There can be no question but that the game should have been won by New York had it not been for the reckless, careless, inexcusable blunder of one player, Merkle. In order that a run could have been scored, Rule 59 applied.

He felt relieved that the official findings of the National League Board of Directors upheld his decision, but he was disturbed by the excessive language used to condemn Fred Merkle.

We can, therefore, come to no other conclusion than that the New York Club lost a well-earned victory as the result of a stupid play of one of its members.

We hold that the New York Club should in all justice and fairness be given a chance to play off the game in question. For that reason we order that the game be played on the Polo Grounds on Thursday, October 8.

Pulliam stood and went to the board's meeting room.

Ebbets saw him first. "You should be pleased," he said.

"It's the correct decision," said Pulliam.

"Harry," said Herrmann, "we're about to release this to the press and then we plan to take some questions from the base ball writers. We'd like you to join us at the podium."

"Certainly," said Pulliam.

"But first," said Dovey, "we need to speak to Murphy and Brush."

"Did you send a copy to Barney?" asked Pulliam.

"I had one sent up to his room," said Herrmann.

"Horseshit," said Murphy when he finished reading the document. "It's our game by forfeit, and Brush owes me a thousand dollars. That's what the rule book says."

"The decision has been made," said Herrmann. "That's the end of it. If I were you I'd think about the game on the eighth."

"I'm thinking about the fucking barnyard mess you boys have made," replied Murphy. "What if the Giants lose today and beat us on the eighth? Then we have three teams tied for first again. How many play-off games will that mean? We'll be playing in the goddamn snow."

Dovey said, "It's a fair decision."

"Fair, George?" said Murphy. He pounded the table. "The goddamn Pirates and the goddamn Giants were both eliminated from this race days ago, and you have let both teams right back in. That ain't fucking right no matter how you look at it." He turned to Ebbets. "This is your doing, Charlie. You've hated the Cubs for years and would just as soon we all got killed on the Polo Grounds that day. So now you're backing this cockeating invert," he gestured at Pulliam, "to give it to us up the ass."

"Bullshit, Murphy," said Ebbets. "You're looking for the pennant to be handed to you instead of playing base ball for it."

Herrmann raised his hands. "Now, now. This will get us nowhere. Calm down everyone. The decision is made."

Pulliam glanced at Brush, wondering why he had said nothing. Brush sensed Pulliam's gaze and turned to meet it. He smiled broadly and said, "Boys, I'm going to leave this room and make a call to New York. I've got to get tickets printed for the game on the eighth. Charlie, I suggest you call Chicago and book the Twentieth Century Express for your team."

There was a knock on the door. A young bellboy entered and went to Herrmann. "The press, sir. They's all ready just like you asked."

Herrmann took a coin out of his pocket and handed it to the boy. "Thank you, Richie. We'll be right out."

"Thank you, sir," said the boy and left the room.

"You all ready?" said Herrmann. He led them out the door.

Murphy, turning red with anger, hurried ahead of the rest of the group. "The decision makes the tangle worse than before," he said to the press. "The Giants were given the best of it without giving them the game direct." But after a few moments he calmed. "We'll play them Thursday, and we'll lick them, too. We'll make it so lopsided that no boneheaded base running can cast a shadow of doubt on the contest."

Brush edged his way next to Pulliam who stood far to one side of the podium. "Of course they'll play us on Thursday," he said in a low voice. "Charlie'll make a lot more money from their share of the gate than the thousand dollars of forfeit money he's bellowing about."

"Murphy would rather have the World's Series money guaranteed," answered Pulliam.

"Of course. I know that. But still, I'd take the risk of playing that game and getting the Series money both." Brush paused a moment. "Say, Harry, are you catching the next train to New York? I'll be on it, too."

"I'm sorry, John, but I will be heading straight for Detroit. I've already made my plans."

"Detroit? And miss maybe the biggest game in the history of our league? Don't seem right. I feel a little insulted, Harry."

"I'm sorry if I've made you upset, John, but think about how much money you'd lose surrounding me with armed guards to keep your fanatics from killing me."

"You can sit with me, Harry. I'll protect you."

"No, thank you."

"What's the matter? Not good enough for you? Have I lost my youthful good looks?"

"Have a nice trip," said Pulliam. "I need to call John Heydler." He walked away and looked for a telephone. They were all taken by reporters. He went to the front desk and requested a telegram form. He sent Heydler a brief summary of the board's decision and then asked if the clerk could reserve him a seat on the next train to Columbus. When the reservation was confirmed, he returned to his room to get his luggage.

Barney Dreyfuss stood at his door.

"Barney? So you haven't left town yet."

"Not yet. I need to talk to you."

"Come on in," said Pulliam. "I'm just going to collect my things and check out. Is this about the decision?"

"No. The decision is of no further concern to me. Look at this." He slapped a sheet of paper on the bed. Pulliam picked it up and read.

"This is ridiculous. But what do you care if the Cubs are sued by a fan who was injured by a ball at their ball park."

"It wasn't just any ball."

"It says here that it was a foul ball off the bat of Abbaticchio."

"It was a fair ball."

Pulliam looked up at Dreyfuss. "Is this the same play the Pirates protested? If I recall, it was a long hit down the line and called foul by..."

"Hank O'Day. Your friend Hank O'Day. Your friend the Chicago-born Hank O'Day."

"Barney, are you suggesting that Mr. O'Day called the hit foul because he's from Chicago?"

"He called Merkle out at second, didn't he? He's been calling games in Chicago's favor all season. Read on. The woman who was hit by the ball detailed exactly where she was sitting which was in fair territory. That hit by Abbaticchio was a two-run home run. Instead he's forced to step back in the batter's box and strikes out and that's the end of my Pirates for the season."

"What would you have me do about it?"

"Uphold my protest. Resume the game from that point. It was the beginning of a Pirates rally, cut short by a bad call."

"Please, Barney. Don't be absurd. The call is final."

"But we have legal evidence that the ball was fair."

"You know I can't change the ruling on the field."

Dreyfuss took a step toward Pulliam and pointed a finger at his chest. "You had better change the ruling, Harry."

"Lower your voice, Barney."

"I will not lower my voice. The whole season rested on the correct call of fair ball for a Pirates home run, but instead my players have gone home when they should be preparing for the World's Series. It's that goddamn O'Day. Chicago-bred and a Chicago fan down in his soul."

"I'll not listen to you accuse one of the best umpires in either league of bias toward any one team."

"First Merkle and then this. O'Day is making sure that his Cubs play in another World's Series."

"Tell me something, Barney, if O'Day leans toward the Chicagos, why did he rule in favor of your Pirates when your Gill failed to run to second base last month?"

"Gill touched second base," shouted Dreyfuss. "He could rule no other way. Why believe Evers? He cheats and always has."

"Please, Barney. Calm down."

"I will not. Your O'Day has cost me and my team a lot of money. I need that money. I am building a new base ball field—the biggest and best in either league." He paused and stared at Pulliam. Lowering his voice to a whisper, he said, "Is it because he's like you, Harry?"

"What do you mean?"

"You know what I mean. Hank isn't married is he? And between seasons he is often with Bob Emslie. They travel together. Hunt together."

"Barney, I cannot believe I am hearing this from you. And I won't listen to it."

"Is that it, Harry? He's one of them inverts, just like you. You all stick together, don't you?"

Pulliam pushed by Dreyfuss and opened the door. "Get out. Leave."

"All right. I'll leave. But who can you turn to now, Harry? You've made enemies of Brush, Murphy, Herrmann, and now your old friend Barney. That's half the league."

"Get out."

Dreyfuss walked past Pulliam and down the hall.

Later that evening, sitting on the train, he concentrated on looking forward to meeting Ted in Columbus, putting, as much as possible, his confrontations in Cincinnati behind him. He had won this battle and would not need to deal with the magnates again until after the World's Series. But he had offended Barney. No, Barney had offended him. Barney had always known what he was like; he had even met Ted once in Pittsburgh. Why had Barney treated him so badly—said those horrible things?

He put his head in his hands. They felt clammy, but he could not remove them. He wondered about O'Day and his motivations. He had always thought him completely honest and straightforward.

O'Day had never married? *Did I know that?* he wondered. He couldn't remember. Nothing about O'Day's behavior hinted that he was not attracted to women.

What about his own behavior? It was obvious that most of the league knew. McGraw and Brush made it obvious. But until now they had left him alone to do his job. Could he do his job effectively in the future? Would the magnates let him?

He would resign. He would confront the league with the issues of gambling, bribery and ticket scalping and then resign and let them sink in their own pit of mud. Then he and Ted would disappear together somewhere. Heydler could take over. He was qualified. He wondered whether Heydler planned to travel to Detroit for the games and then realized that he had neglected to inform him or Lenore of his change of plans—that he would not return to New York. During a stopover in Dayton, he got off the train and found the Western Union counter. He sent another telegram to the office.

NEW YORK, NEW YORK

Mike Donlin was in a good mood as he entered McGraw's pool hall in Herald Square. They had beaten the Phillies four to one and needed only to win the next day's game to finish the year tied with the Cubs for first place. They would then replay the game of September 23 for the 1908 National League Pennant. And the way they were playing he felt good about their chances, especially on the Polo Grounds.

Al Bridwell played eight ball with an old man in a nice suit. Buck Herzog sat nearby nursing a beer and watching his teammate shoot pool. McCormick, Tenney, Seymour, and McGinnity stood at the bar. McGraw, standing behind the bar, noticed Donlin come in and nodded in the direction of a back room. Donlin continued through the smoky hall, past the rows of billiard tables and cue racks. McGraw tossed back a shot of whiskey and led the players at the bar to the rear door

"Hey," he shouted to Bridwell, who missed a shot and looked up. McGraw pointed to the back. Bridwell laid his cue on the table and followed. Herzog hopped off his stool and joined him.

A large, round card table with eight chairs stood empty in the center of the back room, but none of the players sat. They stood around the walls on three sides of the room. McGraw walked to the table and put his hands on its green felt surface, illuminated by a lone ceiling lamp. "By now," he said, "you all heard about what they decided in Cincinnati. They want us to play this game day after tomorrow."

"Fuck 'em," said McGinnity. "Why should we? We beat the Cubs on the twenty-third. We win tomorrow and we should be in first place all alone."

"Maybe you think so, and maybe I think so," said McGraw, "but none of what we think means a bucket of horse piss."

Bridwell stepped forward. "They can't make us play if we all stick together. It ain't right. We won that game, I don't care what Merkle did or didn't do. The Giants refused to play the World's Series in 1904, and we can refuse to play this game against the Cubs. It's the principle of the thing."

"Boys," said McGraw, "It ain't about principle anymore. It's about Brush."

"What's going on here?" asked Donlin. "We're gonna play and win tomorrow, and then we'll beat the Cubs the day after."

"Bull crap," said McGraw. "Don't you mugs see it? It's another game. It's another gate. Brush probably wet himself over the chance to sell more tickets."

"What's your point, McGraw?" asked Herzog.

"See?" said McGraw, "we all have a lot of noble thoughts and are all suitably outraged I'm sure. But all I know is Brush stands to make a shit pile of money on the eighth and there ain't nothing in our contracts that says we get a piece of it."

"He's right," said Donlin. "They'll stuff at least twenty-five thousand in the ball park. They'll have to turn bugs away."

"Shit," said Bridwell. "Brush won't turn anybody away."

Herzog said, "Brush'll have them on the roof of the grandstands and looking over the umpire's shoulder. I say there'll be thirty thousand if there's one fan at all."

"Okay," said Donlin, "Say we don't play Chicago. Then we don't go to the World's Series, and we lose that money for sure."

"Brush'll want us to play the Cubs on Thursday all right," said McGraw, "and I say we call him on it."

"Ten grand to play on the eighth," said Bridwell. "We split it evenly."

"Even Merkle?" asked Herzog.

"Especially Merkle," said Bridwell. "Weren't for him there'd be no extra game."

The other players laughed. McGraw scowled. "We tell Brush we want fifteen," he said. "He'll offer seventy-five hundred and we'll take ten." He looked around the room at each player in turn. "Then it's settled. I got Brush. I'll say we're standing on principle and he'll know better, but it will give him a fine story for the papers."

"What about Matty?" asked Donlin.

"I'll take care of him, too," said McGraw. "It'll truly be a matter of principle for him. I'll ask him to come with me to talk to Brush. Give the proceedings an air of respectability."

"And the rest of the team?" asked Herzog.

"Up to you boys," said McGraw. "Bring them in any way you see fit, but make sure we're all together on this."

"Even Merkle," said Donlin.

"Especially Merkle," said McGraw. "Wasn't his fault." He walked past the players and out the door.

The Western Union boy ran into Heydler as he unlocked the door to enter the National League offices. Heydler read the telegram about Pulliam's travel plans and put it in his pocket as he entered his office. He pulled the door closed, tossed his bowler on a table, and shut his door. Lenore hadn't arrived yet, so he pulled out a piece of paper and began to compose a note to her. But the phone rang. The caller asked for a certain statistic. He took out his ledger and placed it on his desk, covering the unfinished note. He found the information and read the numbers to the caller.

Lenore's phone rang as she walked through the office door. She noticed that Heydler's door was closed, which meant that he was already in his office and did not wish to be disturbed. Pulliam's door was open, his office empty. She crossed to her desk and connected the phone as she removed her hat. "Office of the National League," she said.

A male with a raspy voice said, "Who do I have to talk to about tickets for tomorrow's game?"

"I'm sorry sir but you'll have to contact the New York Giants."

"I've already contacted the New York Giants. They told me to call you."

Lenore scowled. "I don't know why they suggested that you call this office, sir. We have no tickets. All game tickets are under the jurisdiction of the home team, which in the case of tomorrow's game would be the Giants."

"Let me talk to that Pulliam fellow."

"Mr. Pulliam is not in." Another line began ringing. "Please hold for a moment."

She connected to the ringing line. "Office of the National League."

"Pulliam."

"I'm sorry, sir, but he's not in the office."

"My name is Lardner. I met him in Chicago a while back. He told me if I ever—"

"Excuse me, sir. I'll be right back."

She reconnected the first line. "I'm sorry, sir. Perhaps you should contact the Polo Grounds."

"Don't you ever disconnect my line again, missy. Do you know who I am?"

"No, sir, I surely do not. Best of luck finding tickets. Goodbye." She disconnected the line and watched the switchboard until the incoming light went off. She reconnected to the second line.

"I'm sorry, Mr. Lardner. As I said, Mr. Pulliam is not in the office." The first line rang again. "I'll tell him you called."

She disconnected and went back to the first line. "National League."

"Miss Caylor?"

"Yes."

"I need to talk to Mr. Pulliam right away. This is Jim Johnstone."

"Hello, Mr. Johnstone. Mr. Pulliam isn't in the office just yet. Can I have him call you? Is this about tomorrow's game?"

"Yes. I'm at a public phone. He can't call me back."

"Can I give him a message?"

"Tell Mr. Pulliam that neither Klem or me can work tomorrow's game, and I need to talk to him about it right away."

"What do you mean you can't work tomorrow's game? Who will we call? There are only four other umpires available, but they are too far away to get here in time." Heydler's door opened. He exited wearing his hat. "Mr. Johnstone, can you talk to Mr. Heydler?"

Heydler frowned and shook his head.

"Mr. Johnstone, please hold the line a moment." She covered her mouthpiece and looked at Heydler. "Mr. Johnstone says that neither he nor Mr. Klem can work tomorrow's game. Can you discuss this with him?"

"Not at this time. Tell him...tell him to come in tomorrow first thing, and we'll discuss it. I have to leave and won't be back until the morning. In the meantime, get out your list of alternates and look for substitutes. Maybe someone from the American League." He opened the outer door and left the office.

"Certainly. But I think Mr. Pulliam..." The door closed. She uncovered her mouthpiece. "Mr. Johnstone?"

"Yes?"

"I suggest you try again in a little while. I'm sure Mr. Pulliam will be in soon. If you still don't connect with him, Mr. Heydler suggested that you come into the office first thing tomorrow morning."

"But that will be too late."

"Until then we will be looking for replacement umpires."

"Where? You just said..."

"Please don't worry about that. We will handle it."

When she disconnected she decided to call the American League office in Chicago and ask for help, knowing that both Brush and Murphy would scream to heaven and protest the game if American League umpires took the field.

Johnstone called three more times. By the end of the day, when Pulliam had not come in and had not called, she was worried enough to telephone the New York Athletic Club. He was not in his rooms.

——— THURSDAY, OCTOBER 8, 1908 ———
NEW YORK, NEW YORK

Lenore arrived at the office at about ten thirty after running several errands. A tall man in a worn brown suit sat in the waiting area holding a brown bowler on his lap. He stood when he saw Lenore. "Excuse me, ma'am. I gotta talk to Mr. Pulliam."

She continued to her desk, placing her packages on the floor. Pulliam's door was open and his office dark. "I'm sorry. Mr. Pulliam is not in. Can I help you?"

"I gotta talk to somebody."

"May I ask what this is about?"

"It's about that game."

"Which game, sir?"

"That Merkle game."

"The Merkle game. I'm sorry, sir, but the league has made its decision."

"I didn't think it mattered because there was no chance that the season would end in a tie, know what I mean?" he sat back down, letting his bowler drop back onto his lap.

"No one expected that to happen."

"And another thing, the season only ended yesterday. Why do they have to play this game so soon? The Cubs will never get here on time."

"I believe they took the Twentieth Century yesterday from Chicago." She took off her hat and hung it up on the coat rack.

"Then they're here already?"

"I'm sure they're at the Polo Grounds by now."

"I just gotta talk to somebody."

"Excuse me a moment. I have to tell Mr. Heydler that I'm in."

"Heydler?"

"He's the league secretary."

"Maybe I could talk to him? It's real important."

"I'll ask him if he's free."

"Thank you, ma'am."

Lenore stood and went to the door to Heydler's office. She knocked.

"Yes?" answered Heydler from within. Lenore smiled at the man who nodded his appreciation.

"Mr. Heydler, do you have a moment?" asked Lenore through the door.

"Come in, Miss Caylor, come in."

Lenore turned the doorknob and entered. Heydler sat facing two men dressed in umpire uniforms. They turned and looked at Lenore.

"Oh. Excuse me, Mr. Heydler," she said. "I didn't know you had visitors." She turned to leave. Heydler quickly stood.

"No, Miss Caylor. Don't leave. Please come in." She hesitated but then closed the door and took a couple of steps into the office. "Miss Caylor, do you know Mr. Klem and Mr. Johnstone? They're scheduled to be the umpires for today's game. Gentlemen, Miss Lenore Caylor."

"I have had the pleasure of meeting both gentlemen several times during the season."

"Miss Caylor," said Klem.

"Ma'am," said Johnstone.

"Miss Caylor," said Heydler, "I'd like you to witness a statement. Mr. Klem, will you repeat in Miss Caylor's presence what you just told me."

"Well, as I said, they're after me with money."

"They're after me, too," said Johnstone.

"They told me I'd be set for life if the Giants win today," said Klem.

"They told me the same."

"And who exactly told you this," asked Heydler, "or promised you this remuneration if you saw to it that the Giants win today?"

"It was Creamer," said Klem. "That doctor who works for the Giants. Dr. Joseph Creamer. He caught up with me on the train. 'Listen, there isn't enough money in the world to bribe me,' I told him. 'Don't talk such damned nonsense. You're being silly,' I told him. I wanted to duck this man and I wanted no approaches from anyone else. I tried to ditch him by leaving the train at Forty-Second."

Johnstone cleared his throat. "They found me on the train, too."

"They?" asked Heydler. "There was more than one?"

"Yes," answered Johnstone, "but I only knew Creamer."

"There's little time, gentlemen," said Heydler. "We cannot replace you for today's game. As discussed yesterday we have found alternates, but know that they will be unsuitable to the Chicago and New York clubs. But, with Miss Caylor as our witness, we have confirmed your reporting of this attempt to bribe you both by a member or members of the New York Giants organization. I am confident that this incident will have no influence on your handling of the game. We will proceed as originally scheduled." He looked up at Lenore. "Thank you, Miss Caylor." She turned to leave.

The man with the bowler stood again when she came back into the outer office. He approached her desk. "Excuse me, ma'am, but I need to talk to somebody before they play this game today."

Lenore, upset by what she had heard in Heydler's office, said quickly, "I'm sorry, sir, but Mr. Pulliam is out and Mr. Heydler is busy."

"But ma'am, like I was saying, I didn't think it would matter because being a Giants fan, I was so damn sure they'd take the pennant."

"What are you trying to say, sir?"

"That it's my fault they's playing this game today. That's what."

"Your fault? Sir, I hardly think that's possible."

"We was there. Me and my brother. Right above third base. Not far from you, ma'am. I saw you with Mr. Pulliam. I knew him from his picture in the paper. I thought you was his wife."

"I was there with Mr. Pulliam," she replied. "And Mr. Heydler and Mr. Dovey of the Boston Doves."

"Well, that's fine, but I'm here to tell you that we was there when all that crazy stuff happened in the bottom of the ninth."

"Sir, we have statements from the Cubs, the Giants, and the umpires. The board of directors has made its decision. The issue is settled."

"But nobody talked to me and I feel bad about it. I should have come forward before this, but it all wasn't decided 'til yesterday."

"What do you mean 'come forward'?"

"Well, like I said, we was there. Me and my brother. 'Course we didn't know it was going to be the biggest game of the year, but we knew it was big." He paused and looked down at his bowler hat. "We've been following the Giants since...well, since forever, and we couldn't believe that we had these tickets. Got them from Rube Hanson. Like I said. He got us right down behind third base." He looked up at Lenore. "I guess I don't need to tell you about McCormick being on third and all the stuff about that last hit by Bridwell."

"No."

"'Course not. I'm sure you heard your fill on that. We didn't see Merkle at all anyway so I can't say nothing about that. But here's what happened to us." He took a deep breath. "Actually, we was hoping Merkle would take second on his own hit. Take away the force. But he didn't, so we was yelling for Bridwell to connect. And I felt pretty sure about it. You know how you get those feelings? And Pfiester didn't look too good out there. Didn't look like he had much left.

"So I was just waiting for Bridwell to connect and then he did on the first pitch and Moose McCormick crossed the plate and my brother and me we jump up and down and hug and slap each other on the back and slap the backs of every rooter we can reach. It was loud out there. Loud and crazy. I never heard it louder. But you know that.

"So then, without thinking about it, we just follow everybody else onto the field to join the party out there and maybe meet a ball player or two and maybe find a Cub and spit in his eye." He smiled sheepishly at Lenore. "So we're on the grass and I'm looking around and see them Cubs and they ain't left the field yet and I yell at my brother that something fishy's going on out there.

"Now being kind of tall I can see over most heads, especially since most everyone has thrown their hats in the air and is running around bareheaded. I didn't toss mine because I lost a good one New Year's Eve in Longacre Square and bought this new brown one and can't afford to keep buying hats all year, know what I mean?"

When Lenore didn't react he continued. "So that's how I notice Evers because he's standing on second and so I can see his Cub cap up a little higher than everybody else's. Everybody but that home plate umpire who I can see because he's standing up on the mound looking at Evers. And I think, 'What the hell?' Pardon me, miss, but I think, 'What's going on around here?' So I stop and watch and I see the ball fly into the infield. Then I don't see much for a minute or two, and then I see the ball again and it's floating in the air like a lazy pop-up, heading straight for me."

"And you caught the ball," she said.

"Yes I did. Couldn't miss it. It was right to me."

"Did anyone see you catch it?"

"Of course they did. My brother saw me and couldn't believe I had the game ball in my hand. Ain't too many bugs get that kind of souvenir. They don't let you keep them when they hit a foul into the stands, you know."

"Yes, I know. Anyone else see you?"

"Them Chicagos."

"Cubs."

"Yeah. Three of them. We was standing there real pleased with ourselves and then I look up and see these three Cubs coming straight at me, staring at me like I'd just run down their mothers or something. And they ain't letting nobody stop them—pushing people over, punching them, shoving them aside."

"Which Cubs?"

"I don't know. I never seen a Cub this close up before." He waited for her to say something, to ask another question, but she said nothing. "So I know they must want the ball, and I ain't about to give it up so I turn and yell at my brother that we gotta get out of there. And we take off, fighting our way through the crowd just like the Cubs were doing. We get a little ways and I look back over my shoulder and they're still coming. Still fighting and still coming and getting closer. And so I start thinking that the two of us are gonna have to fight the three of them, but being surrounded by Giants rooters, I think maybe we actually outnumber them by ten or twenty thousand." He laughed. Lenore didn't. He took another deep breath. "So about then I figure we better turn and face them which would be better than getting hit from behind. So I pull on my brother's arm and we stop and I put the ball in my pocket and I turn to face them." He screwed up his mouth and nodded once.

"And what happened next? You had to fight the Cubs for the ball, didn't you?"

"Nope. They was gone."

"Gone? That's not what they testified."

"And you believed them? Shoot, I wouldn't believe nothin' no Cub said. They was gone, I'm telling you. I didn't see them nowhere. Just a mob of crazy Giants fans dancing and screaming. Then I look over toward second and see Evers with his mitt high in the air. And I see a ball flying through the air and he catches it."

"Excuse me?"

The man reached into his jacket pocket and pulled out a battered, grass-stained base ball. He held it out for Lenore to take. "I don't know what ball them Cubs threw to second base, but this here is the game ball."

Lenore took the ball and turned it in her hand. The leather was nicked and scuffed with green and brown streaks, the red stitches frayed. She saw Mr. Pulliam's printed signature near the Spalding trademark.

"Wait here," she said and ran across to Heydler's door. She rushed in without knocking. The office was empty, the two chairs that the umpires had been sitting in pushed in random directions away from Heydler's desk. She crossed the room to another door that led directly to the outer hall. She opened it and looked to her right toward the elevators. The hall was empty. She went back into the office to the window and looked down onto the street, but immediately realized that it was hopeless. She returned to the outer office.

She stopped just inside the door and looked at the man. "Why in God's holy name didn't you bring this to our attention before today? Have you any idea what this means to the season, and to Mr. Pulliam?"

"I'm very sorry, ma'am, but I had this ball and I never had one before. I had something I could show my Jimmy and make him proud that I was there. I never thought the season would end in a tie for first. Who did?"

"And your Jimmy—your son?" The man nodded and looked down at his hat. "What will he think of you when he finds out that you cost the Giants the 1908 pennant?"

"He won't never know. Can't we stop the game some way? We got the proof right here that the Cubs never forced Merkle out at second."

"I don't see how, unless...," she paused and thought a moment. "What time is it?"

"About a quarter of two."

"The game starts at three. We may have time to get to the ball park and find Mr. Pulliam."

"I thought you said he ain't around."

"He was supposed to return from Cincinnati yesterday. I expected him in today, but he must have gone straight to the Polo Grounds. I know where he'll be sitting. Come on. The traffic will be terrible." She grabbed her bag, hat, and jacket and ran to the door. Opening it she held it for the man. He stood but hesitated.

"What are you waiting for?" she said, exasperated. "What kind of a fan are you? You can stay here and take the blame poor Fred Merkle has been cursed with, or you can come with me and try to save the year for your team." He put his hat on and went out. Lenore followed, shutting the door behind her.

On the street, Lenore rushed ahead of the man and looked to her right, down Broadway into Madison Square. She saw Thomas at his usual place and waved her arm to catch his attention. He snapped the reins and pulled up to the curb where Lenore stood in front of the St. James Building.

"Polo Grounds, Thomas," she said. "And please hurry."

"Polo Grounds? Sorry, ma'am. I just came from there. The whole city is trying to get into the game. Can't get close."

"But we have to get there."

"So says everybody, but I'm telling you, it's sealed off for blocks around. I could maybe get you to 135th and Broadway, but you'd have to walk about twenty blocks and then try to make your way down Coogan's Bluff into the hollow."

"135th?"

"Sorry, Miss Caylor. And even if I got you there, you couldn't get in. They locked the gates. No one else gets in, even with a ticket."

The man with the brown bowler, standing just behind Lenore, spoke up. "Excuse me, ma'am, but we could take the El. I live downtown and that's how we always go to the ball park."

"The El?" she said. "Yes. Of course. The line ends at the Polo Grounds."

"We can catch it at Twenty-Third and Ninth," said the man.

Lenore looked up at Thomas. "Can you take us to Twenty-Third and Ninth Avenue? If we can get to the Polo Grounds, I think they'll let me in."

"That I can do," said Thomas. He started to climb down to open the door for Lenore, but she had it open and was stepping into the cab, followed by the man in the brown bowler. Thomas clucked his tongue and guided his horse into a U-turn, heading back into Madison Square toward Twenty-Third. Midafternoon traffic was heavy, but Thomas maneuvered his way through the square and turned right onto West Twenty-Third Street where he was able to pick up speed.

Lenore looked out the window at the blurred street scenes. The man in the bowler sat next to her, but they could have been in two different cabs, each lost in their individual worries. She had to find Mr. Pulliam and stop the game. She didn't care that to do so would overturn his ruling and the ruling of the board of directors. She wanted the game called off and the Giants declared winners of the 1908 pennant because McGraw would take Christy Mathewson and the rest of his players into the World's Series, and Brush would get his revenue. Perhaps then they would leave Mr. Pulliam alone. They would all be rooting together for their National League Giants to defeat the American League Detroit Tigers. And maybe the issue of the attempted bribery of the umpires would go away as well. She did not want Mr. Pulliam to confront the Giants organization on yet another issue, especially one as serious as the umpires' accusation. Brush and McGraw would show no mercy. But if there was no game, there could be no crime.

The man in the brown bowler sat hoping he wouldn't run into Rube Hanson. The week had gone well until the ruling of the National League Board of Directors was announced. As Quigley had assured him, the Giants easily swept the Doves, eight to one, four to one, and seven to two. But when the news came out that there would be a playoff game if the Giants won all three, Rube Hanson came after him and found him in the bar on Eighteenth Street and pulled him into the men's room and sucker punched him in the face knocking him back into one of the urinals.

"You stupid fuck," Hanson had spat into his face, his breath reeking of whiskey. "Tammany had a man in Cincinnati, did they? Well Tammany should have worked as hard on that motherfucker Dovey as they did on his team. You shit. Do you know how much money I put on this pennant? You better hope the Giants beat the Cubs on the eighth or you will be chewing on your own balls. Understood?"

That was when he decided to visit the National League office.

The carriage pulled up to the curb near the iron stairwell entrance to the station platform. Lenore and the man with the bowler jumped out of the carriage and ran to the stairs. At the first step Lenore stopped and looked back at Thomas. He had climbed down from his perch and was tying his horse's reins to one of the vertical, iron I-beams that supported the elevated tracks. He took his top hat off and tossed it into his cab.

"Miss Caylor, there's a riot going on up there," he said. "You're going to need help to get in today."

"My God, Thomas," she said. "Of course. Thank you."

The elevated structure vibrated as a train approached from downtown. As they ran up the stairs, Lenore's hat blew off and tumbled over the railing onto the sidewalk. Thomas turned to retrieve it. "Forget about the hat," she screamed over the rattle of the approaching train. Thomas turned back and followed them up the stairs to the station.

Several dozen people stood on the platform watching the train approach. When it arrived and its doors opened, a few passengers got off, but many more shouldered their way on board. Some on the platform gave up and backed away from the cars. The doors closed as Lenore, Thomas, and the man arrived.

Lenore's shoulders slouched in defeat. The man in the bowler immediately looked down the track for another train. Thomas jumped onto the narrow platform above the coupling between two cars. He held out his arms. Lenore, without thinking, jumped into them. The man with the bowler disappeared into the remaining crowd on the platform as the train lurched forward.

Thomas pushed open a door and they entered a crowded car. Dozens of male passengers stood in the aisle, holding the backs of seats, grab bars, and the yellow canvas handgrips that hung from above. Four seated men noticed Lenore and immediately stood and offered her their seats. She nodded to the closest man and sat. "Thank you, sir."

"You are most welcome, ma'am," he answered tipping his hat. He remained in the aisle standing over her.

Thomas nudged his way next to Lenore. "Looks like we lost your friend," he said.

"I just met him," said Lenore. "He wanted to speak to Mr. Pulliam about the Merkle game. I didn't even get his name."

The train sped uptown, stopping next at the Thirtieth Street station, more dense with hopeful passengers than Twenty-Third Street. Thomas strained to protect Lenore as more riders pushed their way on board. She looked past the man sitting next to her and out the window at the crowd pressing shoulder to shoulder on the platform. Some inched their way toward the doors while others looked down the track for another uptown El. She felt the train shake as men jumped on between cars. And then heard footsteps overhead. Many on the car looked up at the ceiling as if they could see through it. Lenore looked out to see men climbing onto the roof of the train, using the windows to gain footing.

The train jerked forward, sending those standing bumping into each other. Lenore heard the sound of tumbling bodies above her. The train picked up speed.

Thomas bent and looked out the window. "Must be behind schedule," he said. "We're moving much faster than usual."

The man sitting at the window looked out. "We're not slowing down for the next station," he said.

Most of the passengers around Lenore then peered out to see the Thirty-Fourth Street station whir by. The train picked up more speed as they sped past Forty-Second, Fiftieth, and Fifty-Ninth at which point the man standing next to Thomas protested loudly. "This can't be right. They have to stop. They can't just take us all uptown to...what's the last stop?"

"Polo Grounds," someone said.

"But that's at 155th Street."

"It looks like we're all on the Polo Grounds express whether we like it or not," said another. "Okay with me. I got a ticket for the game."

"It's not okay with me. I have to get off at 140th Street"

The train continued uptown through another station without stopping. Lenore saw angry passengers on the platform waving their arms. Then something hit an open window pane, and Lenore felt something wet and sticky on her face. She wiped it off to find the red remains of a tomato.

The train slowed to take the curve at 110th Street, which allowed the frustrated passengers waiting on the platform to barrage them with anything handy. Those sitting, including Lenore, ducked, lowering their faces almost to their laps and covering the tops of their heads with their hands and arms. Those standing tried to stoop, contorting themselves in any way they could and positioning themselves to use the seated passengers as shields. Passengers seated next to windows tried to close them. A window shattered. A woman screamed.

Into the end of the turn the train again accelerated, passengers hanging on tightly to the backs of seats and to the handgrips. The car began to shake violently. More screams could be heard throughout the train.

Between stations, Thomas looked at Lenore and said, "They know they're not gonna make it to the game so they're throwing the junk they brought for the Chicagos at us."

"All because of a ball game?" said the man who had given Lenore his seat.

A passenger standing in the middle of the aisle, his arm arched over Thomas's shoulder so he could hold onto a canvas handgrip, spoke up. "This is no mere ball game, sir," he said. "This afternoon the Polo Grounds become the thematic center of the cosmic scheme, and all wish to secure a place within." Other passengers turned and stared at the man. He bowed.

The train began to slow. The man sitting next to Lenore glanced out the window as they approached 155th Street. "Sweet Jesus," he said. "Heaven help us."

Henry and Maureen inched their way along the sidewalk under the El tracks. "We gotta get out of here, Maureen," he said, his mouth next to her ear, shouts and horns and bells and rattles causing a deafening din. "There's no way we'll ever find the guy in this mob."

"We must at least try," said Maureen. "It's our last chance. And we have tickets already. I've been here all day and I'm not going home."

She had arrived at the ball park early that morning to find thousands of other fans in line at the ticket windows. But she waited patiently and bought two bleacher tickets. She didn't know what else to do. Henry wouldn't finish his shift until noon, later if there was a fire, and she was sure the ball park would be sold out by the time he could get there. They would meet under the El, across from the players' entrance, and go into the park and find the man and give him his money back and then enjoy the game with a clear conscience. So she stood and waited and watched as the entire area filled with fans until she had no room to move. She clung to one of the black, iron El support girders until Henry found her at a few minutes before two o'clock.

"It took me forever to get down here," he told her. "You should see the mob from up on Coogan's Bluff. A cop told me that a quarter of a million people are up here. I saw hundreds on the roof of the grandstands."

A sea of people covered sidewalks and streets as far as he could see in every direction up to the walls of the ball park. Manhattan Field, the open sports field across the street from the ball park, was a solid mass of people. Fans clung to every pole, billboard, chimney, and smokestack with a view of the field. Hundreds of police, on foot and on horseback, tried to control the mob.

"At this rate," said Henry, "we won't get to the gate before the fourth inning."

Then the word came down from fan to fan. The gates were locked. No one would be allowed in, not even with a ticket. The crowd grew restless, and then angry, many not knowing where to go or what to do. Henry looked up and saw men perched on top of the billboards that were the back wall of the bleachers. He saw a man shimmying up a telephone pole. Looking through the slats of the train yard above them he followed the moving shadows of hundreds more finding places along the tracks among the out-of-service El cars.

They approached another support pole. "I can at least take a look and see what's going on," he said. He took hold of the girder with his hands and pulled himself up a couple of feet.

"Henry, don't be silly."

"Not to worry. They call me Monkey McBride don't forget. I've climbed worse in buildings that were burning down around me." He smiled and scooted up the girder to the point where it met the underside of the track superstructure.

Around the corner, outside the left field wall, Rube Hanson pushed his way through the crowd, and he was mad. Biggest game in the history of base ball, on which he had bet almost his entire bankroll, and they thought they were going to keep him out of the ball park?

"Bastards," he said to a companion.

"Nothing to be done about it, Rube," said his friend. "Let's get out of here. It's getting dangerous."

"Dangerous, you say? I'll show you dangerous." He pulled out a bottle of whiskey, took a swig, and then started shaking its contents onto the ball park's outer wall.

"What the hell?" said a man nearby. "That's good booze." Others around them laughed.

"Oh, that'll show them," taunted one.

"Hey, pour that on me, you fool," said another.

"You want to get in the ball park?" yelled Rube. "I'll show you how." The bottle empty, he tossed it aside and took out a box of matches. "Here you go," he said, struck the match with his thumbnail and held it to the whiskey-dampened wall. It ignited, a low, rolling blue and orange flame crawling up the planks of wood. "Now," he said, standing back a step, "if you want this to burn a little faster I suggest that some of the rest of you bugs do likewise and donate your spirits to the cause."

Several stepped forward with pint bottles, fifths, and hip flasks and began feeding the growing blaze.

The El train's doors opened and the passengers inched their way onto the packed platform. Sirens, horns, and bells sounded below in a cacophony of mechanical noise. Lenore could see the upper deck of the ball park, a solid mass of derbies, fedoras, and occasional Merry Widow hats. Beyond them to the right, fans crowded the roofs of cars in the train yard, peering over the outfield wall onto the playing field. One of the trains suddenly lurched, starting up to begin its route downtown. Surprised fans screamed and dropped to their hands and knees, holding onto the roof as the train rattled out of the yard. To her left a man had extended a wooden plank across the narrow gap between the tracks and the Polo Ground's outer wall. He stood and collected money from fans who jumped across on the plank and into the ball park. Beyond the makeshift entrance, several uniformed men with clubs ran along the tracks shouting at him. Lenore watched as one of the officers hit him on the back of his head. Another pulled the plank, a fan not quite into the ball park falling into the gap onto fans on the street.

Thomas ran interference for Lenore, pushing through the mob in the station. One man, shielding his small son, pushed back. "Hey, mac," he shouted in Thomas's face. "Make way! My kid is scared to death. What's your hurry anyway? You ain't getting in. All the entrances are chained shut and guarded by cops."

Thomas mumbled a "sorry" and continued on, leading Lenore to the exit. Angry and frightened fans clogged the stairway. Thomas pushed ahead, but then stopped and looked around for the best way off the platform. He suddenly smiled. "Holy mother of God," he said. "Well, what d'ya know? Wait here a minute, Miss Caylor." He found a clear spot near a railing. "Hold on," he said.

Lenore grasped the railing tightly. Thomas disappeared into the crowd on the platform. Fans pushed past Lenore, jostling and bumping her. Less than a minute later Thomas returned holding onto the left arm of the man in the brown bowler hat, suit disheveled and covered in soot and splattered garbage. "Look who I found," said Thomas.

"My goodness," said Lenore. "Where were you?"

"I jumped on the back of the last car," said the man. "I rode the whole way hanging onto the railing."

"Lucky," said Thomas.

"Lucky? Look at me! I was the target of every bum who missed his train from 116th to 145th."

"Well, we're here now," said Thomas. "Let's go." He led the way down the stairway to the street where the mob was worse than on the station platform. Fans clung to every iron pillar of the track structure as high as they could climb. Lenore saw more fans trying to scale the outside walls of the ball park.

From his perch just under the tracks Henry could see some of the outfield and the entire infield. "The players are warming up," he shouted down to Maureen. "You should see the grandstands and the roof and Coogan's Bluff. I've never seen so many people in one place."

Then he caught a whiff of the familiar smell of burning wood. It came from his right. He turned and saw smoke rising from beyond an open section of left field. He couldn't quite see the smoke's source, so he leaned out a little more and shifted his weight to get a better view.

"Henry," cried Maureen. "Be careful up there."

"There's a fire, Maureen. Over there." He pointed, but stretched his arm a little too far. Off-balance, he lost his grip. At first he thought he would be okay, if he tumbled into his fall as he had been taught during training. Maybe a broken leg or a couple of fractured ribs. But then he knew he was in trouble because his foot caught, for just a moment, on one of the rivets of the girder, a shallow bump that he had used as a foothold to climb up the pillar. An image of the girl who had fallen from the tenement flashed through his mind.

As Lenore watched, a man on one of the El's pillars suddenly fell. People screamed in terror as he plunged to the pavement at the feet of a young woman who raised her hands to either side of her face and cried out repeatedly, hysterically. Three policemen swinging billy clubs cleared a space around him, one leaning down to check on him. Even from where she stood on one of the bottom steps of the entrance to the El, Lenore could see by the unnatural angle of his legs and head that he was dead.

Nearby a brawl broke out as fans fought to take the dead man's spot on the pillar.

"Oh God," said Lenore. "Oh no."

"Miss Caylor," said Thomas. "I have to get you out of here. It's too dangerous. We'll never make it to the grandstands."

"How, Thomas? How will we get out of here? The only safe place is in the ball park, and I think I can get in at the office. You remember. It's near the clubhouse in center field. Please."

Thomas silently agreed. They pushed on.

A fire alarm rang somewhere in the ball park. Rube Hanson looked at the wall and decided it was time. "All right, boys," he shouted, "charge!"

He ran at the wall, leading with his left shoulder. When it gave way in a shower of splintering, ashen black wood, the crowd behind him followed, tramping over the smoldering boards into the ball park. Several hundred made it in before police arrived to beat back the rest and seal the area. A fire company approached from the south, but could get no further than the center field outside wall. Nonetheless they found a hydrant and hooked up their hoses. A policeman arrived and told them not to bother, that the fans had stomped out the fire as they stormed into the ball park.

"Get them off the wall instead," said the cop, pointing to where a dozen men made their way up the side of a wall in an effort to climb their way in. Scores more waited below for their turn. One of the firemen turned on the hydrant. Two others handled the unwieldy hose, aiming it at the fans closest to the top of the wall. The water started with a weak spurt, but then quickly built into a pulsing, gushing rush. The fan at the top was stunned when first hit by the water. He tried to hang on, but soon tumbled down the ten-foot wall, taking four other fans with him. They fell in a tangled heap on the wet pavement. The crowd that had gathered at the base of the fence scattered as well as they could as the fireman washed the remaining fans off the wall.

As they approached the office Lenore heard a loud argument between two fans somewhere nearby. But she had seen enough in the chaos that surrounded the ball park and only wanted to get inside. The yelling continued, now desperate.

"No! Stop it! Bastard!"

Thomas grasped her shoulders and pulled her aside. He held her firmly as he raised his eyes to the top of a billboard above the office and clubhouse. Two men rocked back and forth in a stiff clinch, neither giving way, until they lost their balance and together, arms interlocked, fell backward onto the sidewalk. Thomas and Lenore stared as they rolled apart, struggled to their feet, and looked for a way back inside.

As Gregory Mason made his way along 155th Street toward the Harlem River, he realized that his best option was to give up and set off for the Gotham Theater to watch the game on the big electronic board. So he turned and walked against the stream of fans who thought they might get into the park. As he approached the slopes of Coogan's Bluff he passed a man selling tickets and paused.

"Best seats," cried the man. "Best seats! Who needs four?" He looked to be about thirty-five, and he was thin and dressed in a crisp, clean black suit and bowler.

A fan approached him. "What do you want for them?" he asked, stopping a couple of feet in front of the scalper. Another man stopped just behind him. Both stood with hands in pockets, heads cocked, ready to deal.

"Twenty bucks each."

"I don't make that in a month."

"And you won't see a game like this again for the rest of your life. Go ahead and keep walking, though. Worse seats are available for more just up the street."

The fan considered for a moment. "Make it fifteen and I'll take two."

"Fifteen?" said the scalper, incredulous. "Listen, I gotta make a living, too. How much you think I paid for these? I didn't get them at the ticket window."

Twenty dollars, thought Mason, watching the transaction. He had twenty-two dollars and a quarter in his pocket. But if he bought a ticket at these prices he'd be living on soup and crackers for a week. He sighed and took a step toward the man but paused when he heard a commotion from behind him. He looked over his shoulder to see four angry young men approach from the direction of the ball park. They pushed their way through the crowd until one of them stopped and pointed at the scalper. "There he is, boys."

"I can go nineteen and a quarter," said the scalper to his customer, which made Mason recalculate his finances as he watched the four men circle the scalper.

"Hey, you," said another of the men. He held up four tickets and shoved them in the scalper's face. "These are no good. They locked the gates an hour ago and you knew it. You owe us a hundred bucks."

"Those tickets are good," protested the scalper. "The genuine article. It ain't my fault they locked the gates."

"It ain't ours neither," said another of the four men. "So we're pretty damn sure you'll give us our money back."

"Sorry, boys. All deals are final."

"All deals are final?" said the first man. "I'll give you a final deal." He balled up his right hand and punched the scalper between the eyes. He fell back into a small crowd of spectators who had gathered to watch the argument. One of the observers was a police officer, who jumped back out of the way and began laughing as all four large men joined in, punching and kicking the scalper. One of them rifled through his clothes and found a roll of bills. He stood and counted out 100 dollars and then dropped the rest of the money and their four tickets on the prone body of the scalper.

"Come on, boys. I got our money," he said. They looked down at the bleeding, moaning little man on the ground for a moment and then walked away toward the bluff.

Mason approached the scalper and knelt down on one knee. "You all right?" he asked. Before the man could respond someone pushed Mason from behind. He braced himself, but landed sprawled over the scalper.

"You!" yelled a deep voice above him. He turned his head to see the policeman standing over him with a billy club in his hand. "You with him? You want me to run you in on a charge of illegal scalping?"

"No, sir," said Mason. "I was trying to help. He looks hurt."

"And I'll hurt you, too, unless you get the hell out of here."

Mason climbed to his feet and left the area as quickly as possible.

Lenore peered in the office door's window and then rapped on the glass. The door opened a crack and Freddy, pale and harassed, looked out at them. "God almighty," he said. "What are you doing here, Miss Caylor? Jeez, look at you."

"Let me in, please, Freddy," said Lenore. "I've got to find Mr. Pulliam."

"No can do. And I ain't seen Pulliam neither."

"What do you mean? The league office has four seats for every game. Mr. Brush himself assured us they'd always be available."

"Mr. Brush hisself gave orders that nobody from the league was to get no more passes never. So if Pulliam is here—and like I say, I ain't seen him—he bought a ticket like everybody else."

"Now look, Freddy..."

"No, you look, lady. With all due respect, you people from the league office stole a game from the Giants and handed it to the Cubs all wrapped up with a pretty little bow like it's Christmas. So now we gotta play this here game," he jerked a thumb over a shoulder, "and we got all we can do to keep Chance and Evers and the rest of those Chicago bums alive long enough to lose to the Giants today."

"But we've got to stop this game."

"Stop it? What? So Chubby Murphy can scream forfeit again?" Freddy shook his head. "Mr. Brush will tie a boulder around my neck and drop me in the Harlem River if I let you in." Thomas stepped forward, whispered in Freddy's ear, and put something into the palm of his hand. Freddy looked down. "But," he said and looked up, "I'm kind of worried about your safety in these tough conditions. Why don't you step into the office and wait here until all of this dies down." He opened the door wide enough for Lenore, Thomas, and the man in the bowler to squeeze into the office.

"Now what?" asked the man in the bowler.

"As far as I'm concerned," said Freddy, "you folks ain't even here. So I'm gonna get back to work and if you should happen to disappear through that door and down the hall to the right and out into the grandstands, I won't know nothin' about it, and neither will you because if Mr. Brush ever..."

"Don't worry, Freddy," said Lenore. "Your secret is safe with us."

The seats were packed with fans with little room left in the aisles to walk. The area between the bleachers and the rope that marked the border of the outfield was full of standing rooters, with hundreds more sitting on the outfield grass just in front of the rope and in foul territory. Vendors in white uniforms and white paper caps passed among them selling refreshments, seat cushions, and scorecards. Players warmed up on the field.

Lenore looked for Brush's Hewitt. "Mr. Brush sometimes watches the game from his car," she said. "I don't see it, but I know where he sits. Perhaps Mr. Pulliam is with him." She led them through the crowd toward the grandstands along the third base line.

All at once the crowd came to life, standing and screaming. Lenore looked out onto the field to see Frank Chance leading the Cubs out of the clubhouse. The crowd booed loudly.

"Chance, you sonofabitch!"

"Go back to Chicago, you bum!"

"Chance you shit! You thieving shit!"

The Chicago first baseman cheerfully jogged across the field, waving and tipping his cap to the fans, his team following in a ragged line behind him.

Lenore led them through the grandstands to an aisle between third base and home plate. A gray-suited security guard at the top of the aisle blocked the way. "Private section, ma'am," he said. "Sorry."

"I need to speak to Mr. Brush," said Lenore.

"Sorry, ma'am. No fans allowed in this section."

"Tell Mr. Brush it's Lenore Caylor from the league office. I must speak to him. It's an emergency." The guard looked Lenore over and scowled at her companions. "You'd look like this, too, if you had to fight your way through that mob outside."

The guard turned and walked down the steps of the aisle. Near the bottom at the low wall that separated the box seats from the field, he crouched and spoke to someone in a seat to his left. Lenore looked out onto the field while they waited. At home plate Joe McGinnity approached Frank Chance who was taking batting practice. McGinnity carried a bat. They exchanged words. Chance pushed McGinnity aside. McGinnity raised his bat threateningly, and Chance brandished his own bat as a weapon. Both teams ran from their benches and converged at home plate. Several players stood between Chance and McGinnity breaking up the confrontation. The crowd hooted and cheered, but the teams quickly separated and retreated to their benches.

The guard returned to the top of the aisle. "All right, ma'am. But just you." Lenore followed the security guard down the steps. When she arrived at Brush's seat he glanced at her but returned his gaze to the field.

"Afternoon, Ollie's girl," said Brush. "How'd you get in? I left strict instructions that there were to be no tickets left for the league office."

"So I was told. We made our way in anyway."

"I don't suppose it was you that burned down my left-field wall?"

"No. I wouldn't stoop to arson. We found a way in."

Brush laughed loudly, slapping his thigh. "Oh, Ollie's girl, you are a prize." He coughed and spat on the field. "Well, I'm sending the bill for the repairs to Pulliam anyway."

"Is Mr. Pulliam here?"

"Pulliam? That sissy chicken? Excuse the language. He's in Detroit."

"Detroit?"

"I was with him in Cincinnati for the hearings," said Brush. "When we heard there would be a game today, Pulliam met with me and Chubby Murphy to finalize the deal. I didn't like it. Murphy didn't like it. But we agreed. Wasn't that sporting of us?"

"But why didn't he return to New York?"

"Because your noble president didn't want to face spending the day on a train with me, I suppose. Maybe I'm not as pretty as his downtown friends." He turned and glared at Lenore. "Or maybe he was afraid he would catch my disease." Brush laughed hard, causing another violent coughing spasm. "He claimed it would be easier for him to head up to Detroit for the start of the World's Series day after tomorrow. Didn't he tell you?"

"He must have told Mr. Heydler," she said.

"I don't know. He may have forgotten to tell even him. He's been looking poorly lately, don't you think?"

On the field umpire Klem walked toward the infield, took a hand broom out of his back pocket, and cleaned home plate. "Play ball!" he shouted. Sheckard of the Cubs stepped up to the plate to bat.

"Why are they starting the game?" asked Lenore. "It's only two forty-five."

"Because I said so," he said and paused. "Miss Caylor, you're blocking the view."

She crouched in the aisle. On the pitcher's mound Christy Mathewson wound up and delivered the first pitch of the game. Klem raised his arm and called a strike. The crowd cheered wildly.

"What are you doing here, Ollie's girl?" asked Brush. "It ain't no social call, I assume."

"I'm here because," she began, but then paused. "What if I had absolute proof that Merkle was never legally forced out at second? What if I could prove that the Giants won the game of September 23rd? Could you stop this game and give the league a chance to investigate?"

Mathewson pitched strike two.

"You don't need to prove it to me."

Mathewson pitched again and Sheckard swung and missed. The fans jumped to their feet, screaming their approval. Johnny Evers stood near the Cubs bench. He dropped one of two bats he had been swinging and stepped to the plate.

"And why would I want to stop this game?" said Brush. "Look at this crowd. There must be fifty thousand stuffed into this pigpen. Will the League refund their money? Ask Pulliam that for me, if he ever shows his pretty face in this town again."

Lenore heard shouting and arguing behind her and turned to see the man with the bowler run away through the crowd. A security guard ran after him. She saw Thomas up higher in the stands watching her.

Evers grounded out bringing the crowd to its feet once again.

"My so-called loyal players already demanded that we boycott the game," said Brush. "Some stupid matter of principle. I had to offer them an incentive. Will your Harry-boy pay me back the bonus I had to give these bums to play this game? They ain't gonna give it back to me. And you think I'd give up this gate? I got a feeling we're gonna win this one, and then we'll have the money from this game and the Series both."

Lenore stood. "I hope you're not counting on Dr. Creamer to win it for you," she said. Brush snapped his head to the right and looked at her. She paused to let the information sink in. "Good luck today, Mr. Brush." Lenore walked back up the steps.

Johnny Evers knew before the game that Jack Pfiester's trip to see Bone-setter Reese had done little good. His arm was still hurt. *They're rushing him back to the slab too soon,* he thought. But once again Chance and the bastard Tinker had shouted him down. He would have slugged Tinker except for the riot that was waiting to break out on the field.

Didn't need a fight in the clubhouse or on the bench to make matters worse, he thought. *But what the hell? With Pfiester on the slab we don't have a prayer of winning anyway. And after the way we went down in the top of the first, it looks like Mathewson is on his game.*

When Pfiester's first pitch hit Tenney on the arm, Evers glared at Chance, who avoided meeting his eyes. Then Herzog walked on four pitches, and the Giants, without swinging a bat, had men on first and second with no outs. Pfiester looked at Evers from the back of the mound as he rubbed the ball. "I'll get this sonofabitch," he said. And he did, rearing back and using the angles to strike out Bresnahan with a curve. Cubs catcher Kling dropped the ball and Herzog, leading off first base, ran for second. But Tenney didn't leave second base and so Herzog had nowhere to go but back to first. The Cub catcher fired the ball to Chance who tagged Herzog out. The crowd was stunned silent. The freak double play left them with a man on second with two out.

Good enough, thought Evers. But Pfiester was pitching in the first inning as if he had already thrown a hundred pitches. It would be like this the whole game if Chance didn't do something. Turkey Mike Donlin stepped up to the plate, knocked dirt off his spikes, and pointed his bat at Pfiester, daring him to put the ball over the plate.

Lenore glanced onto the field as a security guard led her and Thomas to an exit chute. She watched as Donlin hit a double down the first base line, batting in the first run of the game. She wondered for a moment if Mabel was there, standing and cheering as her husband stood triumphant on second base.

Evers stood next to Donlin at second base. "Look over there, Mike," he said. "There's Frank, our Peerless Leader, screaming at Klem that your double was a foul ball."

"Well, Johnny, it just might have been foul," said Donlin.

"You don't say? Don't matter. Jack ain't got a thing today. If you didn't hit the double on that pitch, you would of on the next."

"That's for damn sure. Or somebody else would've hit it. He's pitching batting practice today." He looked around and took his leadoff as Evers returned to his position for the next batter.

Pfiester walked Seymour. Chance scowled at Evers, but went to the mound, took the ball, and called for Three Finger Brown.

Brown was glad to be away from Chance and Evers and Tinker, the three of them yelling and pointing and nose to nose—so close they was trading snot. He agreed with Evers, Pfiester had nothing. The Giants would get to him eventually and then the season would be over after all the shit they'd been through.

Chance had sent him out to the bullpen beyond the left field wall to warm up and stay loose in case Evers was right and Pfiester got in trouble. Perfectly fine with him. Even though he'd pitched the last game of the year against the Pirates, he had three days rest which was more than plenty. And he was mad. He had a pocket full of letters from Giants fans telling him that he would be killed if he took the mound this day. Some were signed with the stamp of a black hand, as if some Italian criminals would bother to threaten him. Shit, if they were anything like Colosimo's gang in Chicago, they would just shoot him and be done with it without all the letter writing. So he concentrated on placing the stub of his index finger in just the right place and putting the ball in just the right spot in the catcher's mitt.

He knew by the crowd's reactions that the first inning did not begin well for the Cubs. But then the crowd grew quiet, and the fans in the outfield turned and directed their poison directly at him. The Cubs batboy made his way through the mob on the field and told him that Chance was making a change on the mound. He dropped the warm-up ball and began forcing his way through the crunch of fans who parted and let him pass even as they spat on him and cursed.

"We'll cut off your pud to match your fingers, Brown."

"You'll be dickless, too, Three Finger."

He stared straight ahead and replied, "You're welcome to it boys, if you can handle it."

On the mound Chance told him there were two out with two Giants on base. Art Devlin was due up.

"Forget the runners," said Chance. "Get Devlin."

Brown had no trouble striking him out to end the inning.

Thomas knew the area better than Lenore and so suggested they walk along the river and catch the subway at 145th Street. They rode silently downtown to Twenty-Third Street, ignoring the looks from other passengers, and then walked west to Madison Square.

They paused at Fifth Avenue. Lenore turned to Thomas. "If you'd like to come with me to the office," she said, "I'll pay you for your time and reimburse you for the damage to your uniform, and whatever you paid Freddy."

"Tomorrow's fine, ma'am," he replied. "I think I'll just keep going along Twenty-Third here and retrieve my cab."

"I hope it's still there."

"Oh I'm not worried, ma'am. Ol' Wilma wouldn't let anyone else take her reins."

"Then I'll see you tomorrow." She held out her hand. He took it lightly, shook once, and released it. "Thank you, Thomas. I'll never forget your generosity today."

He nodded. "Evening ma'am. Unless you'll be needing a cab to take you home. You already have me for the day."

"No, thank you, Thomas. I'll take the subway."

He bowed slightly and continued west. Lenore turned up Broadway toward the office. As she crossed Twenty-Fourth Street she paused. A crowd had formed in front of the St. James Building, cutting off Broadway traffic at Twenty-Sixth and Twenty-Fifth. *What now?* she thought, grateful that Mr. Pulliam was out of town.

As she continued up the street she saw that the crowd was calm, all eyes riveted on something on the wall of the building. Arriving at the St. James, she saw that an electronic board had been mounted for fans to follow the progress of the game. A sign at its bottom read: "FOR OUR FANS. COMPLIMENTS OF JOHN T. BRUSH AND THE NEW YORK GIANTS." Small electric lights indicated the positions of the players, the batter, and which bases held runners. In their rush to leave the building earlier she hadn't noticed it.

The Cubs had scored four in the third inning, and all the Giants were able to manage was a single run in the seventh to add to the one they scored in the first. There was one out in the bottom of the ninth. A man next to the board raised a large, cone-shaped megaphone and announced the second out of the inning and then, a few moments later, the final out of the game, and of the Giants' season.

Each of the Cubs knew the game was over after the first out in the last inning. So did the Giants, and so did their fans. It took Brown only four pitches to retire the Giants in the ninth, and as he wound up to deliver that last pitch to Bridwell, the Cubs looked around at the fans. On September 23rd the Giants' rooters had stood wild with the intoxication of certain victory, eyes riveted on the batter and base runners. Now they paid virtually no attention to Bridwell in the batter's box. They stared at the Cubs on the field with unbridled hate in their eyes.

Chance glanced at Brown. Tinker looked at Kling behind the plate. At the moment of Bridwell's out, the entire team took off for the clubhouse, not waiting for the dubious protection of Polo Grounds security. Even if they had been diligent about their task, the police were woefully outnumbered. A troop closed in around Evers, Steinfeldt, and Hofman, but Chance, Pfiester, and Kling had to fight their way to the clubhouse. Chance took a punch to his throat that dropped him to the turf. A fan slashed Pfiester's shoulder with a knife. The police drew pistols to control the mob.

After recuperating in the clubhouse, the Cubs decided to follow the strategy of September 23rd and leave one at a time in street clothes.

When two policemen insisted on accompanying Mordecai Brown to the El station, he refused their help saying, "You fellows get away from me. Those uniforms will surely tip me off." He made it to the station, mutilated hand in pocket, without incident.

Rube Hanson followed the man in the brown bowler as he made his way toward the El station. Hanson had spent most of the game, at least since the Cubs took their lead in the third inning, wandering the ball park looking for him. He spotted his hat in the sixth inning and stayed close until the game ended.

With the Giants' loss the man owed him a bundle. He knew he would never collect it, and hated the idea of listening to the man's blubbering at the bar on Eighteenth Street. And he was getting to like the man's wife. They had their little parties, as she called his visits, once in a while, which was a very satisfactory situation, as far as Hanson was concerned. What he didn't need was the man showing up with his brown bowler cocked to one side, charming the wife and kid with little gifts and big promises.

Quigley had told him that Brennan told him that Sullivan approved. The man in the brown bowler was becoming an embarrassment.

The only question was the final resting place. The East River or Harlem River?

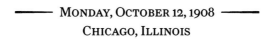

——— MONDAY, OCTOBER 12, 1908 ———
CHICAGO, ILLINOIS

The grandstands at the West Side Grounds were not full. The Chicago Cubs stood on the verge of winning their second consecutive base ball championship, and Joe Rupp estimated that there were maybe 15,000 fans in the ball park, probably less. The rooftops, however, like the one where he stood across the alley from right field, were jammed with fans. He recalled the game he and his wife attended when 30,000 or more had filled the seats and spilled into the outfield grass and foul territory along the baselines. But for game three of the World's Series, there were plenty of empty seats.

"Very odd," Joe said to a man sitting on a large wooden box next to him. He was thrilled to be there because tickets to the games had been very hard to come by, except through scalpers who were asking a lot more than he could afford. That's why he was surprised to see the empty seats.

"Odd?" replied the man. He stood and then stooped down in front of the box. He flipped up several latches and then opened its top.

"Yeah," said Joe. "I couldn't find a ticket to save my life and look out there. There are thousands of empty seats."

The man took a smaller wooden box out of the big one. "You didn't hear about the scalping scheme?"

"Scalping scheme? No."

"Chubby Murphy held back the bulk of the tickets and sold them all to a ring of scalpers. Then he jacked up the prices of the rest of the tickets, the few that were left, so that nobody could afford them." He looked out at the ball park. "Today's even worse than yesterday, but I guess it's a workday. Not too many guys willing to give up a day's pay on a Monday and have to pay Murphy's prices—or some scalper—to get in."

"Ain't that illegal?" asked Rupp.

The man reached over the big box and picked up a wooden tripod. "So you ain't from Chicago?" He spread the tripod's legs and adjusted them while watching the bubble level.

"Yeah, sure I am," said Joe. "You need some help with that?"

"No thanks," said the man. He reached over with his right hand. "George Spoor."

Joe took his hand and shook. "Joe Rupp. Nice to meet you."

"I guarantee you," continued Spoor, "that most of the bugs in those seats out there work for Hinky Dink or Bathhouse John or are friends of Big Jim Colosimo. Or both." The man picked up the smaller box and mounted it on the tripod.

"What're you doing?" said Joe. "If you don't mind my asking."

"Not at all. I'm going to take a moving picture of the game."

"No kidding?"

"Yeah." Spoor reached into the box and took out a crescent wrench. "People still want to see the game. After a pennant race like we had this year Murphy could have sold fifty thousand tickets at reasonable prices. It's embarrassing." Spoor jiggled the camera to make sure it was steady and then inserted a crank on the box's right side. "That's why I'm here. We'll show a flicker of the game in the nickelodeons."

"No kidding? The whole game?"

"Hell no. People won't sit in a theater watching a flicker for two hours. We'll show some highlights. I got a partner in the ball park shooting up close. Then we'll splice something together."

"Interesting."

"You think the Cubs will be coming out soon?"

Joe took his watch out of his pocket. "Yeah. It's time." He looked back onto the field. "The umpires are out there." A moment later, the crowd in the grandstands stood and cheered as the Cubs ran out to their positions. "Will we see that in the moving picture?"

"It'll look like a bunch of white ants scurrying onto a big field," said Spoor. "We're pretty far away." He looked out onto the field as he continued to crank the film through the camera. "Who's that pitching?"

"Pfiester," said Joe.

"Phooey," said Spoor. "He ain't been worth dog shit lately."

Johnny Evers was grateful that it was a seven game series and that after today they would have four more games to win two. He had watched Jack Pfiester warm up and knew that, in spite of only pitching less than an inning on October 8, he hadn't fully recovered from whatever treatment Bonesetter Reese had performed on him. And getting knifed in the shoulder by a Giants fan after the playoff game didn't help. But Evers didn't think he had gotten it any worse than Chance, who could hardly talk from the blow he'd taken to the throat.

Pfiester almost made a liar out of him, looking good through five innings. *Maybe the knife wound made him forget his bum arm,* thought Evers. In the sixth, however, Jack gave up five runs to erase the Cubs' two run lead for good. But Chance wouldn't take him out. Miner Brown was scheduled for tomorrow and Overall the next game. *The Cubs would just have to win it in five,* thought Evers, *instead of a four game sweep.*

"Thanks for the help, Mr. Rupp," said Spoor.

"Call me Joe. My pleasure." He loaded film canisters into one of the boxes. "It was fun talking to you and watching you work, even though the Cubs didn't look too much like champions. Got any more projects you might need help on?"

"You want to get into flickers?"

"Well, maybe on a day off or something. I'd be glad to help. It's kind of interesting even though I don't know nothing about it."

"Oh, it's pretty boring, to be honest with you," said Spoor. "Very slow. A lot of waiting around. Not like this where the action is right in front of you and you have to start cranking or miss it."

"Where you located?"

"Up on Argyle."

"That's north of Lawrence, right?"

"That's right. We're between Clark and Broadway."

"Maybe I'll stop by some day."

"Sure. Essanay Studios. Just ask for me." Spoor picked up the camera box by its handle. "Well, the Cubs'll get them tomorrow. The Tigers ain't no match for them. Cobb or no Cobb."

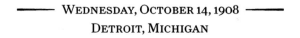

WEDNESDAY, OCTOBER 14, 1908
DETROIT, MICHIGAN

Hank O'Day loved the 1908 World's Series. Compared to the chaotic, violent games of September and early October, the five games between the Cubs and the Detroit Tigers were downright polite, resembling cricket matches, he imagined—never having actually seen a cricket match. He loved the sparse attendance most of all. Today Bennett Park wasn't close to half full. No fans on the grass. No fans in the outfield. Not even enough fans to make a respectable protest to a close play called against the Tigers. Maybe the drizzling rain kept them away. Maybe the fact that the Cubs had handled the Tigers like they were playing a minor league team made this last game a formality in the fans' eyes. And the players on the two teams were getting along just fine, Kling joking with Detroit batters and Chance talking up Tiger base runners. In fact, feelings were so good all around that the two teams would play exhibition games for charity after the Series.

With two out in the bottom of the ninth and Cub pitcher Overall as strong in the last inning as he was in the first, the Cubs two-to-nothing lead looked insurmountable. Not even Cobb could hit him. In the first he had to strike out four batters to get out of the inning, because of a wild pitch on one strikeout, but that didn't faze him. His big curve had the Tigers tripping over themselves all day.

O'Day watched as Tiger catcher Boss Schmidt stepped to the plate. He had "last out" written all over his face. And wasn't he the last out of the 1907 World's Series, too? *Things sometimes happened in pairs,* he thought. *Like the Gill and Merkle plays. Almost identical in everything including all the shit they caused.*

True to form, Schmidt dribbled one a few feet toward the mound. Johnny Kling had no trouble jumping out from his position behind the plate, picking up the ball, and tossing it to Frank Chance to put to rest the 1908 base ball season. None too soon for O'Day. Even the Cubs seemed more relieved than joyous about it, their on-field celebration somewhat reserved seeing as they just won their second consecutive World's Series. *They rule base ball for sure,* he thought. He wouldn't be surprised if they were back again and again over the next several years. But he had the rest of the fall and all winter before he had to think about it again. He looked forward to the first hunting trip of the year with his friend Bob Emslie.

PART III

Pulliam nibbled his breakfast without tasting it and sipped his coffee without noticing that he had not sweetened it, which was his habit. Heydler sat to his right at the front table in a banquet room in Chicago's Auditorium Annex Hotel. Team magnates were scattered around the room at the other tables, but none sat with him.

"I'm serious," Pulliam said. "I hope they dismiss me."

"Harry, please," said Heydler. "We'll get through this."

"Nonsense," said Pulliam. "You will get through this, and you will be the next president of the National League. I will be gone."

He had argued with Barney Dreyfuss again, this time over game scheduling. It was as painful as it was unnecessary. The story of his expelling his old friend from his office was then leaked to the newspapers. Murphy had said to the press that "Pulliam was through," and he didn't care to disagree.

The group of reporters covering the National League winter meetings in Chicago had clamored for an official statement from him, so he gave them one.

> I am weary and sick of the whole ugly mess, and it looks like I would get my release for although I have won all my fights previously, I expect to lose this time because the handicap is too great. There are too many against me, but I will show the men who I think have been most unfair and unjust to me that I am a good loser. I expect to leave on Monday for California for a good rest and for the purpose of forgetting it all.

But not before he exposed the attempted bribery of umpires Johnstone and Klem in New York. He could accept the owners ganging up against him on policy or interpretations of the league agreements and rules, but not outright crimes against the game. They had granted him an "indefinite leave of absence" in an attempt to keep him quiet. He would go away, but he would not remain silent.

A bellboy approached his table. "Mr. Pulliam?"

"Yes?"

"Telephone, sir."

Pulliam turned to Heydler. "Excuse me a moment, John."

"Certainly, sir."

Pulliam pushed back his chair and stood. The bellboy led him out of the banquet room to a phone at a desk near the registration counter. Pulliam tipped the boy and picked up the phone. "Harry Pulliam," he said into the mouthpiece.

"Hello, Harry." Pulliam grimaced at hearing Brush's voice.

"Hello, John. It's a pity you couldn't be here."

"Yes, I'm sure you miss me." He cleared his throat loudly. "Tell me something, Harry. What are your plans for today's meeting?"

"I intend to make a short speech."

"Don't be cute with me, Harry. You know what I'm talking about. What do you intend to say about Klem and Johnstone?"

"I intend to bring the matter to the attention of the league."

"I see. Well, I don't know what information you think you have, but I promise you this, if you do anything to put my business in jeopardy, I will see to it that you are removed from office and arrested on morals charges."

"Arrested? You can't threaten me."

"This is not a threat. You cheated me out of World's Series revenue. Do you think I will sit by and let you take my entire business from me?"

"Your business, sir? Listen to you. No mention of the league and what your meddling might have done to all of our businesses and to the integrity of the game and what it means to the public."

"Very noble. I weep for the game and the humble fan that parts with his nickels for a couple hours of drunken entertainment. But I hear you intend to name names today and that concerns me, and it makes me worry about your precious fans and what they'll think of your game if the press gets wind of it. Murphy's worried, too. He says you want to investigate some nonsense about ticket sales and so-called scalpers. He says you want to change the way he runs his business."

"My eggs are getting cold," said Pulliam.

"Okay," said Brush. "I'll make it simple. If I catch the slightest, foulest whiff that you are going to bring up my name, my manager's name, or my team doctor's name in connection with any alleged bribery scheme, I will have you dismissed and investigated by the police for sodomy."

"Don't be ridiculous."

"And just to make my point very clear I've invited a couple of people you know to Chicago to talk sense into you."

"Goodbye, Mr. Brush."

"Lot of folks worried about you, Harry. You're not a well man. Your brother John traveled all the way down from Wisconsin to help you. He's right there, Harry. Look around." Alarmed, Pulliam looked up and visually searched the lobby. "Listen to your brother, Harry. He's a mighty smart man."

Pulliam dropped the earpiece. Ted and his brother John stood watching him from the far end of the lobby.

"Are you there, Harry?" said Brush, his voice crackling from the desktop. "Listen to your brother, Harry."

The two men approached. Disoriented, Pulliam fumbled for the back of a chair to steady himself. Here were two of the people he treasured most in the world, but he knew, by the way they walked and looked at him, that they had betrayed him to John T. Brush.

"Harry," said his brother, "I got word from New York that you weren't well."

"Harry?" said Ted. "I'm sorry, Harry. He made me come. He said he'd put us on trial, Harry. Jesus, Harry, a public trial."

"Ted?" said Pulliam. "But you should be in Cincinnati with your exhibition. I left a message for you at your hotel this morning."

"Harry, they know all about us."

"Shut up, Ted," said John Pulliam. "Harry, I don't need to tell you what this man Brush and the others mean to do."

Pulliam turned to his brother. "But John. Don't you see? I can't let them do this to the game."

"The game?" said Ted. "The game, Harry? Do you know what this could do to my family? To the Russell name in Louisville? To your family?"

Pulliam looked at Ted and then his brother. "It will be all right. I promise. They will never go through with this. And I know the press. They won't write about it."

"Harry, have you really gone insane?" said his brother. "It will be a sensation. A filthy, sordid sensation. In New York and Chicago and Louisville."

"They can't prove anything. And I have plans."

"What plans?" said John. "California? A leave of absence? A vacation across the world while the rest of us deal with your mess?"

"No. I leave today for St. Louis. I'm to be married. That will put a stop to the rumors."

"Married?" said Ted. "Harry, you don't know what they've said to me. They've been watching us for over a year."

"But don't you see? They can't hurt you if I do this." He turned to his brother. "They can't hurt our family, John. There will be no scandal. We'll have a wedding instead. Don't you see?"

"They know all about it. About your so-called wedding plans. Your friend Barney Dreyfuss just told me. They mean to stop you."

"Is that why you're here, John? To help them stop me?"

"Harry," said Ted, "I have to tell you this. They promised me that if I told them about us they would keep my name out of it."

John Pulliam turned on him. "What's that? You'd do that to Harry? You inverted bastard."

Pulliam turned and walked quickly to the banquet room. At the door he looked back to see John and Ted talking to Gary Herrmann. As he watched, Herrmann nodded and followed him. Charlie Murphy stood just inside the door. Pulliam pushed past him knowing he had watched the entire exchange. He continued to his table and stood behind his chair scanning the room.

"Harry," said Heydler. "Are you all right?"

Pulliam watched as George Dovey joined Murphy at the door. They both left the room. He picked up a knife and rapped it against a water goblet. "Your attention, please. Your attention please." The room quieted.

"To begin today's meetings," he began, "I feel it is my duty to address a matter that was brought before our officers in October of last year. In addition, I must submit to the league that certain members of this organization have threatened officers of the league and warned us not to review the incidents in question." Murphy entered the room. Pulliam watched him as he continued to speak. "I refer to incidents related to the game of October 8, 1908, and to the sale of World's Series tickets in Chicago, which, although the matter is supposedly settled, I wish to revisit, recognizing that a scandal of this nature can cause irreparable harm to the league and to the game." He paused, picked up his water and sipped, his eyes continually moving around the banquet room. He set the glass down.

"On the morning of the eighth of October, Mr. William Klem and Mr. James Johnstone arrived at our offices and spoke to Mr. John Heydler, league secretary. At that time they informed Mr. Heydler that a certain doctor..."

John Pulliam and Ted entered through the open door at the back. Pulliam stopped speaking. His hands began to shake. He lifted his water. As he drank he spilled water down his chin and onto his shirt and tie. He slammed the goblet down on the table, breaking it at its stem and spilling water across the table. Heydler stood and tried to calm him, but Pulliam pushed him away.

"A certain Dr. Joseph Creamer," shouted Pulliam.

"Harry, calm down," said Heydler, grabbing his arm. Gary Herrmann rushed to the table and tried to subdue him.

"A certain doctor...," repeated Pulliam. He pulled himself away from the two men and ran through the room toward the door.

"My God, Harry," said Ted.

"Harry, stop, please," said his brother.

Pulliam pushed past them and continued toward the lobby, his brother, Ted, and Heydler following.

"You're not well, Harry," said John Pulliam. "You need rest. Please, come home with me."

"I'm going to St. Louis."

"And what about the woman in St. Louis," said his brother, "whoever she is. Are you prepared to drag her and her family into all of this?"

"She loves me," said Pulliam. He led them to the coat-check counter. He handed the attendant a ticket and turned to look at his brother and Ted. They stood staring at each other until the attendant returned and gave Pulliam his hat, coat, and a travel bag. He tossed the coat over his arm, put on his hat, and walked out of the hotel.

Barney Dreyfuss stood on the sidewalk watching the traffic on South Michigan Avenue. When he saw Pulliam he went to him and grabbed his arm. "Harry, come on," he said. "Let's go back inside and sort this out."

"I'm going to St. Louis, Barney," said Pulliam. "I'm going to be married."

Dreyfuss stared at him. "Harry, you're breaking my heart." Pulliam said nothing, staring across the street at stark, cold Grant Park. Dreyfuss looked at the row of cabs on the street. "Let me at least get you a cab," he said, almost whispering. He raised an arm and a driver four down in the line snapped his reins and bolted to the front. The hotel doorman opened its door and waited. Pulliam climbed in.

"Dearborn Station," he said. The hansom pulled away from the curb and continued south on Michigan Avenue. At Seventh Street, instead of turning right toward the station, the driver turned the cab around and drove north.

Pulliam looked out the window. "This isn't the way to Dearborn Station," he shouted. "Where are you taking me?" He paused and looked more closely at the driver. "George?"

Boston Doves president George Dovey turned and briefly looked down at Pulliam. "I'm sorry, Harry," he said. "It's the only way. You just won't listen."

"What are you doing?"

"We're all real worried about you, Harry."

"I know what you're worried about. Stop this cab!"

"I can't do that just now, Harry. Please listen to me. I volunteered to do this because you're my friend. You've got to listen."

The cab sped through heavy traffic, dodging horse drawn carriages and automobiles and streetcars.

"Where are you taking me?"

"I'm making sure you don't board that train for St. Louis," said Dovey. "Then, we'll go back to the hotel, and John will arrange a rest for you."

"My brother knows you're doing this?"

"Of course, Harry. He only wants what's best for you."

The cab approached the Art Institute at Jackson. Pulliam looked out the window. He opened the cab door.

"Harry! What the hell?" Dovey tried to control the horse as he watched Pulliam jump out of the cab, coatless, and roll against the curb, losing his hat.

Pulliam slowly stood. The cab pulled to a halt, the horse bellowing in protest. Pedestrians on Michigan Avenue stopped and gawked. Pulliam limped a couple of yards and then ran awkwardly, but with increasing determination.

Dovey jumped down from the driver's bench. He watched Pulliam run in the opposite direction. He returned to the hansom and turned it around. Pulliam looked over his shoulder and saw him coming. He turned into an alley and continued running, avoiding the avenues, making his way through the gangways, alleys, and shadows of Chicago's near South Side.

But Dovey knew where he was going and could get there more directly and much faster. When Pulliam emerged from narrow Plymouth Court just east of the station, he saw Dovey waiting at the curb on Polk Street, in front of the station's main entrance. He pulled his jacket around his ears and continued on Plymouth to a side exit and waited until a group of arriving passengers opened the gate. Nodding his thanks and mumbling excuses, he shouldered past them and entered the station. Satisfied that Dovey was outside, he made his way to the waiting room.

He looked up at the board and saw that the St. Louis express was about to depart. He ran to the platform and jumped onto the train's rear car just as it began to pull away. Catching his breath he turned and, as he watched the station recede, saw Dovey arrive on the platform. The Boston magnate shook his head and waved once, his arm lifted as high as his chin.

—— St. Louis, Missouri ——

Lenore, her uncle Logan, her aunt Florie, and her cousin Amy sat at the dinner table eating supper. To Lenore it felt blessedly normal after the crazy months of the 1908 base ball season and the relentless badgering of Brush and McGraw and the New York newspapers during the off-season. It was a relief to be in St. Louis where the pace of life left time to relax. Mr. Pulliam had insisted that she take a vacation while he was at the winter meetings in Chicago.

"The league will hire a local stenographer in Chicago," he had said. "Please, Miss Caylor. Travel. Relax."

She put up only token resistance, wanting to get out of New York and away from the office. She decided to visit relatives on her father's side after four years of minimal contact via brief, polite letters. "Thank you, Mr. Pulliam," she said. She contacted St. Louis and the following week gave Pulliam her uncle's name and address. "Just in case you need me," she said and smiled. "As you know very well, St. Louis is a short train ride from Chicago. I can be there in a matter of hours."

"I still say," her aunt said, picking up a conversation they had begun in the kitchen, "that the way the Cubs handled Detroit in the World's Series, they deserve to be champions."

"I don't disagree," said her uncle. "They are the best team in base ball. Their pitching staff was almost unhittable all season."

"I hate the Cubs," said Amy. "They always win."

"But the fact remains," said Mr. Caylor, "that the Giants would have won the pennant if Merkle had just touched second base."

"I'd like to go to a World's Series," said Amy.

"Well," said her mother, "there doesn't seem to be much danger of the World's Series coming to St. Louis any time soon."

The doorbell rang. Amy jumped up and ran to the hall. "I'll get it."

"What's she so excited about?" asked Lenore. "Is she expecting someone?"

"More like something," said her mother. "She ordered new clothes from the Sears catalog."

"Lenore," Amy shouted from the front of the house. "Lenore, there's someone here for you."

Her aunt and uncle looked at her. "Are you expecting someone, Lenore?" asked Mrs. Caylor.

Lenore pushed her chair back and rose at her place. "No," she said. "No one in St. Louis knows I'm here except you." She left the dining room and walked down the hall to the foyer where Amy held the front door open. A man stood shaking on the porch, without hat or overcoat. He looked very pale. His head was stiffly set to one side so his ear almost rested on his shoulder.

"He asked for you, Lenore," said Amy.

"Miss Caylor?" said the man.

The familiar, lilting, Southern river town accent horrified her. "Mr. Pulliam?"

"Miss Caylor, I'm sorry."

"But what are you doing here? What about Chicago? Where's your coat? Where's your hat?" She stepped outside, took his arm, and gently led him into the house. "Amy, get a blanket."

"Sure." Amy turned from the door and ran up the staircase to the second floor.

"Who is it, Lenore?" asked her uncle from the dining room.

Lenore took Pulliam down the hall and into the kitchen. She heard her aunt and uncle push back their chairs and follow. She pulled out a chair from the small, wooden kitchen table and guided Pulliam into it.

"What is it?" asked her uncle, stopping at the kitchen door. "Who is this, Lenore?"

She went to the stove, took the kettle off a burner, and went to the sink. As she ran cold water she said, "Uncle Logan, Aunt Florie, this is Mr. Harry Pulliam, president of the National League." She felt herself losing control. She dropped the kettle into the sink. Water from the faucet bounced off of its metal side and splattered onto the counter, the window above the sink, and the front of her dress.

Ten minutes later, Pulliam sat with a plaid blanket draped around his shoulders as Lenore poured a cup of tea. Her uncle entered the kitchen and stood at the table opposite Pulliam. "Mother is getting a room ready," he said.

"Thank you, Uncle Logan," said Lenore.

The doorbell rang again. Amy called from the front of the house, "I'll get it!"

"You should come in by the fire," said Mr. Caylor.

"In a moment, sir," said Pulliam. He lifted the cup but shook so badly that the tea spilled over his hands, scalding them. Lenore took the cup and set it back on its saucer. She turned to the sink, ran the cold water, soaked a towel, and, returning to Pulliam, wrapped his hands in the wet terry cloth.

"Dad," called Amy from the front hall. "Can you come to the door?"

Lenore gently massaged Pulliam's hands. "Uncle Logan's right," she said. "Let's go in by the fire."

"I need to speak to you alone, Miss Caylor."

"I'll be right there, Amy," said Mr. Caylor. "I'll see what Amy wants and then fetch some brandy. I have an excellent VSOP, and I'll get three snifters. Lenore?"

"That sounds very nice, Uncle Logan. Thank you."

Lenore's uncle left the kitchen, leaving the hall door open. Lenore released Pulliam's hands, but he immediately took her hands in his own and looked up into her eyes. "Miss Caylor," he began, clearly struggling. "Lenore. Will you? Please say you will. Will you do me the honor of becoming my wife?"

She pulled her hands away from his. "Mr. Pulliam?"

"You think I'm ill," said Pulliam, "or deranged. But I assure you I'm quite serious."

"I don't know what to say."

"Please, Lenore. We do very well together in the office. We're almost a couple already."

"I certainly wasn't expecting this."

"Are you displeased?" asked Pulliam.

"No. It's not that."

"Then you'll consider it? Please tell me you'll sleep on it and then we'll talk to your mother. We'll notify the press tomorrow."

"The press?"

"Yes. We must," he said, his voice rising. "All the papers. St. Louis. Chicago. New York. Louisville. It's vital. You don't know what they're doing to me. Brush and McGraw. And Murphy. Even George Dovey and Barney Dreyfuss."

"Mr. Dreyfuss?"

"You don't know what they're doing," he said again. "Doing to the game." His head dropped into his hands on the table. He dug his fingertips into his temples and his thumbs into his cheekbones. "You don't know what they're doing to me, Lenore. What it will do to him."

"What happened, Mr. Pulliam?" she asked. "In Chicago?"

"It will kill him. Just kill him. It's what they do to people like us."

"I think, Mr. Pulliam," Lenore began.

"Harry," he interrupted. "Please call me Harry."

"Certainly. Of course," said Lenore.

"You'll be very happy, Lenore," said Pulliam. "I promise."

The sound of men talking came from just outside the kitchen door. Pulliam looked up as Lenore's uncle and another man entered the kitchen. The man looked at Pulliam and said, "Hello, Harry. Why didn't you come to the hotel with me?"

Pulliam stood. "Who are you?"

"This is Mr. Jack Ryan," said Lenore's uncle, "of the Planters Hotel. He says you always stay there when you're in St. Louis. He says he met you at the station, but you ran away from him."

Pulliam's eyes widened as he recognized the visitor. "Jack?"

"Come with me, Harry," said Ryan. "Your room is ready. Remember? Your friends called me from Chicago and I met you at the train."

Pulliam turned to Lenore. "Mr. Pulliam, you can stay here," she said. "You don't have to leave with this man."

Ryan approached Pulliam.

"Lenore," said her uncle, "I think you'd better let Mr. Pulliam go with Mr. Ryan."

"Come along, Harry," said Ryan. "We have a nice dinner and your favorite bourbon whiskey waiting for you."

"Mr. Pulliam should do as Mr. Ryan asks," said Mr. Caylor. "They know what's best for him, Lenore."

Pulliam looked hard at Ryan and then dropped his head.

"What's best for him?" said Lenore. "It's what's best for them, don't you see?"

Ryan took Pulliam's arm, helped him stand, and guided him toward the kitchen door. Lenore moved to intervene, but her uncle stepped in and grasped her shoulders.

"Now now, Lenore," he said. "Calm down. This has nothing to do with us. This man is Mr. Pulliam's friend."

"No he is not!"

Ryan and Pulliam left the kitchen. Lenore watched their backs as they walked through the hall toward the front door.

"He is not our friend," said Lenore, crying.

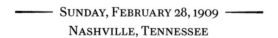

SUNDAY, FEBRUARY 28, 1909
NASHVILLE, TENNESSEE

Lenore paid the cab driver and stepped out of the carriage in front of a house that could have been on the same block as her uncle's home in St. Louis. It was a white, three-story, wood frame structure with a wrap-around porch, twin bedroom windows on the second floor, and an attic window in the gable of the peaked roof. She walked up the narrow sidewalk from the street, climbed the broad front steps, and rang the doorbell. As she waited she turned and looked out at the peaceful neighborhood of similar houses. A single carriage drove along the street, the clomping of the horse's hooves on cobblestone the only sound. The door opened and an elegant, beautiful woman stood at the threshold holding the inner doorknob. Her light brown hair was pulled back in a simple bun. She wore a starched white shirtwaist and deep green skirt. A pale blue and white cameo hung on a silk cord around her neck.

"Mrs. Cain?" said Lenore.

"Yes?" answered the woman, frowning.

"My name is Lenore Caylor. I work for Mr. Pulliam. I'm sorry to intrude. I tried to telephone but couldn't get through. I was wondering if he was still here."

The woman stared at Lenore. "You say you work for Harry?"

"Yes, ma'am," said Lenore. "I'm the league stenographer. I read in the papers that he came here from St. Louis and was planning to go to Florida. I wanted to see him before he left."

"You're not from the papers? I told the papers to stay away. We've disconnected the telephone. Harry needs his rest."

"I'm not from the papers," said Lenore. "Please, Mrs. Cain. If you tell Mr. Pulliam I'm here, I'm quite sure he'll see me."

"I guess it's all right," said the woman, opening the door wider. "You understand that it's been a hard week for us."

"Yes, ma'am."

"Wait here a minute and I'll tell Harry you're here." She turned and walked through an inner door and into a hallway. Lenore stepped into a foyer with a leaded, stained glass window that cast a spectrum of colored sunlight onto its walls. A moment later Pulliam slowly approached through the hallway, silhouetted against daylight streaming into the back of the house. The woman stood behind him.

"Miss Caylor?" he said softly as he arrived at the foyer. He wore a blue sweater over a white shirt with no collar, brown flannel trousers, and red plaid slippers. His eyes looked tired; his complexion was a pasty gray. "What are you doing here?" He turned and held an arm out gesturing toward a room to his right. "Please come in."

Lenore entered the house and followed him into a large parlor furnished with an ornate couch, matching chaise, several upholstered chairs, and small side tables. A fire burned in a stone fireplace built into the far wall. "I'm sorry to bother you," she said, "but I was returning to New York and thought I'd leave a day early and come through Nashville to see you."

"Through Nashville?" he said, puzzled. "Where were you, Miss Caylor?"

She looked at him, saying nothing for a moment. "I was at my relatives' home in St. Louis. You remember, don't you, Mr. Pulliam?"

"St. Louis? Yes, of course. I was in St. Louis, too. Did you know that?"

"Yes, sir. I was there on vacation and you came to St. Louis."

"I stayed at the Planters. Do you know it?"

"Yes, sir." Lenore felt tears welling in her eyes. She turned away from him and approached the couch.

"Please sit down, Miss Caylor. I'll have my sister brew a pot of tea. Did you meet my sister Grace?"

"Yes." She looked toward the hallway and saw the woman watching them. The woman gave her a shallow nod and walked toward the back of the house.

"Please," said Pulliam, "let me take your hat and coat." When he left the room she sat down on the edge of the couch. He returned a moment later and sat in one of the chairs. "It was very kind of you to visit, Miss Caylor," he said. "You must fill out a voucher and be reimbursed by the league for the extra train fare."

"Thank you, sir," she said. "I'll do that."

He leaned back in his chair and crossed his legs. "So, what can I do for you, Miss Caylor? Have you talked to Mr. Heydler?"

"No," she said. "I read in the papers that you were here."

He waved an arm dismissively. "Oh the papers. They have been more of a bother than ever. They claim I've had a breakdown, did you know that?"

"I read something about that."

"Ridiculous. And they say I claimed to be engaged to be married. They make up things like a bunch of dime novelists."

"Yes, sir." Lenore reached into her purse and found a handkerchief. She wiped her eyes and blew her nose.

Pulliam stood. "Miss Caylor, are you all right? What's the matter?"

"Nothing, sir," she said. "I must have caught a cold on the train."

"I can believe it," he said. "I caught a nasty bug on the train from Chicago. Drafty old cars don't keep the heat in at all."

"No, sir. They don't."

"Some nice hot tea will be just the thing,"

"No, thank you. I just thought I'd stop to see if there is anything you'd like me to do while you're gone."

"While I'm gone?"

"Yes. It was reported that you will take a leave of absence."

Pulliam sat back down. "A leave of absence? Yes, that's true. I've had enough of the magnates and their squabbling and money grubbing. Did you read my statement?"

"Yes."

"I'm not sure I'll return."

"I don't blame you."

"I need to sort things out in my mind. I intend to spend some time in Florida. Perhaps I'll attend some ball games and decide how I feel about coming back." When she did not reply he continued. "I'm looking forward to that, Miss Caylor. I can't wait to watch a few ball games without worrying about an umpire's call or a protest by a manager or a magnate. And they have some excellent leagues in Florida."

"It sounds wonderful," said Lenore.

"Yes. Can you imagine it? Maybe I'll grow a beard and watch from the farthest seat so no one will know me. It will be just me and the game."

Lenore stood. "Then there's nothing about the office that you need to tell me?"

Pulliam got up from his chair and faced her. "I don't think so, Miss Caylor. But you're not leaving already, are you? You've just arrived. You haven't had your tea."

"Thank you, sir, but I have to catch my train."

"But how will you get to the station? My brother-in-law has the carriage."

"I can walk, sir. It really isn't so far to the station from here, and it's a nice day. Rather warmer than New York, I should think."

"Yes. They play base ball on colder days than this."

"Goodbye, Mr. Pulliam. Please take care of yourself." She extended her hand. He took it in both of his.

"Don't worry about me, Miss Caylor. And thank you so much for coming." He released her hand and let her out, closing the door gently behind her.

As she descended the front steps, Lenore noticed Pulliam's sister standing on the lawn near the corner of the house. "You're the one, aren't you?" she said to Lenore.

"Pardon me?"

"The one the papers said he was engaged to." When Lenore didn't reply, she continued. "I'm sorry, Miss Caylor. I'm sorry for what you must be going through. He's very sick and confused. At first he didn't even know why he was here. From what I can gather, he snapped while he was in St. Louis. I've been explaining things to him very slowly. That's why he didn't remember seeing you there. He visited you at your family home, didn't he?"

"My aunt and uncle's home."

"But you see, he can't marry."

"I know that, Mrs. Cain."

"It's not his fault."

"No, it isn't."

"I hope he never goes back to New York."

"He'll miss the game," said Lenore.

"The game? The game is killing him. Can you promise me that if he goes back it won't be more of the same?"

"No."

"Then if you have any influence on him at all, don't let him return to New York. You'll miss him. I can see that. But it's hopeless, Miss Caylor."

They said nothing for a moment. Lenore started down the walk but then stopped. "This is difficult, Mrs. Cain, but what about his friend Ted? Has he contacted Mr. Pulliam since he's been here?"

"Friend? That's a laugh. He was in Chicago with our brother John. He was the one who turned against Harry. Did you know Harry stopped in Louisville on his way here and tried to find him? He didn't even remember that Ted had been in Chicago."

"I see," said Lenore. "Well, I guess I'd better be going, Mrs. Cain."

"The train station isn't really very close. But if you walk up the street two blocks you'll come to a busy street with plenty of cabs."

"Thank you, Mrs. Cain."

"Goodbye, Miss Caylor." She turned and walked toward the back of the house.

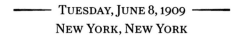

TUESDAY, JUNE 8, 1909
NEW YORK, NEW YORK

Lenore walked up the Twenty-Eighth Street subway station stairs and stepped out onto the sidewalk across from Madison Square Garden. She felt a hand touch her sleeve. She turned to see Mr. Adams standing behind her.

"Hello, Miss Caylor."

"Mr. Adams."

"It seems like a year since we last spoke."

"I think perhaps it has been a year," she said.

"Shall we continue to our respective offices?"

Lenore nodded and began walking toward Fifth Avenue. Adams stepped in beside her. They walked silently for half of the block.

"How is the new season coming along?" asked Adams.

"Well enough. I don't believe the Chicagos will win it again, but there are many, many games left to play."

"I was sorry to hear about Mr. Pulliam. Have you heard from him?"

"Why, yes. He intends to return to work shortly. He says he feels strong and is anxious to get back to the game."

"That's wonderful to hear. He seems like a good man."

"And you, Mr. Adams? How is your year progressing?"

"Very well, thank you. Boats keep arriving and departing from the harbor. Once in a while one sinks." He chuckled.

They stopped at the entrance to the Brunswick Building. "I'll leave you here, Mr. Adams. It was nice to see you again."

"Very nice to see you, Miss Caylor." She turned to go. "Miss Caylor?" She stopped but said nothing. "Miss Caylor, I think you should know that my divorce was finalized three weeks ago."

"I'm sorry for your troubles, Mr. Adams."

"Perhaps I can...perhaps you would allow me to..."

She nodded slightly, turned, and continued on to the St. James Building.

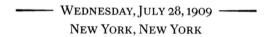

WEDNESDAY, JULY 28, 1909
NEW YORK, NEW YORK

Lenore sat sorting through box scores from the previous day's games. Satisfied, she stacked the sheets and placed them at a corner of her desk. She picked up her earpiece and plugged a cord into her switchboard. She could hear the phone in Pulliam's office ring unanswered through the door. She unplugged the cord, rose, and went to Pulliam's door. She knocked twice. When there was no reply she knocked a little harder. When there was still no reply, she carefully turned the knob and pushed the door open. Pulliam stood staring out his window. Sheets of paper and envelopes lay strewn across his desk. A jumble of papers had toppled onto the floor.

She wished he had never come back from his leave of absence. The magnates wanted to release him during the winter meetings, so why didn't they? Instead, midseason they allowed him back, a shell of himself. Maybe they thought they could control him. Manipulate him. And John Heydler? Instead of supporting Mr. Pulliam and helping him, he ran off almost as soon as Pulliam returned to work. How could a league executive take a vacation as far away as the St. Lawrence River during July with the season in full swing? She had lost all respect for him.

"Mr. Pulliam?" she said, almost whispering. "Excuse me?"

Pulliam turned and looked at her. His eyes were vacant. He held papers in his left hand and a pen in his right. His head was cocked slightly and stiff, as if locked in a permanent tilt toward his right shoulder.

"Mr. Pulliam, Mr. Murphy called long distance from Chicago. And I have yesterday's box scores ready if you would like to take a look at them." She looked closer at him. "Mr. Pulliam, are you all right?"

Pulliam dropped the pen and papers to the floor. "Yes, Miss Caylor. I'm tired, though. I think I'll go home." He walked around the desk, took a hat from the coat stand, and approached the door.

"Of course, Mr. Pulliam," said Lenore. "Yes. That's a good idea. Shall I get Thomas for you?"

"No, thank you, Lenore. I believe I'll walk. It's a beautiful day. A beautiful day for a base ball game."

She stood watching him slowly make his way through the outer office. When he closed the door behind him, she got down on one knee and gathered up the papers. Standing again, she began to sort through them so they would be organized for him in the morning. There was a report from Pittsburgh on the success of the Pirates' new ball park, Forbes Field. She read a brief summary of a lawsuit that had been filed by a woman in Chicago who claimed to have been injured by a batted ball that hit her during a game at the West Side Grounds. The suit had been dismissed. Hugh Fullerton wrote a short note to Mr. Pulliam thanking him for his support of the new sportswriters' organization, the Base Ball Writers' Association of America.

She noticed an elegantly penned note on New York Giants letterhead clipped to a telegram.

Pulliam. Things going well this year. Welcome back! By the way, we received our last note from associates in Chicago. Thought you should see. JTB

She folded the note back and read.

CHICAGO JULY 27, 1909
TO J T BRUSH NY GIANTS ST JAMES BUILDING NY NY
FINAL REPORT STOP TED R LIVING WITH MAN
LEVEE DISTRICT STOP CHANGED NAME TO JOHNSON
STOP DRINKS STOP ARRESTED ASSAULT AND RELEASED
STOP FULL REPORT TO FOLLOW MAIL STOP
PINKERTON

She took the note and telegram to the outer office, ripped them up, and dropped the pieces into her wastebasket.

At eight fifteen that evening Lenore sat on the love seat reading. As she opened a newspaper to the sports page, the telephone rang. She stood and walked toward the hall. Trudie had arrived first and was speaking into the phone. Lenore started to return to the living room.

"Lenore," said Trudie. Lenore stopped and looked back. "It's for you."

"For me?" she replied.

"It's a man."

Lenore went down the hall, took the earpiece, mouthed a "thank you" to Trudie, and turned to the phone, expecting to hear Mr. Adams's voice.

"Hello?"

"Miss Caylor," Pulliam spoke in a hoarse whisper. "Lenore."

"Mr. Pulliam?"

"Lenore, Lenore." Then silence for a moment. "Brush. McGraw."

"Mr. Pulliam, what's wrong?"

"I can't help him anymore."

"Mr. Pulliam, are you all right?"

An explosion at the other end of the line jolted Lenore's head sharply to the left and caused her to drop the earpiece. Bringing her hands to her ears, she screamed. Doors opened down the hall. Trudie and her mother stared out at her. She looked at the earpiece dangling on its coarse brown cord from the wall telephone. She slowly reached down and picked it up. She leaned toward the mouthpiece.

"Mr. Pulliam? Mr. Pulliam? Oh no."

Trudie slowly approached. "Lenore?" she said.

Lenore turned away from the phone and looked down the hall past the women. "Trudie?" she called. "Aunt Trudie?"

"My lord, Lenore, what's wrong?"

"Can I call the police from here?"

"I don't know. I've never done that."

"But I have to. Something's happened."

"But, Lenore, I don't know how."

Lenore ran back to her room, letting the earpiece dangle and bounce against the wall. Trudie picked it up and replaced it on its hook. A moment later, Lenore reappeared wearing a light coat. She ran out the door.

A bored bellboy sat at a switchboard in a room off the main lobby of the New York Athletic Club. A light blinked on the console. The bellboy wondered what to do. He had watched the light blink for half an hour. He knew the jack above the blinking light was to Mr. Pulliam's phone, and he knew that it hadn't been connected to an outside line for over twenty minutes. *Off the hook,* he thought. He plugged a cord into the jack.

"Hello? Is anyone there? Please hang up. Hello? Is anyone there?" Nothing but the hollow sound of an empty room. He thought he could hear the rumbling of Fifty-Ninth Street traffic coming in through Pulliam's window. He stood and went to a door that opened into the night manager's office.

"The light's been lit for half an hour," he said. "It's unusual for Mr. Pulliam. So I plugged in to make sure he's okay, but there's nobody on the line."

The night manager, an overweight middle-aged man dressed in a proper, black three-piece suit, high collar, and black tie, looked up from the ledger he had been studying. "What?" he said gruffly.

"Sorry, sir," said the bellboy. He turned back to look at the switchboard again to make sure that if he convinced the night manager to get up from his desk it would be for a good reason. The light continued to blink. "But Mr. Pulliam's phone's been off the hook for a long time."

"So what?"

A loud commotion coming from the lobby distracted them. "Now what is it?" he said. He threw his pencil at the ledger and stood. The bellboy let him squeeze past and then followed him out of the office.

A doorman struggled near the club's front door, trying to restrain a young woman.

"You've got to let me in," she cried. "It's Mr. Pulliam. I heard a shot. Didn't you hear a shot? Please let me in."

"It's Mr. Pulliam on the third floor," offered the bellboy. "Like I said. That's the phone what's been off the hook."

"Please, madam," said the night manager. "Calm down. This is a men's club and only families are allowed in."

"I am family!" shouted Lenore.

"Excuse me?"

"I am his fiancée."

The manager hesitated, but then nodded at the doorman. He released Lenore. She made the appearance of calming herself.

"Very well, madam," said the night manager. "But please wait here. We will go up and check on Mr. Pulliam and come back and let you know the situation. I'm sure there is nothing wrong, and we will return with Mr. Pulliam himself, or with a message from him."

"Thank you," said Lenore. She sat down on the edge of a leather clad bench. She glanced around the lobby and located the stairway on her right.

The doorman returned to his post at the door. The manager nodded at another bellboy who positioned himself near Lenore. The manager and first bellboy went to the elevator. Lenore watched as one of the sliding elevator gates opened and a uniformed man stepped out. The manager spoke quietly to him for a moment. The elevator operator nodded. The three stepped on and the doors closed.

Lenore looked at her bellboy "guard" and started crying.

"Gee, ma'am," he said, "is there anything I can do?"

She shook her head and looked up at him. "Some water, maybe. Can you bring me a glass of water, please?"

"Yes, ma'am. I'll be right back." He hurried across the lobby and exited through a side door.

Lenore jumped up and ran to the staircase. She took the three flights two stairs at a time, holding on to the banister both to steady herself and to pull her way up. At the third floor she paused at the head of the stairs and, out of breath, looked down the hall first to her left and when she saw nothing there, to her right. The manager and bellboy stood in front of a door, the manager working a key. She waited until they unlocked the door and went in. She ran down the hall as they entered Pulliam's room.

"Mr. Pulliam?" said the manager. "Excuse me, Mr. Pulliam. Are you there?"

"I saw him go up here after dinner," said the bellboy, "and I ain't seen him come down since."

Lenore arrived at the room and, looking in, immediately saw him. "Oh no. Oh no," she said softly, her hands going to her mouth. The night manager and bellboy turned to look at her.

"Now, madam," said the manager. "I distinctly said that you were to wait downstairs." He stopped when he realized that Lenore saw something in the dimly lighted room that they had not. Following her gaze, he made out Pulliam's body twitching on the floor in front of a chaise. A large amount of blood had soaked into the carpet around his head and continued to pulse out of a gaping hole in his right eye socket. A bloody, scorched, jagged wound opened into his right temple. He was dressed only in his underwear, splattered with blood. A revolver lay on the floor near his right hand. The phone's earpiece hung off the edge of a small table next to the chaise.

Lenore tried to push past the two men. The bellboy stopped her and held her by her arms. "No, ma'am. Please," he said.

She struggled against his grip. "Let me go. Mr. Pulliam? Oh God, Harry."

The manager slowly approached Pulliam's prone form, hesitating as if the wounds were contagious. He knelt on one knee, avoiding the wide pool of blood soaking into the carpet.

"Mr. Pulliam?" he said. "Mr. Pulliam? You've been shot. How were you shot?"

Pulliam jerked his head slightly. "I've not been shot," he whispered, his words a liquid garble. His head fell to the floor and he remained still.

——— THURSDAY, APRIL 13, 1911 ———
NEW YORK, NEW YORK

Knocking on her door woke Lenore. She had the feeling that it had been going on for some time, gradually getting louder. "Lenore," called her aunt Trudie from the hall. "Lenore, are you there?"

"Yes," she replied. "Just a moment, please." She sat up and ran her fingers through her hair. Throwing her covers off, she stood, found her way to the door in the darkness, and opened it a crack. "Is something wrong, Aunt Trudie?"

Her aunt stood in the soft yellow glow of the hall light, clutching her worn, cotton-print bathrobe at the neck. "I don't know, Lenore. There's a man at the door. He looks like a cab driver. He asked for you. You weren't expecting a cab, were you?"

"No. Of course not. What time is it?"

"It's almost two in the morning. This is very odd, Lenore."

"Go back to bed, Aunt Trudie. I'll find out what it's about." She closed the door. She waited a moment until her eyes adjusted to the dim moonlight coming in her window and then found her shoes and her housecoat. She didn't bother to fix her hair.

Thomas stood on the front stoop. She hadn't seen him since Mr. Pulliam's death when he began working Columbus Circle instead of Madison Square. He wore a flat cap instead of a top hat, but otherwise looked as he did when he used to stand at the curb at Twenty-Sixth and Broadway ready to open his hansom's door for her and Mr. Pulliam.

"Hello, Miss Caylor," he said before she could speak.

"Thomas," she said. "What is it? Why are you here?"

"You know I wouldn't wake you up like this and disturb your family, especially after all this time, if it weren't something important."

She stepped onto the stoop next to him. A faint breeze rustled the branches of the trees along the otherwise quiet street. "What is it, Thomas?"

"Miss Caylor, like I said, I wouldn't do this except for what all we been through. And except for Mr. Pulliam. But I thought you'd like to see this."

"See what, Thomas?"

"It's the Polo Grounds."

"The Polo Grounds?"

"The ball park's burning down, Miss Caylor."

"Burning down?"

"I just took a fare to the Bronx and passed by. The grandstands are going fast. It may spread to the bleachers."

"My God."

"I dropped them off and was going back downtown and was near your street and thought to myself that maybe you'd like to see it. I mean, like I said, after all we went through. That Merkle game and the game in October that year. You and Mr. Pulliam."

"And you."

"Yes, ma'am. I was there, too."

"Thank you, Thomas. Just give me a minute." She ran back up the stairs to her room and quickly dressed. She stopped a minute and looked at an old handbag on a shelf next to a stack of books. She grabbed it and ran out the door.

Thomas stood at the curb next to an automobile, holding the rear door open.

"Thomas?" said Lenore. "Where's your horse? I'm sorry. I forgot her name."

"Ol' Wilma died last year," said Thomas. "So I signed up for one of these things. It's a French motorcar. Mr. Allen of the cab company imported them."

"I think I'd like to ride with you, Thomas," said Lenore stepping to the front.

"Ma'am?"

"You're not charging me, are you?"

"No, ma'am." He closed the back door and opened the front passenger door.

They rode silently uptown for a few moments.

"It's nice to see you again, Thomas."

"Very nice to see you, Miss Caylor." He glanced at her and then back at the street. "I trust you and your family are in good health."

"Everything's fine, thank you."

"And the Adams gentleman?"

"How did you remember him?"

"Oh, I recall taking you and him from the St. James Building up to Times Square for a show one evening. Seemed like a nice fellow."

"He is."

"And he's doing well?"

"I think he will someday," she said and paused. "He's asked me to marry him."

"Say, no kidding," said Thomas. "That's good news."

"Not yet. I told him I'd think about it."

Thomas laughed. "Miss Caylor, I gotta say, you always were a step ahead of the game, if you don't mind my saying so."

Lenore laughed with him. "Not really, Thomas. But thank you."

As they approached the Harlem River a flickering orange glow illuminated the sky. They turned on the drive at the top of Coogan's Bluff. Automobiles and carriages lined the street. Spectators stood along the curb and on the bluff's boulders in pajamas or evening dress or work clothes or housecoats hastily pulled over whatever they wore to bed. Thomas parked behind a horse-drawn carriage and turned off his engine. Lenore stepped out of the automobile and walked around its broad front hood to see the familiar shape of the Polo Grounds grandstands engulfed in flames, thick clouds of dark gray smoke disappearing into the black sky. Fire wagons sat parked around the ball park vainly arcing sprays of water onto the collapsing wooden structure.

She looked around at the fans who had come out for this last stand of the old ball yard. A few cried. She saw a figure she recognized. John

McGraw stood leaning against a limousine. A Hewitt. She walked toward him. As she approached she noticed that a rear door was open and someone lay prone and propped up on a cot in the back seat. She had last seen him only two weeks before, but he looked as if he had aged ten years since.

McGraw turned and recognized her at once. He pushed himself off the car to face her. "Why, look who's here," he said. "Hello, Miss Caylor. Come to watch the show?"

"Who's that?" said Brush. "Miss Caylor, you say? Well what do you know? Fine night for a fire, ain't it, Ollie's girl?"

"Mr. McGraw," she said in greeting. "Mr. Brush. Couldn't you afford a demolition company? Let me guess. You needed the insurance money to add more seats. Nice timing, by the way. No one will suspect arson at the beginning of the season."

"Tsk, tsk, Ollie's girl," said Brush. "I'm shocked at your cynicism."

"I suppose you already know where you'll play your games."

"Sure," said Brush. "Me and Frank Ferrell talked about it. We'll play at Hilltop Park when the Highlanders are out of town. I mean the Yankees since that's what they want to be called now. In the meantime, I'll build a new ball park. Concrete. Steel. Fireproof."

McGraw leaned back against the car. "I'll miss the old field, though," he said. "I had my own private entrance."

"Was anyone inside?" asked Lenore.

"Come on, Ollie's girl," said Brush. "We're businessmen, not murderers."

"Is that so?"

"I see. You think we had something to do with Pulliam, don't you? Obvious suicide. Coroner said so."

McGraw chuckled. "Come on, Miss Caylor. I wouldn't have shot him in the head. I never would have thought a bullet in the head could hurt him."

"Thank you for clearing that up," said Lenore. "Since the Giants were the only team in either league that didn't send a representative to the funeral, I thought the guilt might have been too hard to live with."

"Guilt?" said Brush. "That's precious. Anyway, I couldn't go all the way to Louisville just for a funeral. I'm a very sick man." He laughed a guttural, phlegm-fueled cackle and began to cough. "McGraw, McGraw!"

McGraw pushed himself off the car. He reached into the back seat and lifted Brush's body up and over the far rear door. Brush tilted his head and spat.

"Nice to see everything's working out for you," said Lenore. "I'm sure you'll build a beautiful new ball park."

"Thirty-five, maybe forty thousand," said Brush as McGraw lowered him back into his position on the cot. "I'm thinking of calling it John T. Brush Stadium."

"Congratulations," said Lenore. "I hope you live long enough to see it."

A loud crash distracted them. They turned to see the upper deck behind home plate collapse onto the lower grandstands in an explosion of smoke and flames and sparks. The spectators on Coogan's Bluff gasped.

"Don't you worry about me, Ollie's girl," said Brush. "We'll open before the Fourth of July."

"So you're ready with the plans," said Lenore. "The contractors, the building materials, the permits?"

"Oh, we've been ready for months," said Brush. "That's why this accidental fire is so fortunate for us. A demolition company would have taken forever and cost me a small fortune."

Lenore turned to go, but paused and reached into her handbag. She took out an old base ball, stained yellow-green and dirt brown. "Well," she said, "here's a souvenir of the old Polo Grounds for you and your new ball park." She tossed the ball at Brush.

McGraw reached out and intercepted it. "What's this?" he said, rolling the ball around in his thick hands.

"I was told it was a game ball," said Lenore.

"Piece of shit," said McGraw.

"Watch your language, McGraw. A thoughtful gift," said Brush. "Will you sign it for us, Ollie's girl? Is it the ball from the Merkle game? I bet it is. Everybody's been wondering where that ball ended up. Evers claimed to have it, but he never caught the actual game ball, did he?

Come on. Sign it in honor of your old boss." He laughed again, the laugh quickly turning into a violent cough. "Funny thing is," he said, struggling to regain control, "funny thing is, Miss Lenore Caylor, Ollie's girl, your boss, Pulliam, he got that call right. 'Bout the only call he ever did get right, but he was right. Merkle was out three different ways. Hope he didn't blow his brains out over that silly play."

Lenore turned and walked away. Thomas stood watching her. He opened the front car door. "Was that the ball?" he stammered. "You still had the ball? The Merkle ball?"

"The man never came back for it," said Lenore.

"But why did you give it to the Giants, Miss Caylor? That ball is cursed."

"Cursed?"

"It's the ball you told me about. The one you had on the El that day," said Thomas. "It's the ball that lost the Giants the 1908 pennant."

"It's just a ball. The man said it was the game ball, but why believe him? He was a Giants fan. He was desperate to get into the game, like everyone else." She paused. "Like you and I."

They looked down at the burning Polo Grounds one last time.

"Take me home, please, Thomas."

Acknowledgments

Special thanks to all of the Sullivans and their spouses who helped in a variety of ways. Also Patrick Creevy who reviewed the manuscript and introduced me to the folks at Amika, and to those folks themselves, Jay Amberg, John Manos, and Sarah Koz. To Ann Wambach for her excellent editing and proofreading work. To Donald G. Evans for reading the manuscript, catching typos, and suggesting edits. To William Brese for his excellent graphic work on the cover. To Tim Wiles at the National Baseball Hall of Fame Giamatti Research Center. To Angelo Louisa and David Cicotello, members, writers, and editors at the Society for American Baseball Research, for their early support of my writing. To the members of the Lancaster, Pennsylvania, fiction workshop where the earliest version of the manuscript was discussed. And to Candy Tingstad, the granddaughter of Harry Pulliam's sister Grace.

ABOUT THE AUTHOR

FLOYD SULLIVAN was born in Chicago and grew up in Oak Park, Illinois. He graduated from the University of Illinois at Chicago with a degree in history. He has written one non-fiction book, *Waiting for the Cubs,* and edited a collection of essays titled *Old Comiskey Park.* He blogs about baseball at Waiting4Cubs on ChicagoNow.com. He works as a freelance writer and photographer in Chicago, where he lives with his wife.

CPSIA information can be obtained
at www.ICGtesting.com
Printed in the USA
LVOW10s1919071217
558994LV00016B/1455/P